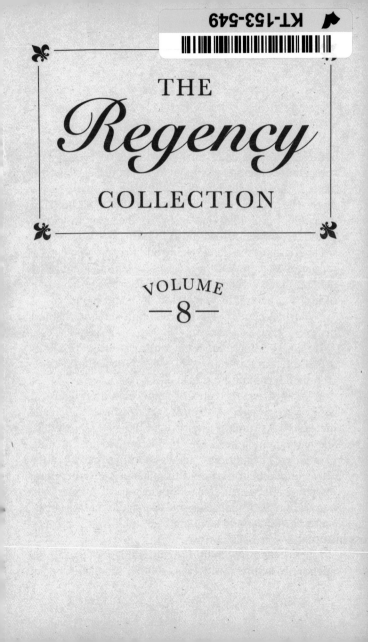

THE

Regency

COLLECTION

VOLUME
—8—

THE
Regency
COLLECTION

VOLUME
—8—

Fair Juno
by
Stephanie Laurens

Serafina
by
Sylvia Andrew

*First published in Great Britain 1999 by
Harlequin Mills & Boon Limited,
Eton House, 18–24 Paradise Road,
Richmond, Surrey, TW9 1SR.*

The Regency Collection © by Harlequin Enterprises II B.V. 1999

The publisher acknowledges the copyright holders of the
individual work as follows:

Fair Juno © Stephanie Laurens 1994
Serafina © Sylvia Andrew 1995

ISBN 0 263 82352 0
106-9912

*Printed and bound in Spain
by Litografía Rosés S.A., Barcelona*

FAIR JUNO

by

Stephanie Laurens

Dear Reader

I've always loved the world of the Regency—a world of wit, of elegance, of drama and romance. The rich tapestry of Regency life, with the balls and glittering entertainments of the London Season, and its frenetic pace, contrasting with the relaxed ambience of country house parties and family life on large country estates, provides a perfect background against which to examine the questions of love and marriage—two subjects that, in the Regency, were not considered necessarily synonymous.

The characters, too, lend themselves to romance— the dashing blades, reckless bucks, the ineffably elegant gentlemen, and the innocent misses, the self-willed young ladies not at all sure they wish to cede their independence, and the eccentric damsels intent on tasting adventure, all these contribute to the depth and passions that can be found in Regency romance.

Working within the Regency has always brought me a great deal of pleasure—I hope my Regency romances bring you the same enjoyment, and take you back in time —to when lovers waltzed under the crystal chandeliers.

Enjoy!

Stephanie Laurens

Born in Sri Lanka, **Stephanie Laurens** has lived mostly in Australia. After qualifying as a scientist, she and her husband travelled extensively through the Far and Middle East, as well as throughout Europe and England. Four years in London gave her the settings for her Regency romances. Now settled once more in Australia, she lives in a comfortable suburban house with her husband, two young children, a mindless but lovable dog, and a cat with a crooked leg.

Other titles by the same author:

Tangled Reins*
Four in Hand
Impetuous Innocent
The Reasons for Marriage**
A Lady of Expectations**
An Unwilling Conquest**
A Comfortable Wife

* linked
** linked

CHAPTER ONE

MARTIN CAMBDEN WILLESDEN, fifth Earl of Merton, strode purposefully along the first-floor corridor of the Hermitage, his principal country residence. The scowl marring his striking features would have warned any who knew him that he was in a foul mood. A common saying among the men of the 7th Hussars had been that if any emotion showed on Major Willesden's face the portents were bad. And, thought ex-Major Willesden savagely, I've every right to feel furious.

Recalled from pleasant exile in the Bahamas, forced to leave behind the most satisfying mistress he had ever mounted, he had landed in gloomy London to face an uphill battle to extricate the family fortunes from the appalling state they had, apparently unaided, tumbled into. Matthews, the elder, of Matthews and Sons, his and his family's man of business, had warned him that the Hermitage was in need of attention and would not, in its present state, meet with his approval. He had thought that was all part of the old man's attempt to persuade him to return to England without delay. He should have recalled Matthews' habit of understatement. Martin's lips thinned. The grim look in his grey eyes deepened. The Hermitage was in even worse case than the investments he had spent the last three weeks reorganising.

As he paced the length of the corridor, the crisp clack of boot-heels penetrated his reverie. In a state bordering on shock, Martin stopped and stared down. There were no runners! Just bare wooden boards and, to his critical eye, they were not even well-polished.

Slowly, his grey gaze lifted to take in the sombre tones of decaying wallpaper framed by faded and musty hangings. A pervasive chill inhabited the gloom.

His frown now black, the Earl of Merton swore— and added yet another item to the catalogue of matters requiring immediate attention. If he was ever to visit the Hermitage again, let alone reside for more than a day, the place would have to be done up. Downstairs was bad enough—but this! Description failed him.

Setting aside his aggravation, Martin resumed his determined progress towards the Dowager Countess's rooms. Since his arrival eight hours ago, he had postponed the inevitable meeting with his mother on the grounds of dealing with the problems crippling his major estate. The excuse had not been exaggeration. But the critical decisions had been made; the reins were now firmly in his grasp.

Despite such success, his hopes for the coming interview were less than certain. Curiosity brushed shoulders with a lingering wariness he had not thought he still possessed.

His mother, Lady Catherine Willesden, the Dowager Countess of Merton, had terrorised her household for as long as Martin could recall. The only ones apparently immune from her domination had been his father and himself. His father she had excused. He had not been so favoured.

He halted outside the plain wooden door that gave access to the Dowager's apartments. Despite all that lay between them, she was his mother. A mother he had not seen for thirteen years and whom he remembered as a cold, calculating woman with no room in her heart for him. How much of the blame for the decay of his ancestral acres could be laid at her door? The question puzzled him, for he knew her pride. In fact, he had a good few questions, including how she would deal with him now; the answers lay beyond the door facing him.

Recognising the instinctive squaring of his shoulders as his habit when about to enter his colonel's domain, Martin's lips twitched. Without more ado, he raised a fist to the plain panels and knocked. Hearing a clear instruction to enter, he opened the door and complied.

He paused just beyond the threshold, his hand on the doorknob and, with a practised air of languid ease, scanned the room. What he saw answered some of his questions.

The tall, upright figure in the chair before the windows was much as he remembered, more gaunt with hair three shades greyer, perhaps, but still retaining that calm air of determination he so vividly recalled. It was the sight of the gnarled and twisted hands resting, useless, in her lap and the peculiar rigidity of her pose that alerted him to the truth. They had told him she kept to her room, a victim of rheumatism. He had interpreted that as a fashionable response to a relatively minor ailment. Now, reality stared him in the face. His mother was an invalid, bound to her chair.

Pity stabbed him, sharp and fresh. He remembered her as an active woman, riding and dancing with the best of them. Then his eyes locked with hers, chilly grey, haughty as ever—and more defensive than he had ever seen them. Instantly, he knew that pity was the very last thing his mother would accept from him.

Despite the real shock, his face remained impassive. Unhurriedly, he closed the door and strolled into the room, taking a moment to acknowledge the round-eyed stare of the only other occupant of the large chamber—his eldest brother's relict, Melissa.

Catherine Willesden sat in her high-backed chair and watched her third son approach, her features as impassive as his. Her lips thinned as she took in his long, powerful frame, and the subtle elegance that cloaked it. The light fell on his features as he drew nearer. Her sharp eyes were quick to detect the hardness behind the elegance, a ruthless determination, a hedonism ill-concealed by the veneer of polite manners. It was a characteristic she was honest enough to recognise.

Then he was before her. To her horror, he reached for her hand. She would have stopped him if she'd been able but the words stuck in her throat, trapped by her pride. Warm, strong fingers closed over her gnarled fingers. Her surprise was swamped beneath a sudden rush of emotions as Martin's dark head bent and she felt his lips brush her wrinkled skin. Gently, he replaced her hand in her lap and dutifully kissed her cheek.

'Mama.'

The single word, uttered in a gravelly voice deeper than she recalled, jolted Lady Catherine to reality. She blinked rapidly. Her heart was beating faster. Ridiculous! She fixed her son with a frown, struggling to infuse an arctic bleakness into her grey eyes. The slight smile which played about his mouth suggested that he was well aware he had thrown her off balance. But she was determined to keep this black sheep firmly beneath her thumb. She could, and would, ensure he brought no further scandal upon the family.

'I believe, sir, that I sent instructions that you were to attend me here immediately you reached England?'

Entirely unperturbed by his mother's icy glare, Martin strolled to the empty fireplace, one black brow rising in polite surprise. 'Didn't my secretary write to you?'

Indignation flared in Lady Catherine's pale eyes. 'If you are referring to a note from a Mr Wetherall informing me that the Earl of Merton was occupied with taking up the reins of his inheritance and would call on me at his earliest convenience, I received it, sirrah! What I want to know is what the meaning of it is. And why, once you finally arrived, it took you an entire day to remember the way to my rooms!'

Observing the unmistakable signs of ire investing his mother's austere features, Martin resisted the temptation to remind her of his title. He had not expected to enjoy this discussion, but, somehow, his mother no longer seemed as remote nor as truly hostile as he recalled. Perhaps it was her infirmity that made her appear more human? 'Suffice it to say that the Merton affairs were in a somewhat deeper tangle than I had understood.' Placing one booted foot on the brass fender, Martin braced an arm against the heavily carved mantel and, with unimpaired calm, regarded his mother. 'However, now that I have managed to spare you some time away from the damnable business of setting this estate to rights, perhaps you could tell me what it is you wish to see me about?'

By the conscious exercise of considerable will-power, Lady Catherine kept surprise from her face. It wasn't his words that shook her, but his voice. Gone entirely were the light, charming tones of youth. In their place, there was depth containing a great deal of hardness, harshness, with the undertones of command barely concealed beneath the fashionable drawl.

Inwardly, she shook herself. The idea of being cowed by this scapegrace son was ludicrous. He had always been impudent—but never stupid. Such languid insolence would be a thing of the past, once she made his position clear. Wrapping herself in haughty dignity, Lady Catherine embarked on her son's education. 'I have much to say concerning how you should go on.'

Exuding an attitude of polite attention, Martin settled his shoulders against the mantelpiece, elegantly crossing his long legs before him, and fixed his mother with a steady regard.

Frowning, Lady Catherine nodded towards a chair. 'Sit down.'

Martin's lips twisted in a slow smile. 'I'm quite comfortable. What are these facts you needs must inform me of?'

Lady Catherine decided not to glare. His very ease was disconcerting. Much better not to let on how disturbing she found it. She forced herself to meet his unwavering gaze. 'Firstly, I consider it imperative that you marry as soon as possible. To this end, I've arranged a match with a Miss Faith Wendover.'

One of Martin's mobile brows rose.

Seeing it, the Dowager hurried on. 'Given that the title now resides with the third of my four sons, you can hardly be surprised if, in my estimation, securing the succession is a major concern.'

Her eldest son George had married to please his family but Melissa, dull, plain Melissa, had failed lamentably in satisfying expectations. Her second son Edward had died some years previously, part of the force which had successfully repelled The Monster's invasion. George had succumbed to the fever a year ago. Until then, it had never dawned on the Dowager that her impossible third son could inherit. If she had thought of it at all, she would have expected him to die, somwhere, on one of his outlandish adventures, leaving Damian, her favourite, as the next Earl.

But Martin was now the Earl; it was up to her to ensure that he toed the line.

Determined to brook no opposition, Lady Catherine fixed her son with a commanding eye. 'Miss Wendover is an heiress and passably pretty. She'll make an unexceptionable Countess of Merton. Her family is well-respected and she'll bring considerable land as her dower. Now you are here and the settlements can be signed, the marriage can take place in three months' time.'

Prepared to defend her arrangements against a storm of protest, Lady Catherine tilted her chin at an imperious angle and regarded the lean figure propped by the fireplace with keen anticipation. Once again, she was struck by the changes, enveloped by a unnerving sense of dealing with a stranger who was yet no stranger. He was looking down, his expression guarded. Unexpectedly curious, Lady Catherine studied her son. Her last memories of Martin were of a twenty-two-year-old, already steeped in every form of fashionable vice—drinking, gambling and, of course, women. It was his propensity for dabbling with the opposite sex that had brought his tempestuous career to a sudden halt. Serena Monckton. The beauty had claimed Martin had seduced her. He had denied it but no one, least of all his family, had believed him. But he had steadfastly resisted all attempts to coerce him into marrying the chit. In a fury, her husband had bought off the girl's family and banished his third son to a distant relative in the colonies. John had regretted that action bitterly, regretted it to his dying day, quite literally; Martin had always been his favourite and he had died without seeing him again.

Intent on finding evidence that the son of her memories had not in truth changed, Lady Catherine acknowledged the broad shoulders and long, lean limbs with an inward snort. He still possessed the figure of Adonis, hard and well-muscled through addiction to outdoor pursuits. His long-boned hands were clean and manicured; the gold signet his father had given him on his twenty-first birthday glowed on his right hand. The hair that curled about his clear brow was as black as a raven's wing. All that she remembered. What she could not recall was the strength engraved in the chiselled features, the aura of confidence which went further than mere arrogance, the graceful movements that created an impression of harnessed power. Those she could not remember at all.

Unease growing, she waited for some show of resistance. None came.

'Have you nothing to say?'

Startled from his reverie, induced by memories of the last time his mother had insisted he marry, Martin

lifted his gaze to the Dowager's face. His brows rose.
'On the contrary. But I would like to hear all your
plans first. Surely that's not the sum of them?'

'By no means.' Lady Catherine threw him a glance
that would have wilted lesser men and wished he would
sit down. Towering over her, he seemed far too powerful to intimidate. But she was determined to do her
duty. 'My second point concerns the family estates and
businesses. You say you've been acquainting yourself
with them. I wish you to leave all such matters in the
hands of those retainers George hired. They're doubtless better managers than you could ever be. After all,
you can have no experience of running estates of such
size.'

A muscle at the corner of Martin's mouth quivered.
He stilled it.

Lady Catherine, absorbed in ordering her argu-
ments, missed the warning. 'Lastly, once you and Miss
Wendover are married, you will reside here throughout
the year.' She paused to eye Martin speculatively. 'You
may not yet realise, but it is my money that keeps the
Merton estates afloat. Remember, I wasn't a nobody
before I married your father. I've allowed what passed
back to me through settlements on your father's death
to be drawn upon for living expenses as the estates are
unable to pay well enough.'

Martin remained silent.

Confident of victory despite his impassivity, Lady
Catherine advanced her trump card. 'Unless you agree
to my conditions, I'll withdraw my funds from the
estate, which will leave you destitute.' On the word,
her eyes flickered over the long frame still negligently
propped against the mantelpiece. The subtle hand of a

master showed in the cut of his dark blue coat; the
pristine state of his small clothes was beyond reproach.
Gleaming Hessians completed the picture. Martin, his
mother reflected, had never been cheap.

The object of her scrutiny was examining the toe of
one boot.

Undeterred, the Dowager added a clincher. 'Should
you choose to flout my wishes, I'll see you damned and
will settle my fortune on Damian.'

As she made this final, all-encompassing threat, Lady
Catherine smiled and settled back in her chair. Martin
had always disliked Damian, jealous of the fact that
the younger boy was her favourite. Knowing the battle
won, she glanced up at her son.

She was unprepared for the slow smile which spread
across his dark face, softening the harsh lines, impart-
ing a devilish handsomeness to the aristocratic features.
Irrelevantly, she reflected that it was hardly surprising
that this son, of the four, had never had the slightest
trouble winning the ladies to his side.

'If that's all you have to say, ma'am, I have a few
comments of my own.'

Lady Catherine blinked, then inclined her head
regally, prepared to be gracious in victory.

Nonchalantly, Martin straightened and strolled
towards the windows. 'Firstly, as regards my marriage,
I will marry whom I please, when I please. And,
incidentally, if I please.'

The stunned silence behind him spoke volumes.
Martin's gaze skimmed the tops of the trees in the
Home Wood. His mother's suggestions were outrageous, but entirely expected. However, while her
machinations were unwelcome, he understood and

respected the devotion to family duty that prompted her to them. Even more to the point, they confirmed his supposition that she had had no hand in the decline of the Merton fortunes. As she was tied to her room, her household under the sway of an unscrupulous factor he had derived great satisfaction from verbally flaying before evicting him in the time-honoured way, he doubted his mother had any idea of the state of the rest of the house. Her chambers were in reasonable condition, better than any others in the rambling mansion. The factor had succeeded in intimidating the rest of the staff and, very likely, had gulled Melissa and possibly even George into believing that the decay was unavoidable. And if the section of gardens he could now see was the only fragment of the grounds still deserving of the title, how could his mother know the rest was wilderness? Martin paused by the window, his fingers drumming lightly on the wide ledge. 'Apropos of Damian, I should point out that he will hardly thank you for rushing me to the altar. He is, after all, my heir until such time as I father a legitimate son. Considering his current pecuniary embarrassments, he's unlikely to appreciate your motives in assisting me to accomplish that deed, and in such haste.'

Lady Catherine stiffened. Martin spared a glance for his sister-in-law, huddled back in her chair, listening intently to the exchange between mother and son while ostensibly absorbed with her embroidery. One brow rising cynically, Martin turned to his mother's fury.

'How *dare* you!' For a moment, rage held the Dowager speechless. Then the dam broke. 'You will marry *as I say*! To think of any other course is out of the question! The arrangements have been made.'

'Naturally,' Martin replied, his voice cool and precise, 'I regret any inconvenience your actions may cause others. However,' he continued, on a sterner note, 'I am at a loss to understand what gave you the impression that you were empowered to speak for me in this matter. I find it hard to believe that Miss Wendover's parents were so ill-advised as to imagine you did. If they have, in truth, done so, their discomfiture is the result of their own folly. I suggest you inform them without delay that no alliance will occur between Miss Wendover and myself.'

Stunned, Lady Catherine blinked. 'You're mad! I would be mortified to do so!' She sat bolt upright, her hands twisting in her lap, her expression one of dawning dismay.

Martin quelled an unexpected urge to comfort her. She would have to learn that the youth who left this house thirteen years before was no more. 'I hesitate to point out that any embarrassment you might feel has been accrued through your own machinations. It would be well if you could bring yourself to understand that I will not be manipulated, ma'am.'

Unable to meet his stern gaze, Lady Catherine glanced down at her crabbed fingers, conscious for the first time in years of an urge to fuss with her skirts. Suddenly, Martin looked very like—sounded very like—his father.

When his mother remained silent, Martin continued calmly, his tone dry. 'As for your second point, I can inform you that, having become thoroughly acquainted with my inheritance, I've rescinded all the appointments made by George. Matthews and Sons and Bromleys, our brokers, together with our bankers, Blanchards, remain. They date from my father's time. But my people are now in charge of this estate and smaller estates in Dorset, Leicestershire and Northamptonshire. The men George hired were bleeding the estate dry. It's beyond my comprehension, ma'am, why even you did not question the story that estates of the size of the Merton holdings were, within two years of my father's death, mysteriously no longer able to support the family.'

Martin paused, tamping down the anger simmering beneath his calm. Just thinking of the state of his patrimony was enough to summon his demons. Surmising from his mother's stunned expression that she needed a few minutes to adjust to his revelations, he let his gaze wander the room.

Lady Catherine's mind was indeed reeling. A niggling memory of the odd look old Matthews had given her when, angry at Martin's inheriting, she had given vent to her frustrations in a long catalogue of his shortcomings, returned with a thump. She had been taken aback by the man's quietly tendered opinion that Mr Martin was just what the Merton estates needed. Martin, expensive profligate that he was, was hardly the sort she had expected Matthews to support. Later, she had learned that Martin had engaged the same firm his family had long used to represent him in his business dealings. It had come as something of a shock to realise that Martin had the sort of dealings with which a firm such as Matthews and Sons would assist. Matthews' comment had bothered her. Now she knew what he had meant. Damn him—why had he not explained more fully? Why had she not asked?

After gazing at Melissa's bent head, pale blonde

flecked with grey, and recalling his conclusion of years before that nothing much actually went on inside it, Martin turned back to his mother. As he guessed rather more of her thoughts than she would have wished, his lips twisted wryly. 'You're quite right in saying that I've little experience in running estates of this size — my own are considerably more extensive.'

Confirming as they did that her third son had changed in more ways than met the eye, his words seriously undermined Lady Catherine's composure. They more than undermined her plans.

At her thunderstruck look, Martin's grin converted to a not ungentle smile. 'Did you think your prodigal son was returning from a life of deprivation to hang on your sleeve?'

The glance she threw him was answer enough. Martin leant back against the window-ledge, long legs stretched before him. 'I'm desolated to disappoint you, ma'am, but I'm in no need of your funds. On my return to London, I'll instruct Matthews to call on you here, to assist in redrafting your will. I pray you hold to your threat to disown me. Damian will never forgive you if you don't. Besides,' he added, grey eyes gleaming with irrepressible candour, 'he needs the support that the news that he's your beneficiary will bring. If nothing else, it should relieve me of the necessity of repeatedly rescuing him from the River Tick. As far as I'm concerned, he may go to the devil in whatever way he chooses. If he uses your money to do it, I'll be even better pleased. However, regardless of what you may choose to do, no further monies from your settlements will be used for the Merton estates, in any way whatever.'

Martin examined his mother's face, sensitive to the encroachments of age on past beauty. After her initial shock, she had drawn herself up, her eyes grey stone, her lips compressed as if to hold back her incredulity. Despite her ailment, there was a deal of strength and determination still descernible in the gaunt frame. To his surprise, he no longer felt the need to strike back at her, to impress her with his successes, to demonstrate how worthy of her love he was. That, too, had died with the years.

'And now to your last stipulation.' He pushed away from the window-ledge, glancing down to resettle his sleeves. 'I will, of course, be residing for part of the year in London. Beyond that, I anticipate travelling to my various estates as well as visiting those of my friends, as one might expect. I also anticipate inviting guests to stay here. As I recall, during my father's day, the Hermitage was renowned for its hospitality.' He looked at his mother; she was staring past him, plainly struggling to bring this new image of him into focus.

'Of course, such visits will have to wait until the place is refurbished.'

'*What*?' The unladylike exclamation burst from Lady Catherine's lips. Startled, her gaze flew to Martin's face, her question in her eyes.

'You needn't concern yourself about that.' Martin frowned. There was no need for her to know how bad it really was; she would be mortified. 'I'm sending a firm of decorators down once they've finished with Merton House.' He paused but his mother's gaze was again far-away. When she made no further comment, Martin straightened. 'I'm returning to London within the hour. So, if there's nothing further you wish to discuss, I'll bid you goodbye.'

'Am I to assume these decorators will, on *your* instruction, redo these rooms as well?' The sarcasm in Lady Catherine's voice would have cut glass.

Martin smothered his smile. Rapidly, he reviewed his options. 'If you wish, I'll tell them to consult with you—over the rooms that are peculiarly yours, of course.'

He could not, in all conscience, saddle her with the task of overseeing such a major reconstruction, and, if truth be known, he intended to use this opportunity to stamp his own personality on this, the seat of his forebears.

His mother's glare relieved him of any worry that she would react to his independence by going into a decline. Reassured, Martin raised an expectant brow.

With every evidence of reluctance, Lady Catherine nodded a curt dismissal.

With a graceful bow to her, and a nod for Melissa, Martin left the room.

Lady Catherine watched him go, then sought counsel in silence. Long after the door had clicked shut, she remained, her gaze fixed, unseeing, on the unlighted fire. Eventually shaking free of her recollections, she could not help wondering if, in her most secret of hearts, despite the attendant difficulties, she was not just a little bit relieved to have a man, a real man, in charge again.

Downstairs, Martin briskly descended the steep steps of the portico to where his curricle awaited, his prize match bays stamping impatiently. A heavy hacking cough greeted him, coming from beyond the off-side

horse. Frowning, Martin ignored the reins looped over
the brake and, patting the velvety noses of his favourite
pair, rounded them to find his groom-cum-valet and
ex-batman Joshua Carruthers propped against the carriage, eyes streaming above a large handkerchief.

'What the devil's the matter?' Even as Martin asked
the question, he realised the answer.

'Nuthing more'n a cold,' Joshua mumbled thickly,
waving one gnarled hand dismissively. He gulped and
stuffed the handkerchief in his breeches pocket, revealing a shiny red nose to his master's sharp eyes. 'Best
get on our way, then.'

Martin did not move. 'You're not going anywhere.'

'But I distin'ly 'eard you say nuthin' on earth woul'
induce you to spen' the night in this ramshackle 'ole.'

'As always, your memory is accurate, your hearing
less so. I'm going on.'

'No' without me, you're not.'

Exasperated, hands on hips, Martin watched as the
old soldier half staggered to the back of the curricle.
When he had to brace himself against the curricle side
as another bout of coughing shook him, Martin swore.
Spotting two stable boys gazing in awe, whether at the
equipage or its owner Martin was not at all sure, he
beckoned them up. 'Hold 'em.'

Once assured they had the restless horses secured,
Martin grasped Joshua by the elbow and steered him
remorselessly towards the house. 'Consider yourself
ordered back to barracks. Dammit, man—we wouldn't
get around the first bend before you fell off.'

In vain, Joshua tried to hang back. 'But——'

'I know the place is in a state,' Martin countered,
sweeping his reluctant henchman back up the steps.

'But now I've got rid of that wretched factor, the rest of the staff will doubtless remember how things should be done. At least,' he added, stopping in the gloomy front hall, 'I hope they will.'

He had given orders that the household should conduct itself as it had previously, in his father's day. Enough of the staff remained for him to expect a reasonable outcome. All locals, many from generations of Merton servitors, they had been overwhelmed by the outsider George had installed over them. Freed from the tyrannical factor, they seemed eager to return the Hermitage to its proper state.

Joshua sniffed. 'What about the horses?'

Martin's lips twitched but he suppressed the urge to smile, assuming instead a repressively haughty attitude. His brows rose to chilling heights. 'You aren't about to suggest I don't know how to take care of my cattle, are you?'

Muttering, Joshua threw him a darkling glance.

'Get off to bed, you old curmudgeon. When you're well enough to ride, you may take a horse from the stables and come on to London. It'll have to be that hack of George's; it's the only animal remaining with sufficient resemblance to the equine species to meet your high standards.'

Not at all mollified, Joshua humphed. But he knew better than to argue. Contenting himself with a last warning—'There's rain on the way, so's you'd best take heed'—he stumped down the hall towards the faded baize-covered door at its rear.

Smiling, Martin returned to his curricle. Dismissing the wide-eyed lads, he climbed to the box seat and clicked the reins. The carriage swept down the weed-choked drive. Martin did not glance back.

As he passed through the gateposts marking the main entry, through the heavy iron gates, half off their hinges, Martin heaved a heartfelt sigh. For thirteen years, his home had glowed in his memory, a place of charm and grace, an Elysian paradise he had longed to regain. Fate had granted him his wish but, as fickle as ever, had denied him his dream. The charm and grace had vanished, victim to the neglect of the years since his father had had it in his care.

He would restore it—bring back the gracious beauty, the calming sense of peace. On that he was determined. Martin's jaw set, his eyes glinted, grey steel in the afternoon sun. In truth, he was glad to leave behind the travesty of his dream. He would remain in London until the work was done. When next he saw his home, it would once again be the place he had carried in his heart through all the years of his roaming. His particular paradise.

The road to Taunton loomed ahead. Checking his team for the turn, Martin cast a quick glance to the west. Joshua had been right—there was rain on the way. Pursing his lips, Martin considered his options. If he stopped at Taunton, London the next day would be a tough order. He would make for Ilchester—he and Joshua had passed the previous night at the Fox in tolerable comfort. Decision made, Martin dropped his hands, letting the horses stretch their legs. From memory, there was a short cut, just south of Taunton, which would see him in Ilchester before the coming storm.

Two hours later, the curricle swayed perilously as the wheels hit yet another rut. Martin swore roundly.

He reined in his team to peer ahead into the gathering gloom. The short cut, dimly remembered as a fair road, had not lived up to expectations. A low mutter came from the west. Martin scanned the horizons, barely visible beneath the low-lying cloud. He doubted he could even make the London road before the storm struck.

He was gently urging the horses over the rutted stretch, dredging his memory in an effort to recall any nearby shelter, when a scream rent the air. The horses plunged. Rapidly bringing them under control, Martin leapt from his perch and ran to their heads. He caught hold of their bits just in time to prevent them rearing as a second scream sliced through the night. No doubt about it, a woman's scream, coming from the woods just ahead. Swiftly, Martin tied the team securely to a nearby gate and, grabbing the pair of loaded pistols from beneath the seat, made for the trees. Once in their shadow, he took care to move silently, thanking the years of his misspent youth, when he had often gone poaching on his father's preserves with young Johnny Hobbs from the village.

Some distance into the wood, he froze. Before him lay a small clearing, a track leading into it from the opposite direction. Sounds of a struggle came from an ill-assorted trio, waltzing in the shadows in the centre.

'Keep still, you little. . .!'

'*Ow*! Gawd! She bit my finger, the doxy!'

As one man pulled away, the group resolved into two burly men dressed in unkempt frieze and a lady, unquestionably a lady, in a silk gown which shimmered in the twilight. The larger of the men succeeded in grabbing the woman from behind, trapping her arms by her sides. Despite her efforts to kick him, he managed to hold her.

'Listen, missus. The master said to hold you 'ere and not to harm a single hair of your head. Now how's we to do that if'n you don't stop still?'

The exasperation in the man's voice brought a sympathetic smile to Martin's face. The clearing was too large to allow him to creep up on them. Quietly, he worked his way around so that the man holding the woman would have his back to him.

'You fools!' The woman and her captor teetered perilously. 'Don't you know the price for kidnapping? If you let me go, I'll pay you double what your master will!'

Martin's brows rose. The woman's voice was unexpectedly mature. Clearly, she had not lost her head.

'Maybe so, lady,' growled the man nursing his finger. 'But the master's gentry and they're mean when crossed. No—I don't rightly see as how we can oblige.'

Holding both pistols fully cocked, Martin stepped from the trees. 'Dear me. Haven't you been taught to always oblige a lady?'

The man holding the woman let her go and swung to face Martin. In the same moment, Martin saw the second man draw a knife. He had a clear shot and took it, the ball passing into the man's elbow. The man dropped the knife and howled. His comrade turned to the source of the sound and so missed the pretty sight of ex-Major Martin Willesden, soldier of fortune and experienced man at arms, being laid low by a right to the jaw, delivered by a very small fist. Martin, his attention on the man he had shot, did not see the blow coming. His head jerked back from the contact and struck a low branch. Stunned, he crumpled slowly to the ground.

Helen Walford stared at the long form stretched somnolent at her feet. God in heaven! It wasn't Hedley Swayne after all! The discharged pistol, still smoking, was clutched in the man's left hand. His right hand held a second pistol, cocked and ready. She darted forward and grabbed it. Catching her skirts in one hand, she leapt over the sprawled form and swung to train the pistol on her captor, hampered in his efforts to reach her by the body between. 'Keep your distance!' she warned. 'I know how to use this.'

Noting the steadiness of the pistol pointed at his chest, the man who had held her decided to accept her word. He glanced back at his accomplice, now on his knees, moaning in pain. He threw Helen a malevolent glance. 'Blast!'

He eyed her menacingly, then turned and stumped over to his mate. Helping him up, he growled, 'Let's get out of this. The master's bound to be along shortly. To my mind, he can sort this lot out hisself.'

His words carried to Helen. Her eyes widened in shock. 'You mean this man isn't your master?' She spared a glance for the still form at her feet. Heavens! What had she done?

The men looked at the crumpled figure. 'That swell? Never set eyes on him afore, missus.'

'Whoever he be, he's goin' to be none too pleased with you when he wakes up,' added the second man with relish.

Helen swallowed and gestured with the gun. Grumbling, the two rogues made their way to the edge of the clearing where stood a disreputable gig pulled by a single broken-down nag. They clambered aboard and, whistling up the horse, departed down the rough track.

Left alone in the gloom with her unconscious rescuer, Helen stood and stared at the recumbent form. 'Oh, lord!'

Thus far, her day had been a resounding disaster. Kidnapped in the small hours, bundled up in a distinctly odoriferous blanket, bustled from one carriage to another until the sounds of London had been left far behind, she had spent the day being battered and jostled, tied and gagged, trussed and trapped in a worn-out chaise. Her head was still pounding. And now she had been rescued, only to lay her rescuer low.

With a groan, Helen pressed a hand to her temple.

Fate was having a field day.

CHAPTER TWO

THE back of his head hurt. Martin's first thought on regaining consciousness convinced him he was still alive. But, when his lids fluttered open, he realised his error. He had to be dead. There was an angel hanging over him, her golden hair lit by an unearthly radiance. A sudden twinge forced his eyes shut.

He could not be dead. His head hurt too much, even though it was cradled in the softest lap imaginable. A delicate hand brushed his brow. He trapped it in one of his. No spectre, his angel, but flesh and blood.

'What happened?' He winced, pain stabbing behind his eyes.

Helen, bending over him, winced in sympathy. 'I'm dreadfully afraid that I hit you. On the jaw. You stumbled back and hit a branch.'

When a spasm of pain—or was it irritation?—passed over her rescuer's strong features, Helen's guilt increased. As soon as the rattle of the gig had receded, she had fallen on her knees beside her victim. Quelling all maidenly hesitation—she was hardly a maiden, after all—she had bent her mind to ministering to the injuries she had caused. His shoulders were abominably heavy, but, eventually, she had managed to lift his head on to her lap, gently stroking back the raven locks that had fallen across his brow.

Martin held on to her hand, reluctant to let his anchor to reality slip. It was a small hand, the bones delicate between his fingers. Gradually, the pounding in his head subsided, leaving a dull ache. He put up his free hand to feel the bruise on his chin. Just in time, he remembered not to try and feel the bump on his head. It was, after all, resting on her lap and she sounded like a lady.

'Do you always attack your rescuers?' Martin struggled to sit up.

Helen helped him, then sat back on her heels to look at him, open concern in her eyes. 'I really must apologise. I thought you were Hedley Swayne.'

Gingerly, Martin examined the lump rising on the back of his skull. Her voice, if nothing else, confirmed his angel's station. The soft, rounded tones slid into his consciousness like warmed honey. He frowned. 'Who's Hedley Swayne? The master who arranged your abduction?'

Helen nodded. 'So I believe.' She should have guessed this man wasn't Hedley—his voice was far too deep, far too gravelly. Feeling at a distinct disadvantage due to the unfortunate circumstance of their meeting, she studied her hands, clasped in her lap, and wondered what her rescuer was thinking. She had had ample opportunity to admire his length as he had lain stretched out beside her. A most impressive length. The single comprehensive glance she had had, before his head had hit the branch, had left a highly favourable impression. Despite her predicament, Helen's lips twitched. She could not recall being quite so impressed in years. Reality intruded. She had hit him and knocked him out. *He*, doubtless, was not impressed at all.

Surreptitiously observing his damsel in distress as

she knelt beside him in the shadowy twilight, Martin could understand his earlier conviction that she was an angel. Thick golden curls rioted around her head, spilling in chaotic confusion on to her shoulders. Very nicely turned shoulders, too. A silk evening gown which he thought would be apricot under normal light clung to her shapely curves. He could not guess how tall she was but all the rest of her was constructed on generous lines. He glanced at her face. In the poor light, her features were indistinct. An unexpectedly strong desire to see more, in better light, possessed him. 'I take it this same Hedley Swayne is expected here at any moment?'

'That's what the two men said.' Helen spoke dismissively. In truth, she could summon little interest in her abductor; her rescuer was far more fascinating.

Slowly, Martin got to his feet, grateful for his angel's steadying hand. His faculties were a trifle unsettled, his senses distracted by her nearness. 'Why did they leave?' She was quite tall; her curls would tickle his nose if she were closer, her forehead level with his lips. Just the right height for a tall man. Her legs, glorious legs, were deliciously long. He resisted the urge to examine them more closely.

'I held the second pistol on them.' Sensing his distraction and worried that she might have caused him serious injury, Helen frowned, trying to study his expression through the gloom. Reminded of his pistols, she bent to retrieve them, her silk skirts clinging to her shapely derrière.

Martin looked away, shaking his head to dislodge the fantasies crowding in. Damn it! The situation was potentially dangerous! Definitely not the time for idle

dalliance. He cleared his throat. 'In my present condition, I feel it might be wise to leave before Mr
Swayne arrives. Unless you think it preferable to stay
and face him?'

Helen shook her head. 'Heavens, no! He'll have a
coach and men with him. He never travels without
outriders.' Her contempt for her abductor rang in her
tone. A sudden thought struck her. 'Where are we?'

'South of Taunton.'

'Taunton?' Helen stood, the pistols hanging from her
hands, and frowned. 'Hedley mentioned estates somewhere in Cornwall. I suppose he was going to take me
there.'

Martin nodded; the explanation was likely, given
their present location. He glanced around to reorientate himself, then reached for his pistols. 'If he's likely
to come with friends, I suggest we depart forthwith.
My curricle's in a lane beyond the wood. I was passing
when I heard your screams.'

'Thank heaven you did.' Belatedly, Helen shook out
her skirts. 'I held very little hope we would be near
any main road.'

She glanced up at her rescuer, to find he was studying her, the shadows concealing his expression.

Martin smiled, a little wryly. His angel was not out
of the woods yet. 'I hesitate to disabuse you of such a
comforting thought, but we're some way from any
main road. I was taking a short cut through the lanes
in the hope of reaching the London road before the
storm.'

'You're going to London?'

'Eventually,' Martin conceded. The branches above
obscured too much of the sky to let him judge the

approach of the rainclouds. 'But first we'll have to find shelter for the night.'

With a last glance about, Martin offered her his arm.

Quelling a rush of uncharacteristic nervousness, Helen placed her hand on his sleeve. She had no choice but to trust him, yet her trust in gentlemen was not presently high.

'Was it from London you were taken?'

'Yes,' Helen felt no constraint in revealing that much but the question reminded her to be wary until she knew more of her rescuer, fascinating though he might be.

Absorbed in negotiating the numerous hurdles in the congested path through the trees without further damaging her gown, Helen felt the calm certainty with which she normally faced her world return. Her rescuer's strong arm assisted her over the blockages. The subtle deference in his attitude effectively dispelled her fears, settling a cloak of protectiveness about her. Relieved to find his behaviour as gentlemanly as his elegance, she relaxed.

Martin waited until they were some distance from the clearing before appeasing his burgeoning curiosity. The question burning his tongue was who she was. But that, doubtless, would be best left for later. He contented himself with, 'Who is Hedley Swayne?'

'A fop,' came the uncompromising reply.

'You mistook *me* for a *fop*?' Despite the potential seriousness of their plight, Martin's latent tendencies were too strong to repress. When she turned her head his way, eyes wide, her lips parted in confusion, his eyes wickedly quizzed her.

Helen caught her breath. For an instant, her eyes

locked with her rescuer's. Three heartbeats passed before, with a desperate effort, she wrenched her gaze free and snatched back her wandering wits. 'I didn't see you, remember.'

At the sound of her soft and slightly husky disclaimer, Martin chuckled. 'Ah, yes!'

A fallen tree blocked their path. He released her to step over it, then turned and held out his hands. From beneath her lashes, Helen glanced up at his face. A strong, intriguing face, rather more tanned and harsh-featured than one was wont to see. She wondered what colour his eyes were. With a calm she was not entirely sure she possessed, she put her hands into his. His strong fingers closed over hers; a peculiar constriction tightened about her chest. Helen glanced down, ostensibly to negotiate the fallen tree, in reality to hide her sudden frown at the ridiculous skitterishness that had attacked her. Surely she was too old for such girlish reactions?

Resuming his place by her side, Martin glanced down at her bent head, perfectly sure, now, that the tremor he had felt in her fingers had not been a figment of his over-active imagination. Highly experienced in the subtleties of this particular form of play, he sought for some topic to get her mind off him. 'I trust you've suffered no harm from your ordeal with those ruffians?'

Determined not to let her ridiculous nervousness show, Helen shook her head. 'No—none at all. But they were under orders to take care of me.'

'So I heard. Nevertheless, I dare say you've had your wits quite addled by fright.'

Despite an unnerving awareness of the presence by

her side, Helen laughed. 'Oh, no! I assure you I'm not such a poor creature as all that.' She risked a glance upwards and saw her rescuer's dark brows rise. The look he bent on her was patently disbelieving. Her smile grew. 'Very well,' she conceded, 'I'll admit to a qualm or two, but when they were plainly being as gentle as they knew how I could hardly quake for fear of my life.'

'I've rescued an Amazon.'

The bland statement floated above her curls. Helen chuckled and shook her head, but refused to be further drawn.

As the trees thinned, she resolutely turned her mind to her present predicament. With the uncertainty of her abduction receding, she was conscious of an oddly light-hearted response to this new set of circumstances. Twilight was drawing in; she was walking through woods, very much alone, with an unknown gentleman. While she was quite convinced of his quality, she was not nearly so sure it was safe to approve of his style, much less his propensities. Nevertheless, trepidation was not what she felt. Unbidden, a smile curved her lips. Not since childhood had such a whimsical, adventurous mood claimed her; the same buoyant exuberance had whirled her through her most outrageous childhood exploits. Why on earth it should surface now, in response, she was sure, to the stranger by her side, she had no idea. But the thrill of exhilaration tripping along her nerves was too marked to ignore. In truth, she had no wish to ignore it—life had been too serious, too mundane, for too long. A little adventure would lighten the dim prospect of her lonely future.

They emerged from the trees. In the narrow lane, a

fashionable curricle was outlined against the gathering gloom, a pair of high-stepping bays restlessly shifting between the shafts. Impulsively, Helen gasped, 'What beauties!'

The lines of both equipage and horses spoke volumes. Clearly, her rescuer was a man of means. Smiling, he released her beside the carriage, going to the horses' heads to run a soothing hand over their noses.

Helen eyed the curricle, wondering if, in her slim evening gown, it was possible to gain the box seat perched high above the axle with reasonable decorum. She was about to attempt the difficult climb when a pair of strong hands fastened about her waist and she was lifted, effortlessly, upwards.

'Oh!' Her eyes widened; she bit back a most unlady-like squeal. Deposited gently on the seat, she blushed rosy red. 'Er. . . thank you.' The smile on her rescuer's face was decidedly wicked. Abruptly, Helen busied herself with settling her skirts, while, under her lashes, she watched him untie the reins.

It wasn't just the fact that she knew she was no lightweight, nor that no man before had ever lifted her like that, making her feel ridiculously delicate. It wasn't even the impression of remarkable strength that lingered with the memory of his hands gripping her waist. No. It was her quite shocking response to that perfectly mundane little intimacy that was tying her nerves in knots. Never in her life had she felt so odd, so thoroughly witless. What on earth was the matter with her?

Her rescuer swung up beside her. He moved with the ease of a born athlete, compounding the impression of leashed power created by the combination of under-stated elegance and sheer size. A deliciously fascinating impression, Helen was only too willing to admit. Then he glanced at her.

'Comfortable?'

She nodded, the simple question dispelling any lingering fears. In her estimation, no blackguard would ask if his victim was comfortable. Her rescuer might make her nervous; he did not frighten her.

A drop of rain fell on Martin's hand as he clicked the reins. The sensation drew his mind from contemplation of the woman beside him and focused it on more practical matters. Night was closing in and, with it, the weather.

He levelled a measuring glance at his companion. When he had lifted her to the box seat, getting a good glimpse of a pair of shapely ankles in the process, he had confirmed the fact that her dress was indeed silk, fine and delicate. Furthermore, his experienced assessment told him her fashionable standing extended to wearing no more than a fine silk chemise beneath. In the wood, the warmth of the afternoon had been trapped beneath the trees but now they were in the open and the temperature was dropping. The neckline of her gown was cut remarkably low, a fact which met with his unqualified approval; the tiny puffed sleeves, badly crushed, were set off her shoulders. Even in the poor light, her skin glowed translucently pale. She was not yet shivering, but it could only be a question of time. 'If you'll forgive my impertinence, why are you gallivanting about without even a cloak?'

Helen frowned, considering. How much was it safe to reveal? Then, unconsciously lifting her chin, she took the plunge. 'I was at Chatham House, at a ball given for Lady Chatham's birthday. A footman brought a note asking me to meet...a friend on the portico.'

In retrospect, she should have been more careful. 'There were...circumstances that made that seem quite reasonable at the time,' she explained. 'But there was no one about—at least, that's what I thought. I waited for a moment or two, then, just as I was about to go back inside, someone—one of those two ruffians, I think—threw a coat over my head.'

Helen shivered slightly, whether from the cold or the memory of her sudden fright she was not sure. 'They bundled me into a waiting carriage—it was still early and there were no other coaches in the drive.' She drew a deep breath. 'So that's why no cloak.'

'I see.' Martin trapped the reins under his boot and reached behind the seat to drag his greatcoat from where it was neatly stowed. He shook it out and flung it about his companion's distracting shoulders, then calmly picked up the reins. 'What makes you think it was this Hedley Swayne behind your abduction?'

Helen frowned. In reality, now that she considered the matter more closely, there was no firm evidence to connect Hedley with the kidnap attempt.

Observing her pensive face, Martin's brows rose. 'No real reason—just a feeling?'

At the superior tone rippling beneath the raspy surface of his deep voice, Helen drew herself up. 'If you knew how Hedley's been behaving recently, you wouldn't doubt it.'

Martin grinned at her prickly rejoinder and infused a degree of sympathy into his, 'How has he been behaving?'

'He's forever at me to marry him—heaven only knows why.'

Pressing his lips together to suppress the spontaneous retort that had leapt to his tongue, Martin waited until his voice was steady before asking, 'Not the obvious?'

Absorbed in cogitations on the vagaries of Hedley Swayne, Helen shook her head. 'Definitely not the obvious.' Suddenly recalling to whom she was speaking, she blushed. Praying that the poor light would conceal the fact, she hurried on. 'Hedley's not the marrying kind, if you know what I mean.'

Martin's lips twitched but he made no comment.

Helen considered the iniquitous Mr Swayne, a slight frown puckering her delicate brows. 'Unfortunately, I've no idea why he wants to marry me. No idea at all.'

They proceeded in silence, Martin intent on the bad road, Helen lost in thought. The land about was open pastures, separated by occasional hedgerows, with not even a farmhouse to be seen. A stray thought took hold in Martin's mind. 'Did you say you were at a ball when they grabbed you? Have you been missing since last night?'

Helen nodded. 'But I went in my own carriage—not many of my friends have returned to town yet.'

'So your coachman would have raised the alarm?'

Slowly, Helen shook her head. 'Not immediately. I might have gone home in some acquaintance's carriage and my message to John got lost in the fuss. That's happened before. My people wouldn't have been certain I was truly missing until this morning.' Her brows knit, she considered the possibilities. 'I wonder what they'll do?'

For his own reasons, Martin also wondered. The possibility of being mistaken for a kidnapper, and the consequent explanations, was not the sort of imbroglio he wished to be landed in just at present—not when he had barely set foot in England and had yet to establish his bona fides. 'You'll certainly cause a stir when you reappear.'

'Mm.' Helen's mind had drifted from the shadowy possibilities of happenings in London, drawn to more immediate concerns by the presence beside her. Her rescuer had yet to ask her name, nor had he volunteered his. But her adventurous mood had her firmly in its grip; their state of being mutually incognito seemed perfectly appropriate. She felt comfortably secure; appellations, she was sure, were unnecessary.

Absorbed in the increasingly difficult task of managing his team over the severely rutted track, Martin racked his brains for some acceptable avenue to learn his companion's name. Their situation was an odd one—not having been formally introduced, he did not expect her to volunteer the information. He balked at simply asking, not wanting her to feel impelled to reveal it out of gratitude for her rescue. Yet, without it, could he be sure of finding her in London? He ought, of course, to introduce himself, but, until he was more certain of her, was reluctant to do so.

Another drop of rain and a low mutter from the west jerked his mind back to practicalities. Skittish, the horses tossed their heads. He settled them, carefully edging them about a sharp corner. The dark shape of a barn loomed on the left, set back in a field and screened on the west by a stand of chesnuts. The mutter turned into a growl; lightning split the sky.

With a grimace, Martin checked the horses for the turn into the rough cart track leading to the barn. He glanced at his companion, still lost in thought. 'I'm afraid, my dear, that before you you see our abode for the night. We're miles from the nearest shelter and the horses won't stand a thunderstorm.'

Startled from her reverie, Helen peered ahead. Seeing the dark structure before her, she considered the proposition of spending the night in a barn with her rescuer and found it strangely attractive. 'Don't mind me,' she replied airily. 'If I'm to have an adventure then it might as well be complete with a night in a disused barn. Is it disused, do you think?'

'In this area? Unlikely. Hopefully there'll be a loft full of fresh straw.'

There was. Martin unharnessed the horses and rubbed them down, then made them as secure as possible in the rude stalls. By now very grateful for the warmth of his thick greatcoat, Helen clutched it about her. She wandered around the outside of the barn and discovered a well, clearly in use, by one side. Before the rain set in, she hurried to draw water, filling all the pails she could find. After supplying the horses, she splashed water over her face, washing away the dust of the day. Refreshed, she belatedly remembered she had no towel. Eyes closed, she all but jumped when a deep chuckle came from behind her, reverberating through her bones, sending peculiar shivers flickering over her skin. Strong fingers caught her hand; a linen square was pushed into it. Hurriedly, Helen mopped her face and turned.

He stood a yard or so behind her, a subtle smile twisting his firm lips. He had found a lantern and hung it from the loft steps. The soft light fell on his black hair, glossing the curls where they formed over his ears and by the side of his neck. Hooded grey eyes—she was sure they were grey—lazily regarded her. Helen's diaphragm seized; her eyes widened. He was handsome. Disgustingly handsome. Even more handsome than Hazelmere. She felt her throat constrict. Damn it! No man had the right to be so handsome. With an effort, she masked her reactions and swept him an elegant curtsy. 'Thank you most kindly, sir—for your handkerchief and for rescuing me.'

The subtle smile deepened, infusing the harshly handsome face with a wholly sensual promise. 'My pleasure, fair Juno.'

This time, his voice sent tingling quivers down her spine. Fair Juno? Shaken, Helen held out the handkerchief, hoping the action would cover her momentary fluster.

Taking back the linen square, Martin let his eyes roam, then abruptly hauled back on the reins. Dammit— he was supposed to be a gentleman and she was very clearly a lady. But if she kept looking at him like that he was apt to forget such niceties.

Smoothly, he turned to a rough bin against one wall. 'There's corn here. If we grind some up, we'll be able to have pancakes for supper.'

Helen eyed the blue-suited back a touch nervously, then turned her gaze, even more dubiously, on the corn bin. Were pancakes made of corn? 'I'm afraid. . .' she began, forced to admit to ignorance.

Her rescuer threw her a dazzling smile. 'Don't worry. I know how. Come and help.'

Thus adjured, Helen willingly went forward to render

what assistance she could. They hunted about and found two suitable rocks, a large flat one for the grinding base and a smaller, round one to crush the corn. After a demonstration of the accepted technique, Helen settled to the task of producing the cornmeal, while her mentor started a small fire, just outside the barn door, where the lee of the barn gave protection from the steady rain.

Every now and then, a crack of lightning presaged a heavy roll of thunder. The horses shifted restively, but they settled. Inside the barn, all was snug and dry.

'That should be suffcient.'

Seated on a pile of straw, Helen looked up to find her mentor towering beside her, a pail of water in one hand.

'Now we add water to make a paste.'

Struggling to keep his eyes on his task, Martin knelt opposite his assistant and, dipping his fingers in the water, sprinkled the pile of meal. Helen caught the idea. Soon, a satisfyingly large mound of soft dough had been formed. Helen carried the dough to the fire in her hands, while Martin brought up the heavy rock.

She had seen him wash an old piece of iron and scrub it down with straw. He had placed it across the fire. She watched as he brought up the water pail and let a drop fall to the heated surface. Critically, he watched it sizzle into steam.

Martin smiled. 'Just right. The trick is not to let it get too hot.'

Confidently, he set two pieces of dough on to the metal surface and quickly flattened them with his palm.

Helen pulled an old crate closer to the fire. 'How do you know all this?'

A slow grin twisted Martin's lips. 'Among my many and varied past lives, I was a soldier.'

'In the Peninsula?'

Martin nodded. While they cooked and ate their pancakes, he entertained her with a colourful if censored account of his campaigning days. These had necessarily culminated with Waterloo. 'After that, I returned to. . .my business affairs.'

He rose and stretched. The night was deepest black about them. It was as if they were the only souls for miles. His lips twisted in a wry grin. Stranded in a barn with fair Juno—what an opportunity for one of his propensities. Unfortunately, fair Juno was unquestionably gently bred and was under his protection. His grin turned to a grimace, then was wiped from his face before she could see it. He held out a hand to help her to her feet.

'Time for bed.' Resolutely, he quelled his fantasies, insistently knocking on the door of his consciousness. He inclined his head towards the ladder. 'There are piles of fresh straw up there. We should be snug enough for the night.'

Helen went with him readily, any fears she had possessed entirely allayed by the past hours. She felt perfectly safe with him, perfectly confident of his behaving as he ought. They were friends of sorts, engaged in an adventure.

Her transparent confidence was not lost on Martin. He found her trust oddly touching, not something he was usually gifted with, not something he had any wish to damage. Reaching the foot of the ladder, he unhooked the lantern. 'I'll go up first.' He smiled. 'Can you climb the ladder alone?'

The idea of being carried up the ladder, thrown over his shoulder like a sack of potatoes, was not to be borne. Helen considered the ascent, then shrugged out of his greatcoat. 'If you'll take that up, I think I can manage.'

Briskly, Martin went up, taking the coat and the lantern with him. Then he held the lantern out to light her way. Helen twisted her skirts to one side and, guarding against any mis-step, carefully negotiated the climb.

Above her, Martin swallowed his curses. He had thought coming up first was the right thing to do, relieving her of the potential embarassment of accidentally exposing her calves and ankles to his view. But the view he now had—of a remarkable expanse of creamy breasts, barely concealed by the low neckline of her gown—was equally scandalous. And equally tempting. And he was going to have to spend a whole night with her within reach?

He gritted his teeth and forced his features to behave.

After drawing her to safety, he crossed to the hay door and propped it ajar, admitting the cool night air and fitful streaks of moonlight, shafting through breaks in the storm clouds. He extinguished the lantern and placed it safely on a beam. Earlier in the evening, he had brought up the carriage blanket from the curricle. Spreading his greatcoat in the straw, he picked up the blanket and handed it to her. 'You can sleep there. Wrap yourself up well or you'll be cold.'

The air in the loft was warmer than below but the night boded ill for anyone dressed only in two layers of silk. Gratefully, Helen took the blanket and shook it out, then realised there was only one. 'But what about you? Won't you be cold, too?'

In the safety of the dark, Martin grimaced. He was hoping the night air would cool his imagination, already feverish. Only too aware of the direction of his thoughts, and their likely effect on his tone, he forced his voice to a lighter pitch. 'Sleeping in a dry loft full of straw is nothing to the rigours of campaigning.' So saying, he threw himself down, full-length in the straw, a good three yards from his coat.

In the dim light, Helen saw him grin at her. She smiled, then wrapped the blanket around her before snuggling down into his still warm coat. 'Goodnight.'

'Goodnight.'

For ten full minutes, silence reigned. Martin, far from sleep, watched the clouds cross the moon. Then the thunder returned in full measure. The horses whinnied but settled again. He heard his companion shift restlessly. 'What's the matter? Afraid of mice?'

'*Mice*?' On the rising note, Helen sat bolt upright.

Silently, Martin cursed his loose tongue. 'Don't worry about them.'

'*Don't*. . .! You must be joking!'

Helen shivered, an action Martin saw clearly as a shaft of moonlight glanced through the hay door and fell full on her. God, she was an armful!

Hugging the greatcoat about her, Helen struggled to subdue her burgeoning panic. She sat still, breathing deeply, until another crack of thunder rent the night. 'If you must know, I'm frightened of storms.' The admission, forced through her chattering teeth, came out at least an octave too high. 'And I'm cold.'

Martin heard the querulous note in her voice. She

truly was frightened. Hell! The storm had yet to unleash its full fury—if he did nothing to calm her she might well end up hysterical. Revising his estimate on which was the safer—spending an innocent night with fair Juno or campaigning in Spain—he sighed deeply and stood up, wondering if what he was about to do qualified as masochism. It was certainly going to make sleep difficult, if not impossible. He crossed to where she sat, huddled rigid beneath the blanket. Sitting beside her, on his coat, he put his arm about her and gave her a quick hug. Then, ignoring her confused reluctance, he drew her down to lie beside him, her head resting on his shoulder, her curls tickling his chin. 'Now go to sleep,' he said sternly. 'The mice won't get you and you're safe from the storm and you should be warm enough.'

Rigid with panic, Helen held herself stiffly within his encircling arms. Heaven help her, she did not know which frightened her most—the storm, or the tempest of emotions shattering her confidence. Nothing in her extensive experience had prepared her for spending a night in a stranger's arms but, with the storm raging outside, she could not have forced herself from her safe haven if the stars had fallen. And she was safe. Safe from the elements outside. Gradually, it dawned that she was also safe from any nearer threat.

Reassurance slowly penetrated the mists of panicky confusion assailing her reason. Her locked muscles eased; the tension left her limbs. The man in whose arms she lay was still and silent. His breathing was deep and even, his heart a steady thud muffled beneath her cheek. She had nothing to fear.

Helen relaxed.

When she melted against him, Martin stifled a curse, willing his muscles to perfect stillness.

'Goodnight.' Helen sighed sleepily.

'Goodnight,' Martin replied, his accents clipped.

But Helen was still some way from sleep. The storm lashed the countryside. Inside the barn, all was quiet. Martin, very conscious of the warm and infinitely tempting body beside him, felt her flinch at the thunderclaps. In the aftermath of a particularly violent report, she murmured, 'I've just realised I don't even know your name.'

Helen excused her lie on the grounds of social nicety; she had been wondering for hours how to approach the subject. Their unexpected intimacy gave her an opening she felt justified in taking. It was part of the adventure for him not to know her name, but she definitely wanted to know his.

'Martin Willesden, at your service.' Despite his agony, Martin grinned into the darkness. He was only too willing to serve her in any number of ways.

'Willesden,' Helen repeated, yawning. Then, her eyes flew wide. 'Oh heavens! Not *the* Martin Willesden? The new Earl of Merton?' Helen twisted to look up into his face.

Martin was entertained by her tone. ''Fraid so,' he answered. He glanced down, but her expression was hidden by the dark. 'I presume my reputation has gone before me?'

'Your reputation?' Helen drew breath. 'You, dear sir, have been the sole topic of conversation among the tabbies for the last fortnight. They're all dying for you to show your face! Is the black sheep, now raised to the title, going to join polite society or give us all the go-by?'

Martin chuckled.

Helen felt the sound reverberate through his chest. The temptation to stretch her hands over the expanse of hard muscle was all but overwhelming. Resolutely, she quelled it, settling her head once more into his shoulder.

'I've no taste for the melodramatic.' Martin shifted his hold, adjusting to her position. 'Since landing I've been too busy setting things to rights to make my presence known. I'm returning from inspecting my principal seat. I'll be joining in all the normal pastimes once I get back to London.'

'"All the normal pastimes"?' Helen echoed. 'Yes, I can just imagine.'

'Can you?' Unable to resist, Martin squinted down at her but could not see her face. He could remember it, though—green-flecked amber eyes under perfectly arched brown brows, a straight little nose and wide, full lips, very kissable. 'What do you know of the pastimes of rakes?'

Helen resisted the temptation to reply that she had been married to one. 'Too much,' she countered, reflecting that that, also, was true. Then the oddity of the conversation struck her. She giggled sleepily. 'I feel I should point out to you that this is a most *improper* conversation.' Her tone was light, as light-hearted as she felt. She was perfectly aware that their present situation was scandalous in the extreme, yet it seemed oddly right, and she was quite content.

Martin's views on their situation were considerably more pungent. Sheer madness designed to make his head hurt more than it already did. First she had hit him on the jaw, and caused him to crack his skull. Now this. What more grievous torture could she visit on him?

With a soft sigh, Helen snuggled against him.

Martin's jaw clenched with the effort to remain passive. A chuckle he could only describe as siren-like escaped her. 'I've just thought. I escaped from the clutches of a fop only to spend the night in the arms of one of the most notorious rakehells London ever produced. Presumably there is a moral in this somewhere.' She giggled again and, to Martin's profound astonishment, as innocently and completely as a child, fell asleep.

Martin lay still, staring at the rough beams overhead. Her admission to a knowledge of rakes and their activities struck him as distinctly odd. Also distinctly distracting. Before his imagination, only too willing to slip its leash, could bring him undone, he put the peculiar statement aside for inspection at a later date— a safer date. Given fair Juno's apparent quality, taking her declaration at face value and acting accordingly might not be wise.

With an effort, he concentrated on falling asleep. First, he tried to pretend there was no woman in his arms. That proved impossible. Then he tried thinking of Erica, the mullato mistress he had left behind. That did not work either. Somehow Erica's dark ringlets and coffee-coloured skin kept transforming to golden curls and luscious white curves. Instead of Erica's small, dark-tipped breasts, he saw fuller white breasts with dusky pink aureoles. His experienced imagination had no difficulty in filling in what the apricot silk gown hid—a subtle form of mental torture. Finally, after making a vow to learn fair Juno's name and track her down once she was restored to her family and no longer under his protection, Martin forced himself to think of nothing at all.

After an hour, he drifted into an unsettled doze.

CHAPTER THREE

EARLY morning sunlight tickled Martin's consciousness awake. Luckily, he opened his eyes before he moved, not something he always did. What he saw stopped him from reacting on impulse to the warm softness in his arms. Biting back his curses, he extricated himself from the clasp of silken limbs and, without disturbing fair Juno, got down from the loft as fast as he was able.

He greeted the horses, then went outside. The sky was clear, the air fresh and clean. The storm had drenched the countryside but the sun now shone bright. A good day for travelling. After stretching his legs, he was about to go inside and wake his companion in adventure when he bethought himself of the state of the roads.

A few paces down the cart track saw his plans revised. Used to travelling on gravel or the hard-surfaced highways, he had forgotten they were on byways not much more than cattle tracks. The track from the barn turned to a quagmire before it reached the road. The road itself was little better. Closer inspection suggested a few hours would suffice to render it passable, at least as far as he could see.

Resigned to the wait, he returned to the barn.

He climbed to the loft and found fair Juno still asleep. The morning sunlight spilled through the hay door, gilding the curls that escaped in random profusion from the simple knot on the top of her head.

Her lips were slightly parted in sleep, her breathing shallow. A delicate blush tinted her perfect complexion. An ivory and gold goddess, or so she seemed to him. He stared long and hard at the vision, drinking in the symmetry of her features, the arch of her brows and the warm glow of full lips. Most of the rest of her was concealed by the folds of the carriage blanket, much to his relief. Only one arm, nicely rounded in a distinctively feminine mould, showed bare, ivory-sheathed, nestling on the straw where he had laid it down.

Who was she? Quietly, Martin descended the ladder. Let her sleep—after the storm, she probably needed the rest.

Once more on firm ground, he rubbed his hands over his face. In truth, he could do with a few hours of extra sleep, but he was not fool enough to try relaxing in the straw by fair Juno's side.

The morning was far advanced before Helen awoke. For a full minute, she lay, confused and disorientated, before recollections of the previous evening returned her to full understanding.

She was alone in the loft. Abruptly, she sat up. Then she heard his voice, dimmed by distance. After a moment, she realised he was outside, talking to the horses. Hurriedly, she scrambled out of the carriage blanket. She shook it and folded it neatly before laying it, along with his coat, on the edge of the loft by the ladder. Then, with a last glance to make sure he was still outside, she gingerly descended the ladder, her skirts hiked to her knees.

Relieved to have reached the ground undetected,

she let her skirts down, brushing ineffectually at the creases. She pulled a wisp of straw from her hair, grimacing at the thought of how she must look. There was a pail of fresh water beside the ladder, the linen handkerchief she had used the day before draped over the side. Quickly, she splashed her face and rinsed her hands. She was patting her face dry when she heard his step behind her.

'Ah! Fair Juno awakes. I was just about to roust you out.'

Helen turned. In daylight, her rescuer was even more distressingly handsome than in lamplight. The broad shoulders seemed broader than ever; his height was no dream. Small wonder he had made her feel weak and small. The aquiline features held a touch of harshness, but the impression might be due to his tan. Helen blinked and found his grey eyes laughingly quizzing her. She prayed her blush was not detectable. 'I'm so sorry. You should have woken me earlier.'

'No matter.' Martin reached for the harness he had left on the wall of the stall. He had wondered what colour her eyes would prove to be in daylight. Pools of amber and limpid green highlighted with gold, they were the most striking features of a remarkably striking package. He thanked his stars he had not seen her in daylight before being forced to spend a night by her side. Her blush suggested she felt much the same. Martin knew for a certainty that relaxing with rakes was much easier in the dark but he did not want her to retreat behind a correct façade. He smiled and was relieved when she smiled back. 'The roads are only just dry enough to attempt the curricle.'

Helen followed him outside, pausing to breathe

deeply of the fresh morning air. She saw him struggling
to harness the restive horses and went forward to help,
approaching steadily so as not to spook the highly
strung beasts. Catching hold of the bit of the nearside
horse, she crooned sweet nothings and stroked the
velvet nose.

Martin nodded his approval, pleasantly surprised by
her practical assistance. Together, they efficiently
hitched the pair to the curricle.

Holding the reins, he went to her side, intending to
lift her to the box seat.

'Er—I left the blanket and your coat in the loft.' The
words tumbled out. Helen prayed that he would not
notice her fluster. Panic had risen to claim her at the
mere thought of him touching her again. After the past
ten minutes' surreptitious observation, she could not
understand how she had had the nerve to survive the
night.

One black brow rose; the grey eyes rested thoughtfully on her face. Then he handed her the reins. 'I'll
get them. Don't try to move 'em.'

He was back in two minutes, but by then she had
steeled herself for the ordeal. He stowed the blanket
and coat behind the seat, then reached for the reins.
Helen relinquished them. An instant later, his hands
fastened about her waist. A moment of weightlessness
followed, before she was deposited, gently, on the seat.

As she fussed about, settling her skirts, Helen
reflected that new experiences were always unsettling.
Just what it was she felt every time he touched her she
could not have said—but she had no doubt it was
scandalous. And delicious. And very likely addictive,
as well. Doubtless, it was one of those tricks rakes had

at their fingertips, to make susceptible women their slaves. Not that her late and wholly unlamented husband had had the facility. Then again, she amended, giving the devil his due, Arthur had never had much time for her, the gawky sixteen-year old he had wed for her fortune and supplanted within weeks with a more experienced courtesan. However, none of the countless admirers she had had since her return to social acceptability had ever affected her as Martin Willesden did.

The curricle jerked into motion. Her eyes fell to his hands, long, strong fingers managing the reins. His ability probably owed more to his undeniable experience—the experience that glowed in the smouldering depths of those grey eyes. Whatever it was, wherever its origin, he was dangerous—a fact she should strive to remember.

The sun found her face; Helen tilted her head up and breathed in the fresh scent of rain-washed greenery. Her mental homily was undoubtedly apt, but, try as she might, she could not take the threat seriously. This was an adventure, her first in years. She was reluctant to allow strictures, however appropriate, to mar the joy. The situation was, after all, beyond outrageous; decorum and social niceties had necessarily been set aside. Why shouldn't she enjoy the freedom of the moment?

'We should reach Ilchester for a late breakfast.'

Helen wished he had not mentioned food. Determined to keep her mind from dwelling on her empty stomach, she cast about for some suitably innocuous topic. 'You said you'd been visiting your home. Is it near here?'

'The other side of Taunton.'

'You've been away for some time, haven't you? Was it much changed?'

Martin grimaced. 'Thirteen years of mismanagement have unfortunately taken their toll.' The silence following this pronouncement suggested that his anger at the fact had shown in his tone. He sought to soften the effect. 'My mother lives there, but she's been an invalid for some years. My sister-in-law acts as her companion but unfortunately she's a nonentity—hardly the sort to raise a dust when the runners disappeared.'

'Disappeared?' Shocked incredulity showed in fair Juno's eyes, echoed in her tone.

Reluctantly, Martin grinned. 'I'm afraid the place, beyond my mother's rooms, is barely habitable. That's why I was so set on heading back to London without delay.' Reflecting that had this not been the case he would not have had the honour of rescuing fair Juno, Martin began to look on the Hermitage's shortcomings with a slightly less jaundiced eye. Considering the matter dispassionately, something he had yet to do, he shrugged. 'It's not seriously damaged—the fabric's sound enough. I've a team of decorators at work on my town house. When they've finished there, I'll send them to the Hermitage.'

Intrigued by the distant look in his eyes, Helen gently prompted, 'Tell me what it's like.'

Martin grinned. His eyes on his horses, and on the ruts in the road, he obliged with a thumbnail sketch of the Hermitage, not as he had found it, but as he remembered it. 'In my father's day, it was a gracious place,' he concluded. 'Whenever I think of it, I remember it as being full of guests. Hopefully, now I've returned, I'll be able to restore it to its previous state.'

Helen listened intently, struck by the fervour rippling in the undercurrents of his deep voice. 'It's your favourite estate?' she asked, trying to find the reason.

Martin considered the question, trying to find words to convey his feelings. 'I suppose it's the place I call home. The place I most associate with my father. And happier memories.'

The tone of his last sentence prevented further enquiry. Helen mulled over what little she knew of the new Earl of Merton and realised it was little indeed. He had clearly been out of the country, but why and where she had no idea. She had heard talk of a scandal, unspecified, in his past, but, given the anticipation of the hostesses of the *ton*, it was clearly of insufficient import to exclude him from their ballrooms and dinners.

While he conversed, one part of Martin's mind puzzled over the conundrum of his companion. Fair Juno was not that young, nor yet that old. Mid-twenties was his experienced guess. What did not seem right was the absence of a ring on her left hand. She was undeniably beautiful, attractive in a wholly sensual way, and the sort of lady who was invited to Chatham House. The possibility that she was a lady of a different hue occurred only to be dismissed. Fair Juno was well-bred enough to recognise his potential and be flustered by it—hardly the hallmark of a barque of frailty. All in all, fair Juno was an enigma.

'And now,' he said, bringing their companionable silence to an end, 'we should put our minds to deciding how best to return you to your home.' He glanced at the fair face beside him. 'Say the word, and I'll drive you to your door.' Entirely unintentionally, his voice had dropped several tones. Which, he thought, catching Juno's wide-eyed look, merely indicated how much she affected him.

'I don't really think that would be altogether wise,' Helen returned, suppressing her scandalous inclinations. He was teasing her, she was sure.

'Perhaps not. I had hoped London starchiness had abated somewhat, but clearly the passing of the years has yet to turn that particular stone to dust.' Martin smiled down into her large eyes, infusing his expression with as much innocence as he was capable. 'How, then?'

Helen narrowed her eyes and stared hard at him. 'I had expected, my lord, that one of your reputation would have no difficulty in overcoming such a minor obstacle. If you put your mind to it, I'm sure you'll think of something.'

It was a decidedly impertinent speech and provoked a decidedly audacious reply. The gleam in the grey eyes gave her warning.

'I'm afraid, my dear, that if you consult my reputation more closely you'll realise I've never been one for placating the proprieties.'

Realising her tactical error, Helen retreated to innocence. How silly to try to deflate a rake with outrageousness. 'Don't you really know? I confess, I'd thought you would.'

For an instant, the grey eyes held hers, suspicion in their depths. Then their quality subtly altered. She was conscious of a stilling of time, of her surroundings dimming into blankness. His grey eyes, and him, filled her senses. Then his lips twisted in a gently mocking smile and he looked away.

'As you say, fair Juno, my experience is extensive.' Martin slanted another glance her way, and saw a slight frown pucker her brow. 'I suspect it might be best if we try for one of the minor inns, just before Hounslow. I'll hire a chaise and escort for you there.' When the frown did not immediately lift, he smiled. 'You may give the coachman instructions once you reach the outskirts of London.'

'Yes,' said Helen, struggling to preserve her calm in the face of the discovery that grey eyes of his particular shade seemed to possess a strange power over her. For a moment, she had been mesmerised, deprived of all will, totally at his mercy. And it had felt quite delicious. 'I suppose that will do.'

Her tone of reluctant acceptance brought a smirk to Martin's lips, quickly suppressed. What a very responsive yet oddly innocent goddess she was. His interest in her, already marked, was growing by the minute. Just as well that they had agreed to part that evening. 'We should reach Hounslow before dark,' he said, eager to settle that point.

They journeyed on in silence. Martin pondered how to broach the subject of her name; Helen pondered him. He was, without doubt, the most attractive man she had ever met. It was not just his physical attributes, though there was no fault to be found with those. Neither could his manners, polished and assured though they were, account for the effect. It was, she decided, something far more fundamental, like the raspy growl of his deep voice and the fire banked like coals in the smoky grey eyes.

'Do you spend much of your year in the country, fair maid?'

The question jolted Helen back to reality. 'I often visit at——' She broke off, then continued smoothly, 'At friends' houses.'

'Ah.'

The quality of the glance that rested fleetingly upon her face confirmed her suspicion. He was trying to learn more of her.

'So you spend most of your year in London?'

'Other than my visits.'

Conversation rapidly degenerated to a game of quiz and answer, he trying to glean snippets of information, she trying to avoid revealing any identifying fact while politely answering all his queries.

'Do you attend the opera?'

'During the season.'

'In friends' boxes?'

Helen threw him a haughty look. 'I have my own box.'

'Then no doubt I'll see you there.' Martin smiled, pleased to have scored a hit.

Realising her slip, Helen had no choice but to be gracious. She inclined her head. 'Countess Lieven often joins me. I'm sure she'll be only too pleased to meet you.'

'Oh.' Stymied by the mention of the most censorious of the patronesses of Almack's, Martin looked suitably chagrined. Then his brow cleared. 'A capital notion. I can sue for permission to waltz in Almack's. With you.'

At the thought, Helen had to laugh. The vision of Martin Willesden stalking the hallowed boards, an eagle among the lambs, setting all the mother ewes in a flap, was intensely appealing.

It was Martin's turn to look haughty. 'Do you think I won't?'

Abruptly, Helen found herself drowning in smouldering grey, warmed and shaken to the core. Dragging her eyes from his, she looked ahead. 'I. . .hadn't imagined you would be attracted to the mild entertainments of the Marriage Mart.'

'I'm not. Only the promise of all manner of earthly pleasures could get me over its threshold.'

Helen was not game to try to cap that. She rapidly became absorbed in the scenery.

A slow smile curved Martin's lips before he gave his attention to his horses. He could not recall ever enjoying thirty minutes of conversation with a female half as much. In fact, he could not recall any other woman he had ever favoured with half an hour of verbal discourse. Fair Juno was a novelty, her mind quick and adroit. Innocent though the information he had gained was, it confirmed his suspicion that she had attained a position in the *ton* normally reserved for older matrons. Or widows.

At the thought, he let his eyes roam in leisurely appraisal over the curvaceous form beside him. She felt his gaze and glanced up, a slightly nervous smile hovering on her rosy lips.

Helen saw the predatory gleam in the grey eyes and accurately read their message. Dragging her dignity about her, the only protection she possessed, she arched one brow in spirited defence, perfectly ready to continue their banter. But the reprobate by her side merely smiled in a thoroughly seductive way and gave his attention to his horses. Helen transferred her gaze to the scenery, her lips irrepressively curving in appreciation. Conversing with a rake while free of the normal strictures, protected from any physical consequences by the fact he had both hands full of high-tempered horseflesh, was every bit as scandalously exciting as she had ever, as a green girl, imagined it would be. It was all deliciously dangerous but, in this case, completely safe. She had realised as much some miles back. It was a game that, in this particular instance, she could play with impunity. She was in his care and, instinctively, she knew he would honour that charge. While she remained under his protection, she was safe from him.

Heaven help her later.

But, of course, there would be no later. Helen stifled a sigh as reality intruded, impossible to deny. The future, for them both, was fixed. When he reached London, he would be the focus of the matchmaking mamas—with good reason. He was titled, wealthy and hideously handsome to boot. Their darling daughters would make cakes of themselves trying to catch his grey eyes. And, inevitably, he would choose one of them as his wife. Some well-dowered, biddable miss with an immaculate reputation. A widow, with no pretensions to property, with a murky marriage to a social outcast behind her and nothing more than her connections to recommend her, was a poor bargain.

Inwardly, Helen shook herself. Reality began in London. There was no need to cloud her day of adventure with such dismal forebodings. She tried to force the image of Martin Willesden paying court to a sweet young thing from her mind. In truth, the tableau was somewhat hazy. It was hard to believe that a man of his tastes, as demonstrated by their dalliance of the past half-hour, would settle to marriage with a sweet young thing. Doubtless, he would be the sort who kept a mistress or two on the side. Well, who was she to complain? Her husband had done the same, with her blessing. Not that her blessing would have been forthcoming had Martin Willesden been her husband.

With a determined effort, Helen redirected her thoughts. He wanted to know her name. She could tell him, but her anonymity was a comforting sop to her conscience. Besides which, when he reached London and learned who she was, he would realise such a connection was unsuitable, for no one would ever believe it innocent. If she refused to tell him her name, he would not feel obliged to acknowledge her when he met her again. Then, too, many men felt widows were fair game and she would hate him to consider her a potential candidate for his extramarital vacancy. All in all, she decided, he did not need to know her name.

Martin wondered what thoughts held his goddess so silent. But the peace of the morning was soothing about them and he made no move to interrupt her reverie. Despite not knowing her name, he felt confident of finding her in the capital. London might be the teeming hub of the nation, but its hallowed halls were trod by few. A gold and ivory goddess would be easy to trace.

The road widened then dipped. A ford lay ahead. Engrossed in contemplation of the predictable delights of waltzing with fair Juno, Martin automatically checked his pair, then sent them into the shallow water at a smart trot.

The horses' hooves clopped on the gravelly surface of the opposite bank; they slowed, then leaned into the traces and strained. The carriage wheels stuck fast, rocking the occupants of the box seat to full awareness of their predicament.

Helen clutched the side of the seat, then turned a wide-eyed look on her rescuer as a muttered expletive was belatedly smothered.

Martin shut his eyes in frustration. He had forgotten that minor fords were often not paved. The heavy rain had washed silt into the ford; his wheels felt as if they were six inches deep.

With a heavy sigh, he opened his eyes. 'We're stuck.'

Helen glanced around at the swiftly moving stream. 'So we are,' she agreed helpfully.

Martin cast her a warning look. She met it with unlikely innocence. Grimacing, he lifted his gaze to scan their surroundings. About them, the silence of woods and fields lay unbroken by human discord. No smoke rose above the trees to give hint of a nearby cottage. Memory suggested they were still some miles from the London road.

With a groan, Martin shortened the reins. 'I'll have to get down and find some stones. Can you hold them, do you think?'

A mischievous grin lit Helen's face. 'I was under the impression that no out-and-outer would ever entrust his cattle to a mere woman.'

Martin grimaced. '*Touché*. I wouldn't—except that I wouldn't give a farthing for their behaviour if I simply tied the reins to the rail. The devils would sense the absence of a master and they'd be off as soon as the stones were in place.' He glanced down into the large green eyes. 'All they need is a light touch on the reins for reassurance—and you seem to know your way about horses.'

Helen reached for the reins. 'I do. But if you spook them by throwing stones, I'll drive off and leave you to your fate. So be warned!'

Martin laughed at her melodramatic tone and relinquished the reins. He stood carefully and removed his coat, placing it over the seat before jumping down from the carriage. The water covered his ankles. With an inward sigh for his gleaming Hessians, he splashed to the bank and cast about for stones to place beneath and before the wheels.

Helen watched, the reins held gently in both hands. Every now and then, she felt a tug as the horses lived up to their owner's expectations and tested their freedom. They were clearly unhappy to be standing stock-still, half in and half out of the stream, rather than stretching their legs along the highway. As the minutes ticked by, Helen became infected with their impatience. Martin had to go further and further afield to find stones to lay in the mud before the wheels. She had no idea of the time, but thought it close to noon. How far were they from London?

Then her reckless self emerged and shouldered aside her worries. This was adventure and in adventure important things took care of themselves. Things would turn out all right; she need not concern herself—fate was in charge.

Determinedly light-hearted, she started to hum, then, as Martin had disappeared upstream, lifted her voice in the refrain from an old country air.

Martin heard the lilting melody as he returned with

yet more rocks. He paused for a moment, out of sight, and let her gentle contralto wash over him, waves of song lapping his consciousness. The sound was close to a caress. With a chuckle, Martin moved forward. A siren's song, no less.

She checked when she saw him, but when he raised one brow in question she raised one back and, tilting her chin, resumed her song.

With a broad smile, Martin settled the stones he carried to best effect and headed back for more. In truth, he found fair Juno's fortitude somewhat remarkable, he who would have sworn he knew all there was to know of women. But this woman had not whined at the delay, nor raised peevish quibbles about the consequences. Consequences neither he nor she could do anything to avoid. Had she realised yet?

An interesting question. Yet, he reflected, fair Juno was no one's fool.

Three more trips and there were enough rocks to attempt to break free of the cloying mud. Hands on hips, Martin stood by the side of the carriage and looked up at his assistant. 'I'll have to push the carriage from behind. Do you think you can hold them, once they gain the bank?'

A look of supercilious condescension was bestowed upon him. 'Of course,' Helen said, then deserted the high ground to ask, 'Do you think they'll bolt?'

With a half-smile, Martin shook his head. 'Not if you keep the reins short.' He moved to the back of the curricle, praying that that was so. 'When I say so, give 'em the office.'

On her mettle, Helen obediently waited for his call before clicking the reins. The horses heaved, the curricle slowly edged forward. Then the wheels gained firm purchase and the carriage abruptly left the water. The horses pulled hard. Suppressing her sudden fear, stirred to life by the strength of the great beasts sensed through the reins, she determinedly hauled back, struggling to hold them. She applied the brake to lock the wheels, and the carriage skidded slightly.

Then Martin was beside her, taking the reins from her suddenly weak fingers.

'Good girl!'

The approval in his voice warmed her; the glow in his eyes raised her temperature even more. To her annoyance, Helen felt herself blushing. An odd sensation of weakness, not quite faintness but surely an allied affliction, bloomed within. She shifted along the seat, making room for him, supremely conscious of the large body when it settled once more by her side.

To her relief, Martin seemed content to resume their journey without further delay, leaving her to the task of shackling her wayward thoughts. Never before had they been so astray. And, if she was any judge at all of the matter, Martin Willesden was the type of man who could sense a wayward feminine thought at ten paces. Her present safety might be ensured, but she did not need to lay snares for her future.

Having learned his lesson somewhat belatedly, Martin devoted as much of his attention as he could summon to driving. The London road was gained without further mishap. Soon, they were bowling along at a spanking pace. Even so, it was past two o'clock when, accepting the inevitable, Martin checked and turned into the yard of the Frog and Duck at Wincanton.

He turned to smile into Juno's questioning eyes. 'Lunch. I'm famished, even if, being a fashionable woman, you are not.'

Helen's eyes widened slightly. 'I'm not that fashionable.'

Martin laughed and jumped down. He reached up to lift fair Juno to the ground, noting her slight hesitation before, without fuss, she drew nearer and let him grasp her waist.

Flustered again but determined not to show it, Helen accepted Martin's proffered arm. He led her up the steps to the inn door, then stood aside to allow her to enter. As she did so, the head groom, having laid eyes on the horses his ostlers had taken in charge, came hurrying to ask Martin's orders.

Alone, Helen crossed the threshold, thankful for the cool dimness within. She was feeling unduly warm. The door gave directly on to the taproom, a large chamber, low-ceilinged and cosy with a huge fireplace at one end. Alerted by the noise outside, the landlord was coming forward from his domain on the other side of the room. Seeing her, he stopped. And stared. Helen became aware that all the other occupants of the tap, six in all and all male, were likewise transfixed. Then, to her discomfort, a leering grin suffused the landlord's face. Faint echoes appeared on his patrons' faces, too.

Simultaneously realising what a sight she must present, and the likely conclusion the landlord had drawn, Helen drew herself up, ready to defend her status.

There was no need. Martin came through the door and stopped by her side. One comprehensive glance was all it took for him to grasp the conclusion the inhabitants of the Frog and Duck had jumped to. He scowled at the landlord. 'A private parlour, host, where my wife can be at ease.'

The growled command wiped the leer from the landlord's face so fast, he had no expression ready to cover the ensuing blankness.

Helen was not sure whether to laugh or gasp. *Wife*? In the end, she covered her left hand with her right and, tipping up her chin, looked down her nose at the landlord, a feat assisted by the fact that she was taller than he. The man shrank as obsequiousness took hold.

'Yes, m'lord! Certainly, m'lord. If madam would step this way?'

Bowing every two paces, he led them to a neat little parlour. While Martin gave orders for a substantial meal, Helen sank, with a little sigh of thankfulness, into a well-padded armchair by the hearth, carefully avoiding the mirror above the mantelpiece. She had little real idea how bad her state was, but could not imagine knowing would help.

Martin heard her sigh. He glanced at her, then said to the landlord, 'We had an accident with our chaise. Our servants are following behind, with our luggage. Perhaps,' he continued, raising his voice and turning to address a weary Juno, 'you'd like to refresh yourself above stairs, my dear?'

Helen blinked, then readily agreed. Led to a small chamber and supplied with warm water, she washed the dust of the road from her face and hands, then steeled herself to examine the damage her adventures had wrought in her appearance. It was not as bad as she had feared. Her eyes were sparkling clear and the wind had whipped colour into her cheeks. Clearly, driving about the countryside with Martin Willesden agreed with her constitution. In the end, she undid her hair and reformed the mass of curls into a simpler knot. Her dress, the apricot silk marred by a host of creases, was beyond her ability to change. Other than shaking and straightening her skirts, there was little else she could do.

Returning to the parlour, she found their repast laid out upon the table. Martin rose with a smile and held a chair for her.

'Wine?'

At her nod, he filled her glass. Then, without more ado, they applied themselves to the task of demolishing the food before them.

Finally satisfied, Martin sat back in his chair and put aside contemplation of their problems the better to savour his wine while quietly studying fair Juno, absorbed in peeling a plum. His eyes slid over her generous curves—generous, ample—such words came readily to mind. Along with luscious, ripe and other, less acceptable terms. Martin hid a smile behind his goblet. All in all, he had no fault to find in the arrangement of fair Juno's dispositions.

'We won't reach London tonight, will we?'

The question drew Martin's gaze to her lips, full and richly curved and presently stained with plum juice. A driving urge to taste them seared through him. Abruptly, he refocused his mind on their problem. He raised his eyes to Juno's, troubled green and concerned. He smiled reassuringly. 'No.'

Helen felt justified in ignoring the smile. 'No', he said, and smiled. Did he have any idea of the panic she was holding at bay by dint of sheer determination?

Apparently, he did, for he continued, more seriously,

'Getting stuck in that ford has delayed us too much. However, I draw the line at driving my horses through the night, not that that would avail us, for I can't see arriving in London at dawn to be much improvement over our current state.'

Helen frowned, forced to acknowledge the truth of that remark. He would not be able to hire a chaise for her if they passed by Hounslow in the middle of the night.

'And, before you suggest it, I refuse to be a party to any scheme to hire a chaise for you to travel alone through the night.'

Helen's frown deepened. She opened her mouth to argue.

'*Even* with outriders.'

Helen shut her mouth and glared. But his tone and the set of his jaw warned her that no argument would shift him. And, in truth, she had no wish to spend the night jolting over the roads, a prey to fears of highwaymen and worse. 'What, then?' she asked in her most reasonable tone.

She was rewarded with a brilliant smile which quite took her breath away. Luckily, he did not expect her to speak.

'I had wondered,' Martin began diffidently, unsure how his plan would be received, 'if we could find an inn where neither of us is known, to put up in for the night.'

Helen considered the suggestion. She could see no alternative. Raising her napkin to wipe her lips, she raised her eyes to his. 'How will we explain our disreputable state—and our lack of servants and luggage?'

The instant she asked the question, she knew the

answer. Deliciously wicked, but, she reasoned, it was all part of her adventure and thus could be viewed with a lenient eye.

Pleased by her tacit acceptance of the only viable plan he had, Martin relaxed. 'We can tell the same story I edified our host with—that we've had an accident and our retainers are following behind with the luggage.'

Still a little nervous of the idea, Helen nodded. Did he intend to claim they were wed?

'Which reminds me,' said Martin, sliding the gold signet from his right hand. 'You had better wear this for the duration.' He held the heavy ring out and dropped it into her palm.

Helen studied the ring, still warm from his hand. Obviously, they were to appear married. She slipped it on to the third finger of her left hand. To her surprise, its weight, in that remembered place, did not evoke the expected horror. Instead, it was strangely reassuring, a source of strength, a pledge of protection.

'Very well,' she said. She drew a deep breath and purposefully added, 'But we'll have to have separate rooms.' Determined to be clear on that point, she raised her eyes to his darkly handsome face and beheld a haughty expression.

'Naturally,' returned Martin repressively. It would undoubtedly be safer that way. Aside from anything else, he would need to get some sleep. He studied Juno's fair countenance and the need to know her real name grew. Given that they were to masquerade cloaked in wedded bliss, he felt that their increasing intimacy justified a request for enlightenment. 'I rather think, my dear, that, given our new relationship, it might be appropriate if I knew your name.'

Engrossed in fantasies revolving around their new relationship, Helen gave a start. 'Oh.' She thought once more of the matter, inwardly acknowledging her reluctance and her reasons for it. Eyeing the handsome face, the strangely compelling eyes fixed on hers, she admitted to an urge to tell him, to confide in a man so transparently at ease in her world. But hard on the heels of that feeling came a premonition of how he would look when he heard her name. He would know of her husband; they would likely have met. What would he feel—pity? Revulsion, albeit carefully cloaked? Doing anything to damage the closeness she sensed between them was repugnant.

Letting her gaze fall, she picked up her napkin, creasing the folds between her fingers. 'I. . .really. . .' Her words trailed away. How to explain what she felt?

Martin smiled a little crookedly. He would have liked her to confide in him but the point was not worth disturbing her over. 'You really feel you shouldn't?'

Helen threw him a grateful look. 'It's just that the adventure seems more. . .complete—and,' she added, determined at least to have some of the truth, 'my behaviour more excusable if I continue incognito.'

Smiling more broadly, Martin inclined his head in acceptance. 'Very well. But what should I call you?'

With a gentle smile that, unbeknown to her, held an element of sweet shyness quite at odds with her years, Helen said, 'You choose. I'm sure you can invent something appropriate.'

Her smile very nearly overset Martin's much tried control. He had thought it strengthened by the years, but fair Juno was temptation beyond any he had ever faced. Invent something? His mind was seething with invention, did she but know it. But, as knowledge of his thoughts would hardly be conducive to allowing her to continue with reasonable calm in his company, he could only be thankful that they did not show in his face.

They did show in his eyes. Even with the table between them, Helen saw the smoke rise and cloud the grey. Stormy heat caressed her. Mesmerised, she sat and waited, breathless and trying to hide it. Heaven forbid that he ever realise how much he affected her!

'Juno,' Martin said, just managing to keep his voice within acceptable range. 'Fair Juno.' His smile was entirely beyond his control, laced with wicked thoughts and scandalous suggestion.

Helen lifted one brow, trying to pour cold water on the flames she could feel flickering around them. 'I hardly think, my lord, that such an allusion is appropriate.'

His smile only gained in intensity. 'On the contrary, my dear. I feel it entirely appropriate.'

Helen tried to frown. Juno—queen of the goddesses. How could she argue with that?

'And now, having settled our immediate future, I suggest we get on our way.' Martin rose and stretched, letting languid grace cloak his haste. If he did not get out of here soon, and back to the relative safety of the curricle's box seat, he would not answer for the consequences. Exposure to fair Juno was sapping all will to resist his rakish inclinations. And he had dinner with her, alone, to look forward to. He had need to recoup what strength he could.

He went around the table and helped her to her feet. Tucking her small hand into the crook of his arm, he led her to the door. 'Come, my lady. Your carriage awaits.'

CHAPTER FOUR

THEY had chosen the Bells at Cholderton as their overnight stop. The small town nestled just south of the London road, the major traffic passing by without pause. The Bells was an old house, less frequented in these days of rapid travel but still in sufficiently good state to hold promise of a comfortable night.

Shown into a private parlour, Helen glanced about at the faded elegance. She nodded in approval, her haughty demeanour supporting their fiction. Martin had told their story, his natural arrogance wiping out any possibility of disbelief. Lord and Lady Willesden required rooms for the night. The landlord found nothing amiss with the request; he was, in fact, only too pleased to see them.

'My good wife will have your supper ready directly, m'lord. There's duck and partridge, with lamb's-foot jelly and a wine syllabub to follow.'

Languidly superior, Martin nodded. 'That should do admirably.'

When the door closed behind the little man, Martin glanced her way, laughter lurking in his grey eyes. 'Just so,' he said, his smile warming her every bit as much as the fire in the grate.

Feeling her nervousness increase as he drew nearer, Helen turned to hold out her chilled fingers to the blaze. When the sun had slipped beneath the horizon, he had insisted she don his greatcoat. Her fingers went to the heavy garment to ease it from her shoulders. Instantly, he was beside her. His fingers brushed hers.

'Here, let me.'

She had to, for she could not have moved if the ceiling had fallen. His gentle touch, so simple but almost a caress, and the velvety quality cloaking his rumbling growl, drowned her senses in dizzying distraction. The effect he had on her was intensifying with time. How on earth was she to survive the evening?

As soon as he stepped away from her to drop the coat over a chair, Helen sank into the armchair by the fire. She drew a deep breath, forcing herself to meet his intent gaze when he turned once more to face her.

Martin studied the vision before him, reading her unease with accomplished certainty. If circumstances had been different, she would have every reason to feel threatened. As things stood, she was safe. Or at least, he amended, safe enough. He knew she could sense his attraction and was hourly more entertained by her efforts to hide her consciousness of him. Entertained and intrigued. Clearly, fair Juno, if widow she was, was not one of those who dispensed her favours with gay abandon.

As he watched, a small frown creased Juno's brow.

'Why aren't you travelling with a groom or tiger?'

Elegantly disposing his long limbs in the chair opposite hers, Martin smiled, perfectly ready to converse on such innocent topics. 'My groom fell victim to a severe head cold. I left him at the Hermitage.' Considering that fact, privately Martin owned to some relief that Joshua had not been perched behind, cramping his style.

'Does the Hermitage have many farms attached?'

'Six. They're all leased to long-term tenants.'

Succeeding questions, which Martin was shrewd enough to know were far from artless, led them to a discussion of farming and the care of estates. He could appreciate Juno's desire to avoid questions on town pursuits; such topics were likely to give him more clues to her identity. Yet her opinions on the organisation of farm labour and the problems faced by tenant farmers were equally revealing. Her knowledge of the subject could not have been acquired other than through first-hand experience. All of which added to his mental picture of fair Juno. She had spent a goodly portion of her life on a large and well-run estate.

A brisk knock on the door heralded the landlord. 'Your dinner, m'lord.' Carrying a heavily laden tray, he entered, closely followed by a buxom woman with tablecloth and cutlery. Together, they efficiently laid the table, then bowed and withdrew.

Rising, Martin held out his hand. 'Shall we?'

Placing her hand in his, Helen ruthlessly stifled the thrill that shot through her at his touch, assuming her most regal manner as she allowed him to lead her to the table and seat her at one end. The slight smile which played about his lips suggested he was not deceived by her worldly air.

Thankfully, the food gave her a safe topic for discussion.

'I have to admit to ignorance of the latest fads. Thirteen years is a long time away from the boards of the fashionable.'

Encouraged by this admission, Helen ignored the laughing understanding lighting his grey eyes and launched into a catalogue of the latest culinary delights.

When the landlord re-entered to draw the covers, Helen grasped the opportunity to retreat to the chair by the fire. She heard the door shut behind their host and wondered, a little frantically, how she was to manage for the next two hours.

'Brandy?'

Turning to see Martin at the sideboard, decanter in hand, she shook her head. Did he but know it, he did not need any assistance to befuddle her wits.

Helping himself to a large dose, undoubtedly required if he was to sleep with Juno, alone, next door, Martin came to stand by the fire, one booted foot on the fender, his shoulders propped against the mantelpiece.

'Your man is not going to be impressed with your boots.'

Martin followed her glance and grimaced. 'I'll have to entrust them to the boots here. Joshua will, in all probability, never forgive me.'

Helen smiled at his nonsense. Despite the tingling of her nerves, due entirely to her company, she felt relaxed and at peace, not a state she had had much experience of over her life. Content, she thought, searching for the right word. Engaged in a most scandalous escapade and I feel content. How odd.

Catching Martin's gaze as it rested lightly upon her, she smiled. He smiled back, a slow, pensive smile, and she felt the heat rise inside her. Her eyes locked with his, smoky grey and intent, and she felt her will start to slip from its moorings.

Sounds of an arrival disrupted their silent communion.

Martin turned to stare at the door. The noise beyond rose until it resolved into the clamour of many voices. An invasion had found the Bells.

Helen frowned. 'What could it be?'

Equally at sea, Martin shook his head. 'Too late for a scheduled stop, I would have thought.' Inwardly, he hoped that whatever company had sought shelter at the inn did not include any who might recognise either Juno or himself. If it ever became known, there was no possibility that their escapade would be viewed as innocent.

The noise outside subsided to a steady hum. Almost immediately, the landlord arrived to satisfy their curiosity.

'Excuse me, m'lord, but it seems a night for accidents. The night coach for Plymouth's lost a wheel just up the road. The smith says as it can't be fixed 'til the morrow, so's we're having to put up all the passengers here. If it be all the same to you and her ladyship,' he said, ducking his head in Helen's direction, 'I've put you in the main chamber. It's got a huge bed, m'lord—you won't be disappointed. But there's more people than we have beds as 'tis, so I didn't think as how you'd mind.'

The man looked hopefully at Martin. Martin looked back, wondering how Juno was taking the news. From his point of view, the disaster was a damned nuisance. But if he insisted on separate rooms, they would probably end up sharing with some less suitable bedfellows—the sort who travelled on the night coach. And, all in all, with the extra men in the house, he would much rather Juno was safe by his side, even if he got no sleep as a result. 'Very well,' he replied in his most languid voice. He heard the hiss of Juno's indrawn breath and suppressed a smile. 'In the circumstances, your best chamber will have to do.'

Obviously relieved, the landlord bobbed his head and departed.

Martin turned to meet Juno's reproving gaze. One black brow rose. 'In truth, my dear, you'll be far safer with me than alone this night.'

There was no answer to that. Helen dragged her gaze from his face and fastened it on the flames leaping and dancing about the large log in the grate. The prospect of sleeping in the same bed as Martin Willesden left her feeling numb. It was shock, she supposed. She had slept in his arms in the loft last night, but a loft was not the same as a bed. Her adventure was taking a decidedly dangerous turn. No— it was impossible. She would have to think of some alternative.

But she had still to discover another way from the impasse when, at Martin's suggestion, they went upstairs to their room, the largest chamber as promised. A welcoming fire burned in the grate, a bed which was every bit as huge as her fevered imagination had anticipated stood against one wall. The room was comfortably furnished, the age of the hangings disguised by the soft candlelight. Martin held the door for her, then followed her in.

The click of the latch jolted Helen to action. She swung to face him, clasping her hands firmly before her. 'My lord, this is impossible.'

He smiled and moved past her to the window. 'Martin,' he said, throwing a mild glance over his shoulder. 'You'd better stop "my lording" me if we're supposed to be married.'

Martin checked the window, opening it a crack to let in some air, then rearranged the heavy drapes. He strolled back to the middle of the room, pausing to shrug out of his coat. He draped it over the back of a chair, then smiled at Juno, still standing, uncertain and nervous, near the door. 'It's not impossible,' he said, beckoning her forward. 'Come here by the fire and let me unlace your gown.' He ignored the alarm flaring in her eyes. 'Then you can wrap yourself in the sheet and be as modestly garbed as a nun.'

Helen considered his words, her nerves in knots, her mind incapable of finding any way out. When his hand beckoned again, with increasing imperiousness, she walked hesitantly forward, her eyes reflecting her troubled state.

With a reassuring smile, Martin took her hand and drew her to face the fire. Behind her, he found the lacings of her silk gown. His practised fingers made short work of the closures. He resisted the temptation to part the sides of the garment and run a fingertip down her spine, clad only, as he had suspected, in a fine silk chemise. 'Stay there a moment. I'll fetch the sheet.'

Helen stared at the flames, her cheeks rosy red. So far, his behaviour had been as reassuringly unthreatening as his words. It was her own inclinations that were undermining her confidence. She was perfectly well aware of how close she stood to having an illicit affair with one of the most notorious rakes in England. All she needed to do was to give him a sign that she would welcome his advances and she would learn what it was that made rakes so sought after as lovers. Martin Willesden was temptation incarnate. But her common sense stood firmly in her way, prosaically pointing out that the last thing she needed was a fling, an affair of the moment, based on nothing more than a passing attraction. That had never been her style.

The sheet descended over her shoulders.

'I'll look the other way. I promise not to peek.'

Helen did not dare look to see just where he was or if he complied. Hurriedly, she slipped the silk dress down, letting it puddle about her ankles while she wrapped the sheet around and about her, tucking the ends in to secure it. She stepped out of her dress and bent to pick it up.

The sheet rustled as she moved and Martin turned around, just in time to see her pick up her dress. He admired the view before she straightened, shooting him an uncertain look. The firelight gilded her curls, sheening softly on the exposed ivory shoulders and arms. The ache in his loins, a niggling pain for the past twenty-four hours, intensified. Determined to ignore it, he grinned at her. 'If you get into bed, I'll tuck you in.'

Discovering the teasing glint inhabiting his grey eyes, Helen glared, but obediently moved to the bed. 'Where are you going to sleep?' There was no armchair in the room.

Martin's grin grew. 'As the landlord said, it's a large bed.' He unbuttoned his waistcoat then started on the laces of his shirt.

Helen stopped and stared. 'What are you doing?'

His control under strain, Martin grimaced. 'Getting ready for bed. I'll be damned if I sleep another night in these clothes.' At the look on fair Juno's face, a picture of scandalised horror, he growled, 'For God's sake, woman! Get into bed and turn the other way. You know you're perfectly safe.'

Which was more than he knew, but the longer she stood there, wide green eyes on him, the more danger she courted. When she blinked, then climbed rapidly on to the bed, curling up on one side and pulling the covers about her ears, Martin let out a sigh of relief.

Nerves skittering uncontrollably, Helen lay and stared at the wall. The candles were snuffed, but the flames from the fire shed enough light to see by. She heard his Hessians hit the floor, then the door opened as he stood them in the corridor for the boots to attend to. He closed the door and she heard the muffled sounds of him undressing. She wished she could stop listening, but her nerves, at full stretch, would not let her. Then the bed at her back sagged. With a small squeak, she clutched the side of the mattress to stop herself from rolling into him.

In spite of his pain, Martin chuckled. He had not anticipated that difficulty. 'Don't worry. You have my word as a gentleman that I won't take advantage.'

That's not what I'm worried about! Helen kept the thought to herself. She was scandalised, tantalised, terrified by the possibilities. It had been a long time since she had been in bed with a man, and that never innocently. Last night in the straw did not count—that had been quite different—that had not been a bed. This was definitely a bed. To her horror, her thoughts kept sliding to how easy it would be to relax, to let herself drift back in the bed, until she met the hard, heavy body indenting the mattress behind her.

In the dark, Martin mentally gritted his teeth. His

loins were as girded as they could get. But the warm perfume of her hair tickled his senses; his body was alive to her nearness. If last night had been difficult, tonight would be torture. As the firelight faded, leaving them in comforting darkness, he realised she was stiff and rigid beside him, definitely not asleep.

'You needn't worry I'll move in the night. I sleep very soundly.' Once I sleep, he added silently. 'I suspect it's something to do with having been in the army. One slept when one could, usually in far from comfortable surroundings.'

'How long were you in the Peninsula?'

Her question, muffled by the bedclothes, reminded Martin of an ascerbic comment made by some high-ranking hostess, to the effect that there was nothing so boring as hearing of men's military exploits. He seized the idea. Within ten minutes, the woman's astuteness was confirmed. He paused in the middle of a detailed description of his second major battle. No sound beyond the crackle of the fire disturbed the stillness of the chamber. Then his straining ears caught the soft huff of Juno's breathing, shallow and even. She was asleep.

He smiled into the darkness, oddly elated, as if he had succeeded in winning another battle. Knowing she was asleep allowed him to relax. As he slipped into slumber, he sternly reminded himself to make sure he woke properly—before he moved.

The reminder was needed. He awoke to find that, as he had expected, he had passed the night without stirring. He was no nearer to where Juno had laid her head than before. Unfortunately, Juno herself had moved. A lot closer. She had somehow insinuated herself into his arms, her head comfortably settled on his chest. One naked arm lay about his waist.

And her sheet had ridden up in the night. He could feel her silken limbs entwined with his.

Martin clenched every muscle he possessed and willed his body to compliance. Carefully, excruciatingly slowly, he disentangled their limbs, trying not to glance at her legs, too worried about waking her to draw the sheet down. He was naked; if she woke now, she was going to get a shock.

It was a relief to leave the warmth of the bed. Quickly, he dressed and escaped downstairs.

He found the landlord in the taproom, serving some of the male passengers from the coach. There were others still asleep on some of the benches. After greeting the man and asking after the weather, Martin casually asked, 'Have our servants by any chance appeared?'

The landlord shook his head. 'No, m'lord. No one's been by this morning.'

Frowning direfully, Martin swore. 'In that case, I'll hire one of your carriages. My wife can go on to town while I back-track to find out what's become of our people.'

The landlord was all sympathetic help. He assured Martin of the quality of his carriage and that the coachman and groom could be trusted to see her ladyship safe into London.

'Very well,' said Martin, tossing a small purse to the man. 'Have the carriage ready. I'll want her ladyship on her way immediately after we breakfast.' Martin glanced about the taproom and remembered the sensation

Juno had caused the previous day. 'Perhaps you could send a tray upstairs?'

'Certainly, m'lord. I'll send my missus up directly.'

Martin returned upstairs, pausing to gather his strength before tapping lightly on the door and entering. To his relief, Juno, fair as ever, was out of bed and fully dressed.

Helen was seated before the small dressing-table, setting her hair once more into a neat knot. She turned when Martin entered, returning his smile as calmly as she could. She had woken to find him gone, but had found herself in the middle of the bed, her protective sheet twisted high on her thighs. The coverlet had been over the top, but she could not begin to think of where he had been when he had awoken. 'Good morning.'

Her pulse accelerating, she turned back to the mirror.

'A fair morning it is.' Martin came to stand beside the dressing-table, propping his shoulders against the wall.

To Helen's sensitised senses, he exuded an overwhelming aura of potent masculinity. Struggling to keep her wits focused, she listened as he told her of his arrangements.

'With luck, you'll be home shortly after midday.'

Despite the fact that home was where she wished to be, Helen was acutely aware of a dull, shrinking feeling as he pronounced the end to their adventure. Suddenly, the morning seemed less bright.

Their breakfast arrived and was laid out on the small table by the window. Bidden to attend, Helen tried to shake off her attack of the dismals and respond to his banter as she should. He had been a knight in shining armour, in truth, and she owed him a great deal. So she put a brave face on her irrational despondency and replied brightly to his comments.

She would have been mortified to know the ease with which Martin read her thoughts. Clearly, Juno had never mastered the art of prevarication. Her expression was open, her eyes a direct reflection of her mood. He accurately sensed her feelings, and her desire to keep them hidden. Wisely, he made no reference to his knowledge, but was inordinately pleased that she should feel saddened at having her time in his company brought to an end. It would make it so much easier to draw her to him when next they met.

Breakfast over, he escorted her downstairs. The day was fine; Juno did not need his coat. He paused, holding her beside him on the steps of the inn. The carriage which was to convey her to London stood ready before them, as neat and clean as the landlord had said. The coachman and groom were burly fellows, both with the open honesty of countrymen. Juno would be safe in their care. He looked down into her clear green eyes. A wry smile twisted his lips. 'I've told them they should take you to London but that you'll make up your mind where you wish to go when you get there. I've paid them fully, so you don't need to worry about that.'

Helen felt breathless. 'I don't know how to thank you, my lord,' she began, her voice soft and low so that none would hear them. 'You've been of inestimable help.'

Martin's smile broadened. 'The pleasure was entirely mine, fair Juno.' He lifted her hand from his sleeve and placed a kiss on her trembling fingertips.

'Your ring,' Helen whispered.

Smoothly, reluctantly, Martin drew the heavy signet from her finger and replaced it on his. He raised his eyes to gaze deeply into hers. 'Until next we meet.'

Helen smiled tremulously, aware of a desire to lean into his warmth, to clutch at his hand.

Quite where the idea sprang from Martin could not later have said. But it suddenly occurred to him that he was masquerading as her husband. And being her husband gave him certain rights. Furthermore, being a rake, he would be mad not to take advantage of those rights. His lips lifted in a wholly devilish smile.

Helen saw the smile. Her eyes widened. But she got no chance to do anything at all. One strong arm slipped about her, pulling her firmly against him, while the fingers of his other hand tipped her face up. His lips closed over hers, confidently, possessively. And time stood still.

For an instant, she held firm against that too knowledgeable kiss, but the subtle invitation to greater intimacy was too compelling to resist. Her lips parted; he took immediate advantage, tasting her, teasing her, languidly, expertly exploring her, sending her mind whirling into fathomless sensation. She was dimly aware of the tightening of his arms about her. She melted against him, seeking to press herself against his muscled length. It was utterly delicious, this invitation to delight. The heady taste of him filled her senses; she was oblivious to all else but him.

Reluctantly, Martin brought the kiss to an end, wishing he could take their interaction further but knowing that was, for the moment, impossible. But at least he had left her with something to remember him by, until he found her in London and continued her seduction.

Looking down into her dazed eyes, he smiled and, too wise to attempt conversation, led her to the carriage. The groom, studiously straight-faced, jumped down and opened the door. Martin helped his goddess into the coach and saw her settled comfortably. He raised her hand to his lips. 'Farewell, fair Juno. ' 'Till next we meet.'

Helen blinked. The message in his eyes was clear. Then the door was shut. A minute later the carriage lurched into motion. She resisted the urge to scramble to the window, to stare back at him until he was out of sight. There was no need. ' 'Till next we meet,' he had said. She had no doubt he meant it.

Still shaken, Helen drew a ragged breath. If only dreams could come true.

In the inn yard, Martin stood and watched the carriage until it disappeared along the road to London. His impulse was to order his curricle and follow as fast as he was able. But she could not escape. He would find her in London, of that he was sure.

She was one goddess he had every intention of worshipping.

CHAPTER FIVE

THREE weeks later, Helen was in her chamber, studying the contents of her wardrobe to determine what could, and could not, be used for the upcoming Little Season, when her maid, Janet, put her head around the door.

'You've a visitor, m'lady.'

Before Helen could extricate herself from the silks and satins and ask who, Janet had gone.

'Bother!' Helen sat on her heels and wondered who it was. The familiar excitement that had simmered just below her surface ever since she had returned to town blossomed. But it could not be him, she reasoned, not at eleven in the morning. With a sigh, she stood and shook out her primrose morning gown, before seating herself before her dressing-table to straighten her curls.

Her reappearance in the capital had caused a minor sensation among her friends but, luckily, thanks to the discretion of her servants, her disappearance had not been broadcast throughout the *ton*. Hence, while she had had to sustain a somewhat strained interview with Ferdie Acheson-Smythe, who had read her a lecture on the ills likely to befall women of her class who kept scandalous secrets, and a much more rigorous cross-examination from Tony Fanshawe, the entire episode had passed off without major catastrophe. Throughout her explanations, she had managed to keep the names of her abductor—for she had no evidence that it had really been Hedley Swayne—and her rescuer—who was far too scandalous to be acknowledged—to herself. In this, she had been lucky. Circumstances, in the form of the birth of his son and heir, had kept her self-appointed guardian, Marc Henry, Marquis of Hazelmere, at home in Surrey. If she had had to face his sharp hazel eyes, she was sure she would have been forced to the truth—the whole truth. Thankfully, fate had spared her.

Descending the stairs, she was conscious of anticipation still pulsing her veins despite the sure knowledge that she would not meet a pair of stormy grey eyes in her small drawing-room. Those eyes, and their warmth, had haunted her; the memory of his lips on hers lay, a jewel enshrined in her memories. But if he looked for her, he would learn her name. And then he would know. Her silly dreams could never come true.

Startling eyes did indeed meet her when she entered her drawing-room, but they were emerald-green and belonged to Dorothea, Marchioness of Hazelmere.

'Helen!' Dorothea jumped to her feet, elegantly gowned as always, her face alight with a happiness so radiant that Helen's breath caught in her throat.

'Thea—what on earth are you doing here? I thought you'd be fixed at Hazelmere for months.' Helen returned the younger woman's warm embrace. They had become firm friends since Dorothea's marriage to Hazelmere, just over a year ago. Helen's connection with Hazelmere dated from her childhood; she was distantly connected with the Henrys and had spent many of her summers with Hazelmere's younger sister in Surrey.

Helen held Dorothea at arm's length, conscious of a

pang of dismal jealousy that she would never experience the joy that shone from Dorothea's face. 'How's my godson?' she asked, smiling determinedly.

'Darcy's fine.' Dorothea smiled back, linking her arm in Helen's. Together, they strolled through the open French windows and into the small courtyard.

An ironwork seat with a padded cushion stood facing the bank of flowerbeds, the sun-warmed house wall at its back. As they sank on to the cushions, Dorothea explained, 'I've installed him on the second floor of Hazelmere House. Mytton doesn't know how to react. As for Murgatroyd—he's torn between pride and handing in his notice.'

Helen grinned. Hazelmere's butler and his valet were well-known to her. 'But how did you convince Marc you were well enough to come to town? I was sure he would keep you in semi-permanent seclusion until Darcy was in leading strings, at the very least.'

'Quite simple, really,' explained Dorothea airily. 'I merely pointed out that if I was well enough to share his bed I was certainly well enough to endure the rigours of the Season.'

Helen's laughter pealed forth. 'Oh, gracious!' she gasped, once she was able. 'What I would have given to have been able to see his face.'

'Yes,' agreed Dorothea, emerald eyes twinkling. 'It really was quite something.' She turned to study Helen. 'But enough of my managing husband. What's this I hear of a disappearance?'

With practised ease, Helen told her tale. Dorothea did not press her for the details she omitted, merely remarking at the end of the story, 'Hazelmere hasn't heard and I don't see any reason to tell him.' With a quick smile, she continued, 'What I came here to do was invite you to dinner on Thursday. Just the family, those who are in town. It's too early yet for anything formal and we'll have enough of that once the Season begins. You will come, won't you?'

'Of course,' said Helen. Then she grimaced. 'Mind you, by then Hazelmere will have heard about my escapade. You may tell him from me that there's no reason for him to concern himself over it and I won't take kindly to being interrogated over the dinner-table.'

Dorothea laughed and squeezed her hand. 'I'll make sure he behaves.'

Reflecting that she had perfect confidence in her friend's ability on that score, Helen smiled at the thought of the mighty Hazelmere being managed, on however small a scale, by his elegant wife.

Dorothea rose. 'I have to hurry for I've yet to catch Cecily.'

Helen escorted her guest to the door.

'Come early, if you can,' Dorothea urged. 'Darcy's always so good with you.' With an affectionate hug and a cheery wave, Dorothea went down the steps to the street and was handed into the waiting coach by her footman.

Helen watched her depart, then, smiling, went back upstairs to see which of her gowns would do for Thursday.

Martin strolled down St James's oblivious of the noise and bustle that surrounded him. He had yet to learn fair Juno's name, an aberration he had every intention of rectifying with all possible speed. Returning to town in her wake, he had expected to be able to make enquiries the next day. Fate, however, had stepped in and engineered a crisis on his Leicestershire estate. His presence had been necessary; the ensuing wrangle had forced him to post down to London in search of documents, then back to the country to see his orders executed. When the dust had finally settled, three weeks had flown.

He had woken this morning determined to make up for lost time. White's seemed the obvious place to start. He had never let his membership lapse, despite the years spent far afield. Consequently, when challenged, he felt perfectly confident in directing the porter to the membership lists. All proved in order. From the man's change in manner, Martin assumed his ascension to the title was common knowledge. He was bowed into the rooms with all due deference.

He strolled through the interconnecting chambers, pausing to scan the scattered groups for signs of familiar faces. As it transpired, it was they who recognised him.

'Martin?'

The question had him turning to meet hazel eyes on a level with his own. Delighted, Martin grinned. 'Marc!'

They shook hands warmly. After they had exchanged their news, and Martin had duly exclaimed over his friend's recent marriage, Hazelmere gestured to the rooms ahead.

'Tony's here somewhere. He's married too. To Dorothea's sister, as it happens.'

Martin turned laughing eyes on him. 'That must have caused comment. How did Tony take the ribbing about always following your lead?'

'Strangely, this time, I don't think he cared.'

They found Anthony, Lord Fanshawe, and various other members of what had once been Martin's set, ensconced in one of the back rooms. Martin's entrance caused a mild sensation. He was bombarded with questions, which he answered with good grace, picking up the threads of long-ago friendships, and, to his surprise, gradually relaxing into what had once been his milieu. With so many present, he put aside his questions on fair Juno. To Hazelmere or Fanshawe, his oldest friends, he might admit to an interest in an unknown widow. But to raise speculation in so many minds was not his present aim.

Leaving the club some hours later, still in company with Hazelmere and Fanshawe, he wryly reflected that at least he had made a start at re-establishing himself socially.

They were about to part, when Hazelmere stayed him. 'I've just remembered. Come to dinner tomorrow—we're having an informal affair, just family. Tony's coming, so you can meet both our wives.' He smiled proudly. 'And my heir.'

'God, yes!' said Fanshawe. 'Come and add to the mood. It'll be chaos anyway.'

Martin could not help his laugh. 'Very well. I have to confess I'm dying to meet your paragons.'

'Six, then. We still dine early at present.'

With a nod and a wave, they parted. Striding along the pavement in the direction of his newly refurbished home in Grosvenor Square, Martin mused that the new Lady Hazelmere might well be one who could assist him in discovering fair Juno's identity.

Letting himself into his front hall, he surrendered his

cane and gloves to his butler, Hillthorpe, who had instantly materialised from beyond the green baize door. Strolling the corridor to his library, Martin was struck again by the silence of the large house. In his memories, there had always been people around— children, friends of his brothers, friends of his parents. All gone now. Only his mother, tied to her room in Somerset, and his younger brother Damian remained. And God knew where Damian was, nor yet how long he was likely to remain. Martin's expression hardened, then he shrugged aside all thought of his younger brother. Damian could take care of himself.

Sinking into a newly upholstered chair, a glass of the finest French brandy in his hand, Martin considered his house. It was empty—indubitably empty. He needed to fill it—with life, with laughter. That was what was still missing. He had rectified the damp and the decay and had cast forth the unscrupulous. The structure was now sound. It was time to turn his mind, and energies, to rebuilding a family—his family.

Hazelmere's transparent pride in his wife and son had impressed him. He knew Marc, and a few hours had sufficed to assure him that the bonds of similarity that had drawn them to each other in earlier years still persisted.

Perhaps that was why fate had thrown fair Juno at his head?

Martin's lips twisted in a self-deprecatory smile. Why could he not just admit that he was besotted with the woman? There was no need to invoke fate or any such infernal agency. Juno was very real and, to him, wholly desirable. And, for the first time in his life, he was not contemplating a temporary relationship, limited by his interest. He was quite sure his interest in Juno would never die.

With a grin, Martin raised his glass in a silent toast. To his goddess. He tossed off the brandy, then, laying down the glass, left the room.

Thursday evening was mild and clear. Martin walked the few blocks to Cavendish Square. He was admitted to Hazelmere House by the butler, Mytton, whom he recognised and who, to his amazement, recognised him.

'Welcome back, my lord.'

'Er—thank you, Mytton.'

Hazelmere strolled into the hall. 'Thought it was you.'

Martin shook hands but his eyes were drawn to the woman who had followed his host into the hall. Fair-skinned and slender, a wealth of auburn hair crowned a classically featured face. Martin glanced at Hazelmere, his brows lifting in question.

The smile on the Marquis's face was answer enough. 'Permit me to introduce you to my wife. Dorothea, Marchioness of Hazelmere—Martin Willesden, Earl of Merton.'

Martin bowed over the slim hand that was bestowed on him; Dorothea curtsied, then, rising, looked up at him frankly, green eyes twinkling. 'Welcome, my lord. We've heard so much about you. You see me positively preening, such is the cachet of being the first hostess to entertain you.'

The low voice invited him to laugh with her at society's vagaries. Martin smiled. 'The pleasure is entirely mine, my lady.' She was, he thought, entirely enchanting, just right for Hazelmere. His gaze shifted to his friend's face. Hazelmere was watching his wife, the proprietorial gleam in his hazel eyes pronounced.

'But do come in and meet the others.' Dorothea took his arm and led him towards the drawing-room.

Hazelmere fell in on his other side. 'You have to exclaim over the heir, too,' he murmured, hazel eyes dancing with laughter.

They paused on the threshold of the large drawing-room. A babble of gay voices, unaffected by polite restraint, filled the air. Martin scanned those present, noting Fanshawe, with a pretty blonde chit at his side, talking to an older woman whom he recognised as Marc's mother, the Dowager Marchioness. Martin remembered her with affection; she was one of the few who had not condemned him over the Monckton affair. By her side was an even older woman in a purple turban. She looked vaguely familiar but he could not place her.

His gaze travelled on to a group before the fireplace—— And froze. A woman stood before the hearth, a baby balanced on one hip, cradled in one cruvaceous arm. The light from the wall sconce glittered over her golden curls. Her ample charms were exquisitely sheathed in topaz silk; pearls sheened about her throat. She was taller than the dandy she had been talking to, a slim, slight figure with pale blond hair. But his entrance had brought an abrupt halt to their discourse. Eyes of pale green, wide with shock, were fixed on him.

With a slow, infinitely wicked smile, Martin made straight for fair Juno.

As he crossed the large room, he was aware of Dorothea by his side, chattering animatedly. Her comments led him to understand that she thought he was interested in seeing her son. Martin's smile deepened; his eyes locked with fair Juno's. The sight of her, with a baby on her hip, affected him more strongly than he wished to admit. No desire, in a life strewn with desire, had ever been so strong. He wanted to see her standing before his fireplace, with his son in her arms. It was that simple.

Helen couldn't breathe. The sight of Martin in the doorway had quite literally scattered her wits. In the middle of a sentence, in reply to a question of Ferdie's, her voice had simply suspended, stopped, her mind totally focused on the rake across the room. And now he was coming to her side! With an effort, she drew breath, and panic rushed in. Her gaze lifted to his and was trapped in clouds of grey. The quality of his smile registered. It was devilish. Repressing a shiver of pure anticipation, Helen dragged her mind free of his spell. Heavens! She was going to have to do better than this—where had her years of experience flown to?

Then Dorothea was there, reaching for her son. 'Let me introduce Lord Darcy Henry.'

Helen handed Darcy over, desperately struggling to find her mental feet. Dorothea held Darcy for Martin to admire. The Earl of Merton barely glanced at Hazelmere's heir.

'He's nearly two months old.' Dorothea looked up to find that her husband's old friend was not even looking at her son. She stared at Martin, then realised he was staring at Helen. Dorothea followed his gaze and beheld her usually impervious friend mesmerised, bedazzled, wholly hypnotised by Lord Merton's grey gaze.

Fascinated, Dorothea was glancing from Martin to Helen and back again when her husband appeared by her side. Ex-rake that he was, Hazelmere took in the scene in one, comprehensive glance.

'Martin, Lord Merton, allow me to introduce Helen, Lady Walford, Darcy's godmother.' Hazelmere turned to his wife. 'Perhaps, my dear, you'd better take Darcy back to the nursery.' With an innocent air, the hazel gaze returned to Helen. 'And perhaps, Helen, you could introduce the others—or at least those Martin can't recall?'

With a benedictory smile, Hazelmere moved off, firmly removing his by now intrigued wife.

Finding his field clear, Martin allowed a rakish smile to surface. He moved to Helen's side, one black brow rising quizzically. 'Revealed by the hand of fate, fair Juno.'

The softly spoken words caressed Helen's ear, sending a delicious shiver down her spine. 'Helen,' she whispered back urgently, searching for some semblance of equilibrium. She dared not look at him until she had found it.

'You'll always be fair Juno to me,' came the outrageous reply. 'What man of flesh and blood could let that image go? Just think of the memories.'

Helen decided she had better not—her composure was rattled enough already.

Calmly, Martin appropriated her hand and dropped a light kiss on her fingers, smiling at the tremor of awareness the action provoked.

Wide-eyed, Helen glanced up at him, only to glance away rapidly. The glow in his eyes suggested he was going to be outrageous; his smile was a declaration of devilish intent.

Indignation came to her rescue. 'I take it you're acquainted with Hazelmere?'

Martin's eyes danced. 'We're old friends—very old friends.'

Of that Helen had not a doubt. For years, Marc had sternly protected her from the advances of the rakes of the *ton*; now, in his own drawing-room, he had all but handed her into Martin Willesden's arms. Typical! Helen repressed a most unladylike snort.

With his usual good manners, Ferdie had drifted away when Martin had approached so purposefully. With a warning glance for the reprobate beside her, Helen raised her voice. 'Ferdie—have you and Lord Merton met?'

It transpired that they had not. Helen performed the introductions, adding for Martin's benefit, 'Ferdie is Hazelmere's cousin.'

Martin frowned slightly. 'The one who rode his father's stallion?'

To Helen's amusement, Ferdie blushed. 'Didn't think anyone would remember that.'

'I've a particularly good memory,' Martin averred, his eyes seeking Helen's. Trapping her gaze, he added, his voice low, 'Particularly vivid.'

It was Helen's turn to blush. Studiously avoiding Ferdie's interested eye, she placed a hand on Martin's sleeve, risking the contact in the pursuit of greater safety. 'Have you met Dorothea's grandmother, my lord?' With a nod for Ferdie, she purposefully steered Martin in the direction of the dowagers, hoping that in their presence he would get little opportunity to exercise his facility for unnerving innuendo.

To her relief, as they circulated among Hazelmere's guests, Martin behaved in a manner which when she later had time to consider it, only confirmed her assessment of his experience and expertise. He chatted easily with whoever she introduced him to, the ready charm she had always associated with the most dangerous species of rake very apparent. However, at no time did he give any indication of wishing to leave her side. In fact, his attitude declared that, had it been permissible, he would unhesitatingly have monopolised her time.

He made his preference so clear that both the Dowager, Marc's mother, and Lady Merion, Dorothea's grandmother, took great delight in twitting them both over it.

'I gather you've been in the colonies for some years, my lord. I dare say it takes time to remember our ways?'

The pointed look Lady Merion bent on Martin should, by rights, have flustered even him. Yet, to her horror, Helen heard his deep voice reply, 'Having but recently laid claim to an exceptional memory, I can hardly now advance forgetfulness as my excuse, ma'am.'

For the life of her, Helen could not resist glancing his way. The grey eyes were glowing and fixed on her face.

'Perhaps, my lord, you should seek guidance in achieving your re-entry to society?' The Dowager Marchioness's eyes were even more innocent than her son's. 'Perhaps Lady Walford would be willing to assist?'

Helen blushed furiously.

'A capital notion, ma'am.' With a smile for the delighted dowagers that relieved Helen of any need to speak, Martin drew her from their questionable safety.

Her composure severely compromised, Helen tried to act calmly, tried to convince herself that, in the present circumstances, it was she who should be in control, not he, but in that she failed miserably. As the evening progressed, and they went into dinner, she was not even surprised to find that Martin had somehow arranged things so that it seemed natural for him to lead her in and sit on her right.

Under cover of an uproarious discussion on the latest of the Prince Regent's peccadilloes, Martin leaned closer and asked, 'Will you consent to a drive with me in the Park, fair Juno?'

Helen sent him a glittering glance, intended to convey her disapproval of his continued use of that name. He received it with an unrepentant smile.

'Good. I'll call for you at eleven tomorrow.'

Before she could do more than gasp at his effrontery, he was offering her a dish of crab. Helen drew a determined breath. 'My lord. . .' she began.

'My lady?' he promptly replied, grey eyes intent.

Frantically searching for some means of bringing him to a sense of his shortcomings in respect of accepted procedures, Helen looked deep into his eyes, saw them calmly predatory, and knew she stood no chance of turning him from his purpose. His gaze held hers and the fire shrouded by the grey glowed bright. One brow rose. Abruptly, Helen looked down at her plate.

Smoothly, Martin turned back to the company, a confident smile curving his lips.

Nerves aflutter, Helen decided she would do well to regroup before she took on an opponent of Martin Willesden's calibre.

When they adjourned to the drawing-room, the men eschewing their port in favour of joining the ladies, a different light was cast on Martin's propensities. It was Cecily, Lady Fanshawe, who opened Helen's eyes to what had, until that moment, escaped her notice, pre-occupied as she had been with Lord Merton's potential for outrageousness. The youthful Cecily, just seven-teen, had bubbled about the company in her usual fashion, but had missed being introduced to Martin earlier. Helen performed the introduction and was slightly startled by Cecily's reaction. The big pansy brown eyes opened wide; Lady Fanshawe simply stared.

'*Ohh*,' she finally breathed, her round eyes taking in as much of Martin as she could.

Tony Fanshawe came up in time to witness his wife's response. With a deep sigh, he took her arm.

'Go away, Martin,' he said, and, with a long-suffering look, drew Cecily around. About to lead her off, he paused and glanced back, wicked lights gleaming in his blue eyes. 'On second thoughts, why not take Helen away, too?'

Helen glared. They were *insufferable*, the lot of them! A gaggle of unrepentant rakes.

Martin's chuckle brought her around to face him. 'What a very good idea.' The nuance he managed to infuse into the words sent her eyes flying wide. Some-how, his fingers had trapped her hand. Held by the glow in his grey eyes, smoky now with an emotion she was coming to recognise, Helen could only stare as he raised her hand to his lips. The gesture was so simple, yet heavy with meaning. The lingering touch of his lips, a warm caress on her fingertips, sent a succession of shivers through her.

In desperation, Helen blinked—and saw him through Cecily's eyes. She was used to men being the same height as she, but Martin was a good half-head taller. His dark hair curled lightly; there was the faintest trace of silver at his temples. The grey eyes, so mesmeric, were watching her from under arched and hooded lids. The lines at their corners suggested that laughter came easily to their owner. His cheeks were lean and tanned, his lips fine-drawn and firm. One glance at his jaw gave warning of his temper.

With a little sigh, Helen acknowledged the face and moved on to the figure. She was a large woman, junoesque in truth, but he made her feel small. His shoulders were wide, his chest broad, leaving an impression of lean muscle cloaking a large and power-ful frame. She knew he moved gracefully, as an athlete would; the idea of waltzing with him was more than just attractive.

As she realised, with a jolt, just how long she had stood staring, her eyes flew to his. Heightened con-sciousness, of him, of her susceptibility, of how much he could see, threatened to overwhelm her. Her breath caught in her throat. She looked away, nervous, con-fused and more at sea than she had ever been. 'Can you see Ferdie anywhere?'

Martin heard the panic in her tone. Smiling, he duti-fully scanned the room. Her response was encouraging but now was not the time to press her further. With consummate ease, he took charge. 'He's by the fireplace.' Tucking her hand into the crook of his arm, he strolled back into the fray of conversation.

Grateful for his understanding, for she knew it was that, Helen took the opportunity he gave her to reassemble her faculties and get her feet back on the ground. As they circulated about the big room, she recalled a comment of Dorothea's that being in Marc's care often felt like being caught in a web, with him, the spider, in the centre. That was exactly how she now felt, except that it was Martin at the centre of her web. It was a protective web; the bonds did not hurt. But they were there, inescapable, unbreakable.

Her relief was very real when Hazelmere approached them, saying to Martin, 'Tony and I are for White's. Gisborne——' he waved in the direction of his brother-in-law '—is coming, too. Are you for the tables?'

Martin smiled. 'Lead the way.'

Hazelmere laughed. 'I didn't think you'd have changed.' With a nod for Helen, he left them.

Martin had taken possession of her hand. Helen glanced up and discovered that the expression in his eyes went far beyond the acceptable, a warm and distinctly intimate caress. He raised her fingers to his lips.

'Until tomorrow, fair Juno.'

It was all she could do to nod her farewell.

Much later, in the privacy of her chamber, Helen stared at her reflection in the mirror, and wondered when such madness would end.

CHAPTER SIX

NOT soon, was Helen's conclusion when, the next day, Martin called as promised to take her for a drive in the Park. Bowling along beneath the trees, their leaves just beginning to turn, perched in her familiar spot beside him on the box seat, she discovered that he intended to give her no chance to ponder the wisdom of the outing. Instead, he seemed intent on following the Dowager Marchioness of Hazelmere's advice and enlisting her aid.

'Who is that quiz in the shocking purple toque?'

Helen followed his glance. 'That's Lady Havelock. She's a bit of a dragon.'

'And looks it. Does she still hold sway with the Melbourne House set?'

'Not so much these days, now that Lady Melbourne lives so retired.' Helen raised her hand in acknowledgement of a bow from a painted fop.

'And who's he?'

At the possessive growl, Helen's lips twitched. 'Shiffy? Sir Lumley Sheffington.'

Oh.' Martin glanced again at the white-painted face above an outrageous apricot silk bow. 'I remember now. I'd forgotten about him—entirely understandable.'

Helen giggled. Shiffy was one of the more memorable figures among the *ton*.

Martin kept up a steady stream of questions—on the

other occupants of the Park, on the happenings in town and whether certain personages were as he remembered them. Engrossed with her answers, Helen did not notice the passage of time. Their hour together vanished more swiftly, and with greater ease, than she had expected.

Descending the steps of Helen's small house in Half Moon Street, having seen his goddess safely inside, Martin startled Joshua, standing at the bays' heads, with an exceedingly broad grin. Gaining the box seat and retrieving the reins, Martin waved Joshua to his perch. 'The day bodes fair, my projects proceed apace—what more could a man ask for?'

Scrambling up behind, Joshua rolled his eyes heavenwards. 'No mystery what's come over you,' he muttered, *sotto voce*, making a mental note to learn more of Lady Walford. In blissful ignorance of his henchman's deductions, Martin gave his horses the office, well-pleased with his beginning.

As the week progressed, he had even more reason for satisfaction. His re-entry to the *ton* was accomplished more easily than he had hoped. A visit to the theatre, escorting fair Juno to view the latest of Mrs Siddons' dramatic flights, had brought him to the notice of the major hostesses. The pile of white cards stacked upon his mantelpiece grew day by day. Eschewing all subtlety, he determined which of the parties his delight intended to grace by dint of the simple expedient of asking. Thus forearmed, he felt assured of enjoying those assemblies he deigned to attend.

Climbing the stairs to Lady Burlington's ballroom for the first of the larger gatherings on his list, Martin spared a moment to contemplate how the *ton* would receive him. Invitations were one thing, but how would they treat the black sheep in the flesh? If he was to marry Helen, the *ton's* approbation was a hurdle he would have to clear.

He need not have worried.

'Lord Merton!' Lady Burlington positively pounced on him. 'I'm so thrilled you could find time to attend my little party.'

Replying all but automatically to his hostess's gushing comments, Martin reflected that, from what he could see, her 'little party' numbered over one hundred.

'Pleased you could come.'

The gruff accents of Lord Burlington were a welcome release. After shaking hands, Martin moved into the room, only to find himself surrounded. By women.

Blonde hair in ringlets, black hair in curls, every shade and hue pressed in on every side. A medley of perfumes washed over him, light fractured in their gems. 'Lord Merton!' was on each pair of lips. The hostesses of the *ton*, many the very women who had, thirteen years before, closed their doors in his face, all but fell over themselves in their eagerness to impress him with their credentials. Manfully quelling an unnerving impulse to laugh in their powdered faces, Martin drew on his experience, cloaking his antipathy with just the right degree of patronising superiority, and accepted their admiration as became one who knew how their games were played.

'I do hope you'll find time to call.'

Martin allowed a black brow to rise at the tone of that particular invitation, coming from a blonde whose eyes vied with her diamonds in hardness. He could hardly be unaware of the heated glances some of the younger matrons were flinging his way. Cynically, he wondered if, had he returned as plain Martin Willesden, unadorned with an earldom and colossal wealth, he would have been welcomed quite so enthusiastically.

Due to the importunities of the more clinging mesdames, it was late before Martin saw Helen. Instantly, he knew she was aware of him, but, unsure of whether he would notice her, she was making every effort not to notice him. With a devilish smile, he nodded a brief but determined farewell to his court and escaped across the ballroom to his goddess's side.

Helen knew he was approaching long before he reached her. It was not simply that the majority of female eyes in the vicinity had suddenly found a common target, nor that Mrs Hitchin, with whom she was conversing, had stopped, slack-jawed, in the middle of a sentence, her eyes fixed on a point beyond Helen's left shoulder. Her flickering nerves would have told her he was near and getting nearer even had she been blindfold.

Quelling her traitorous senses, ignoring her increasing pulse, Helen turned and, smoothly, surrendered her hand into his. 'My lord.' His fingers closed about hers in a warm, possessive clasp. Determined not to fluster, Helen curtsied.

Martin raised her, then, slowly, deliberately, holding her gaze with is, he carried her fingers to his lips.

For an instant, Helen could have sworn that the entire host held its breath. Kissing ladies' hands was a gallantry no longer common; pray heaven that they put it down to his years away. She, of course, knew better.

The glow in his eyes warmed her, the smouldering grey igniting a familiar warmth within.

To her relief, years of ballroom etiquette came to her rescue. 'My lord, pray allow me to present Mrs Hitchin.'

Martin had no interest in Mrs Hitchin. He bestowed a civil nod upon the lady, and a comforting smile. But he did not let go of Juno's hand. Instead, he tucked it into his arm. 'My dear Lady Walford, there's a waltz about to start. I do hope Mrs Hitchin will excuse us?'

Helen blinked. How *dared* he simply walk up and appropriate her? Then full understanding of what he was suggesting broke upon her. A waltz? Held in his arms—and she could imagine just how. Heaven help her—how was she to manage? Just the thought made her feel weak.

In panic, she looked about for assistance. Mrs Hitchin was no use; the woman was positively basking in the glow of Martin's smile. But before she could find a lifeline to cling to, Martin was moving towards the area of the room given over to the dancers.

'I promise not to bite.'

His words, gentle in her ear, stiffened her resolve. She was being silly—missish, she who did not know the meaning of the word. He would not do anything truly outrageous in the middle of a ballroom, would he?

And then he was drawing her into his arms, holding her every bit as close as she had feared. They joined the whirling couples on the floor. A host of emotions she had never experienced before being exposed to Martin Willesden threatened to overcome her. Helen struggled to quell them. She could not—must not—let him get away with this. . .this commandeering of her senses.

'My lord,' she said firmly, raising her eyes to his.

'My lady,' he replied, his tone investing the term with meaning far beyond the mundane, his eyes confirming his intent.

Helen felt her eyes grow round. Great heavens! He was seducing her. In the middle of Lady Burlington's ballroom, with half the *ton* looking on. Rapidly revising her estimates of his potential, she allowed her lids to veil her eyes and sought for a lighter note. 'Does polite society thus far meet with your approval?'

Martin smiled. 'I hardly know. I've had so little in recent years to compare it with.' He felt her relax, and took the opportunity provided by negotiating the tight turn at the bottom of the room to draw her more firmly against him. 'But, as far as the company goes, I've some reservations.'

'Oh?' Thankful that he was prepared to converse reasonably, Helen decided to overlook the almost imperceptible tightening of his arm about her. 'Why is that?'

'Well,' said Martin, frowning as if considering his words, 'it's the female element I have most trouble with.'

Suspicion bloomed in Helen's mind. What did a rake consider reasonable conversation? She felt compelled to give him the benefit of her doubt and asked, 'What is it that particularly troubles you?'

The concerned look he threw her almost had her believing his, 'It's their predatory tendencies that worry me.' When she looked sceptical, he added defensively, 'It's most unnerving to a fully licenced rake to find himself the pursued rather than the pursuer. Just imagine it, if you can.'

'Strange,' said Helen, green eyes glinting. 'I could almost believe I know just how you feel.'

At that he smiled, a dazzling smile that overloaded her senses and sent them spinning. By the time she had collected them, the music had ceased. 'Perhaps I should return to——' In confusion, Helen bit her lip. Heavens, she was no débutante to be returning to a chaperon's side! What was she thinking of—what was it the man by her side made her think of?

Martin chuckled, following her thoughts easily. 'Fear not, fair Juno. Your reputation is safe with me.' He paused then added in a pensive tone, 'As for the rest of you, though. . .' The shocked glance she sent him had him chuckling again.

When, a few minutes later, he relinquished her to Lord Alvanley, still flustered but recovered enough to throw him a speaking glance, he reflected that he had spoken no more than the truth throughout their exchanges. Which was odd enough. But he did, in fact, find the cloying interest of the unmarried females repelling and suspected his feeling sprang, as he had told her, from his liking to be the driving force behind his relationships. Her far more natural response to him was gratifying; her attempts to hide it, believing, correctly, that it gave him far more influence over her than she would like, made her irresistibly attractive to a man of his ilk. Given his long-term plans for her, he had no intention that her reputation should suffer at his or anyone else's hands. And he felt positively righteous that he had gone so far as to give her clear warning of his intent.

Halo glowing, he strolled about the room, waiting
for the time to claim her for supper.

Dancing with friends and acquaintances who
demanded no more from her than polite conversation
gave Helen time to consider Martin Willesden's words.
Not for the life of her could she fathom what he meant.
If it had not been for the fact that he knew she was a
connection of Hazelmere's, she might have suspected
he intended to set her up as his mistress. But she knew
enough of the peculiar code of the rake to know that
Hazelmere's protection would not be challenged by a
friend. But, if not that, then his words could only mean
he was on the lookout for a wife and believed she
would suit.

Inwardly, Helen sighed, and wished it were so. But
he was wrong—and the sooner he learned his error the
better. He was going to break her heart if he did not
desist from his determined pursuit. None knew better
than she that, while her birth was perfectly acceptable
and her connections beyond reproach, being the relict
of a social outcast would not be considered a suitable
background for the new Countess of Merton. That
position should rightly be reserved for one of the
incomparables, or, at the very least, a richly dowered
débutante. She had never been one of the former,
though she had, for a bare month before her marriage,
been one of the latter.

The cotillion came to an end. Lord Peterborough,
whom she had known forever, bowed elegantly over
her hand. 'Thank you, Gerry,' she said, smiling.
'You're always such an eligible *parti*.'

His lordship laughed and offered her his arm. Supper
was being served downstairs. Helen raised her hand to

place it on his sleeve but, to her surprise, warm fingers closed about hers.

'Ah, Gerry. I have to tell you Lady Birchfield is looking for you.'

Lord Peterborough glared. 'Dammit, Martin! Lady Birchfield can look all she likes. The woman's old enough to be m'mother.'

'Really? I'd no idea you were so young.' Martin's eyes gleamed. 'It's just as well I've arrived to escort Lady Walford to supper. It wouldn't do for her to be thought a cradle-snatcher.'

Having deprived both Lord Peterborough and fair Juno of the power of speech, Martin smoothly drew Helen's hand through his arm and, with a genial nod to his friend, steered her in the direction of the supper-room.

By the time Helen found her tongue, she was seated at a small table in an alcove of the supper-room, a plate of delicacies before her. Fixing the reprobate opposite with a steely glare, her bosom swelled. 'Lord Merton. . .' she began.

'Martin, remember?' Martin grinned at her. 'You didn't really believe I'd let you go into supper with anyone else, did you?'

Staring into teasing grey eyes, Helen felt totally befuddled. Should she answer yes or no? If she said yes, he would only take the opportunity to tell her she should have known better—which was true. And saying no was out of the question. In the end, she glared. 'You're impossible.'

Martin smiled. 'Have a lobster patty.'

Helen gave up. It was simply too easy for him to pull the rug from beneath her feet in private. She had yet, she reflected, to learn how to keep him at a proper distance. If she did not master the art soon, it would be entirely too late. Already, she had noticed a few curious looks cast their way. Still, as far as the *ton* knew, he could merely be looking her over, seeking congenial company until the Little Season got into full swing and he set about the serious task of finding a suitable wife.

Pleased by her capitulation, Martin devoted his considerable talents to distracting her, in which endeavour he was so successful that, by the time he returned her to the ballroom, she was thoroughly flustered. In the circumstances, he forbore to claim another dance, contenting himself with placing a most improper kiss in her palm before leaving her to less threatening cavaliers.

The Burlington ball marked the beginning of Martin's campaign. He was assiduous in attending whatever ball or party Helen Walford graced, paying her such marked attention as could not be misconstrued. He took great delight in teasing her, knowing that she, of all who watched him, was the furtherest from divining his purpose. Many had marked his predilection for her company; he did not, in truth, give a damn. He fully intended to go a great deal further than mere predilection.

Everything he learned of her confirmed his certainty that she was the one woman he wanted before his fireplace. She was accepted and respected, unquestionably good *ton*. Her maturity was transparent, but, while she clearly understood the rules of the game, she had never, to anyone's knowledge, played. Not the closest scrutiny uncovered any degree of partiality for the numerous gentlemen who claimed her as friend. She was much admired, by the women as well as the men— no mean feat in these days of cut-throat beauty.

It was a week into the Little Season when his pursuit of her took him to the dim portals of Almack's. The Marriage Mart had never been one of his favourite venues. As a youth, he had labelled it the Temple of Doom—forswear happiness, all ye who enter here. With a grimace, he gathered his resolution and trod up the steps. Helen was within and he had determined to conquer not only her, but this last bastion of the *ton*.

The porter admitted him to the hall, but, not being a regular, there he had to wait for one or other of the patronesses to grant him permission to enter the rooms. As luck would have it, it was Sally Jersey who swept out in response to the porter's summons, her large eyes wide and incredulous.

'Good God! It *is* you!'

Martin grinned wryly and bowed. 'Me, myself and I, alone.' He smiled winningly. 'Will you allow me to enter, dear Sally?'

Lady Jersey was no more immune to rakish charm than the next woman. But she knew Martin Willesden, and knew of the scandal in his past. She was also one of those who had never believed it. She eyed the tower of potent masculinity before her and frowned. 'Will you promise not to cause any undue flutter?'

Martin put back his head and laughed. 'Sally, oh, Sally. What an impossible stipulation.'

When he eyed her wickedly, Lady Jersey was forced to acknowledge the truth of his words. 'Oh—very well!

I never believed that Monckton chit anyway,' she muttered.

Martin captured her hand and bowed low. 'My thanks, Sally.'

'Oh, go on with you!' said Lady Jersey. 'You make me feel old.'

'Never *old*, Sally.' With one last wicked grin, Martin headed for the ballroom.

He had hoped to slip unnoticed to the side of the room, from which vantage point, being so tall, he would have been able to locate Helen. Instead, to his horror, he was mobbed but feet from the door. While he had been speaking to Sally, word of his arrival had gone the rounds. To his incredulous gaze, it appeared that every fond mama with an insipid daughter in tow had gathered near the entrance for the express purpose of accosting him.

'My dear Lord Merton—I'm Lady Dalgleish—a very old friend of your mama's. Pray allow me to present. . .'

'Such an exciting career as you've had, my lord. You must take the time to tell my dear Annabelle all about it—she just *adores* tales of foreign places.'

Never in his life had Martin faced such a trial. It quickly transpired that, as virtually none could claim acquaintance due to his prolonged sojourn overseas, they had all decided to ignore such niceties and introduce themselves. The reason for his thirteen-year absence was entirely overlooked.

'You must come to my soirée next week. Just a *very* select few. You'll be able to converse with Julia so much more easily without such a horde about.'

Even Martin blinked at that. They were shameless, the lot of them. The temptation to tell them all to go to hell was strong, but Sally would never forgive him. And he wanted to see Helen, who was undoubtedly one of the many enjoying the unexpected entertainment.

In the end, Martin simply stood stock still and let them come at him, steadfastly refusing to ask any young lady to dance, nor to accept any invitation to look over a chit's finer points during a stroll around the rooms. He knew that none of the hostesses would be so bold as to suggest he dance with any of the young things, regardless of their parents' wishes. It was the first time he had ever had reason to be thankful for his past.

Finally, the attack faltered. In between deflecting the none too subtle invitations, he had managed to locate Helen in a small knot of ladies at the far end of the room. Sensing a hiatus, he made a bid for freedom before his besiegers had a chance to regroup.

Gracefully, Martin bowed to the stalwart matron planted plumb in front of him, her two freckle-faced daughters flanking her. 'Your pardon, ma'am. I fear I must leave you. So pleasant to have met your daughters.' With a vague smile, he beat a hasty retreat.

Helen had certainly noticed the crowd by the door and recognised the dark head at its centre. It was no more than she had expected—his due, nothing more. With an inward sigh, she made an effort to immerse herself in her friends' discussion. Lord Merton would have his hands full with the debs from now on.

'My dear—my *very* dear Lady Walford.' Martin did not try to keep the relief from his voice. 'What a pleasure it is to see you—at last.'

Helen jumped and turned, knowing who she would

see before she did. No one else had a voice that could frazzle her senses. 'My lord.' She curtsied. As usual, he raised her and appropriated her hand, as if she had made him a present of it. She had come to accept that particular trick as inevitable, knowing no way of stopping him. But she had yet to come to grips with the warmth in his eyes as they rested on her, and the promise that glowed in their depths.

Breathlessly, she introduced the three ladies in her circle. To her surprise, Martin did not try to remove her but stayed by her side, chatting politely, charming her friends utterly.

When Helen's friends moved away, to talk to other acquaintances among the growing crowd, Martin dropped the reserve he employed in such social situations. He glanced down into Helen's green eyes, his own entirely devoid of guile. 'You'll have to be my mentor in this particular theatre of war. Where else can we go to be safe?'

Helen looked her astonishment. 'Safe?'

Martin smiled a little ruefully. 'I'm claiming your protection.' When she still looked bemused, he added, 'In return for my earlier efforts on your behalf.'

A slight blush staining her cheeks, Helen let her eyes slide over his impressive length. 'However could *I* protect *you*? You're bamming me.'

'No such thing—rake's honour.' Hand over his heart, Martin grinned. 'The matchmaking mamas are out to leg-shackle me, I do assure you. They're hunting in packs, what's more. If I'm to retain any degree of freedom, I'll need all the help I can get.'

Helen smothered a giggle. 'You can't just not take any notice. You'll have to choose a wife some time.'

The grey eyes holding hers suddenly became intent. But his voice was still even when he asked, 'You don't seriously suppose I'd marry any of the delicate debs?'

'But. . .it's what's expected of men of your position.' Helen coloured, then abruptly glanced away. Not only was this a most improper conversation, but she had nearly blurted out that hers had been such a conventional marriage. That, she was the first to admit, was hardly a recommendation.

To her unease, the grey eyes were still trained on her face. She could feel them, compelling her to return his regard. Unable to withstand the subtle pressure, she glanced up. Her eyes locked with his.

Martin smiled gently, and raised her hand to his lips, his eyes holding hers steadily. 'I'll never marry one of the debs, my dear. My tastes run to women of more. . . voluptuous charms.'

If Helen had had any doubts over what he intended her to understand by that, the look in his eyes would have dispelled them. For good measure, when she blushed, his eyes dropped to caress the ripe swell of her breasts, more revealed than concealed by the current craze for low necklines. Helen felt her cheeks flame.

'Martin!'

His eyes returned to her face, gentle laughter in the grey depths. 'Mmm?'

What could she say? She should talk to him of reality, of all the reasons she was ineligible. Now was the time. Determined to halt his mad schemes before they went any further, before her heart was totally torn in two, Helen raised her eyes to his. 'My lord, you cannot marry me. My husband was Arthur Walford— you must have known him. He committed suicide, but only after being hounded from the *ton*. He gambled away everything he owned, including my settlements. With such a background, I'm no suitable wife for you.'

All Martin's levity had flown. The expression in his eyes, intent yet infinitely gentle, did not waver; his thumb moved caressingly over the back of her hand. 'My dear, I know all this. Did you think I would care?'

The room was whirling. Helen could not breathe. 'But. . .'

Martin's smile grew. Confidently, he drew her to stroll beside him. If they remained stationary for much longer, someone would stop to talk. 'My dear Helen, I've never been one to act in accordance with society's dictates. I've been a rake and a gamester for as long as anyone here can recall. I assure you, none will think it the least odd that I, of all men, should choose to marry a more mature woman rather than saddle myself with some mindless flibbertigibbet.'

A nervous giggle assured him that she had accepted the truth of that. 'Now enough of your quibbles. If this is merely a ploy to deny me your protection, I take leave to tell you 'tis a shabby trick.'

'As if you need my protection.' Helen followed his lead in moving from the topic of marriage, trying to regain their usual, lightly bantering tone. Her mind was in a whirl. What he had suggested was beyond her wildest dreams; she would need time to consider the possibilities. Her brain was too overloaded to make much sense of it now, particularly not with him by her side. 'I'm quite sure you could rout all the matchmaking mamas without difficulty.'

'Unquestionably,' agreed the rake by her side. 'But, having done so, I'd be cast out from these hallowed halls, bidden never to return, and thus would be unable to see you on Wednesday nights. Not a prospect I relish. So, in the interests of your Wednesday nights, madam, will you consent to act as my protector?'

Helen could only laugh. 'Very well. But only within strict limits.'

Martin frowned. 'What limits?'

'You must not misbehave with me.' She glanced up, trying for stern implacability. 'No dancing more than two waltzes, and never two together. In fact,' she added, recalling his ability to think up new and ever more disturbing ways of dealing with her, 'no going beyond the line in any way whatever.'

'Unfair! How do you imagine I'll control my rakish tendencies? Have pity, fair Juno. I can't reform in an instant.'

But Helen stood firm. 'That's my best offer, my lord.' When his brows rose, she added, her own brows rising, 'You'd hardly ask me to place my own position here in jeopardy?'

Martin sighed in mock-defeat. 'You drive a hard bargain, sweetheart. I capitulate. In the interests of my own skin, I accept your conditions.'

It was a full minute before Helen registered the ineligible epithet and by then it was too late to gasp.

To her considerable relief, Martin did behave impeccably for the rest of the evening. She had no illusions as to how outrageous he could be if he put his mind to it. His 'rakish tendencies', as he called them, were remarkably strong. But not even the highest stickler could have faulted his performance—beyond the fact that he remained anchored to her side.

* * *

After the excitement of Almack's, Helen had expected to endure a sleepless night. Instead, drugged with unaccustomed happiness, she had slept the sleep of the innocent. Unheralded but sure of his welcome, Martin had called to take her driving at eleven. What with entertaining a small procession of afternoon visitors, all agog to hear anything she might have to say about the Earl of Merton, and then dressing for dinner at Hatcham House, Helen found herself once more in Martin Willesden's arms, waltzing down a ballroom, without having had more than a moment to spend in consideration of his words of the previous night.

'Tell me, fairest Juno, is it normal for such affairs as this to be so refreshingly free of the *jeunes filles*?'

Martin's voice in her ear summoned her wits from besotted contemplation of how very strong he was and how helpless he made her feel. Helen blinked. 'Well,' she temporised, glancing about at the crowd and noticing he was right, 'I suppose it's because the Hatchams are rather out of the deb set—their own children are all married. And Lord Pomeroy is giving a ball for his daughter tonight, too, so many of the younger folk will be there, I expect.'

Martin frowned slightly. 'I don't suppose I can convince you to eschew the larger balls—at least for this year?'

Helen returned his mock-frown with one of her own. 'After avoiding the *ton* and the matchmaking mamas for the past thirteen years, the least you can do is allow them a try at you.'

'But just think how pointless such an undertaking on their parts will be.' His expression became earnest. 'Shouldn't I, in the interests of the social good, and the matchmaking mamas' constitutions, simply give them all the go-by?'

The music ceased and they whirled to a halt. Taking his arm all but automatically, Helen fell to strolling by his side. 'By no means!' She could not yet see where his conversation was taking them. 'It's your duty to be seen at the major functions.'

Martin grimaced. 'You're absolutely sure?'

Warily, Helen nodded.

'Ah, well.' He sighed. 'In that case, just as long as you're there to protect me, I suppose I'll have to attend.'

'My lord, I cannot be forever at your side.' She could see where he was headed now.

'Why not?'

The grey eyes, impossibly candid, held hers.

'Because. . .' Helen struggled to assemble her reasons—her rational, sensible reasons. But, under the power of his grey gaze, they went winging from her head. They had halted by the side of the ballroom and she had turned, the better to look into his face. The eyes holding hers seemed to look deeper, reach deeper, to touch some chord within her and make it sing. Then, as she watched, he was distracted. His eyes left hers, focusing on some vision a few feet behind her.

'Speaking of protection. . .' Martin drew her hand through his arm, securing her by his side.

'Martin—*darling*! How positively *thrilling* to see you again—after all these years!'

Helen stifled a wince at the arch tones. Small wonder that Martin wished to avoid the mesdames if that was the treatment they accorded him. She felt the muscles of his arm tense beneath her fingers. Helen shifted slightly, to stand more definitely by his side, where she sensed he wanted her, and found herself staring at blonde curls much paler than her own, arranged about a face rather older than her own. But not old enough to be a matchmaking mama. The woman cast the barest of icy smiles in her direction before turning big, pale blue eyes on the new Earl of Merton.

The new Earl remained stubbornly silent.

The lady continued unabashed. '*Such* a surprise, my dear. You should have called.' A look of unlikely ingenuousness suffused the pale face. 'Oh! Of *course*. You wouldn't know! I'm Lady Rochester now.'

For Helen, the penny dropped with the name. She stifled the urge to look up at Martin, to see what he was making of her ladyship's performance. Lady Rochester was a widow of some years standing, one of those who, while credited with birth sufficient to enter the *ton* and title sufficient to open most doors, was nevertheless on the outer circle of polite society. No scandal had ever touched her name, but consistent rumour still tarnished it.

Martin's silence was beginning to strain her ladyship's smile. But her voice was determinedly conspiratorial when she said, 'My dear Martin, I've so much to tell you. Perhaps, such old friends as we are, we should repair to some place rather more private to review our histories? If Lady Walford will excuse us?'

The last was said with a dismissive smile. Her ladyship reached for Martin's other arm. Helen stiffened, and would have drawn her hand from Martin's sleeve except that his hand, covering hers, tightened, strong fingers gripping hers.

'I think not.'

Helen blinked, very glad that Martin did not use that particular tone to her. Shafts of ice and arctic winds would have been warmer. Intrigued by this by-play, for it was transparently obvious that there was more to the exchange than she yet knew, she watched Lady Rochester's face pale to blank-white.

'But——'

'As it happens,' Martin continued, repressive coldness in every syllable, 'Lady Walford and I were about to take a stroll on the terrace. If you'll excuse us, Lady Rochester?'

With a distant nod, Martin steered Helen past the importunate Lady Rochester, leaving her ladyship to stare, dumbfounded, at their backs.

Within minutes, they were strolling on the long terrace in relative isolation. Helen felt the tension ease from Martin's long frame. Who was Lady Rochester that she should draw such a violent, albeit suppressed reaction from Martin? Out of the blue, the answer flew into Helen's head.

'Oh! Is she the one who——?' Abruptly, she cut off her words; embarrassment rose to smother her.

Beside her, she felt rather than heard Martin's sigh.

'She's the one who engineered the little drama that saw me exiled from England.'

Engineered? What drama? Helen wished she had the nerve to ask.

Martin stared out over the darkly shadowed gardens, seeing the shadows from his past. He did not want them to cloud his future. There was no one within earshot. 'When I was twenty-two, Serena Monckton, now Lady Rochester, was a débutante. She quite literally threw herself at my head.' He glanced down at Helen's face, and saw the little frown of concentration that dragged at her brows. He smiled. 'As I told you, I have a constitutional dislike of being pursued. In this case, however, I underestimated the opposition. Serena engineered a compromising situation—and then cried rape.'

Helen's brows flew but she said nothing.

'Unfortunately, that little contretemps came on top of the discovery by my father of a rash of gambling debts—nothing overly outrageous, only what was to be expected from a youth such as I was. But my father was determined to keep me in line. Serena's little ploy was the last straw. He issued an ultimatum.'

Despite his clipped tones, and the effort he was making to tell his story without emotion, Helen heard the pain, dulled by the years but still there, an undercurrent that had sprung to life immediately he had mentioned his father.

'Either I married the chit or he'd send me to the colonies. I chose the colonies.' Martin raised his brows, considering his life in brief. 'All in all, that was the luckiest decision of my life.' His lips curled. 'Perhaps I should thank Serena. Without her efforts, I doubt I would be worth quite as much as I am today.'

Helen threw him a soft smile. Hesitantly, and only because she was desperate to know, she asked, 'Did your father learn the truth later?'

There was a distinct pause before the answer came. 'No. I never saw him again. He died two years after the event, while I was still in Jamaica.'

Helen did not need to ask herself if she had heard the truth. Every particle of her being knew that she had. No matter how accomplished an actor, no man, she felt sure, could manufacture the emptiness, the intense loss, that vibrated in the deep, gravelly voice. She had heard vague murmurings of the scandal in his past. She was pleased that he had told her of it—now she could disregard it.

They paced the length of the terrace to where a series of shallow steps led down to a fountain surrounded by an area of parterre. A number of couples were strolling in the fresh night air, seeking relief from the closeness of the ballroom.

Glancing at the serious face beside him, Martin smiled. She was so easy to read. He felt curiously honoured that she should concern herself with his long-ago hurts. But it was time she smiled again. 'Can I tempt you from the terrace, fair Juno? I promise not to abduct you.'

Helen looked up and smiled as the implication of his words registered. A disavowal of any negative response to being abducted by him had almost reached her lips before, horrified, she stilled the words. Fancy admitting to a desire to be kidnapped—by a rake, no less! Her wits were becoming thoroughly untrustworthy when he was by her side. She covered her confusion by drawing away and sweeping him a curtsy. 'Why, thank you, my lord. A brisk turn about the fountain will doubtless clear my head.'

Martin's brows rose. 'Does it need clearing? What's it full of?'

You, was her thought. But his eyes were quizzing her. Determined not to be jockeyed into making any revealing disclosures, Helen put her nose in the air and her hand on his arm. 'The fountain, my lord.'

His soft laugh set every nerve tingling.

'As you command, fair Juno.'

CHAPTER SEVEN

THE Little Season progressed and, with it, Martin's
campaign. By the time the first flurry of balls had faded
into memory, and the trees in the Park had begun to
shed their leaves, he felt it was time to re-evaluate his
position. Helen Walford was his—that was quite clear
to him. Hopefully, it would, by now, also be quite clear
to the *ton* at large. Watching his fair Juno from the
side of Lady Winchester's ballroom, his shoulders
propped against the panelled wall, he spared a moment
in fond amazement that she, alone, was still uncertain
on the matter, unsure that the future he had planned
for her would ever come true.

He had taken great delight in conveying, by every
subtle means at his disposal, just how exciting her
future would be. She was fascinated. Her insecurity
stemmed, he surmised, from her unhappy marriage—a
fact he had no difficulty believing. Arthur Walford
must have been all of fifteen years her senior.

'I wonder. . .is it possible to tempt you to the card-
room?'

At the familiar languid tones, Martin smiled and
shifted his gaze sideways to the Marquis of
Hazelmere's face. 'Unlikely.'

Hazelmere sighed. 'I thought not. I'll have to hunt up
Tony.' He clapped Martin on the shoulder and was
turning away when he paused to add, 'Just remember—
the sooner you resolve this matter, the sooner you can

join us. It doesn't do to forget your friends.' With a smile of the most complete understanding, Hazelmere moved on.

Turning back to the ballroom in time to see Helen throw a laughing smile at her partner—Alvanley and therefore perfectly safe—Martin smiled wryly. He had only just arrived, yet the urge to monopolise Lady Walford's company was growing stronger by the minute. He would resist the tug yet awhile; there was a limit to all things—even the leniency of the *ton* towards one who they were now convinced had been wrongfully slighted. Martin's smile grew. In truth, the past no longer haunted him. His only concern was for the future. But the approbation of the *ton* would be important to the future Countess of Merton, so he was pleased to have secured that elusive cachet.

As to the future itself, he had no doubts. In fact, if he was forced to the truth, he would have to admit that he had made up his mind to wed Helen Walford the instant he had seen her standing before the Hazelmeres' fireplace. The only consideration that had kept him from a declaration was a desire not to startle her—or the *ton*. The *ton* was now taken care of. She was still slightly nervous over what she knew would shortly be her fate, but, if anything, that touch of the wide-eyed innocent only made him more eager to make her his.

The music came to an end and the guests milled across the floor. Conversation rose to cloak the scene lit by the heavy chandeliers. The curls in the ladies' artfully arranged coiffures sheened; jewels winked about their throats. Their gowns swirled, the colours of spring flowers about the trunks of the darker-garbed males.

Juno had her own little court. Over the heads of the throng, Martin watched as she smiled and traded quips. Her gown of palest amber became her fair charms to admiration. With an inward glow, he noted the way her eyes lifted every now and then to scan the company. She had yet to see him. Then, as he watched, waiting for the right moment to make his presence known, a fop in a coat of a peculiar shade of green insinuated himself at Helen's side.

Martin came away from the wall. He started across the floor, automatically smiling and nodding at those he knew, his attention focused on the man beside Helen. He had noticed him, and his interest in Lady Walford, before. Discreet enquiry had elicited the information that he was one Hedley Swayne, Esquire, of a small but prosperous estate in Cornwall. Despite the lack of firm evidence, it was entirely possible that Hedley Swayne had indeed been behind Helen's kidnapping. The *ton* had noted a singular tendency for Mr Swayne to pay assiduous court to Lady Walford but had dismissed this as a mere smokescreen erected by the gentleman with a view to being regarded as fashionable; none could imagine the undeniably fashionable Lady Walford having any serious interest in a man a good half-head shorter than herself and distinctly less high in social rank to boot. Martin had seen Hedley Swayne at numerous gatherings, but this was the first time the fop had had the temerity to approach Helen.

Long before he reached her side, Martin sensed Helen's unease. Mr Swayne had picked his moment;

there were none but the more youthful of her cavaliers at present about her. As he paused to dutifully exchange compliments with an ageing dowager, a friend of his mother's, Martin saw Helen frown.

'I assure you, Mr Swayne, that I am not such a weakling as to need to repair instantly to the terrace immediately a dance is ended.' Helen tried not to sound waspish but Hedley Swayne would try the patience of a saint.

'I merely wished to explain——'

'I don't believe I wish to hear any explanation, Mr Swayne.' Helen wished it were permissible to glare. She came as close as she could, viewing the pale face and long, pink-tipped nose of the unfortunate Mr Swayne with every evidence of aversion. If the man had any sensibility at all, he would leave. Her court had deserted her, prompted by his declared intention of walking with her on the terrace. As if she would risk a terrace in his company! But she knew from experience that Hedley Swayne was all but irrepressible. She compressed her lips in reluctant resignation as she watched him draw breath to put forward his next suggestion. Why wouldn't he just leave her alone?

'Mr Hedley Swayne, I presume?'

The languid tones surprised Hedley Swayne, making him look rather like a startled rabbit. As his eyes rose to take in the gentleman now by her side, the huge floppy bow at his throat, hallmark of the well-dressed fop, all but quivered in agitation. Swallowing a sudden urge to giggle, Helen turned slightly, putting out her hand to Martin. He took it and tucked it into his arm, but spared only a glance for her before returning his attention to her persecutor.

Under the grey gaze, Hedley Swayne blinked nervously. 'Ah—I don't believe we've been introduced, my lord.'

Martin noticed he did not say he did not know who he was. He smiled coldly. 'Not exactly. Your reputation goes before you, you see. I believe we just missed each other—in Somerset, some weeks ago?'

At the heavy meaning underlying the polite words, Hedley Swayne's pale eyes grew round. He blanched, then flushed. 'Er. . .ah. . .'

Martin's gaze grew steely. 'Just so.'

Helen watched in appreciation. It must have been Hedley behind her kidnapping after all. Then the musicians started playing the music for the next dance—a waltz.

Eyes still holding Hedley Swayne's, Martin smiled, letting dire warning show beneath his urbanity. 'My dance, I believe, my lady. Mr Swayne.' With a nod for the hapless Hedley. Martin drew his future wife firmly into his arms, a little shocked at how intensely possessive he felt.

Slightly surprised at being denied the opportunity to take proper leave of Mr Swayne, irritating though that gentleman was, Helen nevertheless could not find it in her to cavil. Waltzing with Martin was a heavenly delight—she had no intention of losing so much as a moment of her rapture over something as inconsequential as a fop called Hedley Swayne.

'Has he been bothering you?'

Helen glanced up to find a frown gathering in the grey eyes fixed on her face. Bother Hedley! She shrugged. 'He's totally innocuous, really.'

'Innocuous enough to have you kidnapped.'

This time, Helen sighed. 'There's no need to worry about him.'

'I assure you it's not Hedley Swayne I worry about.'

Helen looked up and was trapped in his grey gaze. Suddenly, she felt breathless, her pulse accelerating. 'You worry too much, my lord,' she whispered, dragging her eyes from his.

At her tone, Martin shut his lips on his retort. He was tempted to order her to avoid Hedley Swayne, but, as yet, his jurisdiction did not stretch that far. He placated his urge to ensure her safety with the reflection that, soon, he would be in a position to make sure she saw nothing more of Mr Swayne.

Despite his not having uttered his decree, Helen got the message quite clearly. She felt thoroughly disgruntled when the music ceased, denying her the chance to dwell further on the peculiarly addictive sensation of drifting, light as air, in Martin's arms. His discussion of Hedley had distracted her and now their waltz—the last one of the night, what was more—was over.

Nevertheless, she made the most of the rest of her evening, going into supper on the Earl of Merton's arm. She had given up trying to tell herself he was not serious. He was perfectly serious when he wished to be and on the subject of her future he was unshakeable. It was simply not possible to mistake the intentions of a gentleman who made it patently clear that he attended the *ton* parties purely to dance attendance on one woman. Being that woman made her more nervous than she had ever been in her life.

It was the first time she had been in love—the first time she had been the object of love. She comforted herself that it was only the novelty that sent her senses skittering in delicious disarray whenever she heard his voice. Doubtless, the effect would wane with time. A niggling suspicion that it would not, and that she had no real desire that it should, undermined her fragile confidence.

The truth was, she could not quite believe it was all real, that the rainbow that had appeared on her horizon would not simply vanish with the next dawn. Love was something she had convinced herself she would have to do without—to have it served up to her on a gilt-edged, solid-silver platter was well beyond her expectations. Helen Walford had never been so lucky.

Reconciling herself to her sudden change in fates was an uphill battle, her difficulties compounded by his persistent presence and the distraction of his grey eyes. As her carriage wheels rattled over the cobbles, taking her home to her lonely bed, Helen sat back with a sigh and sent a silent prayer winging heavenwards. Please God that this time would be truly different, that this time the fates could find it in them to be kind. That this time her dreams would not turn to dross, that happiness like Dorothea's would at long last be hers.

With a little shiver, Helen closed her eyes. And willed it to be so.

Damian Willesden returned to the capital the next day. Forced by the exigencies of financial commitments to endure a repairing lease with a friend in the country until quarter-day had brought relief, he sauntered into Manton's Shooting Gallery determined to find congenial company with which to make up for lost time. Instead, he found his brother.

The broad shoulders encased in a perfectly cut coat of the best superfine were quite unmistakable. Martin was shooting with a party of his friends.

Beyond informing him that Martin had indeed returned, hale and whole, and was busying himself taking up his inheritance, his mother had been unusually reticent on the subject of the new Earl. Damian had interpreted this as another display of her well-known indifference to Martin and all his exploits. Even more than she, he had lived in the confident expectation that his reckless older brother would have managed to get himself killed, leaving the title to him. Martin's continued existence had been a rude shock. To him and his creditors.

A further surprise had awaited him when he had applied to Martin for assistance. That interview, conducted within days of Martin's return, had left him convinced that he would see little of the Merton revenues while Martin lived. His memories of Martin had been hazy at best; ten years separated them—they had never been close. But he had vaguely supposed that his brother, having spent so many years in the backwaters of the colonies, would be easily enough persuaded to part with his blunt. Instead, the interview had proved *most* uncomfortable. Pulling the wool over his brother's sharp grey eyes was not something he would try again soon.

He comforted himself with the reflection that a man of Martin's known propensities could be counted on to die young. It could only be a matter of time.

Watching the steadiness of the hand that levelled one of Joseph Manton's famous pistols at the slimmest of wafers propped as target twenty paces down the gallery, Damian reflected that such skills were presumably required in order to support the rakehell status his brother enjoyed. The pistol discharged; the smoke cleared. A small charred hole had appeared in the very centre of the wafer. As Manton himself came forward with congratulations, Damian decided that any hope that an indignant husband might put a term to his brother's life was nothing more than wishful thinking.

Turning from Desborough and Fanshawe to lay aside his pistol, Martin saw Damian lounging just inside the door. He nodded and watched his brother reluctantly approach. He could not prevent his lips curving in a knowing smile as the fact that it was two days after quarter-day dawned. Damian saw the smile; his expression turned sulky. Martin felt his own expression harden. Studied critically, there was nothing in Damian's dress to disgust one—his coat was well-cut, although not of the finest quality; the same could be said of his breeches and boots. It was his demeanour that raised brows. At twenty-four, he should have attained the age of reason, together with a little maturity. But his petulant attitude coupled with his expectation that his family must necessarily support his wastrel ways convinced Martin that his brother still had considerable maturing to do.

He raised his brows as Damian halted before him. 'Returned to the delights of town?'

Damian shrugged. 'The country's too slow for my taste.' He considered asking for an advance on his allowance but rejected the idea. He was not that desperate yet. He nodded at the target. 'Pretty shooting. Learned in the colonies, did you?'

Martin laughed. 'No. That was a talent I'd polished

long before I departed these shores.' He paused, then suggested, 'Why not try your luck?'

For an instant, Damian wavered, drawn to the prospect of joining his magnificent brother in such a fashionable pursuit and in such august company. Then his eye fell on the gold signet on Martin's right hand and childish resentment clouded his reason. 'Heaven forbid,' he said, waving away the pistol Martin held out. 'Not my style. *I* ain't in any danger from irate husbands.'

A little stunned by his own gaucherie, and less than sure what reaction it might provoke, Damian abruptly turned on his heel and walked rapidly from the Gallery.

Tony Fanshawe, standing on Martin's other side, an unintentional auditor to the scene, threw Damian a curious glance. 'That pup wants training,' he said. 'Deuced bad manners, walking away from an invitation like that.'

Martin, his eyes on his brother's retreating back, nodded absent-mindedly. 'I'm afraid,' he said, 'that my brother's manners leave a lot to be desired. In fact, my brother himself falls rather short of the mark.' Making a mental note to the effect that some time he was going to have to do something about Damian, Martin turned back to his friends and their game of skills.

He loved her.

That refrain replayed in Helen's head as she revolved about Lady Broxford's ballroom firmly held in Martin Willesden's arms. There was no doubt in her mind of its truth; her heart soared as she finally allowed the prospect of spending the rest of her life under

Martin's smoky grey gaze to take definite shape in her mind. The pot of gold at the end of the rainbow was to be hers at last.

She looked up to find the warm grey eyes upon her, a caress in their depths.

'A penny for your thoughts, my lady.'

The deep, slightly raspy voice sent a cascade of sensations tingling through her. Suppressing a shiver of pure delight, Helen narrowed her eyes in consideration. 'I don't know that telling you my thoughts would be at all wise, my lord. Certainly, all precepts dictate I should stay silent.'

'Oh? They can't be that scandalous.'

· '*They're* not scandalous. You are,' Helen retorted. 'I'm sure it's written somewhere—in the *Handbook for Young Ladies* under the heading of "How to Deal with Rakes"—that it's *most* unwise to do anything to encourage them.'

The grey eyes opened wide. 'And knowing your thoughts would encourage me?'

Helen tried to return his intent look with one of the greatest blandness. Her partner was undeterred.

'My dear Helen, I suspect your education was somewhat circumscribed. You certainly never finished that chapter, or you would have read that it's even *more* unwise to whet a rake's appetite.'

At the unrestrained promise in the gravelly voice, Helen's eyes grew wide. To her relief, they had come to the end of the room and Martin had to give his attention to turning them around. His arm tightened about her, leaving her even more breathless than before. She felt like a lamb about to be devoured by a wolf. For some reason, the idea was quite attractive.

Her wits had obviously scattered. With an effort, she sought to collect them.

Martin glanced down at Helen's face. The eau-de-Nil silk sheath she wore moulded to her ample curves, sliding and sussurating against his coat with every gliding step they took. With the shifting silk to distract her further he doubted her ability to reorientate her thoughts from the salacious direction he had given them. Thoroughly satisfied with her state, he forbore to press her to converse, giving his mind instead to the vexed question of when? When should he ask her to marry him?

He had planned to propose as soon as he was sure she had accepted the idea of being the Countess of Merton and had got over her apparent nervousnes regarding a second marriage. His experienced assessment was that any doubts she had harboured were now things of the past. As the last bars of the waltz sounded, he made his decision. There was no reason to wait.

But the ballroom was crowded, the event a 'sad crush'. The ante-rooms, he knew, would be full of dowagers trying to escape the heat. He would have to reconnoitre.

The music ceased; they whirled to a halt amid the glittering throng. Breathless, wondering what came next, Helen raised her eyes to Martin's face. Their eyes met, their gazes locked, but before either had time to speak Lord Peterborough materialised from the crowd.

'There you are, Helen. I must speak to you about this bad habit of yours—letting this reprobate monopolise your time. Won't do, m'dear—not at all.'

'Gerry, how long has it been since someone told you

you talk too much?' Martin released Helen to allow her to greet their old friend.

Peterborough slanted a shrewd look at Helen's radiant countenance. 'Don't seem to be having much effect in this case.' To Helen, he said, 'Aside from all the other dangers, I dare swear he's trodden all over your toes—been in the colonies for too long. Come and waltz with a man who knows how.'

With a flourish, he presented his arm to Helen. Laughing, she took it, throwing one last smile at Martin before consenting to be led back to the floor.

Free, Martin embarked on a perambulation designed to explore all potential sites for a declaration among the rooms made available to Lady Broxford's guests.

Helen was glad of the opportunity dancing with her usual court gave her to reassemble her treacherous wits and still the fluttering of her heart. She had lived in anticipation of Martin's declaration for the past week; a sense of acute expectation now had her in its grip. She laughed and smiled, teetering on the brink of the greatest happiness she had yet known.

After Peterborough, she danced with Alvanley, then Desborough and even trod a measure with Hazelmere, spared to her by a radiant Dorothea.

After the first few figures of the cotillion, Hazelmere raised a languid brow. 'I take it the pleasures of this Little Season met with your approval?'

Sensing a deeper meaning hidden beneath the urbane drawl, Helen threw him a suspicious glance but answered airily, 'Why, yes. It's all been most enjoyable.' Nothing could keep the sheer happiness from her voice.

Both black brows rose; the hazel eyes watching her

were as sharp as ever. 'I wonder why,' Hazelmere mused. To Helen's heartfelt relief, her long-time protector forbore to tease her, although his hazel eyes suggested that her joy was transparently obvious.

As he raised her from her final curtsy, Hazelmere said, 'I fear I should draw Miss Berry to your notice. She's been trying to attract your attention for some time.'

Following his gaze to where small, bird-like Miss Berry perched on a sofa at the side of the room, Helen chuckled. 'Poor dear. I dare say she feels she's missing out on things, now she's so deaf.'

Hazelmere's lips quirked but he refrained from further comment. He escorted Helen across the room, leaving her ensconced on the sofa, lending a sympathetic ear to Miss Berry.

From the opposite side of the ballroom, partially screened by a potted palm, Damian Willesden eyed the voluptuous figure in eau-de-Nil silk. He frowned, chewing his lip in vexation. He had come to the Broxfords' without an invitation, knowing no hostess would turn him from her door. But doing the pretty by a lot of curst females was hardly his style. He had only come because of what his friend Percy Witherspoon had let fall, of the bets regarding his brother's impending marriage.

He had refused to believe Percy but the entries in Boodle's wagers book had been too numerous to ignore. He stared across the room at Lady Walford; disaster stared back at him. Supremely confident that he would eventually inherit the Merton estates together with the sizeable fortune his mother insisted on tying to the title, sublimely sure that Martin would never trade his free-wheeling rake's existence for one of dull matrimony, he had borrowed until he was ear-deep in debt. Damian swallowed convulsively. It was a wonder the cent percenters were not hounding him already.

No—not yet. They would wait until he was no longer Martin's heir before they moved. Even then, they would start slowly, expecting him to be able to persuade his brother to fish him out of the River Tick. But when they found out Martin had no intention of rescuing him... Never one to dwell on uncomfortable fact, Damian let that thought fade.

He hugged the shadow of the palm and cogitated on his fate—and how to escape it. Ever fertile in subterfuge, his brain fastened on the essential element of his discomfort. It was all quite simple, really. He would just have to see what he could do to prevent this ill-advised marraige.

Having evaded all Miss Berry's leading questions, Helen finally rose, leaving the old lady with a fond smile. She looked about the room, but could not spot Martin's dark head amid the throng. Knowing he would seek her with the Hazelmeres and Fanshawes, in whose company she had come to the ball, she headed in the direction of the chaise on which she had last seen Dorothea.

She had moved but mere feet into the crowd when a hand on her arm halted her.

'Lady Walford?'

Helen turned to see a youth—no, a man, she revised, acknowledging the unformed features that had led her astray. Pale blue eyes returned her regard. There was something vaguely familiar about the gentleman, something about the set and shape of his head, but she was sure she had never met him before. 'Sir?'

Damian summoned a smile. 'I'm Damian Willesden—Martin's brother.'

'Oh.' Helen returned his smile readily. 'How do you do?' Did Martin know his brother was here?

Damian bowed over her hand. 'I haven't seen Martin yet. Is he here?' He knew it was imperative that no hint of the distance between Martin and himself should show.

'I saw him earlier in the evening.' Helen raised her head to glance around. 'I'm sure he's still about, somewhere, but it's so hard to find anyone in this crush.'

Damian fastened on the comment eagerly. 'Perhaps we could move to that alcove there.' He pointed to where a curved niche in the wall held a statuette. 'I'm most curious as to how Martin's been faring, getting back into the swim of things.'

Helen took his proffered arm, wondering why he was not addressing such queries to his brother direct.

'I've just returned from the country and haven't had a chance to speak to Martin yet. But,' said Damian, striving to infuse his light voice with meaning, 'I have heard certain rumours, linking my brother's name with that...of a certain lady.'

Helen blushed. 'Mr Willesden, I would suggest that rumour is an insubstantial entity and that you might be wise to wait for confirmation before you jump to conclusions.'

Damian looked grave, 'I can appreciate your feelings, Lady Walford, and if the case were straightforward I would share your reservations. However...' he paused, frowning '...I feel a certain degree of...affection for

Martin and would be sorry to see him in difficulties once more.'

'Difficulties?' Helen was entirely at sea. What difficulties was Martin's brother alluding to—and why to her? 'Sir, I'm afraid you will have to be a great deal more direct if I'm to understand you.'

Bowing his head to hide an irrepressible smirk, Damian obliged. But when he spoke again, his voice and features were serious, as befitted his assumed role. 'As you doubtless know, Martin returned from the colonies to take up his inheritance. Naturally, what wealth he now has derives entirely from the Merton estates. And, due to past bad management, the Merton estates are kept afloat by my mother's funds.' Pausing to let the implications sink in, Damian gave thanks for his eldest brother's failings. Thanks to George's incompetence, he had the perfect threat to remove Lady Walford from Martin's scene. What woman would marry a man forced to hang on his mother's sleeve? A hostile mother, at that. And, once Lady Walford drew back from the well-publicised relationship, other ladies similarly disposed would, with any luck, have second thoughts. 'Unfortunately,' he continued, 'Martin and the Dowager have never been on good terms. My mother naturally demands that Martin marry as she dictates. Or else. . .'

Cold fingers had laid hold of Helen's heart, squeezing until it hurt, leaving nothing but numbness behind. But she had to hear all of it, understand the whole story. 'Or else what?'

Damian saw the stricken look in the large green eyes and was momentarily taken aback. Then his own future prospects arose in his mind, stiffening his resolve. 'Or

else she'll withdraw her funds. The estate will collapse.
Martin will be destitute, unable to support the lifestyle
he's accustomed to, the lifestyle expected of the Earl
of Merton.'

And he will lose all chance of restoring his home.
Helen recalled all too vividly Martin's face, lit by
enthusiasm as he had described the Hermitage and
told her how it would be once he had finished refur-
bishing it. As it had been in the days of his father, he
had said. In the past weeks, she had heard even more
of his dreams and had come to realise how important
they were to him. A bridge, a living link to the father
he had lost. The destruction of those dreams was a
blow he would feel most cruelly—if he married against
his mother's wishes.

If he married her.

None knew better than she that few mothers would
approve of an eligible son marrying the widow of a
social outcast—a reprobate who had gone well beyond
the invisible line and had subsequently taken his own
life. She was, she knew, unsuitable.

It had never occurred to her to question Martin's
right to choose his own wife. He had seemed so much
in control, she had never thought of him as being in
any way under another's sway. But his brother's tale
rang chillingly true.

Dull emptiness and the cold taste of despair
swamped her senses.

Chilled to the bone, deaf to the babel about them,
she held out her hand to Martin's brother. 'Thank you
for telling me.' Her voice didn't sound like her own—
it was cold and distant, as if she were speaking from a

long way away. She put up her chin. 'You may be sure I'll do nothing to encourage Martin to harm his future.'

Her voice threatened to break. She could say nothing more. Withdrawing her hand from Damian's, she turned and walked into the crowd, all but unaware of her direction, oblivious of the odd looks cast her way.

By the time she found Dorothea, on a chaise by the door, Helen had regained some semblance of composure. If she appeared before Hazelmere, or his equally intelligent wife, with her soul in her eyes, she would never escape explanations. Yet the very thought of Martin and her hopes of happiness, now all gone awry, was enough to bring her to the brink of tears. Resolutely, she shut her mind against the pain and forced herself to act normally.

'Is anything wrong?' was Dorothea's opening gambit.

Helen smiled weakly. 'Just a slight headache—no doubt due to all this noise.' She sank on to the chaise beside her friend.

'Well,' said Dorothea, correctly interpreting Helen's wish to have nothing made of her indisposition, 'I've determined to leave soon, so I can take you up with me.'

After a fractional hesitation, Helen nodded dully. 'Yes, that would be best, I expect.' Martin would expect to see her again that evening, but if she escaped with Dorothea, pleading a headache, then he would not worry. He would call at her home tomorrow, and then she would have to explain. But by then she would have had time to get herself in hand, enough, at least, to face him. For, despite the cold fogs shrouding her mind, there was one point that was crystal-clear. She could not, would not, marry Martin Willesden. She could not face the prospect of being the death of his dream. His interest in her was real—that she knew without reservation. His interest in other women of the *ton* was non-existent. If she was out of contention, he would no doubt allow his mother to find him a bride and so would achieve his ambition—an ambition entirely appropriate to his station.

Glumly, Helen stifled a sniff and struggled to force a smile to her lips. She would sit quietly by Dorothea's side until it was time to leave.

Unfortunately for her well-intentioned plans, Martin appeared by her side but minutes later. Helen's heart leapt in her breast at sight of him; she could not keep the welcoming smile from her face. But he instantly noted its tremulous quality. Drawing her to stand close beside him, he bent his dark head close to ask, 'What's the matter?'

With a calm she was far from feeling, Helen reiterated her story of a headache.

Martin frowned at the press of bodies about them. 'Hardly to be wondered at. Come for a stroll—some fresh air will help clear your head.'

Before she had time to protest—not, she suspected, that he would have listened—Helen found herself strolling by Martin's side along a suspiciously deserted corridor. Her heart started to beat rather faster.

Her suspicions were confirmed when they reached the door at the end of the corridor and Martin opened it to reveal a small walled garden, deserted and entirely private.

He led Helen to a stone seat worked into the rockery

and waited while she settled her skirts on the thyme-cushion growing over it before sitting beside her. On his knees was the prescribed pose, but, given he was thirty-five and she a widow of twenty-six, he felt he did not need to do such violence to his feelings, or to his satin knee-breeches.

She turned to stare up at him. The moonlight gilded her features, features he had come to know very well over the past week. Her green eyes widened, her lips were slightly parted. Because it seemed the right thing to do, and because he had long ago ceased to stop himself doing whatever he wished to do, Martin drew her smoothly into his arms and kissed her.

Helen tried, really tried to hold firm against that kiss, against the invitation to melt into his arms. She had been gathering her strength to speak—to avert any possible declaration, when his dark head had bent and his lips had slanted over hers. But it was impossible to hold back the tide of longing that swept her. Yielding to the inevitble, she softened against him and felt his arms tighten about her.

It was scandalously wrong to sit in a deserted garden and allow a gentleman she was not going to marry to kiss her. Particularly to kiss her like this.

The touch of his lips on hers was sheer bliss. She let her hands settle against his shoulders and leaned into his warm embrace.

Later. She would have to speak later. But for now she might as well enjoy the delicious sensations he stirred within her. He was unlikely to stop soon and at least while he was thus engaged he could not propose to her. Perhaps he did not intend to propose just yet— was merely indulging in a little dalliance further to enthral her? As the pressure of his lips increased, Helen gave up any attempt at thought.

When he finally raised his head, Martin looked down on glittering green eyes, wide and slightly stunned. She was quite speechless and, if experience was any guide, was probably having difficulty stringing two thoughts together. He smiled. It hardly mattered. She would not need to think to answer his question.

'Will you marry me, my dear?'

Helen's mind fell into place with a thud. She felt her eyes widen even further. She struggled to assemble the right words but none would leap to her tongue. When she saw the grey eyes sharpen and become intent, she swallowed. 'No.'

It was such a small sound, Martin thought he had misheard. But the expression in her eyes, the wordless pain, convinced him he had not been mistaken. Somehow, he had muffed it. When she drew her hands from his shoulders, he smiled and tried to make light of her problem, hoping to learn what it was. 'My dear Helen, I'll have you know it's not done to kiss a man and then refuse his suit.'

To his increasing unease, she hung her head. 'I know.'

Helen found she was wringing her hands, something she had never done in her life. 'Truly, my lord, I'm more than honoured by your proposal. But I. . .' Heavens—what was she to say? 'But I've not thought of remarrying.'

'Well, try thinking about it.' Martin strove to keep the edge from his tone. This was not how this interview was supposed to have gone. In fact, the more he thought of it, the whole business was deucedly odd. What had happened?

'My lord, I must make you understand——'

'No—it's I who must needs make you understand. I love you, Helen. And you love me. What more is there to it than that?'

Helen swallowed and forced her eyes to his. The moon shone from behind him, leaving his features in shadow and her with no real idea of his expression. She imagined it was forbidding. Suppressing a shiver, she tried to speak calmly. 'My lord, you know as well as I that there's a great deal more to it than that.'

Martin stiffened slightly, then remembered that he was atrociously rich. She must be referring to his past, but he had told her about that. Didn't she believe him? 'I'm very much afraid, my dear, that you'll have to be rather more specific if I'm to follow your thread.'

Helen's courage was fast deserting her. How to tell a man—an arrogant, proud man—that you knew he was his mother's pensioner? She shifted back on the seat and felt Martin's arms fall from about her. Instead of bringing her relief, the withdrawal of his protection left her feeling more lost than ever. She pressed her hands together and in a very small voice said, 'I was thinking of what your mother would say.'

His reaction was every bit as violent as she had anticipated.

'*My mother*?' Martin was dumbfounded. 'What the devil do you imagine my mother has to do with this?' He had almost forgotten his mother's plans. Had news of her machinations reached town? 'I'll marry who I damn well please! My mother doesn't have any say in the matter.' The idea that Helen thought him the sort of man who would allow anyone to interfere in such a matter made his tone even more steely.

Helen had winced at his questions; by the time he had finished his vehement denial she was more than flustered. Her nerves were jittery; she could not think straight. Her head throbbed in earnest. Of course he would deny it. What more could she say? How could she smooth things over and make him understand?

Martin saw her agitation. Immediately, he sought to cut through the morass they had somehow landed in and bring her to peace again. 'Helen, my dear, I love you. Even if my whole estate were in the balance, I'd still want to marry you.'

He spoke simply, from the heart. He was not prepared for her reaction. Wide eyes turned his way; her breath seemed to catch in her throat. Then her full lips trembled and the moonlight glistened on the tears hanging suspended from the tips of her long lashes.

'Oh, *Martin*!'

The whispered words caught on a sob.

Abruptly, Helen looked down, at her fingers tightly twined in her lap. She had never loved anyone as much as she loved him; she could not let him make such a sacrifice.

Becoming more worried with every passing second, every totally confusing minute, Martin frowned at Helen's bent head. He reached for her hand.

The door from the house opened.

'This way, m'dear.'

Helen would have leapt to her feet, but Martin's hand on hers restrained her. He moved slightly, so that his bulk shielded her from the intruders. As two guests emerged into the small walled court, Martin rose languidly then turned and helped Helen to rise.

'Oh!' said Hedley Swayne. 'My goodness! I'm afraid we didn't realise this area was occupied.'

One of Martin's brows rose. His gaze went from the frippery sight of Mr Swayne to the slight young thing wavering on his arm. 'No matter, I was just about to escort Lady Walford inside.'

He turned to offer his arm to Helen. She took it, trying to appear as unaffected as possible, with her nerves in knots and her heart in her shoes.

'Oh, Lady Walford,' the slight young thing warbled nervously. 'Would you mind if I came inside with you?' Without waiting for assent, the girl turned to Hedley Swayne. 'I really don't think I wish to view the gardens just at the moment, Mr Swayne.'

She bobbed a curtsy and hurried to Helen's side.

Swallowing his frustration, Martin was forced to escort Helen and her unexpected protégée back to the ballroom. Once under the light of the chandeliers, he saw how badly affected Helen was. Feeling very much as if his world had stopped turning, he resigned himself to letting the matter lapse until a more suitable opportunity to speak privately with her could be arranged. He left her with Dorothea, lifting her hand to his lips with a murmured, 'I'll call on you tomorrow,' before taking his leave.

Dorothea took one look at Helen's face, then, without comment, called for her carriage.

Dawn was streaking the skies before sleep finally closed Helen's eyes. The pillow beneath her cheek was damp, her lids decidedly puffy. But she had managed to make the decisions that had to be made. There was no hope of explaining things to Martin—he would not accept her refusal any more than she would accept his suit. So she would have to avoid him—make it plain by her behaviour that their association was at an end. It would cause talk, but nothing serious. The *ton* would wonder what she was thinking of, but there were too many waiting in the wings to claim his attention for the gossipmongers to dwell on her peculiar whims for long.

She would have to give him up, even though it would be easier to cut out her heart. Instead, she would have to live with it, a leaden weight in her breast, evermore. He would be hurt by her withdrawal and even more hurt by her lack of explanation. But if she tried to explain, he would refuse to accept her decision. She could not see him readily acquiescing; who knew to what lengths he might go to attain his goals? No—there was only one way forward.

As she snuggled her cheek deeper into the down, she sighed. She should have known how it would end—happiness of that kind was not for her—would never be hers.

The pot of gold at the end of the rainbow had always been beyond her reach.

CHAPTER EIGHT

'WHAT will you have?'

Martin waved his hand in the direction of the well-stocked drinks tray reposing on the sideboard in his library.

'If memory serves,' said Hazelmere, sinking into the comfort of an armchair, 'your father was a particularly fine judge of Madeira.'

A grin twisted Martin's lips. 'Quite right. And George had no taste for the stuff. Apparently, there's three full racks in the cellar.'

He poured two glasses and carried one to his guest before settling in the armchair on the other side of the empty fireplace. A companionable silence fell. Hazelmere, well aware that Martin had asked him to his home for some purpose, was content to wait for his friend to open his budget. Martin, equally well aware of his friend's understanding, was in no hurry to do so.

The matter was a delicate one. He had called on Helen the morning after the débâcle of his first declaration, two nights ago. Hours of intense concentration had yielded no clue as to what it was that had made her balk at his proposal. Nevertheless, he had gone to her small house in Half Moon Street, confident of ironing out whatver wrinkles had insinuated themselves into the fabric of their relationship. That was when he had realised how serious her problem, now their problem, was.

161

She had refused to see him, sending her maid down with a story of indisposition. For the first time in his life, he had been totally nonplussed. Why?

There had to be a reason—she was not a dim-witted miss, a flibbertigibbet. It had been his avowal of love that had thrown her, though why that should be so he could not imagine. Eventually, he had come to the conclusion that there had to be some hidden bogey in her past that his words, or the meaning behind them, had conjured up.

And the one person who knew enough of Helen's past to be of use was seated in the armchair opposite, a deceptively lazy look in his hazel eyes.

Martin grimaced. 'It's about Helen Walford.'

'Oh?' A look of reserve veiled Hazelmere's sharp gaze.

'Yes,' said Martin, ignoring it. 'I want to marry her.'

His friend's features relaxed in warm approval. 'Congratulations.' Hazelmere raised his glass in the gesture of a toast.

'Premature, I'm afraid. She won't have me.' Martin bit the words out, then sought solace in a hefty draught of finest quality Madeira.

A puzzled frown settled over Hazelmere's black brows. 'Why, for heaven's sake?'

'That's what I want you to tell me.' Martin settled back in his chair and looked pointedly at Hazelmere.

Hazelmere frowned back, an exasperated look in his eyes. 'She likes you. I know she does.'

'So do I—it's not that.'

Uncharacteristically at sea, Hazelmere threw Martin a thoroughly bemused look. 'What then?'

Martin sighed. 'When I told her how much I loved

her. . .' He threw a warning glance at Hazelmere before continuing, 'She nearly broke down and wept.'

Hazelmere showed no sigh of treating the subject lightly. If anything, his frown deepened. Eventually, he said. 'That. . .is bad. Helen hardly ever cries. I've known her since she was three and she's far more likely to argue than weep.'

'Quite.' Martin paused, then added diffidently, 'I had wondered whether there was anything about her previous marriage that would account for it.'

Hazelmere's brows rose. Sitting back, he considered the point, absent-mindedly twirling the stem of his glass between his long fingers. Then, abruptly, as if having reached a decision, he looked at Martin. 'As you seem set on marrying her, and, even if *she* doesn't know it yet, *I* know that means she'll be the next Countess of Merton, I'll tell you what I know.' At sight of Martin's quick grin, he added, 'But I warn you, it's not much.'

His features impassive, the expression in his eyes much less so, Martin waited with what patience he could muster while Hazelmere fortified himself with a pensive sip of honey-gold liquor.

'I expect I'd better start at the beginning.' Hazelmere settled his shoulders against the back of the chair. 'Helen's parents presented her at sixteen—a mistake, for my money. She'd been a tomboy, a hoyden, for years and had yet to grow out of her adventures. But her parents had her life all arranged—a marriage to the son of an old friend, Lord Alfred Walford. The son, Arthur Walford, I think you knew?'

At Hazelmere's questioning glance, Martin nodded curtly. 'We met once or twice before I left for the West

Indies. Hardly the sort of man careful parents would have in mind for a beautiful and wealthy sixteen-year-old.'

A fleeting smile lit Hazelmere's face. 'Ah—but you didn't know Helen then. I know it's hard to believe, seeing her now, but, take it from me, at sixteen she was a Long Meg—and a dreadfully scrawny one at that.' When Martin looked sceptical, Hazelmere waved the point aside. 'Not that it mattered. It wouldn't have made an ounce of difference if she'd been Cleopatra incarnate. The parents, both hers and old Walford, had settled on the alliance long before. It was intended as a dynastic marriage of the most calculated sort. Helen's parents were both ambitious in an odd sort of way. They never mixed much and lived in seclusion in the country, but they were determined to marry their daughter into one of the oldest families about.' Hazelmere paused, his gaze far away, remembering. 'There were many who tried to dissuade them, my parents among them, but they were fixated on the idea. Walford the elder was keen, because of Helen's dowry. Arthur Walford was amenable for much the same reason. So Helen was married to Walford a bare month after her come-out.'

'A *month*?' Incredulity sharpened Martin's tone.

'Precisely,' affirmed Hazelmere, equally sharp. 'The newly-weds repaired to Walford Hall. Less than a month after that, Walford reappeared in town. Helen stayed in Oxfordshire. That situation continued, apparently without change, for close on three years. During that time, all the senior players in the drama died— Walford the elder, and both Helen's parents. The crunch came when, against all odds, Walford succeeded in running through his funds. He had lost his own estates and those that had come to him through Helen. Only Walford Hall remained, as it was entailed. He returned there, not to take up residence but to see what more he could wring from the place. By then, Helen was nineteen. She had still not attained the stature she now has, but she had improved considerably on sixteen.'

Hazelmere paused, studying the glass in his hand. 'I don't know to this day what actually happened, but the upshot of it was that Walford struck Helen—during an argument, she said. For her part, she promptly broke a pot over his head and left.' Hazelmere drained his glass before glancing at Martin. 'She came to me. She had grown up with my sister Allison and we had always considered her one of the family. I sent her to my estate in Cumbria—well out of Walford's way should he try to find her. The story of his treatment of Helen got out—as such things do. It became something of a *cause célèbre*. The upshot was that Walford was hounded from the *ton* and comprehensively ruined. He took his own life rather than face Newgate.'

Hazelmere paused, considering the past, then shrugged. 'Later, many of those who had won stakes from Walford donated money to set up a fund for Helen. I manage it for her. It pays the rent on her house in Half Moon Street and keeps her in her current style—but little else. None of her estates was salvaged.'

Martin frowned, his chin sunk in one hand, his gaze fixed on the Turkey rug gracing the floor between them. Carefully, choosing his words, he asked, 'Is there anything in what you know of her that would lead you to suppose Helen feels any deep-seated revulsion towards marriage? An aversion to the physical side of matrimony?'

Hazelmere's lips thinned. His eyes on his glass, he shook his head. 'I couldn't say—but, conversely, I would not be at all surprised.' He lifted his gaze to Martin's face. 'You know what Walford was like.'

Slowly, Martin nodded. 'Could it have scarred her —so that she has difficulty bringing herself to contemplate marriage again?'

Hazelmere shrugged. 'Only Helen could answer that, but I would have thought it a distinct possibility.'

Almost imperceptibly, Martin's expression lightened. His eyes narrowed in consideration.

Hazelmere noticed. 'What is it?'

A crooked grin was Martin's answer. 'I was just thinking—who better to cure such a malady than I?' He shot Hazelmere a quizzical glance, then sat back, supremely confident, one brow rising arrogantly. 'All things considered, I would have to be the perfect candidate for the job of convincing Helen Walford of the earthy benefits of matrimony. If, with my extensive experience, I can't overcome that particular hurdle, I don't deserve the lady.'

For a long moment, Hazelmere's hazel eyes remained serious, while their owner pondered what was, after all, a distinctly scandalous threat to a lady whom many, including himself, regarded as under his protection. But, if he read things aright, Helen's future happiness was at stake. She had made her partiality plain. And he trusted Martin Willesden as a brother— Helen would come to no harm at his hands. Slowly, a grin twisted Hazelmere's lips. Inclining his head in tacit approval of Martin's avowed intention, he raised his glass in salute.

'Spoken like a true rake.'

Helen settled her skirts and waited for Martin to join her on the box seat of his curricle. The wind whipped loose tendrils of hair about her face and brought colour to her cheeks. As Martin sat beside her and picked up the reins, she flashed a bright smile in answer to his. Then they were off.

With the raucous cries of the Piccadilly street vendors ringing about her, Helen sat, at peace and oddly content, and wondered that it could be so. It was remarkable, she reflected, that, given Martin's painful declaration just over a week before, they should be able to be together like this, companionably setting out for a drive in the Park. For her part, she would not have credited it. But, to her relief, Martin had behaved in the most honourable way.

He had claimed her for a waltz at the Havelocks' rout, the next major function they had both attended. Nothing in his manner had altered; he had behaved every bit as proprietorially as before. Only she had heard his whispered words, 'Trust me. Just relax— there's nothing to worry about.'

Strangely enough, she had. From beneath her chip bonnet, Helen glanced up at his profile, so harshly handsome. His eyes were fixed on the road ahead, his hands steady on the reins. A smile on her lips, Helen returned her gaze to their surroundings. Relaxing in Martin's company had been made a great deal easier by the fact that he no longer sought to befuddle her senses with his particular brand of wizardry. She was determined to keep her traitorous senses in line; his power over them was just as strong, but, if she was intent on her course, she could not afford to let them gain the upper hand. Thankfully, Martin seemed to understand. It was clear that, now she had brought the matter to his mind, he had, however reluctantly, accepted that, given his circumstances and hers, they could not marry. And, gentleman that he was, he was intent on keeping their situation from the world. All she was called on to do was respond to his lead, to make it appear as if there were no rupture between them. It was, she had realised, the sensible course. Now, as time passed, they would be able to draw apart without either being exposed to the avid interest of the scandalmongers.

The Park was reached without incident. They embarked on a slow circuit about the leafy avenues, stopping time and again to chat with their acquaintances. It was during one of these halts that Ferdie Acheson-Smythe approached. His bland expression totally devoid of guile, he nodded to Martin then reached up to shake hands with Helen.

'Hello, Ferdie. Is that a new coat?' Helen knew any question of fashion was guaranteed to appeal to the immaculate Mr Acheson-Smythe. She had known Ferdie, Hazelmere's cousin, forever and was truly fond of the elegant dandy.

'Yes,' replied Ferdie, unwarrantably brief. 'But that wasn't what I wanted to tell you.' His pale blue eyes flicked to Martin, engrossed with some friends on the other side of the curricle, then returned to her face, a slight frown in their depths. Leaning closer, he said, 'I know you've made a damned habit of this, but do you really think it's wise?'

With Ferdie, there was no point in pretending to misunderstand. Helen smiled affectionately at his brother-like concern. She lowered her voice. 'You needn't worry. I'm perfectly safe.'

'Humph!' Ferdie snorted, his gaze once more on Martin's profile. 'That's what I thought about Dorothea and look how wrong I was. Point is, rakes don't change. They're damned dangerous in any circumstances.'

Helen laughed. 'I assure you this one's tame.'

The comment earned her a highly sceptical look, but Ferdie said no more on the matter, turning his attention instead to complimenting her on her new apricot merino pelisse. When a short while later Martin looked around, ready to move on, Ferdie bowed elegantly and stood back, contenting himself with a warning look addressed to Helen's account.

Martin saw it. His brows rose superciliously, but by then Ferdie Acheson-Smythe was already dwindling in the distance. Then Martin's sharp ears caught the muffled giggle as his companion tried to suppress her reaction. Martin relaxed. 'Tell me, fair Juno, am I still considered "too dangerous", despite my exemplary behaviour of recent times?'

Helen shot a startled glance up at him. Reassured by the teasing glint in his grey eyes and the laughter bubbling through his deep tones, she smiled and gave due attention to his question. Considering the matter dispassionately was a decidedly tall order. Eventually, knowing he was waiting on her answer, she ventured, 'I fear, my lord, that there are some who see your "exemplary behaviour" as merely the wool beneath which a wolf is disguised.'

Martin's heavy sigh startled her anew.

'And here I was thinking none could discern the truth.'

Helen's eyes flew wide. His tone held equal parts of dejection and chagrin but the expression in his eyes was still gently teasing. She tried to read his meaning in their depths, but the subtle glint defeated her. Was he warning her that Ferdie was right. Or was he merely making light conversation, teasing her, knowing she was easy to twit on that score?

Uncertain, Helen spent the next ten minutes inwardly wrestling with the possibilities while outwardly playing the social game. They had finished their first circuit when Martin broke into her thoughts.

'I still haven't made the final decisions on the pieces for the parlour.'

'Oh?' Helen had heard about the redecoration of his London home, now in its terminal phase, in some detail. Discussions on the relative merits of damasks and chintzes and the impracticality of the current craze for white and gold décor had filled many of their hours together.

Martin was frowning thoughtfully. 'There's a piece of furniture on which I would greatly appreciate your opinion. It's at a house not far from here.' He glanced at Helen and raised an enquiring brow. 'Can you spare me a few moments of your time, my dear?'

Swallowing her instinctive response that such matters should be reserved for the consideration of his bride, Helen smiled her acquiescence. One subject she had no intention of mentioning was matrimony. 'I dare say I could manage a moment or two.'

Courteously inclining his head in acceptance of her boon, Martin headed his team for the gates, a slow smile of satisfaction curving his lips. They were wending their way through the traffic when Helen asked, 'What is this piece?'

'An occasional sofa.'

Seeing his attention was fixed on his horses, given to nervously jibbing in the crowded streets, Helen forbore to press him for details. Doubtless she would learn soon enough why there was any question about the suitability of this particular sofa.

To her surprie, Martin drew the horses to a halt in front of an imposing residence in Grosvenor Square. He turned to smile down at her. 'This is it.' Relinquishing the reins to Joshua who came running from his perch at the rear, Martin jumped to the pavement and turned to assist Helen. Once on his level, Helen eyed the elegant façade then realised the sofa in question must presently be in the possession of the owner of the mansion.

Surrendering to the subtle pressure of Martin's hand in the small of her back, Helen went up the steps before him. Martin paused before the door and glanced down, his eyes locking with hers, an unfathomable expression in the steely grey. Suddenly, Helen could not breathe. But before she could register more than a flush of unnerving excitement, Martin raised a gloved fist and beat a peremptory tattoo on the polished oak. The door was opened immediately by an imposing if portly butler, who bowed them into a spacious hall.

'M'lord.' The butler turned to her. 'My lady.' He

reached for her coat. Uncertain, Helen raised an
enquiring brow at Martin. When he nodded, she surrendered her pelisse and bonnet. Clearly, the Earl of
Merton was well-known to this household.

'The room at the end of the hall.' At Martin's nod,
Helen walked forward over the black and white tiles,
towards the door that stood open at the far end of the
hall. Martin started in her wake, then hesitated and
turned back, handing his gloves to the butler. Hearing
his footsteps falter, Helen glanced back. Martin smiled
his encouragement. Reassured, Helen continued.

As she drew closer to the open door, she noticed a
peculiar light glowing from within the room. Almost as
if the curtains were drawn and the fire ablaze. Puzzled,
Helen gained the threshold and looked in.

'We don't wish to be disturbed, Hillthorpe.'

Helen's gasp stuck in her throat. It did not need the
butler's deferential 'Yes m'lord' to confirm her wild
conjecture. The proof that, in the case of Martin
Willesden, rake of the highest standing, she had been
wrong and Ferdie perfectly right lay before her startled
gaze. The heavy velvet curtains were indeed drawn,
the fire fully stoked and crackling voraciously. A bottle
of wine, uncorked, reposed in a silver bucket of ice
on the sideboard. Automatically, irrelevantly, Helen
searched the room for the sofa she had come to see—
the occasional sofa. At first, she could not find it. Then
her eyes widened in shock as they focused on the large
piece of furniture standing squarely before the hearth.
The most massive daybed she had ever seen.

Flee! was her first thought—immediately followed
by, *How*? Martin's footsteps rang on the tiles; he was
but feet behind her. If she turned and tried to escape,

he would simply pick her up and carry her through the door. Certainly, his butler would be no help.

Helen drew a deep breath. Danger lay across the threshold. She tried to step back into the relative safety of the hall, only to find that she had hesitated too long. Martin, directly behind her, slipped an arm about her waist and she was swept, effortlessly, into the room.

'Martin!' Breathless, Helen swung to face him, to see him shut the door and turn the key. She was only slightly relieved to see that he left the key in the lock. It was him she had to escape; after that, escaping the room would be child's play. Summoning her defences, she took refuge in indignation. Drawing herself to her full height, in this case unfortunately insufficient to allow her to intimidate the reprobate before her, she fixed him with an affronted glare and prayed her voice would not betray her. 'You tricked me!'

A slow grin twisted Martin's mobile lips. ''Fraid so.' His gaze, heated grey, rested, intent, on her face. Slowly, he moved towards her.

He did not look the least bit contrite.

Helen tried to ignore her skittering pulse and let her temper grow. It was the only thing that might save her. She narrowed her eyes, shutting out as much of the potent male presence approaching slowly but, as far as she was concerned, far too fast, as she could. Forced to tilt her chin up as he drew nearer, she struggled to overcome her suddenly breathless state. 'Your behaviour over the past week has all been a sham, hasn't it?' To her horror, it was all she could do not to squeak. What was he about?

Stopping directly in front of her, Martin allowed his grin to develop into the deepest of smiles, a smile of disturbing magnitude and unnerving intent. 'You've unmasked me, fair Juno.' Eyes glinting, Martin spread his hands in supplication. 'What can I say in my defence?'

Transfixed by the warmth in his gaze, Helen struggled to collect enough wit to tell him.

Smoothly, confidently, Martin reached for the comb that held her curls in a knot on the top of her head. With a deft flick, he drew it free, sending golden tresses cascading over her shoulders, down her back.

Helen gasped, instinctively putting up her hands to stem the tide. But Martin caught them gently in his and drew them down. Glinting, his eyes roamed the tumbled gold. 'You've no idea how often I've considered doing that.'

The idea that he might have done that in the middle of some fashionable ballroom suspended the few faculties Helen had managed to reassemble. His hands released hers, long fingers rising to slip in among the silken strands. The fingers played, sampling the texture, removing loose pins and dropping them like rain on to the floor, then they firmed about her chin, tilting her head up until her eyes locked with his.

Held mesmerised by the smouldering heat in the cloudy grey gaze, Helen felt all thought slipping from her. Martin's hands left her face; he reached for her and drew her into his arms.

Belatedly, self-preservation jolted Helen back to reality. She braced her hands against Martin's chest. 'My lord—Martin!' she amended, accurately reading the comment in his eyes. 'This is unseemly. Scandalous—and worse! If you wish to atone for your behaviour—your deceit—you can escort me back to your curricle this instant!'

She tried to sound firm but her tone was weak and wavering, her diaphragm refusing to lend strength to her words. The smile on the dark face hovering closer and closer to hers only deepened. His arms, already about her, tightened.

'I've a much better idea of how to atone for my sins.'

Martin kissed her. And kept kissing her until every vestige of resistance was overcome, overwhelmed, drowned beneath their passion.

Trapped in his embrace, Helen reluctantly admitted that it was *their* passion—not his alone. That was what made Martin so very hard to resist. His scandalous advances drew an equally scandalous response from her. Caught on a crest of burgeoning desire, so sweet in its novelty that she was unable to resist, Helen gave up the unequal fight, softening against him. She felt his arms tighten further, crushing her to him. Then they shifted; his hands moved over her back, moulding her yielding form to his hard frame.

Helen struggled against the insidious invitation of his kiss, a blatant temptation to lose her wits and drown in a sea of sensuous sensation, striving instead against the steadily mounting odds to retain some fragment of lucidity.

Martin raised his head to glance down at her, his eyes glowing. 'Relax,' he breathed. His lips brushed her forehead. 'Don't worry—we'll take it *very slowly*.'

As his lips returned to hers, Helen wondered if he intended the deep, gravelly words as a threat or a promise. For a full minute, she considered the implications as her will sank slowly beneath the warm web of

sensation evoked by Martin's sure hands. With a mental jerk, she called her wits to order. What was she to
do? The way he was progressing, slow or not, she
would only have a few more minutes in which to
decide.

It was patently obvious to the meanest intelligence
that Martin had reverted to form and intended to
compromise her beyond all possible doubt, in fact as
well as reputation. Helen had not the slightest doubt
that he thought thus to force her acquiescence to their
marriage, to overcome her refusal to accept his suit.
But she was determined to give him his dream—
nothing, not even he, could shake her resolution.

However, she admitted, feeling the gentle tug of
long fingers at the buttons of her gown, any thought of
escape from such a masterful seducer was fantasy.
What he had in mind was undeniably scandalous. To
her, it was undeniably attractive. If she followed her
heart, her truest impulse, she would do as he had said
and relax.

Fate had dealt against her, but that did not mean she
could not enjoy him, take the moment he offered—this
once. This was all the chance she would ever have.
Her one touch at happiness—her one chance to touch
the pot of gold at the end of the rainbow. She had
never been there before, had never known the joy she
surmised must exist, wrapped in the clouds of love.
Martin's fingers skimmed her shoulders, easing her
carriage dress from her. With a little sigh, Helen drew
her arms from the long sleeves, letting her dress fall to
the floor along with her reservations. Glancing shyly up
from beneath her lowered lashes, she lifted her arms
and draped them about his neck in tacit acceptance of

what was to come. Anticipation throbbing its dizzying pulse through her veins, she waited to see how he would manage her light stays.

Aware, as only one of his extensive experience could be, of the import of Helen's tentative movement, Martin drew a deep breath and fought to shackle a desire so strong, it threatened to addle his wits—a thoroughly undesirable outcome. Juno needed to be wooed slowly, gently, seduced like the veriest virgin, skittish and shy. He applied himself to the task with devotion.

Soon, Helen's mind was whirling, giddy with pleasure. Her past had held no clues to the passion that now engulfed her. Her introduction to wifely duties had been mundane in the extreme; her mother had told her what to expect—she had got that and nothing more. The entire procedure had been so basically boring, she had been only too glad when her husband had returned to his mistresses post haste. But, in the long lonely years since then, she had come to the conclusion that there had to be more to it than that, a positive side to the undertaking she had never experienced—for surely it was that that brought the glow to Dorothea's pale complexion and the stars to her eyes.

She had thought she would never learn what it was. But fate had decided to hand her one chance—a consolation prize in the lottery of life. Who better to teach her of the delights of love then the man in whose strong arms she was trapped?

For he was a trap, to her senses at least. She would do well to acknowledge that, and remember it when the time for explanations arrived. He was going to be angry. Very angry. He would ask her to marry him, confidently expecting her, overwhelmed by his loving, to agree. And when she refused, he was not going to be particularly interested in her reasons. Which was just as well, for she had no idea how to make him understand and was in two minds whether it was safe to do so.

But right now two minds were two minds too many for her wits to cope with. He had stolen them, along with her stays—and she had not even noticed how he had accomplished the deed. All she knew was that she felt more enthralled, more consumed with desire than ever before in her life. Martin filled her mind, over-whelmed her senses—and took control completely.

There was nothing she could do to stem the tide of urgent need welling within and between them, engulf-ing them both in its heated embrace. Martin stopped and lifted her, carrying her to the daybed and laying her amid the silken covers. He hovered over her, his lips dipping to hers, his hands skilfully weaving webs of delight over her fevered flesh. Then his lips touched her eyelids, placing a kiss on each.

'Keep your eyes shut.'

Helen sensed he was about to undress. She wanted to watch. 'But——'

'No buts,' came the gravelly voice, even deeper and raspier than usual. 'Do as I say. Just lie there and relax and everything will be wonderful.'

The gentle persuasion in his tone had its effect. Helen lay still, feeling the warmth from the fire flickering over her skin, contrasting with the shimmering touch of the silks and satin on which she lay. Her lips curved slightly at the thought of his lordship's scandalous taste in furniture. The rustle of starched linen came eto her ears. The temptation to peek from beneath her lashes grew.

Helen opened her eyes a fraction. A heavily muscled back filled her view. She watched as Martin divested himself of his clothes, staring for as long as she could until, as he joined her on the daybed, she led her lids fall before allowing them to flicker innocently upwards.

Martin smiled gently, encouragingly. His shoulders were angled over her once more, limiting her view of him. He studied her expression but could detect no hint of panic. Yet. 'Good girl,' he murmured, struggling to harness the passion that vibrated in his voice. He lowered his lips to hers and was relieved when her lids fluttered closed once more. In truth, he had little idea what might scare her but, if she had had a difficult time accommodating Walford, seeing him naked was not going to help.

He released her lips to give more attention to the rest of her, all the while soothing her with comforting, reassuring words. It was not his habit to waste time with talk in such situations but this case was different, unique. He kept watch for any signs of withdrawal or distress, ready to backtrack at the first hint that he was pushing her too fast.

Helen heard his words, letting them wash over her, unable to concentrate on the sentences buried beneath his sensuous rumble. She wished he would stop talking and give all his attention to fulfilling her needs. Her hands itched to explore, but, never having been visited by such a desire before, she was unsure of the etiquette involved. In the end, when, driven by her need, she tentatively spread her hands over the muscles of his back, Martin moved and caught them, trapping them in one of his and drawing them over her head.

'Not yet, sweetheart. We don't want to rush things.'

If she had been capable, Helen would have glared. Why not? she wanted to know. She felt as if she wanted to devour him whole and all he would say was 'Not yet'. Her body felt overheated but all she wanted was more heat.

'Martin——'

'Hush.' He silenced her with a kiss. 'Trust me. You'll enjoy it. This time will be different, I promise.'

Inwardly, Helen frowned. Of course this time would be different—she loved him. She had never loved anyone before. Her inward frown grew. She wished she could shake her head to rid herself of the niggle that there was something here that she was missing, something she did not understand.

'There's nothing to be frightened about. We'll take it slow and easy. No pain at all—only pleasure. Trust me this once and I'll show you how wonderful it can be.'

The gentleness in his voice, overlaying the suppressed desire, gave Helen the vital clue. Her eyes flew wide but Martin, busy kissing her, missed the shocked response. Quickly, realising her error, Helen shut her eyes again, willing her body to remain in the languid, floating state he had induced.

He thought she was sexually crippled—or, at least, had a broken bone or two. An aversion to lovemaking of some major degree. If he had not been kissing her, Helen would have shaken her head in amazement. How had he come to such a crazy conclusion? Arthur had never hurt her—he had simply failed to engage her passions. Now that she knew what passion between a man and woman was, she knew the truth. She was not the least averse to making love with Martin Willesden—but why had he thought she was?

This, however, was no time for imponderables.

Her wits were barely up to recognising facts, let alone dealing with their ramifications. As Martin deepened their kiss, Helen felt her conscious mind melt. Thought, in any form, became all but impossible. Sensation washed through her; joyfully, with abandon, she surrendered to the warm tide.

To Martin's gratification, not the slightest ripple of panic, not the smallest quiver of maidenly nerves, marred the response of the beauty in his arms. Nevertheless, he kept a tight rein on his passions, enforcing ruthless discipline in the face of extreme provocation. It was hard work, seducing a goddess—slowly. Painstakingly, he stoked the fever between them, blowing the embers to flame and pouring desire upon them until the conflagration had her firmly in its grip. It started to singe his control. Still, he held back, ensuring her pleasure beyond all doubt. When he finally brought her to the peak, and held her there for that most fleeting of instants, he felt the most intense surge of satisfaction, before his mind was swamped by his own delight.

The chimes of the elegant French carriage clock sitting on Martin's marble mantelpiece penetrated the pleasured fogs shrouding Helen's mind. Four o'clock.

Four o'clock! With a start, she opened her eyes. An expanse of tanned male chest, liberally sprinkled with curling back hair, met her bemused gaze. Her questing senses detected a heavy, muscled arm lying, relaxed, about her.

Stifling a moan, Helen closed her eyes. What now? Languid pleasure still had her in its grip, drugging her mind and body. It would be easy just to lie here, enjoying the warm intimacy, and let fate take its course. Then he would wake, and ask her to marry him, and she would have to refuse him, while lying naked in his arms.

Helen grimaced. She opened her eyes and slowly raised them to Martin's face. He was still sleeping. With a small sigh of relief, she set about carefully extricating herself from his loose embrace, untangling her legs from the silk sheets he had drawn over them, Luckily, she was lying on the outer edge of the daybed.

Once free, she dressed quickly. While she wrestled with her stays, she allowed her gaze to roam lovingly over the large frame lying sprawled amid the rumpled sheets. She smiled a trifle mistily. At least she now understood just what it was that lay at the end of the rainbow, what it was that gave rise to the glow of anticipation in Dorothea's eyes whenever she looked at Hazelmere. Martin had transported her to the end of the rainbow, had given her a moment of sheer delight beyond any she had ever experienced. She would hold the memory of that moment, enshrine it in her heart, to light the lonely years ahead.

Stifling a sigh, she stepped into her dress and eased it up over her petticoat. When he asked for her hand, how was she to answer him? Despite the passing of a week since her last attempt, no simple way of explaining her view to him had occurred. In fact, her cogitations had led her to conclude that explaining at all could itself prove dangerous. Martin was not the sort of man to accept her sacrifice tamely. He would argue, threaten, run the gamut of all means available to sway her. She was not going to be swayed; despite the glory of the past hours, or, perhaps, because of them, she was even more firmly determined to give him his dreams. She loved him—more deeply than she had realised, more completely than she had understood. Self-sacrifice was an undertaking of which she had considerable experience. Her girlish dreams had been jettisoned for her parents' ambitions, her pride for her husband's greed. Martin was more worthy of her sacrifice than any other; she would make it willingly, if sadly.

Calmly determined, Helen allowed her gaze to rest on the strong features only slightly gentled by sleep. She would never succeed in making him accept her view—it would be better not to try. If she offered no explanation, but simply held firm to her refusal, he would be exceedingly angry, but impotent to pressure her to change her mind.

He was not going to like it but it was for his own good.

The buttons down the back of her gown were proving refractory. Seeing her soft carriage boots on the floor, Helen slid her feet into them while glancing about at the elegantly furnished room. Each piece had been chosen with a judicious eye. The theme was simplicity of line and form, an austerity which balanced the stark black, blue and gold décor. In truth, the room suited its owner. She could not imagine him in less expensive surrounds; this was his milieu, this was where he rightly belonged. This, she was determined, was where he would stay.

Her eyes went once more to the handsome face. Helen smiled as she recalled his efforts to ease her imagined hurt. Her smile faded. In refusing him, she was going to cause him even more hurt than anger. She was going to land a blow where it would hurt a great deal. Her refusal to succumb to his lovemaking was going to place a very large dent in his rake's pride.

Helen paled and felt suddenly chilled.

At sixteen, she had learned that her life was not destined to be easy. She had borne unhappiness and loneliness and put a brave face on her misery. But what she could not understand was why fate had singled her out for such continually harsh treatment. Why her?

Resolutely, Helen straightened, pushing her depression aside. Her fingers were still fumbling behind her, the small buttons sliding on the silk. Muttering a few choice curses, she attacked them with renewed vigour, only to find them slipping from her grasp.

Exasperated, she glanced up—straight into warm grey eyes, laced with lazy laughter. As she watched, Martin's smile grew.

'You should have woken me.' His voice was still several tones deeper than normal, a warm, raspy invitation to illicit delight.

Helen blinked, struggling to focus her wits. She had to keep calm. Trying for her usual brisk tone, she said, 'It's late and I need to get home. I suspected waking you before I got dressed would not necessarily be supportive of that aim.'

Thoroughly relaxed, Martin chuckled. 'You read me so well, fair Juno.' He beckoned. 'Come here.'

Helen eyed him suspiciously. 'Martin, I really *do* need to go.'

Martin's eyes flicked to the clock. His brows rose in resignation. 'I suppose you do.' He sighed. 'In which case, you had better let me do up your dress.' He sat up and swung his leg over the side of the bed, the sheet slipping down to his waist. When he waved her towards him, Helen reluctantly came to stand before him. Martin's strong hands closed about her waist. For one heart-stopping moment, their gazes locked. Mesmerised, her breath trapped in her throat, Helen watched as the slow smile she knew so well twisted his lips. Then he turned her about.

His strong fingers made short work of her buttons. But before she could move away, his hands fastened about her waist and he drew her down to sit on one sheet-swathed knee.

The feel of her warm body between his hands made Martin wish again that she had woken him earlier. He seriously considered pulling her back to the sheets and wrestling her out of her clothes. Who cared what the world thought? With a wry grin, he acknowledged that such wildness would no longer do, not if he intended to assume his social position as the Earl of Merton with his Countess at his side. Speaking of which. . .

He turned fair Juno about so that he could look into her face. He smiled devilishly, the complete rake. 'Did you like it?'

Helen's eyes flew wide. She blushed furiously.

Martin laughed, raising one finger to caress her cheek. 'Say you'll marry me and we can enjoy such delights every day—or at least every night.' His second proposal, he reflected, but in circumstances much more to his taste. He smiled confidently and waited for fair Juno's assent.

Helen could not meet his eyes. As the silence stretched, she felt Martin tense. Feeling a chill creep over her skin, she tried to ease from his hold. He let her go, his hands falling from her as she stood and moved to the fireplace before turning to face him.

Steeling herself, she raised her eyes to his. Cold grey stone would have held more warmth than the grey gaze steadily regarding her. His features were impassive, set like granite; his hands were fisted on his thighs. The light from the dying fire gilded the heavy musculature of his bare chest. He looked very powerful—and deeply angry.

'Martin, I cannot marry you.' Helen forced herself to enunciate the words clearly, calmly. Inside, she felt dead.

'I see.' The words came like a whiplash. Helen hung her head. 'You'll willingly share my bed but you won't *marry* me.' During the pause that ensued, she kept her eyes down, too frightened that she would weaken if she looked up and saw his disillusion.

'Why?'

The confusion and hurt in that single word nearly overset her. She pressed her palms together and forced her head up. 'I'm sorry. I can't explain.'

'*Sorry*?' Abruptly, Martin surged to his feet.

Startled, Helen glanced away, colour flaring in her pale cheeks. With a strangled curse, Martin stalked to where a silk robe had been left lying over the back of a chair. He shrugged into it, struggling to bring order to the chaotic and violent emotions seething through his brain. 'Let me just get one point clear,' he ground out, savagely yanking the sash tight. 'You were willing, were you not?'

'Yes.' Helen brought her head up, relieved to see him decently garbed. Her admission should have sunk her beyond reproach, shaken her to the core. Yet it was the truth; she admitted it without a blink, all her energies concentrated on the difficult task of persuading him to let her go. 'But that alters nothing. It is simply not possible for me to marry you.'

'Why?'

This time, the question held more demand. Martin stalked back and forth before her, a wounded beast. Helen stifled the instinctive urge to offer him comfort. She had to hold firm. 'I'm sorry, I can't explain.'

Eyes narrowed to steely slits, Martin stopped directly in front of her. 'Can't explain why you'd make a high-class harlot of yourself rather than marry me? I'm hardly surprised, madam!'

Inwardly flinching, Helen held herself proudly, refusing to quail under the glittering grey gaze. She felt sick. He was not impassive now; hurt pride was clearly etched in his forbidding features. But she could not regret their afternoon of delight; she did not intend to feel guilty over the greatest joy she had ever known.

Martin held her gaze, willing her to back down. When the clear green gaze remained steady, unwavering, he growled and flung away. He felt violent. He wanted to shake her—to take her back to the bed and reduce her to a state where she would do, and say, anything he wished. But that was no real solution. He threw a furious glance her way. She was still standing, with a calm he knew was assumed, before his fire-place—where he wanted to see her, but without the mantle he wished to place on her shoulders. He could push her to become his mistress, and she might just give way. But he wanted her as his wife.

With a growl of frustration, Martin turned and stalked back to her. 'If my honest proposal is repugnant to you, my lady, I would suggest you leave. Before my baser instincts drive me to make you a far more insulting offer.'

Helen's eyes widened. Martin's fingers closed, vice-like, about her arm. Stifling a gasp, she allowed him to march her, unresisting, to the door. It was better this way. If she had to depart of her own accord, leaving him hurt, wounded and without explanation, she might waver and fail. His furious rejection might break her heart but it might also save his.

In a muddled, befuddled fury, Martin strode into his hall, dragging Helen with him. 'Hillthorpe!'

Instantly, his butler emerged from behind the green baize door. At sight of them, his demeanour underwent a subtle change.

Martin ignored the evidence of Hillthorpe's surprise. 'Lady Walford is leaving. Get a hackney for her ladyship.' He released Helen and, with the curtest of nods, turned on his heel and strode back to the parlour.

When the door slammed behind him, Helen drew a ragged breath. She felt as if her world had crashed about her very ears. Her head was spinning; she felt queasy inside. But there was nothing to do but face the disaster with as much dignity as she could. Her hair was still down, but her pins were irretrievable; she would have to make the best of it. She refused to permit herself to break down and cry, much as she wished to, until she was safe in her chamber. Reaching that sanctuary with all posible haste was her immediate goal.

One glance at Martin's butler showed he was as stunned as she at Martin's rudeness but, unlike her, had no idea from where the uncharacteristic reaction sprang. 'If you would get my hat and coat?'

Her quiet question jolted Hillthorpe out of his state of shock. 'Yes, of course, my lady.' Never in his extensive experience of Mr Martin had Hillthorpe seen him in such a temper. Which, he thought, as he bowed to Lady Walford and hurried to do her bidding, was a damned shame. The servants had been particularly pleased when Mr Martin had inherited. Of the four sons of the house, he had always been their favourite. He was a hard but fair master; they were relieved that the estate was once more in capable hands. Not since the late master, his father, had they felt so secure. And, as servants did, they had kept abreast of his endeavours to secure his Countess. The news that he had chosen Lady Walford for the position had been greeted with considerable relief. Many were the instances when men such as his lordship married youthful misses who led everyone a dance and set the household by the ears. But Lady Walford was well spoken of, kind and generous, a lady in truth.

As he held her ladyship's coat for her, Hillthorpe frowned. She was upset, as she had no doubt every right to be. What was the master thinking of? A hackney? He would summon the unmarked carriage instead. As she turned to face him, buttoning up her coat, he bowed low. 'If you'll just take a seat in the drawing-room, ma'am, I'll summon the carriage directly.'

Grateful for the man's smooth handling of the matter, Helen followed him, battening down her emotions until it was safe to set them free.

From the bend in the spiral staircase two floors above, Damian Willesden watched her disappear down the hall. His eyes widened in surprise. Slowly, he slumped on to the stairs, the better to consider the implications of what he had just seen.

So—Martin had run true to form and seduced the beautiful Lady Walford? That thought pleased Damian no end. With a little crow of delight, he gave thanks for Martin's rakish tendencies. Lady Walford might be his brother's mistress but she would not be his wife. Her ladyship could be crossed off the list of potential candidates for the position of the Countess of Merton.

Or could she?

Damian sobered and gave the matter due thought. He could not imagine why a man such as his brother would marry a woman he could have as his mistress but the unpalatable truth was, such things had been known to occur. All too often. Particularly with unmarried peers.

The front door opened and shut. Lady Walford was gone.

But *he* was not yet safe. Damian frowned and drummed his fingers on his knee. He could not believe that Martin would want to marry the lady now, particularly after that abrupt dismissal, but that did not mean she might not try to entrap him later. Adrift in social straits he normally eschewed with a vengeance, Damian pondered deeply. In the end, he concluded that it would quite obviously be better all round, for Martin as well as for himself, if Lady Walford were not in a position to demand that Martin marry her.

And she could not do that if her reputation was already in shreds.

Aside from anything else, the Dowager would not stand for it. Damian had immense confidence in his mother. And her money.

With a smug smile, Damian rose and sauntered down the stairs. It would be easy, so easy, to ensure his peace of mind. He called for his hat and cane and, once supplied with these necessary items, issued forth from the house of his fathers, determined to make sure that it would one day be his. He turned his footsteps in the direction of St James.

CHAPTER NINE

THE Barham House ball was to be held that night. Wearily, Helen acknowledged that it was impossible for her to miss the event—the Barhams had stood her friends for years. Hopefully, Martin, not so constrained, would not go.

With a dismal sniff, she hauled herself out of the comforting softness of her bed and gave her eyes one last pat with her sodden handkerchief. Janet would have to find some cucumber to take the swelling down. Her bout of tears had done no more than ease her immediate hurt; the deeper pain would linger, undimmed by any show of misery. With an effort, Helen stood and crossed the room to tug the bell-pull. Then she ventured to her wardrobe.

Black was what she felt like wearing, but in the circumstances, dark blue would have to do. The heavy silk was edged with gold ribbons; more ribbon cinched the high waist. In it, she knew she looked austere and a little remote. Perfect for tonight. With any luck, the solid colour would help disguise her paleness.

A bath restored some semblance of vitality. Janet fussed and fretted and coaxed her to eat some lightly broiled chicken. Her cook had tried, but the food might as well have been ashes.

And then she was in her carriage, bowling along to Barham House. What would she do if Martin did attend? Helen drew a long breath and buried that

thought deep. In her present state, it was far too
unnerving to contemplate.

The Barhams greeted her warmly. In the ballroom,
she found Dorothea and Lady Merion already present.
In the comfort of her familiar circle, she relaxed,
allowed a mask of calm unconcern to cloak her bruised
heart.

Midway through the evening, her mask slipped
alarmingly. She was waltzing with Viscount Alvanley
when she became aware that Martin had indeed
attended the ball. He was standing by the side of the
ballroom, powerful shoulders propped against the wall,
a look of brooding intensity darkening his features. His
gaze was fixed unwaveringly upon her.

Even Alvanley, genial chatterer that he was, noticed
her start. 'What's up?' he asked, peering at her over
the folds of his monstrous neckcloth.

'Er—nothing. What were you saying about Lady
Havelock?'

Alvanley frowned at her. 'Not Havelock,' he said,
piqued. 'Hatcham.'

'Oh, yes,' said Helen, praying that he would resume
whatever anecdote he had been pouring into her ears.
She kept her eyes on the Viscount's face, inwardly
struggling to calm her panicky breathing and the erratic
pounding of her heart. To her relief, Alvanley happily
took up his tale.

Helen tried to ignore the grey gaze from across the
room, tried to keep her mind engaged with all manner
of distractions, afraid that if she allowed herself to
meet Martin's eyes her fragile control would break.
She could not let that happen—not in the middle
of the Barhams' ballroom. Aside from anything else,

Martin in his present mood was perfectly capable of taking advantage of such weakness to force her either to explain, or, if she was truly overcome, to accept his suit. Irrelevantly, Helen belatedly recalled Ferdie's warning. Her old friend had been right—rakes were dangerous in any circumstances.

Despite the sea of fashionable heads separating them, Martin's senses, finely tuned where Helen was concerned, detected her unease. Through the veils of rage that still clouded his reason, he realised she did not wish him to approach her. He was tempted to ignore her wishes and claim her for a waltz. Only his uncertainty over what might happen if he did, an unnerving occurrence in itself, kept him from doing so. He was not even sure why he was here, other than that there had been nothing else he had wanted to do. Seeing Helen every evening had become a habit—a habit he was damned if he could break—a habit he had no wish to break. The events of the afternoon had left him more than confused. Anger still rode him, a potent influence, effectively countering all efforts at rational thought. From experience, he knew his mind would not function properly until he had worked it out of his system. How to achieve that laudable goal had him presently at a loss.

He knew his continued staring at Helen was causing comment but he could not stop. His mind was totally consumed by her; his eyes simply followed his thoughts. He saw Hedley Swayne and spared a moment to scowl at him. The fop took fright and disappeared into the crowd.

'Martin! How pleasant to see you again.'

Martin looked down as a hand touched his arm.

Seeing Serena Monckton—no, she was Lady Rochester now—smiling up at him, he repressed the urge to shake off her hand. He nodded casually and came away from the wall. 'Serena.'

Lady Rochester preened. It was the first time since he had reappeared as the Earl of Merton that she had managed to get Martin to use her first name. Perhaps there was hope for her yet?

Martin saw her reaction and inwardly cursed. He had studiously kept Serena at a distance, knowing how cloying her attention could be. He also trusted her not at all, a fact he felt was excusable. With his mind engrossed with Helen, he had forgotten to keep his defences up. Now he would have to repair the damage.

'I do *love* waltzing.' Coquettishly, Lady Rochester smiled up at him. 'So few of the men these days know how to do it properly. But you were with Wellington at Waterloo, weren't you?'

Stifling a curse, Martin reflected that no moss grew on Serena Monckton. She was shameless, propositioning him in such a way. Particularly him. He opened his mouth to put her in her place, when it suddenly occurred to him that perhaps here was an opportunity to demonstate to another shameless woman just what it felt like to be rejected. The very same shameless woman who had spent the afternoon on his daybed and then rejected him. A single glance over the crowd showed that Helen was sitting out the dance, seated on a chaise by Dorothea's side. Martin's eyes dropped to Serena's eager face, his lips curved in a practised smile. 'I do believe that's a waltz starting up now. Shall we?'

He did not have to ask twice. But, immediately his feet started to circle, Martin wished he had thought twice. Dancing with Serena felt all wrong; she was not the woman he wanted in his arms. Gripped by a sudden sense of foreboding, Martin glanced over the heads of the dancers. Helen had not seen them yet. But many others had. He had made a habit of dancing with Helen Walford alone; his sudden appearance on the dance-floor with another woman in his arms, Serena Monckton at that, while Helen was in the room and unengaged, was, Martin belatedly realised, a somewhat obvious insult. The full enormity of his mistake hit him when he again looked Helen's way. They were much closer now. She had seen them; the expression in her large green eyes cut him to the core. Abruptly, she looked down and away, saying something to distract Dorothea, who was staring at him in undisguised fury.

Martin felt chilled. He waltzed automatically, paying no attention at all to Serena's chatter. When their revolutions took them past the chaise where Helen had been, he saw that it was empty. The third time around, and Dorothea was back, alone, staring daggers at him.

Helen had left the ball.

Because of him. He had hurt her and she had fled, not something she would readily do, having, as he knew, no liking for appearing in *on-dits*.

An odd numbness had closed about his heart; his mind refused to function at all. As soon as the dance ended, Martin bowed over Serena's hand and, leaving her standing by the side of the room, paid his respects to his by now curious hostess and left.

From the shadows of a potted palm decorating the side of the room, Damian watched Martin depart and rejoiced. Better and better. After that little scene, there was no chance of his brother and Lady Walford patching things up. Particularly not when the story he had spent the evening seeding into fertile soil took root. It would take a day or so, but after that he would be home and hosed, past the post, safe and sound.

He had decided that, in the circumstances, he would do well to attend a few of the *ton* assemblies, just until the danger of Lady Walford was past. Clearly, he would not have to suffer such boring gatherings for much longer. Virtually the entire ballroom had noticed the incident. Inwardly, Damian hugged himself. Whatever had possessed Martin to take such drastic action he could not imagine but he had to admit that, when his brother struck, he was effective. Lady Rochester was still standing a little way away, trying to pretend that Martin had truly been interested in her. Not that anyone would believe that. Feeling in unexpected charity with his brother, Damian decided to do him a favour.

He strolled to her ladyship's side and waited until the ageing roué who was currently bending her ear departed before nodding his greeting. 'Helpful of you to give Martin a hand.'

Serena scowled. 'Whatever do you mean, sir?'

Her peevish tone brought out the devil in Damian. 'Oh, I think you know.' He watched as Lady Rochester's face purpled. 'Who knows?' he continued smoothly before she could explode. 'Perhaps Martin might be grateful in a way you'd appreciate, now he's terminated his relationship with Lady Walford and will no longer be availing himself of her charms.'

Serena's eyes grew round, and then even rounder as the full implication of what he was saying sank in. 'You mean. . .?' Her voice was an incredulous whisper.

Damian looked surprised. 'Didn't you know? I thought everyone did. Ah well.' He shrugged. 'Just goes to show, don't it?' And with that he moved away, perfectly sure he had warned Lady Rochester off, too. For if Martin could seduce and ruin a woman of Lady Walford's calibre, it stood to reason that he would make short work of such as Lady Rochester.

Left alone, Serena took a long moment to sort out how what she had just heard could be used to greatest effect. She was perfectly well aware that Martin had only waltzed with her to hurt Helen Walford. The fiend had not so much as glanced properly at her—she was finished with trying to attract his notice. But she could not believe he was finished with the beautiful widow. From where she had stood, it had been blatantly obvious that he was still obsessed with Lady Walford. She had no quarrel with Helen Walford, just as long as she did not marry Martin Willesden. She herself held no illusion that she could ever fill that position—not now. But she drew the line at the thought of Martin enjoying his wife. Better anyone than Lady Walford. The rumour Damian was spreading, true or not, would surely cook Lady Walford's goose. And, if Martin was truly enamoured of Helen Walford, as Serena had every reason to suspect, then such an outcome would cause him grief.

Coolly, Lady Rochester smiled. None knew better than she that her long-ago claim of rape had been entirely without foundation. None knew better than she how furious Martin Willesden had made her by denying it and then accepting exile rather than marry her. Time had healed some of the wounds, but she saw no reason not to do what she could to spread Damian's delightful rumour.

Buoyed by a pleasant sense of mischief, she moved into the crowd to see what she could do.

His frown still black, Martin strode into his library. He shut the door with a decided click, then crossed to the sideboard and poured himself a generous quantity of brandy before slumping into the armchair by the fire.

Why? What had possessed him to make such an error of judgement? Never before had he made such a wrong-footed move. He had let his temper take control and it had led him off track. His equilibrium was out of kilter—he was dangerously adrift.

If this was what love did to a man, he was not sure he approved.

With a frustrated groan, he placed his glass on the table beside him and ran his hands over his face. He had hurt her. Dammit—all he wanted to do was make the wretched woman happy. Instead, he had succeeded in making them both miserable. The urge to go around to Half Moon Street and knock on her door until she let him in grew.

Reluctantly, Martin quashed the impulse and reached for his glass.

Enough of histrionics—they had landed him in a worse state than he had been in before. He was more than old enough to know better.

And, speaking of knowing better, did he really want to marry a woman who allowed herself to be seduced while having absolutely no intention of marrying her seducer? A difficult question, given that he had been the seducer and he had not married anyone before.

Martin grimaced and took a long sip of brandy. Regardless of present appearance, regardless of her words, he knew, as only a rake could, that Helen Walford was not promiscuous. Why then her refusal?

For a long while, he stared at the fire while the long case clock in the corner ticked on. The sheer fury he had felt when he had understood her intention of refusing him again, when he had realised that the woman he wanted to place before his fireplace was the sort who could walk away from intimacy without a second thought, still seethed, scrambling his wits.

He shook his head in frustration. It was no good. He could not think straight with his mind in such turmoil. Best to get away, to get out of it, until his temper died and he could consider the matter more calmly. Right now, he was not even sure what he wanted any more, let alone how best to achieve it. His agent at Merton had written, begging his attendance. The decorators were there, making his dream a reality; he should see how they were progressing. He would go down for a few days. Perhaps the peace of the Hermitage would help him sort things out, decide where he stood, what he wanted to do.

Decision made, Martin rose and drained his glass. For a long moment, he stood stock-still, staring at the embers dying in the grate. Then, deliberately, he flung the glass into the fireplace. With a brittle tinkle, it shattered, sending crystal shards flying.

His jaw set, Martin swung on his heel and left the room.

Th first intimation Helen had that anything at all was wrong came two days later, when she finally stirred herself from her lethargy to go driving in the Park with Cecily Fanshawe. It was her first outing since the disaster of the Barham House ball. Thankfully, Cecily had missed the ball through indisposition. As always bubbling with enthusiasm, she prattled on, giving Helen every opportunity to rest her weary mind.

She was worn out—depressed, hurt and heart-weary. The sight of Martin waltzing with Lady Rochester had caused her far more pain than she had been prepared for. She had thought she would be able to weather any such sight, knowing it would come some time. Her nerves had not been up to it that night. His action and her reaction would have caused comment, she knew. Consequently, when she detected the first few whispers, she made nothing of them.

But by the time she and Cecily had gone halfway around the circuit, Helen knew that something more serious was in the wind. There was a coolness in the air. A number of matrons with marriageable daughters drew back from her smile.

It was Ferdie who confirmed her suspicions. He waved to them from the side of the carriageway in the most popular section of the route. When the carriage came to a halt, he opened the door. 'Want to talk to you,' he said to Helen. He nodded to Cecily, with whom he was well-acquainted, then climbed into the carriage. 'Rather think it's time you dropped Helen home. I need to talk to her alone.'

Cecily frowned. 'But we've only just arrived.'

'Never mind. Plenty to keep you busy at home, I dare say.'

Cecily glared at Ferdie; Ferdie stared vacantly back.

It was Cecily who gave way. 'Oh, very well!' she said, and leaned forward to give her coachman directions.

Helen had not thought her heart could have sunk lower than it already had, but, as Ferdie engaged them both in inconsequential patter, she felt the leaden weight in her chest descend to her slippers. But she refused to let herself worry—not until she had heard what Ferdie had to say.

Cecily dropped them off in Half Moon Street, airily declining an offer of refreshment. 'I hope I know when I'm not wanted,' she said, looking pointedly at Ferdie.

Ferdie grinned. 'Not up to snuff yet, I'm afraid. Being married don't make you older.'

Cecily put her nose in the air and, miffed, departed.

Inside her drawing-room, Helen found another visitor waiting. Dorothea was pacing before the unlighted fire. She looked up as they entered. 'Thank goodness!' she said. 'I hoped you wouldn't be long.'

Ferdie entered behind Helen. Dorothea greeted him with relief. 'You're just the person we need.'

Ferdie took the unusual welcome in his stride. 'Got rid of your sister, though. Didn't think she'd take it too well. Never know what she might dash off and do.'

'Very true,' Dorothea agreed feelingly.

'Do you mind,' said Helen, sinking into an armchair, 'telling me what all this is about?' She had a nasty suspicion but she wanted to hear it stated plainly.

The simple question succeeded in striking both her visitors dumb. They looked at her, then, rather uncomfortably, at each other.

Helen sighed. 'Is it about me and Martin Willesden?'

Dorothea sank on to the chaise. 'Yes.' She waited while Ferdie drew up another chair and sat down.

'There are rumours going the rounds. Perhaps one might expect it, after the Barham ball. But what I've heard this morning seems rather more than can be excused.' She raised her large green eyes to Helen's in a gently questioning glance.

Helen held Dorothea's gaze for a moment, then sighed and looked to Ferdie. 'You've heard them, too?'

Ferdie, unaccustomedly serious, nodded. 'At White's.'

Helen closed her eyes. White's. That meant it was all about town.

'The tales suggest,' Dorothea began, 'that you. . . have been. . . Martin Willesden's mistress.' She waited, but Helen did not open her eyes. 'Is it true?' she asked gently.

'Would it matter?' Helen returned, her weariness very evident in her tone. She opened her eyes, raising her brows in disdain.

It was Ferdie who answered. ''Fraid not.' He paused, then continued, 'The thing we need to do now is decide how to quash 'em.'

'Yes,' agreed Dorothea. 'And I'm very much afraid, Helen, that you'll have to face it out. Marc's furious. After all, you first met Martin in our house. It was all I could do to persuade him to do nothing until I'd talked to you.'

Helen's eyes widened. Hazelmere after Martin? In truth, she could not predict who would be the victor in such a contest—they were both extraordinarily power-ful men in every way. But Hazelmere had solid social acceptability on his side—and Dorothea. Abruptly, Helen sat up, reaching across to lay a supplicating hand on Dorothea's sleeve. 'You must promise me you'll make Marc promise not to do anything—anything at all—until he hears from me.' Helen stared at Dorothea earnestly. 'Promise?'

A worried frown in her eyes, Dorothea grimaced. 'I promise to *try*. But you know as well as I that on some issues Marc won't be led.'

That was indisputably true. Helen nodded her acceptance of Dorothea's limited offer. She sank back into her chair. 'I need to think.'

'Best thing to do is to carry on as usual,' said Ferdie. 'Merton'll have to play his part. If neither of you gets the wind up, it'll all blow over.'

Dully, Helen nodded. 'Yes. I suppose that's true.' With a visible effort, she put aside her depression to smile at her guests. 'With friends like you, I'm sure we'll get by.'

Dorothea rose, shaking out her skirts. 'I'll leave you to your thoughts. If you need any additional support, you know you can call on us for whatever you need. Meanwhile, we'll do what we can to dampen the interest.'

Helen nodded her thanks.

Ferdie rose, too. 'I'll come with you,' he said to Dorothea. 'Might help if I saw Hazelmere.'

Both Dorothea and Helen welcomed this magnanimous offer.

After seeing her guests out, Helen returned to her small drawing-room to slump, even more weary than before, into her armchair. She struggled to make sense of what had happened. How had the story of her afternoon with Martin got out? No one had seen her leave Martin's house—his careful butler had seen to that. And, against Martin's orders, he had sent her home in one of the Merton coaches, but an unmarked one, with no crest on the door to give her away.

Had Martin spread the tale—to hurt her? Given the fact that he had deliberately and so very publicly flayed her feelings by waltzing with Lady Rochester—of all women—under her nose, she felt reasonably sure that he was capable of anything. Knowing that her standing in society was one of the few assets she had left, had he set out to strip her of that, too? Helen bit her lip. A sickening sense of betrayal threatened to engulf her. Determined to see things clearly, she forced herself to think long and hard but, in the end, could not believe it of him. He might strike out at her in anger, as he had done at the Barhams', but to seek to pull her down by making public what they had shared that afternoon was not the action of a gentleman. And, beneath his rakehell exterior, Martin Willesden was every inch a gentleman.

The only proof she needed of that was her memory. He had taken great pains to keep her safe, from himself as well as all others, on their unorthodox journey to London. An unscrupulous rake would have taken advantage; she blushed as she recalled their night at Cholderton—he had certainly had opportunity enough.

No—whoever had spread the tale of their afternoon together, it was not, could not be, Martin. Nevertheless, the uncertainty added yet another bruise to her already battered heart.

After half an hour's painful cogitation, she succeeded in convincing herself that she would have to see Martin, to discuss what they should do. He must have heard the rumours by now.

Reluctantly, Helen rose and crossed to the small escritoire which stood before the window. She sat and pulled a blank sheet of paper towards her. After mending her quill, she spent fifteen minutes staring fruitlessly into space. In the end, she shook herself in disgust. Without allowing herself any time to think further, she dashed off a note to the Earl of Merton.

The answer came back two hours later. The Earl of Merton, wrote his secretary, was presently in the country. It was not known when he would be back but her letter would be shown to him instantly on his return.

Helen stared at the plain note, reading the two sentences over and over. Ten minutes passed, then twenty. Finally, as the light started to wane, she stirred. Crumpling the note into a ball, she dropped it into the grate. Then, slowly, she went to the door and climbed the stairs to her chamber.

She lay on her bed and stared at the ceiling. She was alone. Not an unusual occurrence in her life, but it felt much worse this time. Insensibly, Martin had been with her ever since their first meeting in the woods. Now he had withdrawn, at the very moment when she most needed his strength.

What was she to do? That refrain played over and over in her head. The shadows lengthened. Outside, darkness fell. Inside her chamber, the outlook was bleak. In Martin's absence, she could not readily face down the rumours, scotch the scandal by simply denying its truth. Together, they could have pulled it off easily enough, even though, given their present situation, the effort would have cost both of them dearly. Without Martin, she did not have the strength to hold her head high until his return. Who knew when he might come back?

What were the alternatives? Helen bit her lower lip and frowned. If she retired from town for the rest of the Season, there was every likelihood that some other scandal would blow up to eclipse hers. Hazelmere, she knew, would not support such a course, tacitly admitting as it did that there was some substance to the rumours. But she was not a green girl. She was a widow of twenty-six. The *ton* was inclined to turn a blind eye to such matters, as long as the affair was not paraded before their collective eyes. As theirs had been. The cheapest price to secure her future acceptance seemed to be a sojourn in the country. She had little doubt that next year she would be able to return to town and join in the Season as if nothing untoward had occurred.

So the country it would be. But where? Unseeing, Helen stared into the gathering gloom. Hazelmere's estates were always open to her but, given that her absence from town would be against his wishes, she did not feel at ease with such a solution. There was Heliotrope Cottage, of course—her only remaining land, all five acres of it, in west Cornwall. The cottage was a tiny place, just big enough for Janet and herself. Hazelmere had always been against her staying there, on the grounds that she would be without male protection.

But Cornwall was a long way from London. Perhaps, in the isolation of the country, her broken heart would mend faster?

With a sigh, Helen sat up and swung her feet to the floor. There was no sense in thinking further—there was nowhere else to think of. Heliotrope Cottage it would have to be. She rose and crossed to the bell-pull. If Janet packed tonight, she could close the house in the morning and hire a chaise to take them down. Three days would see her far from the capital, far from the grey eyes that haunted her dreams.

Late that night, with all her plans made and her orders given, Helen sank into her bed and closed her eyes. She had decided not to tell anyone of her decision. They would only argue and, at the moment, she was not up to arguing back. No one would worry, however, for, with the knocker off the door and Janet gone, they would know she had shut up her house and gone away. Her dearest friends, those whose approval she valued, were all close enough to respect her wish for privacy. After Christmas, perhaps, she could visit Dorothea once her friend had returned to Hazelmere.

With a little sigh, Helen tried to relax, waiting for sleep to claim her, wondering irrelevantly how long it would be before slumber ceased to bring the image of grey eyes in its train.

CHAPTER TEN

HAMMERING still echoed throughout the ground floor of the Hermitage. Martin paced around the new conservatory, added at the back of the ballroom, admiring his new domain. It was all coming together much as he had planned.

The decorators would take another week to complete their work; the carpenters were expected to leave tomorrow. The sharp tang of new wood mixed with the smell of freshly mown grass. Not to be outdone by their house-bound rivals, the small army of gardeners he had hired to transform the wilderness back into landscaped grounds had taken full advantage of the fine weather. He had noticed the change immediately he had arrived. The drive had been cleared and newly gravelled, the huge wrought-iron gates that had hung for centuries at the main entrance to the estate had been cleaned and rehung. At the sight, Joshua's grumbles, all but constant since London, had abruptly ceased.

Martin leaned both hands on the sill of an open window and breathed deeply. Everywhere he looked, the evidence of his success leaped forward to greet him. Soon, his dream would be a reality; the Hermitage would be fit to take its rightful place as a centre of fashionable living once more, a suitable home for him—and his family.

At the thought, his mood clouded.

His success on one front had not been mirrored on the other. And now he was no longer sure which was the more important. Before he had met Helen Walford, restoring the Hermitage had been his principal goal. Now, with that goal in sight, he was looking far further ahead, beyond having his house, to fulfilling what he recognised as an even more basic need. He would soon have his house—he needed a family to fill it.

And, try as he might, there was only one woman he could picture in that all-important position before his fireplace. His mind was not capable of letting go of the image of Helen Walford, the flames gilding her glorious hair, with his son balanced on her hip.

From being merely an aim, marrying Helen Walford had become an obsession. He knew himself well enough to accept that if he did not marry her he would marry no one. His dream of a family inhabiting his home would never materialise.

He was determined that it would—every bit as determined as she seemed to be to fight shy of marrying him.

She was in for a shock.

He was not giving up.

Martin smiled a twisted smile. The life of a rake, a rich, well-born rake, was hardly conducive to teaching one self-sacrifice. He had no intention of giving up his dream. But how to convince Helen to go along with it was more than he had yet worked out.

Noticing the shadows lengthening, he shook free of his reverie. He would think more on the matter later. Right now, he was due for some light entertainment.

Quickly crossing the conservatory and striding

through the refurbished ballroom, he paused to cast a critical eye over the now elegant dining-room before taking the stairs two at a time. He strode towards his mother's rooms, noting with deep satisfaction how different the atmosphere in the long corridors now was. Gone was the must and the damp. Newly painted woodwork gleamed, and the floor was well-buffed and covered with bright runners. Windows, long stuck, had been repaired and the fresh autumn air danced in. Slim tables stood along the walls, some overhung by paintings, others sporting vases filled with bright flowers. Martin stopped by one such and chose a pink for his buttonhole.

Tucking it into position, he fronted his mother's door. He knocked. When she called to him to enter, he grinned in wicked anticipation and obeyed.

Catherine Willesden looked up as he entered, unsurprised, for she knew his knock by now. To her amazement, Martin had taken to dropping by her room in the late afternoons, not to cause any furore but merely to chat. At first she had been stunned, then disarmed. He had a sharp eye and a ready wit, very reminiscent of his father. She had enjoyed his company far more than she would ever admit.

Regally, she nodded and watched as he appropriated one of her gnarled hands and bent to kiss it. Then he placed a dutiful kiss on her cheek and stood back.

'I've a surprise for you.' Martin smiled down at her.

Lady Catherine struggled to remain immune. 'Oh? What?'

'I can't possibly tell you, or it wouldn't be a surprise.' Martin watched his mother's eyes narrow.

'My dear sir, if you think I'm about to play guessing games with you, you're mistaken.'

'Naturally not,' Martin replied. He found his mother's acerbity refreshing and took the greatest delight in teasing her. 'I would never presume to play games with you, ma'am.'

'Huh!' was his mother's instant response.

'But you're distracting me from your surprise. You'll have to come downstairs to get it.'

Lady Catherine frowned at her son. 'I've not been downstairs for well nigh ten years—as you well know.'

'I know nothing of the sort. If you were well enough to look about the place six weeks ago, you must be well enough to see my surprise.' Martin watched as his mother's crabbed fingers picked at the edge of her shawl.

'Oh,' said the Dowager. 'You heard about that.'

'Yes,' Martin said, his tone several shades more gentle. 'But there was no need for you to see it like that.' He had learned that, when he'd left so abruptly after his first visit, she had insisted on being carried down to view the state she had by then guessed the house had disintegrated into.

'It was awful.' Lady Catherine shuddered. 'I couldn't even recognise some of the rooms.'

Her grief for her lost dreams, the images she had carried for so many years destroyed when she had seen the decay of her home, shadowed her voice.

'Enough of the past. It's all gone.' Martin stooped and scooped her into his arms. Lady Catherine bit back a squeal and clutched at him, then glared when he smiled at her. Reflecting that Helen was at least twice his mother's weight, Martin swung towards the door.

His eyes fell on Melissa's bent head. 'Melissa—are you coming? Dinner will be downstairs tonight—come with us by all means, if you've a mind to see the workings, or come to the drawing-room at six.'

Melissa gawked at him. Dismissing her from his mind, Martin strode towards the door.

'*Downstairs*?' Lady Catherine finally found her tongue. 'I have my dinner up here. On a tray.'

Martin shook his head. 'Not any more. Now that we have a habitable dining-room, while I'm in residence, you'll take your proper place at the end of my table.' He made his voice sound stern, as if he was issuing an order.

He glanced sidelong at his mother. She did not know what to say. On the one hand, she did not like to accept what might just be his charity; on the other, she longed to be seated at her table again. Martin grinned and strode along the corridor to the stairs.

Catherine Willesden barely noticed the bright new furnishings through the veil of tears clouding her eyes. She had never, ever valued Martin and his arrogant, impulsive ways as he deserved. She knew quite well that it was because he had never been tractable, as his brothers had always been. But, while George had brought the place to ruin, Martin had set it to rights. Her heart had been broken when she had finally understood the full sum of the mess—Mr Matthews had been distressingly blunt when she had asked. Now it was as if a magic wand had been waved—it was even better than she recalled.

Not that she could tell Martin that—the rogue would be insufferable. As they reached the bottom of the stairs, she blinked rapidly. Martin eased her into a chair which had been set waiting. She settled her skirts as he stood back.

Suddenly, the chair started to move.

'Martin!' The Dowager awkwardly grabbed at the arms of the chair.

Her reprobate son chuckled—actually chuckled!

'It's all right. I've got hold of it.' Martin pushed the chair slowly forward. 'It's a wheelchair. Set on wheels so you can be moved about easily. See?' He stopped and showed her the wheels. 'I saw it in London. I thought you might find it useful.'

'I dare say,' said his mother, vainly trying to sound as forbidding as usual.

She failed. Martin pushed her on to the drawing-room, a smile of satisfaction on his face.

He took her through all the main rooms, explaining how those yet unfinished were to be decorated. To his surprise, she made no demur at any of his choices, going so far as to add some suggestions of her own. At five o'clock, totally in charity one with the other, they parted to dress for dinner.

The meal was the first they had shared in over thirteen years. Despite that fact, there was no constraint, beyond that provided by Melissa, who sat, dumb, throughout. Martin tried to include her in their conversation; in the end, his mother grimaced at him and shook her head.

But at the end of the evening, after tea taken in the comfort of the fashionable blue and white drawing-room, his mother declined his offer to carry her upstairs.

'Melissa can go,' she said, waving her ineffectual

daughter-in-law away. She turned to look at Martin. 'Are you going to sit in the library?'

Martin eyed her suspiciously. 'Yes.'

'Good! You can wheel me in there. I want to talk to you.'

Reflecting that his mother had not changed all that much in thirteen years, Martin complied, a rueful smile hovering about his lips.

The library had been the first room rendered habitable by the efforts of his decorators. It had always been the room in which his father had sat. Simple but elegant furniture in the classic style Martin favoured was scattered in a deceptively ad hoc manner throughout the long room; warm wooden bookshelves, ceiling high, were packed with leather-bound tomes. Martin dutifully wheeled his mother in, wondering just what she had on her mind. But, when he had settled her before the fireplace, she did not seem to know where to begin.

The Dowager Countess tried to remind herself she was just that, and the mother of the gentleman lounging at his ease in the latest style of wing chair opposite her. She eyed the elegant figure, clad in a simple yet exquisitely tailored blue coat and black knee-breeches, with some hesitation. What she felt she had to say was sensitive—or at least likely to be, given her relationship with this unpredictable son. She drew a careful breath and began. 'As you know, I have always been kept informed of happenings in town by my friends. They write to me, telling me all the latest news and *on-dits*.'

Martin suppressed the impulse to put an immediate halt to the conversation. Instead, he raised one brow coldly. 'Indeed?'

The Dowager stiffened. 'You needn't be so defensive,' she said. Really, he was his father all over again. One only had to mention something he did not want to discuss and he withdrew. 'I merely wished to tell you,' she went on before he had a chance to hinder her, 'that it has come to my notice that you appear to have a great interest in Helen Walford. To wit, everyone expects you to offer for her. As you never were witless, I assume that means you do intend to marry her. My only aim in mentioning the matter is to assure you that I will not raise any objection—even though I'm perfectly aware you wouldn't pay any attention if I did,' she added ascerbically. 'I recall Lady Walford's story and was a little acquainted with her parents. From everything I've heard, she's eminently suitable to be your countess.'

To Martin's astonishment, Lady Catherine paused, frowning, then added, 'I must say, I couldn't imagine you taking a bright little deb to wife—you'd probably strangle her before the honeymoon was over. Or, more likely, dump her on me.'

The Dowager raised her eyes to her son's, and beheld the amusement therein. Her eyes narrowed. 'Which brings me to my point. I don't know what state the Dower House is in, but if you would make arrangements to have it refurbished by this firm you're dealing with I'd be obliged.'

When Martin made no immediate comment, she added, 'I'll stand the nonsense, naturally.'

'Naturally be damned.' Martin put his glass of port down on a table beside his chair and leaned forward so that his mother could see his face clearly. 'You've lived in those rooms above stairs for. . .oh, yes—the past ten years. You've lived in this house for close on fifty. Neither I nor my wife would wish to see you leave.'

For a moment, his mother stared at him, wanting to accept his decree yet unwilling to be suffered out of pity.

'Don't be daft,' the Dowager eventually returned, although the phrase lacked strength. 'Your wife will hardly want me and Melissa cluttering up her house.'

Martin laughed and leaned back in his chair. 'I'd forgotten Melissa,' he admitted, his eyes twinkling. 'Who knows?' he said, his smile twisting. 'Perhaps Fair Juno will be able to get her to speak.'

'Who?'

With a quick smile for his parent's confusion, he brushed the question aside. 'Regardless of all else, I can assure you Helen will expect you to continue here. I suspect you'll deal famously. Aside from anything else, I imagine I'll be facing an unholy alliance every time I want to do anything the least unconventional. You never know, she might need your support.' When the Dowager still looked unconvinced, he added pensively, 'And then there's always the children to be looked after.'

'Children?' His mother's stunned expression suggested she had leaped rather further than he had intended.

Martin grinned. 'Not yet. Rake though I am, I suspect that they had better come after we are wed.'

His mother looked decidedly relieved.

'And now, if I've put all your worries to rest, I'll take you upstairs.' Martin rose. He scooped his mother, thoughtful and silent, into his arms. They were on the stairs when she asked, 'So you are going to marry Helen Walford?'

'Indubitably,' Martin replied. 'As the sun rises in the east, as one day follows another—you may count on it.'

Later, when he had returned to the library and his port, his words echoed in his mind. He had spoken the truth. The only question remaining was how to get his prospective bride to agree.

He lounged in his chair, stretching his long legs before him. Why she insisted on refusing his suit was still a mystery. But he felt certain, now, that he had misunderstood the nature of the hurdle which stood in his path. It was clearly not physical—which was something of a relief. Her reticence had to stem from some more simple problem—possibly a reluctance to place any faith in a man's avowed devotion? Martin raised his brows. Given her first husband's reputation, that was not hard to believe. Whatever the problem, he was confident of finding the answer. His anger at her apparent promiscuity had receded, draining away even as his need for her grew more acute. Rational thought now prevailed; he knew she was not promiscuous; her acts were driven by some deeper motive. He still faced a problem but it was not insurmountable. But he needed to solve it soon. With every passing day, he missed her more. There was nothing—*nothing*—that was more important to him.

With a gesture of decision, Martin drained his glass. There were no objections to be considered, no ramifications to be weighed. Tomorrow, he would return to town and see her.

He would woo her—he would win her. And then he
would bring her home.

Two days later, at the fashionable hour of noon, Martin
turned his bays into the familiar precinct of Half Moon
Street. He drew them smartly to the kerb before
Helen's narrow-fronted house. Joshua jumped down
and ran to their heads. Martin threw him the reins. 'I
don't know how long I'll be. Walk 'em if necessary.'

Martin strode purposefully up the steps. She was
going to say yes this time. He was not going to leave
until she did. He raised his hand to the knocker—and
froze.

The knocker was off the door.

He stared at the empty hinge from which it normally
hung—a small brass weight in the shape of a bell. Only
its outline remained.

Helen had gone out of town.

Abruptly, Martin turned on his heel and strode back
to his curricle. Surprised by his master's sudden return,
Joshua glanced up and opened his mouth, then shut it
again. Silently, he handed his master the reins and
scrambled up behind. From long experience, he knew
better than to ask questions when Mr Martin looked
like thunder.

Heading his team back into the traffic, Martin considered the Park, then decided against it. The last thing
he needed was inconsequential chatter. He turned his
horses towards Grosvenor Square mews. Soon, he was
striding back and forth before the fireplace in his
library, feeling caged and impotent.

Why? Why had she left?

The talk after the Barhams' ball could not have been

that bad. He might have committed a blunder under stress but he knew his London. The tattlemongers would have twittered over it for all of twenty-four hours, then forgotten it entirely.

So why had she gone?

To avoid him?

Martin thrust the thought aside, then, when no other explanation offered, reluctantly brought it back for examination. Too restless to sit, he prowled the room. Could she have thought he would repeat his performance—with Selina or whoever—and make her life a misery? With a frustrated growl, he shook his head. No—no he could not believe she would imagine he would hurt her—well, not more than the Barham effort. Given that they had developed a degree of understanding through the long hours they had spent together, she would know he would calm down after that—after he had seen her distress. Hell, he wanted to marry the woman—she could not believe he would hurt her. Could she?

Sunk in semi-guilt, Martin prowled the room.

A sudden realisation brought him to a halt. He raised his head and stared, unseeing, at his own reflection in the mirror above the mantelpiece. She could not have gone off to escape him—because he had taken himself off. With a sigh of relief, he sank into a chair. She would have realised within a day or so that he had left the capital. He doubted her friends would have sanctioned a withdrawal before that. So. . .

So why had she left? Perhaps the reason had nothing to do with their relationship? She had no immediate family; her friends were a select few, all of whom were presently residing in London. Perhaps Dorothea had taken ill and retired to the country? Recalling the last sight he had had of Hazelmere's lovely bride, Martin rejected that idea as unlikely.

Had Helen been forced to leave by something else entirely? The thought jerked Martin upright. After a moment's cogitation, he rose and tugged the bell-pull, insensibly relieved to have something concrete to do.

When Hillthorpe answered, he asked for Joshua.

Moments later, 'You wanted me, guv'nor?' broke across Martin's thoughts. He raised his head and beckoned Joshua closer.

'That gentleman I had you watch—Hedley Swayne. You mentioned you'd struck up a relationship with his man?'

Joshua wriggled his shoulders. 'Not so much a relationship as a drinking partnership, if you take my meaning?'

Martin did. He smiled, a touch grimly. 'That will do admirably. I want you to get over there now and find out what you can of Mr Swayne's recent exploits. Particularly, if he's had any unusual visitors—or if he's dressed down to attend any meeting. I expect that's something his man would notice.'

'Oh, he'd notice right enough. Went on a treat over the gent's new coloured silk neckerchiefs last time I saw him. The way he tells it, the swell only thinks of the rags on his back.'

Martin raised a brow. 'That's certainly the way he appears—but I know for certain there's at least one other thing Hedley Swayne exercises his wits over.' He fixed Joshua with a commanding eye. 'I want to know what Hedley Swayne's been up to this week—and I want to know as soon as possible.'

'Right-ho, guv'nor.'

With a cheery half-salute, Joshua left.

He was back far faster than Martin had anticipated.

'He's gone—bolted.'

'*What*?' Martin exploded out of the chair he had slumped into. 'When?'

'Seems like the gentleman's taken hisself and his man and his usual escort—whatever that might mean—off to his estates. In Cornwall, they be, so the housekeeper said. They left two days ago.'

'Two days,' Martin mused, pacing back and forth on the hearthrug. 'Any reason given?'

Joshua shook his head. He watched his master stalk the room, then, when no further orders came his way, he asked, 'D'ye want me to keep watch—to see when he returns?'

Martin stopped his pacing. He looked at Joshua, then slowly shook his head. 'I've a nasty suspicion that when he returns it'll be too late.' With a nod, he dismissed Joshua and renewed his striding. It helped him to think.

There was no necessary connection between Helen's leaving town and Hedley Swayne's departure. That did not mean there wasn't one. Martin swore. He wished he had followed up the peculiar Mr Swayne's abduction attempt. His preoccupation with making Helen Walford his wife—and thus safe from such as Hedley Swayne—had pushed that little incident to the back of his mind. His memories of it had been overlaid by far more interesting recollections of Helen herself.

Shaking such recollections aside, Martin acknowledged his worries. He wanted answers and the only way of finding them was to ask questions—of the right people. And, in this instance, the right people were undoubtedly the Hazelmeres.

When a rapid reconnoitre of the gentlemen's clubs drew a blank, Martin presented himself at Hazelmere House. To his surprise, although Mytton was as gracious as ever and went immediately to inform his master, ensconced in his library, of his arrival, he was kept kicking his heels in the black- and white-tiled hall for what seemed like an age. Eventually, the library door opened.

Dorothea emerged, the heir in her arms.

If she had looked daggers at him at the Barhams', this afternoon she had added spears and crossbows to her armoury. Bemused, Martin reflected that he should, by all accounts, be dead.

With a decidedly cool nod, Dorothea turned on her heel and climbed the stairs. The stiffness of her spine bespoke her disapproval.

Martin raised his brows slightly at the sight. He was not overly surprised that she should still be so starchy—he had yet to make his peace with Helen and Dorothea was, after all, Helen's closest friend. But there was a haughtiness in her disapproval that evoked memories of how the matrons had looked at him thirteen years earlier.

Mytton approached. 'His lordship will see you now, my lord.'

There was nothing, of course, to be learned from Mytton's impassive countenance. Martin followed him to the library.

Inside, he discovered that his pricking thumbs were justified. Hazelmere was standing by the long French windows, open to the afternoon breeze. His stance, rigid and unyielding, warned Martin that something indeed was up, even before he drew close enough to see the stony hazel gaze.

Martin stopped by a chair, laying one hand on its back. He raised a laconic brow and sighed. 'What am I supposed to have done now?'

There was an infinitesimal pause while Hazelmere assimilated the information underlying that question. Then his features eased. 'Don't you know?' he asked, his voice slightly strangled.

'Other than losing my head at the Barhams' the other night, I'm not aware that I've transgressed any of the immutable laws.'

'Not even *before* the Barhams' ball?'

At the quiet question, Martin's gaze locked with his friend's. After a long moment, Martin moved around the chair in front of him and slowly sank into it. 'Oh.'

'Precisely.' Slowly, Hazelmere came forward to sit in the chair facing his guest. 'I take it I don't need to ask if it's true?'

Martin threw him a grimace. 'I did say I was going to cure her, didn't I?'

Hazelmere acknowledged that with a resigned nod. 'I hadn't, however, imagined you would allow such an item to become public property.'

'*Public property*?' Martin was on his feet and pacing. 'Bloody hell!' he growled. 'How the hell did that get out?'

Hazelmere viewed his friend's agitation with transparent satisfaction. 'I didn't think you knew anything about it.'

He spoke softly, but Martin caught the quiet comment. He swung about, brows knit in a furious frown.

'Of course I knew nothing of it! Why on earth. . .?' He stopped, struck, his face drained of expression. Slowly, he sank back into the chair. 'Dorothea—and everyone else—thinks I let the information slip?'

Succinctly, Hazelmere nodded. 'To Lady Rochester,' he added. 'She was spreading the tale shortly after you danced so briefly with her at the Barhams.'

Martin groaned and sank his head into his hands. How had Serena found out? A more worrying thought surfaced. He looked up. 'Helen can't believe that surely?'

A frown had invaded Hazelmere's face 'To be perfectly honest, I don't know what Helen thinks—I haven't had a chance to ask her. She's disappeared—gone out of town. I'd hoped you might know where she was, but obviously that's not the case.'

'I came to ask if you knew where she was.' Martin straightened, his worry overcoming his frown. 'I left town early on the morning after the ball. What exactly happened?'

Hazelmere told him, briefly, concisely. 'So Dorothea and Ferdie left her to think things through. The next morning, she left.'

'Damn!' Martin stood again, automatically falling to pacing before the hearth. With an effort, he forced himself to evaluate the situation coolly. 'Luckily, the position's not irretrievable. Once we marry, it'll cease to be news.'

Hazelmere inclined his head in agreement. 'True. But, if you don't mind my curiosity, when, exactly, is the wedding?'

The glance Martin shot him contained equal parts of

frustration and sheer exasperation. 'The witless wanton wouldn't accept.'

For once, the hazel eyes opened wide in honest surprise. Black brows rising, Hazelmere considered his wayward charge. 'What on earth is she about?' he eventually asked.

'Damned if I know,' Martin muttered. 'But if I can lay hands on her, you can rely on me to shake some sense into her.' Tired of pacing, he returned to his chair. 'Have you any idea where she might have gone?'

Hazelmere frowned. 'There aren't all that many options. I know she hasn't gone to one of my estates— I'd have heard by now. I can't imagine her going to an inn or any such.'

Martin shook his head. 'Too risky by half.'

Nodding sagely, Hazelmere continued, 'Which leaves Heliotrope Cottage.'

Martin looked his question.

'As I recall, I told you that none of Helen's properties was saved from the collapse of the Walford estates?' At Martin's nod, Hazelmere said, 'As far as substance goes, that's true. But Heliotrope Cottage was considered beneath the dignity of any gambler. Consequently, it's the one part of Helen's patrimony that remains hers. It's a tiny place on barely five acres. In Cornwall.'

'*Cornwall*?'

At Martin's incredulous exclamation, Hazelmere blinked. 'Yes. Cornwall. You know—it's that bit beyond Devon.'

Martin brushed his levity aside. 'I know where the damned place is but, what's more to the point, so does Hedley Swayne. His estates are there, too.'

Hazelmere's hazel gaze was confused. 'Quite a few people have estates in Cornwall.'

'But,' said Martin grimly, getting to his feet once more, 'none of the others has tried to kidnap Helen.'

Hazelmere blinked. 'I beg your pardon?'

Pacing again, Martin threw his explanation over his shoulder. 'I first met Helen not here but in a wood in Somerset, not far from Ilchester. She'd been grabbed from a ball by two ruffians. They were waiting with her for their client to arrive. From everything I've learned, that client was Hedley Swayne. Helen thought it was at the time.'

Hazelmere met his glance, then fell to considering the facts. 'It doesn't make sense,' he eventually said.

'I know it doesn't make sense,' Martin growled.

'We've all seen Swayne dancing about Helen's skirts, but I wouldn't have thought he'd have any real inclination in that direction.'

Martin shook his head. 'He's definitely not one of us.' A moment later, he added, 'There must be some reason that we can't see. But whatever it is I'd much rather Helen was safe before I shake the answer from Hedley Swayne.'

With that, Hazelmere was in complete agreement. 'Will you go down or will I?'

'Oh, I'll go, if you'll give me her direction. I intend having a very long talk with your wife's dearest friend. After that, I rather think we'll return by way of Merton.' At the thought of taking Helen to the Hermitage, Martin's features eased for the first time that day.

Hazelmere nodded and stood. 'I'll write the route down—it's not exactly straightforward.'

Armed with a complicated set of directions which

Hazelmere assured him would take him to the door of
Heliotrope Cottage, Martin departed from Hazelmere
House, pausing at the last to request Hazelmere to
speak to his wife regarding her killing glances.

As soon as he crossed his threshold in Grosvenor
Square, Martin issued a stream of orders, which culminated in his sending Joshua scurrying to harness the
bays while he strode upstairs to throw a selection of
clothes into a bag. Laying shirts and a supply of freshly
laundered cravats in the base of the bag, Martin grimaced. He would have to get a valet if he was set on
observing all the niceties. Men such as he were
expected to have one, but he had managed well enough
without throughout his eventful life. Nevertheless, if he
was to settle down to socially acceptable wedded bliss,
a valet seemed inevitable. The idea of marriage halted
him mid-stride.

Who knew what situation he would face in Cornwall?
Who knew to what lengths he might have to go to
convince Helen to say yes? All in all, the insurance of
being able to secure his prize the very instant she
agreed to his proposal seemed advisable.

A wry grin twisted Martin's lips. He resumed his
packing, mentally rehearsing his plea to the Bishop of
Winchester, a connection of his father's who would
doubtless be only too pleased to do what he could to
entangle a rake past redemption in the sacred toils of
matrimony.

The bed at the Four Swans was lumpy. Ruefully reflecting
that easy living had exacted a toll from his tolerance,
Martin stretched out and closed his eyes. The day had
been unwarrantedly full.

First, his arrival in London, full of his plans for fair Juno, plans which were dashed by her absence. Then his interview with Hazelmere, and his preparations for his journey. As it had been his secretary's day off, he had decided to go through the pile of mail placed waiting on his desk before quitting his house for an indeterminate time. He had found Helen's brief note in the pile, with a scrawled message from his secretary appended. Initially, he had been downcast that she had appealed for his help and he had not been there to assist her. Then the implication of her appeal had struck him.

Despite the hurt he had inflicted, she had not balked from summoning him; she had clearly envisaged being able to play a part, with him by her side to conceal their illicit liaison. All in all, it would not have been hard, together. They would simply have pretended nothing was amiss—none, he was sure, would have pressed the point.

But the important feature of her call for help was that she had been prepared to see him again, to speak with him again. That was, Martin felt, definitely encouraging.

He sighed and settled his shoulders. Things were looking up. The drive from London to Winchester had been accomplished in time for him to be invited to sup at his Grace's board. His ageing relative had proved much as he had imagined, but more curious than censorious. A special licence had been duly provided. Thus armed, he was looking forward to the second day after the next with keen anticipation.

Even if he left early the next morning, it would still take him more than two days to reach Heliotrope

Cottage. Two more days in which to polish his apologies and frame his proposal while keeping his cattle on the road. He had nearly landed them in a ditch this evening. He would have to make sure he kept sufficient wits functioning to drive; he could not bear any further delay.

He still could not fathom how the fact of their afternoon together had been broadcast to the *ton*. However, rake that he was, he recognised the added weapon the potential scandal gave him. It would have to be wielded with care, of course, and only if Helen still showed reluctance. No woman liked to feel jockeyed into any decision; none knew that better than he. Somehow, he would have to ensure that the idea of marrying him as the most socially acceptable course was subtly conveyed to his love.

No light had yet glowed on her reasons for refusing him; in truth, if she was simply too wary to try marriage again, the only way he could think of to convince her was to marry her and consequently demonstrate how wrong she was. A little gentle persuasion was surely excusable in such circumstances?

With a slight frown, Martin shook aside such quibbles and let his usual positive attitude resurface. He wanted Helen Walford to wife, therefore, however it came about, she would marry him. It was in her own best interests, after all.

The moonlight streamed in through the open window, a slight breeze wafted the net curtains. Martin felt sleep take hold. His dreams would doubtless be of the last inn bed he had slept in—and his fair companion in dreams.

CHAPTER ELEVEN

WAS it two spoons of milk or only one? Helen rubbed a floury hand across her brow and struggled to remember Janet's instructions. She had sent her maid to the mill just outside the tiny village half a mile away, to buy more flour. Meanwhile, she had decided to use what was left and make some bread.

She had never cooked anything before—other than the pancakes she had assisted with during that night in the old barn. Even then, *he* had actually done the cooking. At the thought of him, whom she refused to acknowledge by name in the vain hope that that would assist her mind in forgetting him, Helen's eyes filled. Annoyed, she blinked rapidly. She sniffed. Damn! She had never been the sniffy sort but, ever since leaving London, she had hovered on the brink of tears. It would not do—she had to pull herself together and get on with her life. No matter how lacking in all enticement that life now seemed. For a while, he had filled her with hopes for the future. They had come to nought, but her life was not, in truth, any more drab than it had been before. She tried to reason with her emotions, to no avail. All they seemed capable of dwelling on was her misery at losing him.

Helen gritted her teeth and plunged both hands into her dough. Her sudden urge to action was simply an attempt to get some purpose, however inconsequential, into her life. The past five days had disappeared in a dull daze, the fine weather outside clouded by her misery. Heliotrope Cottage was comfortable enough but, without menservants, Janet had to do everything. Helen poked at the dough disparagingly and reflected that she would have to see about hiring a young girl to come in and help with the cleaning and cooking, and maybe find a gardener as well.

The kitchen was a sunny nook, part of the large room that made up the ground floor of the cottage. A window beside the table at which she stood looked out over the small kitchen garden. The plot was currently overgrown, choked with a full season's weeds, but reddish earth showed in one corner where Janet had made a start on clearing it. Helen breathed deeply of the tangy breeze wafting in through the open door of the cottage, to play with her curls before whisking out again through the back door. With a grimace, she regarded the floury mass in the copper basin. It must have been two spoonfuls.

She was replacing the milk jug on the dresser when the sound of horses' hooves and the sliding thump of heavy carriage wheels rolling down the rutted lane came to her ear. Helen froze. Then her heart started to pound, faster and faster as anticipation rose.

The cottage stood at the end of the lane; there was no passing traffic. Who was it who had come to visit her?

The likely answer addled her wits.

Then she heard a voice, a light voice, giving instructions, and knew it was not the Earl of Merton who had called.

Disappointment sent her back to despair.

Consequently, when a sharp rap came on the doorframe, she made no move to take her hands from the copper basin, but called out, 'Come in!' in as interested a tone as she could manage.

To her surprise, it was Hedley Swayne's slight figure that appeared in the doorway. 'Lady Walford?'

Helen stifled her sigh. Country hospitality demanded that she at least invite him in for refreshment. 'Come in, Mr Swayne.' She waited until her unexpected visitor had mincingly picked his way across her small front room, his features registering disapproval of her rustic surrounds, before commenting, 'I had hardly looked to see anyone from London hereabouts. To what do I owe the pleasure of your visit?'

'Dear lady.' Hedley Swayne bowed effusively. 'Just a neighbourly visit.' When Helen looked her confusion, he added, 'I own Creachley Manor.'

Creachley Manor? Helen blinked. If that was so, Hedley was, in fact, her nearest neighbour. The lands attached to the Manor all but enclosed hers; it was the largest single holding in the immediate area.

'I see,' she said. 'How very thoughtful of you.' She waved a whitened hand at a nearby chair and watched as Hedley disposed himself upon it, fussing about the arrangement of his coat-tails. Dismay was her predominant reaction—to his visit and to the news that he was so closely situated. She did not trust his airy excuse one bit. 'But how did you know I was here?'

For an instant, Hedley's pale eyes went perfectly blank. 'Er. . .ah, that is to say. . .heard about it. On the village grapevine, if you know what I mean.'

Helen inclined her head civilly. Having lived in the country for most of her life, she knew perfectly well what he meant, but, although it often amazed her with its speed, no village grapevine worked that fast. She and Janet had arrived late in the evening; their post-chaise and post-boys had immediately returned to the road for London. Today was the first day anyone in the village could know of their arrival and that only through Janet's appearance at the mill. Hedley Swayne was lying, but to what purpose?

'Could I offer you some tea, sir?'

Hedley looked slightly perturbed at the suggestion. His roving gaze alighted on a small decanter on the sideboard. Helen saw it and correctly divined that the fastidious Mr Swayne did not partake of tea. 'Or perhaps some cowslip wine would be more to your taste?'

To this, Hedley Swayne agreed readily. Sending silent thanks to her cook in London, who had slipped a bottle of her delicious wine into the provisions Janet had packed, Helen lifted her hands from her basin and looked in consternation at the gooey mess covering her fingers.

'Er. . .perhaps if you'd just tell me where the glasses are?'

Appeased by this show of neighbourly good sense, Helen directed Hedley to the cupboard beneath the sideboard. She watched as her visitor arose and helped himself, her brow creasing as she struggled to understand just what he was about this time. His visit was not driven by pure neighbourly concern, of that she was sure. But what did he hope to achieve? His dress was as finicky as ever, better suited to the Grand Strut than a small cottage in deepest Cornwall. The coat of puce cloth was offset by yellow pantaloons; a wide floppy yellow neckerchief tied in a bow proclaimed his allegiance to fashionable fripperies. As with most of the fops, he disdained the highly polished Hessians of the Corinthians, opting instead for heeled shoes, in this case sporting gold buckles. There was a gold pin in the neckerchief and a huge fob watch vied with a range of seals for prominence against a perfectly hideous purple embossed silk waistcoat. Considering the spectacle, Helen reflected that it was almost as if Hedley had dressed to impress. Unfortunately, in his present surroundings, he only succeeded in looking woefully out of place.

Her own dull olive gown, with its round neck and simple sleeves, was far more in keeping with the country atmosphere. Its colour did nothing for her complexion, drawn and sallow after days of weeping. Not that she cared. There was no reason to make the most of herself; she did not desire to impress her neighbours—not even be they Hedley Swayne.

Pouring himself a generous measure of cowslip wine, Hedley returned to his chair. 'I must say, dear Lady Walford, that it's a pleasure to see a woman such as yourself engaged in such a womanly pursuit.'

Helen eyed his smile warily. His attitude was one of a man well-pleased, almost smug, as if he had solved some fiendishly difficult problem and was looking forward to claiming his prize. Helen's unease grew, but she merely nodded, wondering what to say next. Luckily, Hedley had an inexhaustible flow of patter. He rambled on, and, at first, she thought his direction aimless. Then, as she followed his recitation of *ton* events, she started to perceive a pattern to his revelations. They were all concerned with recent scandals and how these had adversely affected the women involved. In particular, how the unfortunate proceedings had affected the subsequent marriageability of the women involved. She made the right noises at the right places, which was all Hedley required to keep him going while she wondered if she dared guess at his summation.

It was as she had suspected.

'Actually,' he said pausing to take a sip of his wine, 'I left the capital six days ago. So ennervating—the Season—don't you think?'

Helen murmured appropriately.

'And then, too,' said Hedley, examining his fingernails, 'there was a distressing rumour going the rounds.'

And that, thought Helen, is enough. 'Indeed?' She infused the single word with arctic iciness. To her dismay, the effect was not at all what she had hoped.

'My dear, dear Lady Walford!' Hedley Swayne was on his feet and approaching.

Helen's eyes grew round as she saw him place his glass on the table. She stood rooted to the spot in surprise as he advanced on her, arms spread wide as if intending to scoop her ample charms into his embrace. When one arm slipped about her, Helen came to her senses with a jolt. 'Mr Swayne!' She brought up her hands to ward him off. To her surprise, he jumped back, as if she had threatened him with a burning brand. Then she focused on her fingers and realised they were still liberally coated with dough.

When Hedley stared, nonplussed, at the threat to his immaculate suiting, Helen struggled to swallow her giggles. Determinedly, she replaced her hands in the dough. As long as her fingers constituted such deadly weapons, she was safe. 'Mr Swayne,' she reiterated, striving for calm. 'I have no idea what rumours you have heard, but I assure you I do not wish to discuss them.'

Hedley Swayne frowned, clearly piqued at having his orchestrated performance cut short. 'All very well for you to say, m'dear lady,' he said peevishly. 'But people will talk, y'know.'

'I dare say,' Helen replied discouragingly. 'But whatever they might say is of no concern to me. Rumour is rumour and nothing more.'

'Ah, yes. But this rumour is rather more specific than usual,' Hedley continued, then, when he glanced up at his hostess and saw the wrath gathering in her clear eyes, he hurriedly expostulated, 'But that wasn't what I came here to say—dear me, no!'

'Mr Swayne,' said Helen, suddenly very weary of his company, 'I really don't think that you could have anything to say, on that subject or any other, that I wish to hear.'

'Now don't be too hasty, dear lady.' Hedley Swayne took a step back and, to Helen's wary gaze, seemed to reorganise his forces. 'I suggest you listen to my reasoning before you make any intemperate judgements.'

Helen's lips thinned. Her gaze as bleak as she could make it, she steeled herself to hear him out.

Encouraged by her silence, Hedley Swayne drew a portentous breath. 'I regret the need to speak plainly, m'dear lady, but your recent indiscretion with a peer— who shall remain nameless—is the talk of the town. We all understand, of course,' he went on, 'that this association is at an end.' He took several paces towards the door, then turned to look sternly at Helen. 'Naturally, the entire episode, and the consequent publicity,

has left you in an unenviable position. That being so,'
he stated, pacing back towards her again, 'you must be
glad of any offer that will reinstate you in the eyes of
society—the censorious eyes of society.'

Helen had no difficulty restraining her laughter at
his measured periods; she could see where his argu-
ments were headed.

'Thus, my dear Lady Walford, you see me here in
the guise of a knight in shining armour. I am come to
offer you the protection of my name.'

There was no help for it but to make her refusal as
gracious as she could. Helen suspected his motives
were not nearly as pure as he made out, but had no
wish to antagonise the man unnecessarily, a neighbour
at that. 'Mr Swayne, I do most sincerely value your
proposal but I'm afraid I have no intention of marrying
again.'

'Oh, there's no need to fear I'll claim any rights over
the marriage dear lady. A marriage in name only is
what I propose. Why, you're a widow and I—I'm a
man about town. I'm sure we'll deal famously. No need
for you to entertain any worries on that head.'

Unbeknown to Hedley Swayne, his declaration, far
from easing Helen's fears, only added to the deadening
misery threatening to pull her down. Martin had
offered her so much more—and she had had to refuse
him. How cruel of fate to send Hedley Swayne with his
mockery of a proposal in the Earl of Merton's place.
'Mr Swayne, I truly——'

'No, no! Don't be hasty. Just think of the advantages.
Why, it'll put paid to all the rumours—you'll be able
to return to London immediately, rather than languish
in this backwater.'

'I enjoy the country.'

'Ah. . .yes.' For a moment, Hedley's lights dimmed. Then he brightened. 'Well if that's the case, you can take up residence at Creachley. No problem there. Can't abide the place myself, but there's no need for you to come back to town if you don't favour it.'

Helen drew herself up haughtily. 'Mr Swayne, I cannot—will not—accept your proposal. Please,' she said, holding up one dough-encased hand to halt his reaction, 'say no more on the matter. I have no intention of remarrying. My decision is final.'

Hedley's weak-featured face turned sulky. 'But you must marry me—stands to reason. Merton won't marry you. He's ruined you and now there's nothing left for it but that you must marry. You should marry me, indeed you should.'

What little reserve was left to Helen evaporated at his petulant tone. 'Mr Swayne, I am not constrained to marry anyone!'

Hedley returned her glare belligerently.

Just how long they would have remained so, locked in a contest of wills, Helen was destined never to learn, for at that moment the sounds of an arrival reached them. Another carriage, wonder of wonders. Her breathing oddly suspended, Helen waited, eyes glued to the door, to see who it was this time.

When a large, well-remembered broad-shouldered figure blocked out the light, she was not sure whether to feel relieved or apprehensive. She might have guessed Martin would come to find her.

The cool gaze swept the room, alighting on the occupants frozen in a most peculiar tableau. Martin instantly realised he had walked in on an altercation of sorts. As if on a stage, Helen stared at him from the other side of a deal table, her hands sunk in a copper basin, her golden curls rioting about her face. One glance was enough to tell him that she had not been taking care of herself as she should. Annoyance at her unwise bolt from the capital, which had developed over the long miles from London, grew. But his immediate concern was to relieve her of the obviously unwelcome presence of Hedley Swayne.

Martin nodded coolly to Helen and strolled into the room. Then he turned his attention to Hedley Swayne. 'Swayne.' With the curtest of nods, Martin acknowledged Hedley Swayne's flustered bow. The man's face was evidence enough that he had heard the rumours. Had he had the temerity to approach Helen with them? Martin decided that the sooner Hedley Swayne left, the safer it would be—for Hedley Swayne. 'But I believe you were about to leave, Mr Swayne?'

Hedley Swayne swallowed. He glanced nervously at Helen.

Helen sensed his glance but did not return it, too busy drinking in a sight she had convinced herself she would never see again. It meant that she would have to argue with him again, but, right now, she did not care. Just the sound of his deep, raspy voice had sent tingles down her spine. She was alive again. Her eyes roamed the large figure, noting the broad shoulders stretching the blue material of his coat, and the long sweep of muscled thighs encased in buckskin breeches. One lock of thick dark hair had fallen across his brow. She had forgotten the excitement his mere presence generated; for a moment, at least, she would bask in the warmth.

'Actually—no.'

The tentative response concentrated Martin's attention firmly on the flustered fop. 'What do you mean, no?'

Sheer aggression vibrated in Martin's growl. Helen blinked and realised the danger. Good God—the last thing she needed was to have to save Hedley Swayne from annihilation by throwing herself into the breach! Knowing Martin, that was what it would take, once he got started.

'What I mean, my lord,' said Hedley, screwing his courage to its highest pitch, 'is that before you interrupted, her ladyship and I were engaged in a delicate negotiation and I really don't think it would be at all considerate of me to leave before we've come to an agreement on the matter.'

A black scowl had invaded Martin's face. When the stormy grey gaze flicked her way, Helen was no longer sure which of her suitors it was safest to encourage. Martin radiated menace. He also looked very determined. His jaw was set, his eyes were cold. Just how far he would go to gain her consent to their marriage she did not feel qualified to judge. Hedley she was sure she could manage; Martin she was sure she could not.

Martin stalked the few paces to the other side of the table. 'Just what sort of "delicate negotiation" were you discussing?'

Helen wished she could have kicked Hedley but he was too far away. Predictably, the fool thrust his chin in the air and stated. 'As a matter of fact, we were discussing a topic I doubt you have any interest in, my lord. We were discussing marriage.'

Martin's black brows flew. 'I see. Whose?'

Helen closed her eyes.

Hedley blinked. 'Why—ours, naturally.' He bridled, but before he could say more Martin's deep voice, carefully controlled, cut him off.

'Contrary to your suppositions, I rather suspect I'm close to becoming an expert on marriage proposals.'

His grey gaze flicked Helen's way. Opening her eyes in time to catch it, she suppressed a wince.

'As it happens, I've already proposed to Lady Walford. I'm here to repeat that proposal and ask for her ladyship's. . .final answer.'

Hedley Swayne's jaw dropped.

Helen resisted the impulse to close her eyes and fake a faint. The subtle emphasis on the last two words did not escape her. Martin was telling her this was the last time—the last chance she would have to grab happiness. He had turned until he was facing her. The grey eyes were watchful, sharply acute. Then, as she watched, a slight smile twisted his long lips.

'Well, my dear?' The grey gaze became slightly mocking, distinctly untrustworthy. 'Now that our liaison is public property, it would seem the only respectable solution for you is marriage. It seems you have a choice. The Countess of Merton or Mrs Swayne. Which is it to be?'

Helen only just managed to swallow her gasp. *Outrageous*! He had jockeyed her into the position of accepting one of them, or appearing a reckless wanton, blind to society's rules. Her instinctive response to his manipulation was to reject them both summarily. Martin, at least, knew she did not have to marry. He, damn his grey eyes, was merely using the situation to

further his ends. She opened her mouth but was forestalled by his deep, gravelly voice.

'Think carefully, my dear, before you choose.'

The look in his eyes warned her that flat rejection of
them both would not work. Helen drew a tortured
breath and struggled to think. Hedley Swayne was
looking at her in fascinated wonder. The fact that she
had not immediately leaped to accept Martin's proposal no doubt gave him heart. If she refused them
both, then she would face continued pressure, not just
from one, but from both. Martin might say it was her
final chance—she did not believe him. He was determined and she suspected few had successfully gainsaid
him—not in the past thirteen years. Hedley, on the
other hand, would hold out hope undiminished if she
rejected Martin. He, too, would persist—he had for the
past twelve months, with even less encouragement.

Her gaze locked with the grey eyes across the table,
Helen felt all her strength drain. Frowning, she dragged
her eyes from Martin's and, automatically, put up her
hand to push back her curls. Both men moved to stop
her. Startled, she remembered the state of her hands
and, just in time, used her wrist instead. 'Give me a
moment to think,' she pleaded.

Her tone twisted through Martin. He frowned. What
the devil did she have to think about? He loved her,
she loved him—there was no reason to cogitate. She
looked so weary, he was tempted to pick her up and
put her to bed—to sleep. Which said a great deal about
the state to which love had reduced him. Right now,
all he wanted was a yes to his proposal, and after that
Helen badly needed looking after—all else took second
place. The presence of Hedley Swayne was a bonus.

He knew Helen's instinctive dislike of the man—nothing overly strong but simply the natural antipathy of a beautiful woman for a man who had no use for beautiful women. It was, he suspected, just the situation to break down her barriers. He needed her to say yes—after that, he was prepared to devote his life to ensuring that she never regretted it—in fact, to ensuring that she enjoyed her second marriage as completely as she had disliked her first. He waited for her answer, supremely confident as to what it would be.

Helen wished the ground would open up and swallow her, that Janet would arrive and break the deadlock, anything at all to get out of making her choice. She did not want to marry Hedley Swayne. But, with every passing minute, that fate took firmer shape.

She had not expected to see Martin again, not after his brutal dismissal of her and his slap in the face at the Barhams' ball. That had all been reaction, of course, natural, no doubt, in a man of his temperament. But she had imagined that that would be the end of it; why, then, was he here? The answer was staring her in the face, stated plainly in his words. Her heart contracted painfully. He had come because of the scandal.

How could she have forgotten? Agonised as she imagined what his feelings must be, finding himself once more forced to make an offer by the weight of the *ton's* displeasure, she pressed her hands tightly together inside her dough. He was now the Earl of Merton and would be expected to play by society's rules. Thus, he would be expected to offer for her. But if she accepted, his mother would, she felt sure, have no compunction in disinheriting him. He would lose his dream. She could save him from both fates—social ignominy and maternal retribution—by the simple expedient of marrying Hedley Swayne. If she were already engaged to marry Hedley, Martin would be absolved from offering her his name in place of her reputation. He would then be free to marry a lady of whom his mother approved, and thus gain his most desired objective.

Martin shifted his weight. Helen noticed; her time was running out. She glanced up and met his gaze. Something of her decision must have shown in her eyes, for, as she watched, his brows descended and his eyes grew stormy.

'I've made up my mind,' she announced, afraid that if she did not get it out quickly her courage would fail her. Her eyes remained on Martin's face an instant longer before she turned to Hedley Swayne. 'Mr Swayne, I accept your proposal.'

Hedley Swayne gawked at her. 'Oh. I mean—yes, of course! Delighted, m'dear.'

The silence from across the table was awful. Helen forced herself to look. Stunned astonishment held Martin's features immobile for a fleeting moment, then the hurt she had expected showed for the briefest of instants before a mask of impassivity put an end to all revelations. With dreadful civility, he bowed, his natural grace so much more polished than Hedley's flamboyant rendition.

'You've made your choice—I wish you happy, my dear.' He glanced up and met her gaze. His eyes were cold and stony, grey upon grey, his face a mask. 'I pray you'll not regret the bargain you've made this day.'

His eyes held hers for one last, agonised minute, then he turned on his heel and left.

Helen stood by the table, slowly extricating her hands from the mess of her dough. She was deaf to Hedley's garrulous self-congratulations, her ears straining to catch the sound of Martin's retreating carriage. When the rumble had finally died in the distance, she moved slowly to the chair by the end of the table and sank into it. Then, as the full measure of what she had lost, of what she had committed herself to, became clear, she leaned her arms on the table and, laying her forehead upon them, gave way to her tears.

The crackle of flames came from behind him but, although he felt chilled to the bone, Martin made no move to turn his chair to the fire. If he did, he would see the mantelpiece. Which in turn would remind him of the woman he had left to her fate that morning in Cornwall.

He could not believe she had accepted Hedley Swayne over him. His frown turned to a scowl. He took a long swig of the amber fluid in his glass. The most damning thought of all was the certain knowledge that by forcing his unholy ultimatum upon her he had driven her into Hedley Swayne's arms. That thought threatened to drive him mad. He felt like howling with rage. Instead, he drained his glass and reached for the decanter on the small table at his elbow.

Outside the uncurtained windows, the stars shone in a black sky. It had been full dark before he had reached the Hermitage, even driving in a frenzy as he had been. Joshua had been silent the entire way, a sure sign of dire disapproval. How long he had sat in the darkened library, drowning his sorrows in the time-honoured way, he did not know. Pentley, his new butler, had entered to suggest dinner but he had ordered him out. All he wanted to do was wallow in his misery—and drink himself into a stupor sufficiently deep to let him sleep.

He had lost her—irretrievably; nothing else mattered any more.

The doors to the hall opened. Martin glowered through the dark, preparing an acid rebuke for whoever had dared to disturb his despair. His eyes, adjusted to the gloom, detected no one until, awkwardly, a chair came hesitantly into the room. It stopped just inside the doors, then they shut behind it.

Stifling a curse, Martin rose to his feet. His mother had come down to him. Who the hell had told her he had arrived?

Drawing on considerable experience, he summoned the skills required to cross the long room to his mother's side. He kissed her hand, then her cheek. 'Mama. There was no need for you to come down—I would have called on you at a more fitting hour tomorrow.'

'Yes, I dare say you would prefer me to leave you in peace to drink yourself into oblivion, but, before you've entirely lost your wits, there's something I have to tell you.'

Through the dark, Martin frowned. 'I'm not in the mood to listen to homilies or any such, ma'am.'

Catherine Willesden's lips twisted. 'This is more in the nature of information. Information I think you would wish to hear sooner rather than later.' When her aggravating son made no effort to move, she grimaced. 'Do come to, Martin! You can't be *that* addled yet. Light a candle for goodness' sake; I'm not particularly fond of the dark. And, if you please, you can push me nearer the fire.'

With a deep sigh, Martin accepted the inevitable and did as he was told. He could not imagine what she had to tell him, but in his present befuddled state, he was not up to arguing with her. But once he had lighted a single candle and placed the candlestick on a table beside her chair, drawn up before the fire as requested, he retreated to his own chair, still engulfed in shadows, moving it back so that he could see his mother but still be largely screened from the mantelpiece.

As he sat, he noticed that her face was more drawn and pinched than he recalled. 'Have you been well?'

With a little start, she raised her eyes to his face. 'Oh, yes. Quite well. But,' she temporised, 'I've had rather a lot on my mind, of late.'

'Such as?'

She threw him a darkling glance. 'For a start, I suppose I should tell you that, as far as the question of Serena Monckton goes, I've known for some considerable time that her charge was without foundation.'

Silence stretched, then, 'Did my father know?'

Catherine Willesden shook her head. 'No, I only learned the truth from Damian some years after John died. But I gather most people now suspect the truth.'

For a long moment, she kept her gaze on her interlaced fingers, then, when no comment came, she glanced up through the shadows.

Martin shrugged. 'It doesn't matter any more. That's all history.'

Slowly, his mother nodded. 'I did consider sending for you, but, from everything I'd heard, it seemed you were enjoying yourself hugely and, very likely, wouldn't have heeded the summons anyway.'

A bark of laughter answered her. 'Very true.' Martin reached for his glass.

The Dowager caught the flash of the flames on the cut crystal and decided she would do well to make a long story short. 'Ever since you've returned and rejoined society, I've heard tell of you, from my friends' letters. What worried me was that, despite the fact he's been on the town for close to four years, I've never heard anything of Damian. That led me to ask some questions of my closest acquaintances. The answers were hardly conducive to a mother's peace of mind.' She paused to stare through the shadows at Martin. 'Is it true Damian is one of the louts who frequent such places as Tothill Fields, drinking gin and getting up to all manner of disgraceful exploits?'

There was a long pause before Martin answered. 'As far as I know, that's true.'

Catherine Willesden looked down at her hands and sighed. 'I suppose that explains some of what's happened. I just couldn't credit it that a son of mine could have behaved as he has, but clearly he's been off the tracks for some time.'

'In my esteemed brother's defence, I feel compelled to point out that he's had precious little guidance from any source. But what's he done now?'

The question flustered the Dowager. In her lap, her stiff fingers laced and unlaced awkwardly. 'I'm very much afraid that something I said put the whole business into his mind. You mustn't blame him entirely.'

Slowly, Martin sat up. 'Blame him for what?'

The Dowager winced at his tone. But she stuck to

her guns, determined to present the matter in the most accurate way. If Martin wished to disown them all after hearing it, so be it. 'As you know,' she began, 'Damian was always my favourite—more than anything else because he was the last of you and so much younger. Also,' she added, determined to be truthful, 'because he was more ingratiating than the rest of you. You, certainly.'

'I know all this.'

'Yes, well what you may not know is that Damian has long imagined that he would eventually succeed to the title. If not to George, then to you. The catalogue of your past exploits reads like a deathwish. Furthermore, you'd shown not the smallest desire to wed. Naturally, Damian thought that, in time, the Hermitage would be his.' The Dowager paused to assemble her thoughts, then hurried on. 'However, more importantly, Damian has been in the habit of coming to see me on flying visits, and when he has done anything he feels is particularly clever he tells me about it.'

'Boasts about it, I suppose.'

The Dowager nodded. 'Yes. I must confess that, when I was making plans for you, before you arrived, I mentioned them to Damian.' She paused, then looked up. 'I dare say you recall what those plans were?'

'Marrying me to some dull frump, as I recall.'

'Yes. And forcing you to it with the threat of disinheritance.'

Martin nodded. 'So?'

The Dowager drew breath. 'So, when Damian saw you getting too close to Helen Walford, he repeated my threat against you to her. He didn't know it wasn't the truth.' She glanced up and swallowed. Martin was no longer lounging in his chair. The shadowy figure was tense and intent.

'Are you telling me that Damian led Helen to believe that if she married me I'd lose all my supposed wealth?'

The suppressed energy vibrating beneath the slowly enunciated words all but paralysed the Dowager. Feeling very like prey in the presence of an enraged predator, she nodded.

'Aaaaaagh!' Martin sprang from his chair and strode about the room, all feeling of indolence vanquished. Halfway down the room, he abruptly turned and came back to stand in front of his mother. 'Was Damian the agent who spread the tale of Helen's spending the afternoon at Merton House?

The Dowager looked up into eyes like flint. All inclination to defend her wretched fourth son evaporated. She nodded. 'Yes, he admitted that, too. However, it seems as if he believed he was doing you a favour at the time.'

Martin paused in his pacing to throw an incredulous glance her way. '*Favour*?'

'I gather he was certain you'd broken off with Lady Walford. He thought to protect you from any claim made by her ladyship by ensuring that her reputation was already destroyed.'

When Martin simply stared at her, Catherine Willesden nodded. 'I know. He's not really very clever at all. He doesn't seem to understand how people should behave.'

Martin groaned. 'Where is he?'

'At the Bascombes', near Dunster. He said he'd be back in a few days.'

Martin nodded. 'I'll deal with him later.'

For five minutes, he paced the room, his brow furrowed as he pieced together the tangled web of his proposals and Helen's refusals. The damn woman had put him through hell, believing she was saving him from financial ruin. With an inward groan, he recalled his comment of not caring for his fortune, only for her. He had tripped himself up with his passionate avowal. But he had it all clear at last. Damian, of course, would have to be licked into shape, but first he had to extricate Helen from the mess her penchant for self-sacrifice had landed her in. Now he understood her steadfast refusals. She had decided to save him and nothing he had been able to say had swayed her. Gratifying, that, even if it had proved frustrating.

With an exasperated snort, Martin halted before the mantelpiece. His raving about his plans for the Hermitage and Merton House had doubtless played their part—he had gone out of his way to share his dreams with her, to make her see she was part of his life. Couldn't she see that his dreams would not be complete without her, here, where she belonged, in front of his hearth? How could she have believed he would value a house more than her—more than their love? Clearly, fair Juno required intense instruction on the whys and wherefores of a love match.

Glancing up, Martin noticed his mother's grey eyes, watching him in open concern. He smiled, for the first time that day. Going to her, he turned her chair from the fire. 'Thank you for your information, Mama. I'll take you to your rooms.'

'And then?' His mother twisted her head to look up at him.

'And then I'm for bed. At first light, I'm heading for Cornwall.'

'Cornwall?'

'Cornwall. I've a goddess to rescue from a fate worse than death.'

When his mother looked her question, Martin added, 'Being married to a fop.'

CHAPTER TWELVE

Wisps of fog wreathed outside the leaded panes of Helen's bedchamber window. She stood before it, listlessly brushing her hair, at one with the dismal chill of early morning. If she had had any sense, she would have stayed in bed. But she could not sleep; there had been no point in lying there, imagining what might have been. Trying to block out the future.

There was no escape. By her own choice, she had cast the die. Now she had to pay the price. She just had not expected the account to be presented quite so soon.

Hedley had a special licence. The man was a bundle of contradictions but could, apparently, organise himself well enough when sufficiently moved. And he had certainly been moved last night.

Helen bit her lip, her eyes fixed, unseeing, on the gloom outside. She had indulged in a rare exhibition of tears after Martin had left, sobbing for what had seemed like hours. Janet had returned and held her, rocking her like a child, soothing her with comforting nonsenses until, finally, she had been numb enough inside to stop. Only then had she become aware that Hedley Swayne was still there.

When he had explained the arrangements he had made, she had realised that he had left, but had returned to tell her of their wedding. The next day.

Today. This morning, in fact.

With a deep sigh, Helen moved listlessly to the window-seat and sank on to the simple cushions. She had spent half an hour arguing with Hedley, why she could not now recall. Martin was gone; it did not really matter when she married Hedley. In fact, for her purposes, perhaps sooner was best, as he had said? Once the knot was tied, Martin would be forever safe.

Again, Helen sighed. She could barely summon the energy to stand, let alone think. Thinking was too painful. If permitted to roam, her errant thoughts showed a depressing tendency to dwell on the bounty she would have reaped as Martin's wife, throwing into stark contrast the dismal prospect of marriage to Hedley. He had made it plain, in a burst of quite remarkable candour, that he considered theirs to be a marriage of convenience, nothing more. She was coming to understand that he was truly indifferent to her but, for some unfathomable reason, was equally steadfast in his desire to marry her.

Shaking her head, she raised her brush once more to her tresses, which were tangling about her shoulders. Hedley was beyond her understanding. More definitely within her grasp was the realisation that, in just a few hours, she would say the words which would condemn her to purgatory a second time around. Like a wet grey cloak, despair sat her shoulders, dragging her down. She would have to put on a brave face at the church, although she doubted there would be many there. Janet, of course, and Hedley's servants, but she did not know anyone else in the village. She did not even know the vicar.

Her brush stilled. Tears filled her eyes, then slowly

welled over to course down her cheeks and fall, unheeded, into her lap.

Minutes ticked by and the fog lifted, yet still the cloud of cold despair shrouded her heart.

Eventually, Janet came to her rescue. The maid fussed and prodded and poked and cajoled and at last she was ready—or as ready as she would ever be. Her bronze silk dress was the only one she had brought with her that was halfway suitable for the occasion, and even that was stretching tolerance a bit far. The low neckline and clinging skirts were intended for *ton* parties, not religious ceremonies. She had no bouquet but chose a small beaded purse to clutch. Her curls were set in the simple knot she preferred; she waved away the rouge pot, dismissing Janet's criticisms of her wan complexion.

Hedley had sent a carriage. Resigned to her fate, Helen allowed herself to be helped aboard.

The short journey to the village was accomplished far too fast. Descending before the lych-gate, Helen was surprised to find a small crowd gathered, country folk all, eager to view the unexpected happenings. She plastered a smile to her lips. As things were shaping, these people might well be her neighbours for the rest of her life.

Buxom farmers' wives bobbed their round faces in smiling greeting; their husbands, broad and brawny, grinned. Between the adults, children swarmed in a continuous stream. Suddenly, a freckle-faced miss bobbed up in Helen's path. Bright eyes, glowing with delight, looked up into Helen's face. A small hand held out a tightly packed bunch of flowers—daisies, lilies and assorted hedgerow blooms.

For an instant, Helen's determination faltered. She swayed slightly, but the necessity of taking the offering and suitably thanking the child took her past the dangerous moment. She would *not* think of what might have been—she could not afford his dreams and hers, too.

Relief swept through her when the cool dimness of the church porch engulfed her. Dragging in a deep breath, Helen saw that the tiny church was packed with locals, most likely Hedley's people from Creachley Manor, for they did not have the look of farmers, like those outside. Everyone had noticed her arrival. As she stood, frozen, at the entrance to the short nave, all heads turned slowly to view her.

With a last, desperate breath, Helen raised her head and walked forward.

Martin cracked his whip above the bays' ears, more to relieve his frustrations than to exhort his cattle to move faster. They were already rocketing along, the well-sprung curricle swaying dangerously. Joshua had been silent ever since they had passed out of the gates of the Hermitage just before sunrise.

Squinting against the glare, Martin took a blind curve at full speed. Six hours of sleep had cleared his head; the brandy he had consumed the evening before had been enough to ensure his slumber free from worry. But immediately the effects had worn off, he had woken—to a full realisation of the potential for disaster. Just because he now knew Helen's reasons for refusing him, it did not mean that he could afford to sit back in comfort and plan how to best reassure her of his wealth and the lack of necessity for her sacrifice.

Not when he had left her primed to make that sacrifice. Doubtless if he had been less experienced in the ways of the world, he would accept the widsom that, having got Helen's agreement to marriage, Hedley Swayne was unlikely to rush her to the altar. But he had not amassed a sizeable fortune in commodities by taking unnecessary risks—why should he take risks with his future?

Aside from anything else, a species of sheer terror rode him. What if he had misjudged Hedley Swayne? What if the fop really did desire Helen. What if he forced her to marry him forthwith? What if, given she was promised to him, the blackguard sought a down payment on his husbandly rights?

The whip cracked again; Martin gritted his teeth. Reason told him that, although pre-empting the marriage ceremony was precisely the sort of behaviour he would contemplate without a flicker of conscience, Hedley Swayne was not of that ilk. Reason was not enough. He wanted to make sure of Helen without delay.

As he checked his team for the turn into the narrower road leading to the village of St Agnes, Martin reviewed his options for getting rid of the redundant Mr Swayne. If necessary, he would buy him off. At the thought, Martin's lips twitched in a self-deprecatory smile. His father had paid a small fortune to extricate him from Serena Monckton's clutches. Now he was prepared to pay an even larger fortune to release Helen from her misguided promise to Hedley Swayne. Doubtless, as fair Juno herself had once observed, there was a moral in this somewhere.

It was market day at St Agnes, which proved a

severe trial to Martin's temper. He carefully edged the
curricle and his high-bred horses through the mêlée,
muttering curses at the delay. Then they were through
and heading out of the village to the hamlet of
Kelporth, beyond which Helen's little cottage lay.

Joshua had not thought it possible to be glad to see
such an out-of-the-way place as Kelporth again. Yet,
when they gained the crest of the small hill before the
village and went smartly down the lane towards it, he
heaved a decidedly heartfelt sigh of relief. He glanced
about at the neat little cottages, set back from the road
with their neat little gardens, tinged with autumn's
colours, before them. Ahead, to their left, a gaggle of
children were playing about the back of a carriage
drawn up to the side of the road. As they drew nearer,
Joshua made out the dark mass of a lych-gate and
surmised that a church must lie beyond. He paled, then
looked at the straight back of his master, presently
fully occupied with his fretting horses. Joshua coughed.
'Master, I don't rightly know as how this is important
but take a look to the left.'

'What now?' Martin snapped but did as directed.

The horses plunged, hauled to a halt so abrupt that
the curricle rocked perilously, nearly flinging Joshua
from his perch. He hung on grimly, then, as soon as it
was safe, jumped to the ground and ran as fast as his
stiff legs would allow to the horses' head. His master
had already sprung down, throwing the reins haphaz-
ardly towards him.

As Martin stared at the children playing in the dust
behind the carriage decked with white ribbons, his
blood ran cold. Slowly, he dragged his eyes from the
horrifying sight and raised them to the church door,

just visible through the lych-gate. What if she had married him already?

The thought jerked him into action. He ran up the path to the church, all but skidding to a halt in the stone-flagged porch. A few of the heads near the door turned his way, but he ignored them, his eyes going to the sight which held most of the congregation spellbound.

Was he too late? His heart was pounding so hard he could not hear. Martin clenched his fists and forced himself to calm down. Gradually, his hearing returning. He frowned. As he was not familiar with the words of the marriage ceremony, it was an agonising three minutes before he realised he had one last chance remaining. Hard on the heels of relief came the vicar's sonorous tones, 'Therefore if any man can show any just cause, why they may not lawfully be joined together, let him now speak, or else hereafter forever hold his peace——'

Martin waited for no further invitation. 'Yes!' he declared, adding, 'I do,' just in case the vicar had misunderstood. He strode forward, his boots echoing on the flags, his gaze fixed on the object of his desire.

At the totally unexpected sound of that deep voice, a voice she had convinced herself she would never hear again, Helen froze. Abruptly, she lost all feeling, all sense of time and place. Her breathing suspended, her eyes had grown round with disbelief even before she turned to find Martin all but upon her, his grey eyes clear and bright and burning with determination.

To her amazement, he took her arm in a vice-like grip.

'I want to talk to you.'

He would have drawn her out of the church then and there but for the combined expostulations of the vicar and the putative groom.

'I say, Merton, she agreed to marry me, y'know!'

'What *is* the meaning of this, sir?'

Martin looked at the vicar, a frown rapidly developing.

But the vicar, secure in his own house and thoroughly disapproving, was not readily cowed. 'This is a marriage ceremony. How dare you interrupt?'

Glancing up into Martin's arrogantly handsome face, Helen saw the cynical gleam in his eyes. Her heart sank. Oh, God! He was going to be outrageous.

'But you asked for objectors to speak up,' Martin replied reasonably. 'I'm merely obliging.'

For one instant, as the truth dawned, the vicar looked blank. Then he looked thunderstruck. 'You're *objecting*?' His gaze took in Martin's austerely expensive dress, and his commanding visage. Then the vicar turned to gaze at Hedley Swayne. 'I knew I should never have agreed to such a hubble-bubble affair,' he said snapping his bible shut.

'No such thing!' Hedley had turned several shades of puce and was all but flapping in agitation. 'Ask him what his objection is—this is nothing more than some lark because he knows she agreed to marry *me*!'

Hedley glared at Martin. Helen felt ready to sink. But the grip on her arm eased not one whit.

The vicar glanced uneasily from Hedley to Martin. 'If you could, perhaps, tell me what your objection is?'

Without a blink, Martin said, 'Lady Walford agreed to marry me.'

Hedley gasped at what was, quite obviously, a brazen

lie. Helen decided it was time for her to take a hand. Despite all, Martin could not be allowed to give up his dreams—not after all the mental agony she had been through to save them for him. 'I did not, nor have I ever, agreed to marry you, my lord.'

Martin looked down at her. As she watched, a glow of warm appreciation filled his eyes, shaking the grip she was endeavouring to keep on her senses. Her eyes widened as that look was superseded by an expression she could only describe as unholy. 'You did, you know,' he said with a slow smile. 'When you were in bed with me that afternoon.'

Helen felt her mouth fall open. Her cheeks were aflame. How *dared* he say such a thing? In church, with the entire congregation for witness?

The vicar threw up his hands in scandalised horror. 'I should have known better than to have anything to do with fashionable folk. London folk,' he added, glowering at Hedley. 'In the circumstances, I must ask you—all *three* of you—to leave the church immediately! And I most seriously advise you to look to your souls.' And with that parting shot the vicar turned and marched into the sacristy.

The congregation erupted. Under cover of the ensuing uproar, Martin dragged Helen through a side-door and into the graveyard. They were midway across the grassed expanse, dotted with worn headstones, before Helen found the strength to haul back, bringing them to a halt.

'My lord! This is ridic——'

The rest of her words disintegrated under the force of his kiss. Fiery passion seared her lips, then, when they surrendered, threatened to cinder what was left of her wits. She struggled, trying to escape a too well-desired fate, trying to deny the hunger that rose up to overwhelm her reason. In response to her ineffectual wriggling, Martin's arms tightened about her, pressing her more fully against his hard chest, until, at last, she admitted defeat and melted against him.

Only when all trace of resistance had been vanquished did Martin risk releasing her lips. She was a stubborn goddess, as he had every reason to know.

'Don't talk,' he said, laying one finger across her reddened lips to enjoin her obedience. 'Just listen.' Gazing down into her wide green orbs, he smiled and enunciated clearly, 'My fortune is mine. Not my mother's, not even vaguely dependent on her whim. I'm excessively wealthy in my own right and have every intention of choosing my own bride. Do you understand?'

The wide eyes widened even further. Helen could barely find the breath to speak. 'But your brother said . . .' was all she could manage.

'Regrettably,' said Martin, his jaw hardening, 'Damian was labouring under a misapprehension.'

Helen detected his anger but knew it was not directed at her. 'Oh,' she said, struggling to decide what it all meant.

'Which means I'm going to marry you.'

The decisive statement brought Helen's eyes up to Martin's grey ones. His stern, not to say forbidding expression gave her pause. 'Oh,' was all it seemed safe to say.

'Yes, "Oh",' Martin repeated. 'I've asked you three times already, which is more than enough. I've given up proposing. You're going to marry me regardless.'

Helen simply stared, too enthralled by the vision of the rainbow rising once more on her horizon.

When she said nothing, Martin went on, entirely serious, 'If necessary, I'm prepared to lock you in my apartments at the Hermitage and keep you there until you agree.' He paused, brows rising. 'In fact, that's a damned good idea—far more appealing than proposing.'

Helen blushed and looked down. Things were moving so fast; her head was spinning, her heart was beating an insistent but happy tattoo. She could barely formulate a thought, with her mind whirling with the giddy promise of happiness his words had implied. Could it really be true?

Martin examined her flushed countenance, conscious of a medley of emotions coursing his veins. Relief that she was once more in his arms was slowly giving way to pride that she had loved him so much she had been willing to accede to another meaningless marriage to save his dreams. An urgency to secure her hand, beyond all possible loss, was slowly growing. He was about to speak, to assure her that he now understood her odd behaviour, before showing her that he appreciated it as he should, when, from the corner of his eye, he saw Hedley Swayne, also leaving the church by the side-door. The fop saw them and turned away, disgruntlement visible in the slump of his shoulders as he made his way jerkily through the headstones.

Reluctantly, Martin released Helen. 'Wait here. And don't move!' He enforced his command with a meaningful look, then strode after Hedley Swayne.

Mr Hedley Swayne had tried very hard to get Helen to marry him—why? Martin held no fears for his future wife—he intended to keep her safe from all danger. But the stone of Hedley Swayne's interest was too intriguing to leave unturned.

Hedley heard him and stopped, all but sulking with disappointment. 'What do you want now?' he asked as Martin drew near.

'One simple answer,' Martin said, coming to a halt directly before the slighter man. 'Why did you want to marry Lady Walford?'

Hedley scowled, then, after a pregnant pause, gave a petulant shrug. 'Oh, very well. You're bound to learn of it sooner than late, what with your business connections.' He eyed Martin with resignation. 'That little cottage of hers is on land bordering my estate. I own many of the tin mines around here. But the purest deposit my people have ever found lies under those five acres. Can't be accessed by any other route.'

For one long moment, Martin stared at the fop, now seen in a new light. Abruptly, he made up his mind. 'Here,' he said, pulling out his note-case, and extracting a card. 'Come and see me when we get back to town. We can discuss a lease then.'

'A lease?' Hedley took the card, speculation dawning in his pale eyes.

Martin shrugged. A crooked smile twisted his lips. 'I warn you you'll have to wait a few months but by then I think it very likely that both Helen and I will feel somewhat in your debt.'

With a nod, he left Hedley Swayne pondering over that cryptic utterance.

Helen was seated on the marble coping of a grave, trying to see her way forward. Could she safely agree to all Martin said—or was he making their situation appear more rosy than it, in reality, was? He wanted to marry her—that was beyond question. He was ruthless and determined and very used to getting his own way. Was it really in his best interests to marry her? And, most importantly, how could she find out? She looked up as he approached, a frown nagging at her fine brows.

Martin ignored it, holding out his hands to her. Dutifully, Helen put her hands in his and he pulled her to his feet. 'And now, fair Juno, it's time for us to depart.'

'But Martin——'

'I'll leave Joshua here to collect your maid and baggage. We can send a carriage for them from the Hermitage.' Martin paused to glance at her dress. 'Where's your coat?'

'In the carriage. But Martin——'

'Good. If we leave straight away, we should be able to reach the Hermitage by nightfall.' He guided her down the shallow steps to the roadway and fetched her coat from Hedley's carriage.

Taking her arm, Martin led her to his curricle. Beside him, Helen allowed her eyes to seek the heavens for one brief instant. If this was how he was going to behave, she would never learn anything to her purpose. With her own determination growing, she put her hands on his arms as he reached for her waist. 'My lord, I cannot simply go with you like this.'

Martin sighed. 'You can, you know. It's quite simple. But if it's all the same to you, my dear, while I'm perfectly ready to discuss our future together in whatever detail you desire, I'd rather not do so in such a public location.'

He stood back to allow Helen a clear view of the churchyard, now filled with a sea of curious faces. Her eyes grew round. 'Oh,' she said. She held her peace while Martin lifted her to the box seat, shifting across to give him room. He paused to give directions to his groom, before mounting beside her. Within two minutes, they had left Kelporth, and her past, behind them.

Helen took a moment to savour the fresh tang of the breeze on her face, to allow the feeling of having escaped a dismal prospect sink in. Ahead, the future beckoned, exciting and beguiling. But largely unknown. Drawing a deep breath, she turned to view the man beside her, noting the strong hands on the reins, the slight frown—was it of concentration?—tugging at the black brows. 'My lord——' she began.

'Martin,' promptly came back.

Despite her determination, Helen's lips twitched. 'Martin, then.' She raised her eyes to his face. 'Is it really true that marrying me will not alter your state?'

The smile Martin turned on her was dazzling. 'I very much hope it will alter my state.' At her confusion, his smile grew. 'But if you mean will it affect my financial state—no. Other than making suitable settlements on you, marriage to you will not seriously erode my fortune.' When she remained silent, he added, 'I did say so, you know.'

'You also said I'd agreed to marry you!' Helen countered, indignation at the way he had said it returning.

His grin was unrepentant. 'Ah, well. Needs must when the devil drives, I'm afraid.'

Helen swallowed a snort and looked away. He was impossible and, she was quite sure, would remain so, behaving outrageously whenever it suited him, making amends with a wicked smile in the sure expectation of being excused. For the space of a few miles, she let the steady swaying of the carriage soothe her ruffled sensibilites. 'I didn't want you to lose your home,' she eventually said, her voice rather small. Without that information, she was not sure what he might make of her own behaviour.

'My home—and my dreams of restoring it?' Martin asked gently.

Wordlessly, Helen nodded.

'Finally, despite the dust you and fate seemed intent on throwing into my eyes, I figured that much out. You'll be pleased to know that my dreams are all but reality, as far as the Hermitage goes. However, there's an even more important dream that I'm very keen to see transmuted to reality—one you can help me with.'

'Oh?' Helen glanced up at him, not sure any longer if he was serious or just trying to cheer her up. But the grey eyes were perfectly clear and intent, holding an expression which made her feel quite breathless.

'Yes,' said Martin, slowly smiling before giving his attention to the road again. 'It'll take some time to achieve, this dearest dream of mine, but I'm more than prepared to devote myself assiduously to its achievement.'

Helen puzzled for a moment before asking, 'What is this dream of yours?'

Martin considered long and hard before shaking his head. 'I don't think I should tell you just yet. Not until we're wed. In fact, possibly not even then.'

'How am I supposed to help you attain it if I don't know what it is?' Helen threw him an exasperated look, wondering again if he was merely trying to distract her. But his face remained serious.

'If I tell you what I want,' said Martin, frowning in earnest as he tried to unravel the tangle of his thoughts, 'then, with your propensity for giving me what I wish regardless of your own feelings in the matter, how will I ever know if you're helping me because you really wish to, rather than because you want to give me my heart's desire?'

Helen stared at him in total confusion. What on earth was this latest dream of his?

Seeing her confusion, Martin laughed. 'I promise to tell you if I need your—er—active assistance.' With an effort, he kept his face straight, despite the wild scenes his rampant imagination was fabricating. Thankfully, his horses gave him excuse enough to keep his eyes on the road.

As the miles fell beneath the powerful hooves, Helen brooded over Martin's disclosures, but could make all too little of them. His assurance about his home had relieved her mind of its most persistent worry, but there still remained one potential cloud hovering over his rainbow. 'Tell me about your mother,' she said. 'She lives at the Hermitage, doesn't she?'

Martin was only too ready to supply his bride-to-be with information on that subject, eliciting her ready sympathy for his ailing parent. 'And regardless of anything Damian may have said, she most definitely approves of my offering for you. In fact, it was she who told me of Damian's interference. Although she didn't say so, I have reason to suspect she was somewhat disappointed that I didn't leave to come after you last night.'

Privately, Helen considered that a reasonable reaction. Her thoughts must have shown in her eyes, for, when she glanced up and found Martin's gaze upon her, he smiled and added, 'I didn't because, quite apart from the state of the roads, I was—er...somewhat under the hatches. Your fault, I might add.'

Understanding this to mean he had been drinking rather more than usual because of her, Helen felt an odd inner glow warm her. As the curricle shot past a farmer's cart, she reflected that it was just as well Martin was not drunk now, for he was driving at a shocking pace.

Martin kept his horses well up to their bits, only easing them when absolutely necessary. They were a strong pair of Welsh thoroughbreds and made short work of the relatively level roads. Lunch was a hasty affair—some bread and cheese washed down with ale, taken in a small inn at Wadebridge. Even so, by the time they left Barnstaple, and Martin headed the horses on to the road to South Molton, the sun was sinking in the west, the way ahead lit by its slanting rays. Realising that they would not reach the Hermitage, just north of Wiveliscombe, until evening, Martin bethought himself of a pertinent point he would do well to inform fair Juno upon.

'We'll be married tomorrow.'

The bald statement jerked Helen's slumbering wits to life. Tomorrow? She looked up in time to catch Martin's glance. He was deadly serious. As she watched, one dark brow rose arrogantly. 'I've a special licence, supplied by the Bishop of Winchester.'

Helen straightened in her seat. 'Don't you think...?' she began lamely.

'No,' said Martin. 'I want to marry you as soon as possible and that's tomorrow.'

Seeing his jaw firm and the line of his lips narrow, Helen resigned herself to walking up the aisle at the earliest possible hour the next morning. But she was beginning to feel that her overbearing suitor was having things a great deal too much his own way. Consequently, she composed her features to calm and stated, 'That's as maybe. However, despite whatever outrageous claims you may choose to make to the contrary, I have not yet agreed to marry you, Martin.'

A worried frown, tending black, was thrown at her. For a moment, he said nothing. Then, 'All you have to do is say yes.'

The low growl suggested that was her only option. Helen put her head on one side, to consider his point. 'I would really feel much happier waiting until after I've met your mother.'

'You can meet her tonight and spend all tomorrow morning with her. We can be married in the afternoon.'

'But I've nothing to wear,' Helen said, appalled as she realised this was true. She had not thought anything of marrying Hedley Swayne in whatever was to hand, but the idea of becoming the Countess of Merton in a worn ballgown was too hideous to contemplate. 'No, Martin,' she said, her voice increasing in firmness. 'I'm very much afraid you'll have to wait at least until I get a suitable gown. I will not marry you otherwise.'

A groan of surpassing frustration fell on her ears. The horses were hauled to a halt; she was hauled into Martin's arms and ruthlessly kissed.

'Woman!' he growled when he eventually raised his

head. 'What further tortures do you have planned for me?'

With an enormous effort, Helen focused her faculties. Heaven preserve her, but if he realised she lost her wits every time he kissed her she would be in serious trouble. 'Is it torture?' she asked, quite fascinated.

That question got her kissed again. 'Dammit—I want you, don't you know that?'

She did, but Helen also wanted a wedding to remember. Her first, she had spent years trying to forget. And, despite the facts, a rushed wedding would be food for the gossip mills. Suppressing the shiver of delight that Martin's gravelly tone sent coursing through her, she set herself to the task of winning him over. 'It'll only take a few days—a week at the outside,' she offered.

Martin snorted disgustedly and released her. Helen watched as he took up the reins again and set the horses forward. The cast of his features suggested, at the least, disenchantment, at the worst, downright aggravation. She cast about for some gesture, some facet she could add to her plan, which would make the delay more appealing to him. Then she remembered his home and his hopes for it. She sat up straighter. 'You said your father used to entertain a great deal at the Hermitage and that you wanted to do the same.'

Martin shot her a glance from under lowered brows. 'So?'

'So why not make our marriage the first occasion you throw open your refurbished house?'

For a few moments, the horses' hoofbeats and the regular rattle of the wheels were the only sounds about them. Then Helen saw Martin purse his lips in consideration. When she saw his dejection lift, she inwardly hugged herself.

'Not a bad idea,' he eventually conceded. He glanced down at her. 'We could invite the Hazelmeres and Fanshawes and Acheson-Smythe and a few of the others.'

Helen smiled brilliantly, and slipped a small hand through his arm. 'I'm sure they'll come.'

The grey eyes glinted down at her. Then Martin humphed and gave his attention to the road. 'Just as long as you say yes at the appropriate time.'

CHAPTER THIRTEEN

THE Hermitage was much bigger than Helen had expected. Even allowing for the deceptive perspective of twilight, the many-windowed two wings stretched deep into the formal gardens. They approached the house from the rear, Martin having driven the curricle around to the stables. The formal front façade, holding court before the sweep of manicured lawns leading to a lake on one side and a stand of majestic horse chestnuts on the other, had been impressive. The back of the mansion was even more appealing, with the pergola-like glassed conservatory positioned at the end of the ballroom in the centre of the main block. The conservatory steps led to a small fountain, centrepiece of the formal gardens enclosed within the wings. Beyond, Helen could just make out the outliers of a wood and the mellow brick wall of the kitchen garden.

Her hand firmly trapped on Martin's sleeve, she was led to a door at the end of one of the wings.

'I suppose I should take you around to the front door, but it's quite a long way.' Glancing down into her upturned face, Martin forbore to add that she was looking tired, which she was. Hardly surprising, for she had had a long day. But at least she was smiling and her eyes were alight. He patted her hand. 'You'll want to freshen up before we have dinner.'

Helen came to an abrupt halt, her eyes widening as she realised what he intended. Then her eyes went to her creased and crumpled bronze silk gown. 'Oh, Martin!' she all but wailed.

Swiftly, Martin pulled her to him and kissed her soundly. 'My mother would welcome you if you were dressed in rags. Now don't fret.' He smiled down into her anguished eyes. 'I'll take you to Bender, my house-keeper. I'm sure she'll be able to help.'

Twenty minutes later, Helen gave thanks for Bender. The large, round-faced woman, in country plaid rather than the regulation bombazine, had immediately understood her wordless plea. While she washed her face and hands and brushed her hair free of the dust of the road, her dress was ruthlessly shaken, then quickly pressed. It would never be the same again, of course, but at least it looked halfway respectable. When Martin tapped on the door of the pleasant bedchamber Bender had taken her to, Helen was ready to face what she privately considered her final hurdle— the final hurdle before she could reach for her rainbow.

Martin's presence by her side, large and infinitely reassuring, helped her hold her head high as she crossed the threshold of the drawing-room, her eyes opening wide as she beheld quite the most elegant room she had entered in years. At the sudden thought that, if the fates were at last disposed to be kind, she would soon be mistress here, Helen's confidence fal-tered. But then Martin was speaking, introducing her. Helen looked down into the grey eyes watching her, and blinked in surprise.

How alike they were, was her first thought, super-seded almost immediately by the recognition of subtle differences. Martin's mother's dark brows were much finer than her son's, though her features were equally arrogant in cast. Her chin and lips were much softer in line, and the grey eyes, so startlingly similar, lacked the wicked glint often lurking in her son's. Helen realised she was staring. With a little start, she bobbed a curtsy.

'I'm most honoured to meet you, ma'am.'

Catherine Willesden eyed the golden-haired beauty before her and was not displeased with what she saw. An unusually tall woman and well-built with it—she could readily see just what in Helen Walford had excited her son's interest. And she looked the sort who could carry children well and would enjoy doing so, even more to the point. But what decided the Dowager in Helen's favour, beyond the slightest qualms, was the look of untold pride that lit her son's grey eyes whenever, as now, they rested on his bride-to-be. That, thought the Dowager, was what counted above all.

'Believe me when I say that it is I who am most thoroughly pleased to see you, my dear.' The Dowager threw a meaningful look at her son before, with an effort, she raised her hands to grasp Helen's cold fingers.

Realising the Dowager's difficulty, Helen immediately took hold of the frail claws and readily bent to place a kiss on the older woman's lined cheek.

From then on, it was fair weather and plain sailing between the Dowager and the soon-to-be Countess. Pleased with their ready acceptance of each other and not a little entertained, Martin drew back, leaving the two women to find their own way about each other. But when, after they had left the dining-table for the comfort of the drawing-room, and spent half an hour discussing the details of the wedding and planning the week-long house party, they turned their attention to the wedding feast, he had had enough.

'Mama, it's late. I'll take you upstairs.'

His mother's eyes widened. She opened her mouth to protest, then, catching his eye, closed it again. 'Very well,' she agreed. She turned to Helen, holding out one frail hand. 'Sleep well, my child.'

Martin wheeled his mother out before she could think of any more witticisms. He returned from the Dowager's rooms to find Helen wandering the hall, examining the landscapes on the wall.

'Come for a stroll. The light's not yet gone.'

Helen smiled and calmly placed her hand on his proffered sleeve. Inside, she felt anything but calm. Her heart was leaping about, turning cartwheels and somersaults with sheer happiness. The Dowager was no dragon and clearly well-disposed. The house— Martin's home—pleased her beyond her wildest dreams. She already felt drawn to it, at home within its spell, though whether the feeling owed anything to the house itself, rather than being a reflection of her all-encompassing love for Martin, she could not have said.

As they stepped from the terrace to stroll, arm in arm, along a gravelled path into a landscaped shrubbery, she felt contentment such as she had never known lay its hand upon her.

'We can send letters to the Hazelmeres and the rest tomorrow.'

Martin's murmur wafted the curls by her ear. Helen turned to smile her acquiescence, then, fleetingly, pressed her temple against his shoulder. With no need for words, they wended their way about the low clipped hedges of a miniature maze, to stand by the small fountain at its centre. Smoothly, Martin drew her around, so that the back of her shoulders brushed his chest. His arms slipped about her waist, steel bands holding her against him. He bent his head and his lips grazed her bare shoulder. Helen felt a giggle bubble in her throat. Only a very accomplished rake, she felt sure, would choose the middle of a maze to play at seduction. However, she was not in the mood to deny him. Obligingly, she tilted her head away, giving him access to the long column of her throat. She did not try to stifle the shiver of pure delight that ran through her at the intimate caress.

A crackling twig brought Martin's head up. His eyes scanned the bushes, then the grassed path leading around to the stables. Just discernible in the gloom was the figure of a man, temporarily immobile. With an oath, Martin released Helen and gave chase, leaping over the low hedges, making directly for the man who, after an instant's hesitation, had taken to his heels.

Martin's long legs gave him a telling advantage. He caught up with Damian before he had reached the wood. Catching hold of one padded shoulder, Martin spun his brother about before sending him to grass with a punishing right cross.

For an instant, Damian simply lay, eyes closed, stretched out on the turf. Then he groaned. Perfectly certain that he had not hit his brother with sufficeint force to do permanent injury, Martin stood over him, hands on hips, and waited for him to get up. When it became clear that Damian was not going to get up without assistance, Martin's jaw hardened. He was reaching for his brother's coat when Helen erupted out of the darkness behind him and caught hold of his arm.

One glance at Damian, cringing on the ground, confirmed Helen's guess. 'Don't kill him,' she pleaded, gasping to catch her breath. Abruptly deserted by the fountain, she had spent no more than a minute staring in amazement. Then she had followed. But her escape from the maze had been a great deal slower than Martin's. She could not leap over the low hedges in her gown and, without Martin's asistance, she had not known how to get out of the maze. In the end, glancing about through the gathering gloom and deciding that the gardeners would long since have gone home, she had hiked her skirts to her thighs and clambered over the bushes.

Now, finding Martin looking as if he was preparing to thrash the life out of his brother, her only thought was to stop him.

To her relief, Martin promptly drew back, his hands coming to hold hers, his eyes searching her face in the last of the twilight, a curious expression in their grey depths. 'I wasn't about to,' he replied mildly. 'But I shouldn't have thought that, in the circumstances, you would mind.'

Still out of breath, Helen shook her head. She had learned the full sum of Damian's iniquity from the Dowager. 'If it were that simple, you could have at him with my goodwill. But if you kill him, you'll be tried for murder and where would that leave my rainbow?'

'Your what?' Martin's smile gleamed white in the dark.

Helen felt her cheeks burn with embarrassment.

Still smiling, Martin patted her hand. 'Never mind. You can explain it to me later.' He slipped an arm about his bride-to-be's waist and drew her to his side.

Then he looked down at his brother, still sprawled at his feet. He shook his head. 'For God's sake, get up! I'm not going to hit you again, though, as God is my witness, you deserve to be horse-whipped.'

Damian half rose, but at the strengthening of his brother's tone he froze.

Martin looked down at him in exasperation. 'You may thank your soon-to-be sister-in-law for deliverance from any punishment I might otherwise have been inclined to mete out.' When Damian said nothing but simply stared, Martin snorted in disgust and turned away. 'Get to your room. I'll see you tomorrow.'

Drawing Helen with him, Martin started back towards the house, then bethought himself of one last warning. He turned to find Damian weaving on his feet. 'In case you're planning a sudden departure, I should warn you I've already given orders that, once here, you are not to be permitted to leave again. Not until tomorrow, when you'll depart under escort for Plymouth.'

'Plymouth?' Damian all but shuddered. 'I won't go,' he said, but to Helen his tone lacked strength.

'I rather think you will.' Martin's tone, on the other hand, radiated strength. 'Mama and I have decided a sojourn in the Indies might well be of as much benefit to you as it was to me.' He paused, then added in a more pensive tone, 'I rather think you'll find it a tad difficult, living in London, once it becomes known that both Mama and I have withdrawn our support.'

Even in the dim light, Helen could see how Damian paled. Obviously, Martin's threat was well-aimed. Martin did not wait to see how his brother reacted. He turned once more in the direction of the house, tucking her hand into the crook of his arm. Obediently, Helen paced by his side.

There was a storm brewing. Large ruffled clouds of deepest grey were blowing up from the west. After a few minutes, Helen glanced up to find that Martin's forbidding expression had disappeared. In its place was a pensive look she rather thought she should distrust.

'Now, where were we?' he murmured, before flashing her a devilish smile. 'Wherever, I rather think we had better go indoors. The evening grows cold and you're without a shawl.'

Forbearing to point out that her lack of a shawl was entirely his fault, Helen happily permitted him to escort her within doors. He led her upstairs, picking up a candelabra from the table in the hall to light their way. In the long gallery, he showed her the portraits of past Willesdens, hanging between the long velvet-curtained windows.

Picking the most scandalous of the family's tales of yore as the most suitable for his purpose, Martin had Helen in stitches as they moved on through the long corridor that led to the west wing. Embellishing freely, he ensured that she was completely enthralled long enough for them to reach the door at the end of the wing.

It was only then that Helen, catching a sudden gleam in Martin's mesmerising grey eyes, looked about her and realised she was lost—in company with a thoroughly untrustworthy host. Far from feeling threatened, she revelled in the delicious anticipation that stirred in her breast. She looked at the door before her—a very large, well-polished oak door—and then looked at Martin, one brow rising in question.

All he did was smile, successfully scattering her wits, then leaned forward to set the door wide.

Feeling very much as if she was taking some irretrievable step, Helen crossed the threshold. The room was huge—and so was the four-poster bed that stood against the wall, long windows flanking it open to the balcony, their fine lace curtains streaming in with the freshening breeze. She watched as Martin closed the shutters. The only light came from the candelabra, which he had placed on a table by the bed. The glow centred on the bed, drawing Helen's awareness with it. A heavy silk counterpane, embossed with what she recognised as the Willesden arms, covered the expanse in deep blue-grey. Silken tassels of the same colour hung from the cord holding the bed curtains back. The oak headboard was heavily carved, again incorporating the family arms, meshed within twining vine leaves.

Nervousness crept up on her, but then Martin was there, drawing her firmly into his arms. Before he could kiss her, and render her witless, Helen placed her hands on his shoulders and smiled up into the stormy grey eyes. 'Is this where I say yes?' she asked, and was surprised at the husky quality of her own voice.

Martin smiled slowly, so slowly that Helen had plenty of time to feel her heart somersault and her stomach contract.

'Actually,' he said, 'given the difficulty you seem to have with that word, I've decided some practice would not go astray.'

His tone feathered over her stretched senses, teasing and tantalising. Helen opened her eyes wide. 'Practice?' she asked in as innocent a voice as she could muster.

'Mmm,' Martin murmured, bending his head to brush his lips across hers. 'I'd rather thought to make you say it a great. . .many. . .times.' His last words were punctuated by light kisses, firm enough to whet her appetite, insubstantial enough to leave her hungry.

Helen felt her will slowly seep from her but she retained sufficient curiosity to ask. 'How will you make me do that?'

Martin did not answer.

Instead, he showed her.

Much later, Martin reached out with one hand and snuffed the candles by the bed. His other arm was occupied, cradling Helen's warm body by his side. She was asleep, thoroughly exhausted, having said the word he had wanted to hear a great many times indeed. Martin smiled into the dark. She still needed more practice—he was quite certain he would be able to convince her of that later. With her head once more on his shoulder, her soft curls like silk at his throat, he listened to the storm passing overhead. Wind lashed the trees in the Home Wood, rain pelted down on the gravel walks. Helen had not even noticed the tempest without, being too much caught up in the tempest they had created within.

With a deep sigh, Martin closed his eyes. Contentment coursed his veins like a drug, bringing peace and satisfaction in its wake. His house was in order, fair Juno safe by his side. Tonight, with any luck, he would get some sleep. Maybe not much, but some. And, unlike the last stormy night he had spent with fair Juno, the torture between times would be much more

to his taste. He closed his hand over one full breast.
And fell asleep.

Helen awoke to rub her nose, then realised that the
curly black hair tickling it was attached to Martin's
chest. She stifled a giggle and pushed it aside, then
glanced up to find lazy eyes watching her, a suspicious
twinkle in their depths.

With a smile, Helen stretched, cat-like, and watched
the twinkle intensify to a satisfying gleam. As she felt
the arm about her tighten, she pressed her hands
against his chest. Heavens! She needed at least two
minutes to think! 'What is your latest dream, my lord?'
she purred, hoping to distract him and appease her
curiosity in one stroke.

Martin relaxed and laughed, the warmth in his eyes
spreading like a languorous flame over her skin.
'Should I tell you?' he asked rhetorically. Then, 'Perhaps I should.' His eyes held hers, mock-serious. 'I
don't think it'll be too hard for you to handle.' His
smile grew. 'Well within your capacity, so to speak.'

Feeling the rumble of his laughter, Helen scowled.
'Martin!'

'Ah—yes. Well, having had an opportunity to assess
your abilities, my love, and having ascertained that you
really do enjoy our recent activities for their own
delight, as it were, I feel secure in the knowledge
that, once you hear of my dream, you'll not be called
on to sacrifice any feelings of your own in its
accomplishment.'

Helen glared at him. 'Martin! What is it?'

Martin eyed her a little warily. 'Promise not to
laugh?'

Puzzled, Helen's glare turned to a stare. 'Why should I laugh?' she asked. When he said nothing further, she grimaced. 'All right. I promise not to laugh. Now, what is this dream of yours?'

'I have this vision of you standing before the mantelpiece—I think the one in the library at Merton House. . .' Martin paused, then went on in a rush, 'With my son balanced on your hip.'

Helen blinked. 'Oh,' she said, her voice non-committal. But she could not stop the smile that curved her lips, then deepened to light her eyes. Gazing deep into the grey eyes that held hers, and seeing the hesitant expression that lingered there, Helen decided that she had clearly reached the end of her rainbow and found her pot of gold. Rapidly blinking to clear her eyes of the tears of happiness that threatened, she swallowed and said, 'Oh, Martin!' before throwing her arms about his neck and burying her face in his shoulder.

His arms came up to close about her, holding her close. 'I take it that means you approve?'

A mumble which was clearly an assent answered him. Martin grinned and hugged her more tightly, conscious of the dampness of tears on his shoulder.

Once she had regained her composure, Helen could not resist asking, 'Is that a typical dream for a rake?'

'I assure you it's this rake's dream.' Martin moved to glance down at her. He smiled slowly. 'Now come and do your bit to make it real.'

Helen's smile answered him. 'Gladly, my lord.'

She reached up and drew his lips down to hers and, in truth, there was no dream in her mind beyond the attainment of his.

SERAFINA

by

Sylvia Andrew

Dear Reader

Love, laughter and some tears, drama, a sense of style,
a flavour of the language of the period—these are what
attract me in writing 'Regency Romances'. And since
I am, after all, a woman of the twentieth century, I
like the idea that women of that period, unlike their
Victorian daughters, were allowed to display spirit and
intelligence.

I hope you enjoy reading about my lovely, spirited
Serafina, as much as I enjoyed writing about her.

Sylvia Andrew

Sylvia Andrew taught modern languages for years, ending up as Vice-Principal of a sixth form college. She lives in Somerset with two cats, a dog, and a husband who has a very necessary sense of humour, and a stern approach to punctuation. Sylvia has one daughter living in London, and they share a lively interest in the theatre. She describes herself as an 'unrepentant romantic'.

Other titles by the same author:

Perdita
A Darling Amazon
Serena
Eleanor
Francesca
Rosabelle Volume One } *The Christmas Belles*
Annabelle Volume Two

CHAPTER ONE

IT HAD been a lovely afternoon. Even though summer was quite definitely over the sun was dazzling as it shone through the leaves of the oak tree, and Mr Hartley Pennyworth was forced to shade his eyes when he looked up. As he peered through the foliage he had a tantalising glimpse of a figure perched on a branch some way up. Its legs were stretched out along the branch, and it was leaning comfortably against the trunk of the tree. Hartley drew nearer. Now he could see that the figure held a half-eaten apple in one hand and a book in the other.

'Miss Feverel!'

The figure gave a sigh, leaned over to look down and said, 'Gracious, it's you, Hartley! Who told you I was here?'

'Rafe.'

Miss Feverel's frown boded ill for her youngest brother, but Mr Pennyworth was not to be deterred. 'Miss Feverel, I have come to ask you to marry me!'

'Oh, Hartley, I thought we had settled all this! You know I don't wish to marry you, and I am sure you would regret it if I did. Has your mother been at you again? It's too bad of her.'

Mr Pennyworth ignored this. He had come, in his mother's words, to 'act like a man', to storm the citadel and to return to Pennyworth Lodge affianced to

Serafina Feverel, and, since he was a man of few but
fixed ideas, nothing was going to put him off.

'Miss Feverel——'

'And I do wish that you would not keep calling me
Miss Feverel in that idiotic way. We have known each
other forever, and until this summer you have always
called me Serafina. Why have you suddenly decided to
change?'

'Because we are no longer children,' said Mr
Pennyworth in throbbing accents. 'I am a man with a
man's needs, Miss Feverel, and I love you.' His tone
changed and he said somewhat peevishly, 'I wish you
would come down, Serafina. It is very awkward proposing to you when I can hardly see you.'

'But I don't want you to propose! I thought I had
made that more than clear. Oh, very well, I suppose
I'll have to come down. My afternoon's reading is quite
spoiled anyway.'

Serafina threw her apple away, put her book in the
capacious pocket of her old-fashioned jacket, shook
herself and started to climb down. As she did so one
of her boots slipped off and it fell, narrowly missing
Mr Pennyworth. A man with a greater sense of humour
might have been amused at the contrast between
Serafina's slender, white-stockinged ankle and delicately arched foot and the heavy boot, obviously not
meant for a lady. But Mr Pennyworth was devoid of a
sense of humour, and, what was more, he was a man
in love. He caught the foot as she descended and kissed
it.

'Oh, Miss Feverel,' he cried. 'My life will be in ruins
if you will not say you'll be mine.'

'Your life will more likely be ruined if I do say so.

Stop talking like a Gothic romance, Hartley, and let go of my foot. I need it to stand on,' she said coldly, wrenching it away from him and jumping lightly to the ground. 'And if you do such a ridiculous thing again I shall complain to your mama.'

'She would understand. Mother knows how much I adore you. In fact it was she who told me to make my feelings plainer, and she is usually right.' He looked sorrowfully at Serafina's frowning face. 'But I think I have only made you angry.'

Serafina sighed and said, 'I am sorry to cause you pain, Hartley. But we really shouldn't suit, you know. You are too...too worthy a man for a harum-scarum like me. Besides, I like reading and discussion, and things like that, and you do not. You always become quite agitated when I argue with you and frequently end up in a sulk. And you don't like it when I laugh at you, either. How on earth should we get on if we were married?'

'Mother says that things would be different then. As my wife, you would naturally defer to me.'

'I see. Well, since I am most unlikely to change my ways for any husband, whatever your mama says, you must abandon the thought of marrying me and try someone else. What about Lizzie Beaminster? She would suit you so much better, and I know for a fact that she admires you.'

'She does?' Hartley was so little used to admiration from anyone but his mother that he was obviously impressed by this piece of information. Then his face clouded over and he said heavily, 'But it is you I love! I cannot sleep for thinking of you. I cannot eat for thinking of you. Mother says I am wasting away. No one else could possibly make me happy!'

'What rubbish!' said Serafina briskly, eyeing Mr Pennyworth's well-fed figure. 'Really, I haven't time or patience for any more of this nonsense—it must stop! You have been cozening your mother most shamefully, Hartley, just as you did when you were a little boy and sulked until she gave you what you wanted. Remember the fuss you made over a parrot you saw in Brighton? And then you gave it away again, not a year later. Well, I am not a parrot, and this is something that your mama cannot arrange for you. Indeed, I am surprised that she wishes to! I have no fortune, and the Feverel estate will go to Gabriel.'

'That's what she said—that we can afford to over-look your lack of dowry where others might not, and that you ought to be delighted to accept such a hand-some offer. And she said that, if you didn't, she feared you would end up an over-educated old maid——' Here Mr Pennyworth, realising that this last sentence was hardly likely to advance his cause, stopped short.

'How very kind of her,' said Serafina with a glitter in her eye, 'to have such concern for my future! Do, pray, thank your mama for her solicitude.'

Mr Pennyworth looked doubtful. 'Er…what do you wish me to say to her, Serafina?'

'That I…will…not…marry…you. Not now. Not ever. In any circumstances! Nor do I wish to see you again before you have recovered your senses. Good-bye, Hartley.'

Mr Pennyworth flushed unbecomingly and turned away. He stopped after a few yards, however, and said, 'You're too clever for your own good, Serafina

Feverel! Don't think I shall ask you again, for I shan't.
My eyes are open at last. My mother was right—who
wants an opinionated bluestocking for a wife?' With
this parting shot he disappeared. Serafina watched him
go without regret. Mrs Pennyworth would doubtless be
relieved to hear that Hartley had finally given up—if
indeed he had. As a doting mother, who had never
denied her son anything in his life, Mrs Pennyworth
had encouraged him in his plans only because his heart
had seemed set on marriage to Serafina. But she would
now work hard to help him to forget. Serafina cordially
wished her rapid and complete success, and turned
towards the house.

Halfway up the drive she was met by a girl accompanied by a little boy. 'Ah, Rafe! I have a bone to pick
with you. . .'

'No, honestly, Sally, I didn't mean to tell him! It
slipped out before I could stop it.'

'Are you going to marry Hartley Pennyworth?'
asked the girl.

'What do you think, Angy?'

'She's not such a clunch!' Rafe exclaimed scornfully.

'No more I am, Rafe, but if you wish to please me
you'll try for once to keep it to yourself. Gentlemen
don't like gossip about unsuccessful offers. Understand, both of you? Promise?' Rafe solemnly drew his
finger across his throat, and Angelica, as befitted a
young lady of fifteen summers, nodded sedately. They
set off again.

'Where's Michael?' Serafina asked.

'He's gone with Colonel Smithers to see the militia
exercising. Sally, where's your other boot?' asked
Angelica. They all looked down, and Serafina stared at

her feet—one in a boot and one in a white stocking—
and started to laugh. 'It's under the tree. I dropped it.
Oh, my goodness, look at my stocking!'

'I'll fetch it for you!' Rafe ran back to where the
forgotten boot lay.

'Mama will scold and Hetty will complain about the
holes in this stocking,' mourned Serafina as she put the
boot on again.

'Mama will say that you shouldn't use Michael's old
boots at all,' said Angelica. 'They're too big, and you
will never learn to walk as a lady should while you
continue to wear them.'

'But they're much more use for walking on rough
ground and climbing trees and fences! Ladies' thin
slippers are useless.'

'Ladies don't climb trees and fences, either,' said
Angelica primly. 'I'm afraid Mama is quite right, Sally.
You are a hoyden.'

Rafe was quick to defend his beloved elder sister.
'You're just saying that because she's better than you
at climbing trees. And at riding. In fact, she's better
than you at anything!'

'She is not! She's older, that's all!'

'She is so, she is so!' crowed Rafe, happy to have
roused Angelica into losing a little of her dignity.

The quarrel went on until they reached the house.
Serafina ignored it—she was used to these spats
between her brothers and sister and they didn't mean
anything. Later today, or tomorrow, or whenever it
pleased them, Angelica and Rafe were quite likely to
join forces against Michael or herself. Basically the
family was a happy one, though, since they had all

been brought up to have minds of their own, it was never dull.

Lucius Feverel, Serafina's father, was a genius. He was not only a noted scholar, he also had that rarest of gifts—the ability to convey his own interests and enthusiasms to his children. Except for Gabriel, the eldest boy, who was now up at Oxford, he taught them for the most part himself. Mornings were devoted to formal lessons, but his true genius revealed itself in the children's regular afternoon walk. Then the natural history, geography or mathematics they learned in the schoolroom came to life while they splashed about in the stream which meandered along the boundary of their estate, roamed the woods and fields round their home, or calculated the numbers of ears of corn in Mr Halkyn's Five Acre field.

Among their neighbours the Feverels were regarded as eccentric, for Lucius did not behave as other fathers behaved. He seldom scolded or punished his family, and he treated his daughters exactly the same as his sons, setting them the same high standards. At twelve Serafina had been able to read Latin and Greek with ease. At fifteen, after the widow of a French emigré had stayed with them for a year, she was fluent in French. Now she had a good working knowledge of most other European languages, too. She had been trained in the more advanced principles of mathematics and logic, and since Gabriel's departure to Oxford she had been the object of her father's particular attention. He often read out to Serafina the letters and articles he sent regularly to various learned journals, and was disappointed if she was not prepared to comment on them. Mr Feverel was proud of all his children, but Serafina, the eldest, was his special pride and joy.

Few of the neighbours, it was true, could boast that their own offspring were as handsome as the Feverel family. But to the outside world the five Feverel children were an undisciplined, noisy gang—girls as well as boys. They roamed the countryside looking like blond gypsies, and on the few occasions when visitors called the children had little, if any, notion of how to behave in company. The ladies of the neighbourhood were shocked that neither of the Feverel girls had had a single lesson in deportment or dancing in her life, and they particularly deplored Serafina's lack of interest in her clothes and appearance. The gentlemen, though impressed with her beauty, quickly came to resent her readiness to give an opinion on matters which they did not consider to be suitable for a lady, and, even more, they resented her ability to express herself with clarity and logic. It had to be said, and the neighbours said it often, that Serafina, or Sally as her family called her, was an opinionated hoyden—gifted, well-read and exasperatingly lovely, but a hoyden none the less. Poor Mrs Feverel.

Mrs Feverel was a talented artist, but she was an invalid, often confined by a debilitating disease to her sofa or her bed. Her family, including her husband, all adored her. The only time the children ever saw Mr Feverel angry was when his wife had been upset, whatever the reason. They spent much of their leisure devising ways of amusing her, and the weekly playlet in which they entertained her with village news in dramatic form was the highlight of Saturday evenings. They sought small gifts for her to paint, too—a lilac-grey dove's feather from Rafe, an interesting bunch of roadside flowers from Angelica, shells, berries or leaves from Michael and Serafina. She received them all with loving gratitude.

It was not easy to keep some kind of order in this strange household, but Mrs Feverel had decided long ago that the best discipline she could exercise was one of love. Of course she worried about them. Gabriel, the eldest boy, was very young to be on his own at Oxford, though he was doing well there. And the girls—they should be presented soon. Indeed, Serafina was already more than old enough. But Mrs Feverel shuddered to think what would happen if her daughters were launched on an unsuspecting world without a great deal of expensive preparation. And then careers for Michael and Rafe would soon have to be considered. Yes, Mr Feverel would have been astonished if he had known how much Mrs Feverel worried. He himself had a mind above economic cares.

Mrs Feverel sighed now as her elder daughter came into her room. Serafina had changed out of her shabby skirt and disreputable jacket, but she was without shoes, and one of her stockings looked decidedly the worse for wear. She looked guilty.

'What is it, Serafina?'

'I'm afraid I have spoilt my stocking, Mama.'

'The second pair this week, my daughter. How did you do it this time?'

'It really wasn't my fault! At least, I suppose it was, because I did forget my—er—shoe——'

'One of Michael's boots?'

'Well, yes. And it came off. But I would have

remembered it except for the fact that I was so annoyed with Hartley Pennyworth. He found me up the oak tree, and I had to listen to a proposal from him yet again. I think I may have finally disillusioned him today. But why does he persist so, Mama?'

'He thinks himself in love with you.'

'In love! How ridiculous!'

'Hartley may not be your ideal, Serafina, but he is not ridiculous. Love is very painful, not funny at all.'

'But Mama, he has no reason to believe himself in love with me!'

Mrs Feverel laughed. 'Reason has little to do with it, child!'

'I suppose you are right.' Serafina shook her head. 'It is odd that people can suffer from such an irrational emotion. It makes life very hard for them, and I am sure it is better avoided. However much in love with me Hartley might have been, Mama, he must have known that it would be madness to *marry* me! I have no fortune, we haven't a single interest in common, and I'm not at all the amenable sort of girl he needs.'

'Perhaps he has seen that now—just like all the other young men of the neighbourhood. Perhaps you are too nice in your requirements for a husband, Serafina. Or do you intend never to marry at all?'

'Oh, I should like to marry—a man with understanding, perhaps. Someone like Papa, I suppose. An intelligent man who...who doesn't moon over me, but is prepared to listen to what I have to say, and treat it seriously. Someone who would share my interests and is prepared to treat me as a human being, not a cross between a mindless doll and some sort of goddess. But I would certainly not dream of marrying for anything so irrational as love! Literature is full of the most dire examples of what happens when you allow your heart to rule your head.'

Mrs Feverel looked curiously at her daughter. 'And your heart has never ruled your head?'

Serafina considered this seriously. 'I don't think so... Certainly nothing to cause me to behave as stupidly as Hartley. I'm not sure it ever will.' She smiled suddenly and added, 'But I love you, Mama. I might do foolish things for you.'

'I'd like you to do sensible ones, Serafina. Such as wearing your own shoes, and remembering to keep them on!'

'Well, then, I will!'

When she considered Serafina's cool assessment of her future, Mrs Feverel was inclined to believe that such a marriage would work for her. Serafina was a level-headed, intelligent girl. Her real interest had always been in matters of the head, not the heart, and an undemanding relationship with a man she respected would suit her very well. If she ever married at all. Mrs Feverel sighed. Unless she was introduced to Society quite soon, Serafina would miss her chance altogether.

A short while before, in an effort to solve this problem, Mrs Feverel had invited Serafina's god-mother, who was now a childless widow, for a visit. Lady Chilham had admired Serafina's looks, and had been very impressed with the girl's devotion to her mother. The children had exerted themselves to entertain her, and their Saturday evening entertainment had been a considerable success. The great news of the week had been the curate's engagement to Miss Twitch, and the visitor had laughed as much as anyone at Serafina's portrayal of the shy little spinster—the downcast eye and modestly folded hands, hampered by her insistence on propriety, but with an ill-concealed eagerness to accept her suitor's offer. Lady Chilham had appeared to be in such good humour and so impressed with Serafina that Mrs Feverel's hopes that she would do something for her were very high.

But Lady Chilham had expressed strong disapproval of the manner in which the two girls were being educated. 'It is too much! They do not need all this Latin and Greek! And politics!' Lady Chilham's nose had wrinkled in distaste. 'Sarah, I warn you, they are both in danger of becoming unmarriageable bluestockings—Serafina in particular.'

Mr Feverel had been outraged, and he and Lady Chilham had almost quarrelled over the matter. Only the regard they both shared for Mrs Feverel had prevented an open breach. Mrs Feverel had decided to postpone any attempt to gain Lady Chilham's help until matters had calmed down a little, and had waited until the last day of her friend's visit before she'd finally spoken. Lady Chilham had proved to be so sympathetic that Mrs Feverel had revealed rather more of the family's financial worries than she had intended.

'It's the girls I worry about most, Elizabeth. Once we have paid for Gabriel at Oxford, and Michael——'

'Does Michael wish to go to Oxford, too? He seems to me to be less academic than his brother.'

'No, he wishes for a career in the army, which as you know can be ruinously expensive. And heaven knows what Rafe will want to do when he is older!'

'Well, I am glad that you have confided in me at last, Sarah. I shall do something for Serafina, of course. But

in fact there is an obvious solution to your problems, if
you would care to make use of it. If you were not
married to a crank you would have thought of it
yourself before now.'

'You have never understood Lucius, Elizabeth. He
is an idealist, not a crank,' said Mrs Feverel with a
smile.

'Idealism don't pay bills!' was Lady Chilham's crisp
reply. 'But I believe my views on that topic are already
known to you. However, it is my considered view that
the family's greatest potential asset is Serafina—I say
potential, you'll note. I still have to establish how much
damage has already been done by her extraordinary
upbringing.'

'Serafina? How?' asked Mrs Feverel, ignoring this
provocation.

'The girl is lovely enough to make a wealthy match,
if all went well. Indeed, she could aim very high. I have
not seen such a lovely face for several seasons. Think
of what a wealthy son-in-law could do for the family!'

'But——'

'And,' said Lady Chilham firmly, 'the girl deserves a
better fate than wasting her beauty down here. Neither
her looks nor all this education will help her when she
has to choose between marrying a country bumpkin or
becoming her brother's pensioner. How many offers
has she had, may I ask?'

'Only one,' said Mrs Feverel. 'From someone she
regards as a joke. The rest of the young men of the
neighbourhood are frightened of her. She does most
things as well if not better than they do. And she
argues with them.'

'What did I tell you? Now, in London I am sure it

would not be difficult to find a sensible man, with a reasonable fortune, whom she could respect. But she will never attract the kind of offer I have in mind until she has more worldly sense. She must learn that being clever is a handicap to a woman, not an asset. She moves gracefully enough, and her voice is attractive — I could soon put her in the way of ladylike behaviour. She could even be one of next season's successes! If you wish, I will arrange something.'

After Lady Chilham had gone Mr Feverel had been ready to pour scorn on the idea of employing Serafina's gifts in such an unworthy cause. Besides, he would miss her! But he'd been silenced when he'd seen that his wife, frightened by Lady Chilham's prophecy of Serafina's future if she remained in Sussex, and worried about the rest of her children too, had set her heart on it. Serafina herself would not have been normal if she had not been excited at the prospect of a visit to London.

A few weeks later word came from Lady Chilham. She had decided to invite Serafina for a brief visit before Christmas.

There is little by way of entertainment at this time of year, but I feel that Serafina and I could get better acquainted with each other. The season doesn't start till next May, but if I decided to present her she would have to be carefully prepared for it, beginning in about March. What she needs most, of course, is to acquire some worldly sense!

The letter continued in a very kindly tone, but it was obvious that Serafina was to be on trial before her godmother would agree to sponsor her during the next season. Mrs Feverel was nervous of her husband's reaction, but to her surprise he raised few objections, merely saying that he would miss his daughter, but that she should take what advantage she could from a visit to London. The British Museum was particularly worth a visit. Preparations for Serafina's trip were put in hand with a number of visits to the dressmaker and the shops in Brighton. But she still found time to visit old haunts.

Over the hill from Feverel Place and the village of Hardington was a mansion which had been unoccupied for some time. Blanchards had once been a handsome estate—a beautiful house, built in the reign of Queen Anne, surrounded by well-kept grounds and gardens. But during the past thirty years it had been sadly neglected. The house was somewhat isolated, and old Mrs Dacre, who had been a recluse, had leased out most of the land many years before. After she died Blanchards remained unoccupied. Now it lay forgotten and deserted, slowly falling into ruin. Mrs Dacre had been a connection of the Aldworth family, and her estate had been left to them. For a while it had been hoped that Lord Aldworth would restore the house and make it habitable again, but then tragedy had struck the Aldworth family twice in quick succession. First old Lord Aldworth had died, then Gervase, his son, had succumbed to an illness quite soon afterwards. Charles, the younger son, had succeeded his brother to the title, but he was a diplomat and spent most of his time abroad. None of the Aldworths bothered with Blanchards, and Sam Eckford, the caretaker, remained its sole employee.

For two of the Feverels at least, this continuing

neglect of Blanchards had come as a relief. Sam
Eckford was idle, and in any case had little reason to
worry overmuch about his masters. He was seldom to
be seen anywhere near the house, contenting himself
with a brief tour round the outside each morning and
remaining in the lodge the rest of the time. He never
went near the gardens. This meant that the Feverel
children could roam there more or less at will whenever they were free.

Serafina and Michael had discovered the walled
garden behind the house some time before. The overgrown tangle of currant bushes and raspberry canes
testified to the years of neglect, but earlier in the
summer they had found some fruit. Best of all, an old
vine still flourished in the greenhouse set against the
ancient south-facing wall—the sole survivor of a once
luxuriant collection of exotic fruit trees. The children
had tended this vine all summer, and were now reaping
the results of their labours. Mrs Feverel had already
received several baskets filled with bunches of sweet-
tasting grapes.

A short time after the arrival of Lady Chilham's
letter Serafina and Michael were in the greenhouse at
Blanchards. Serafina was once again wearing her
shabby skirt and disreputable jacket, together with a
woolly cap and Michael's boots. After all, it was only
sensible to wear boots for clambering over stone walls!
The slight breeze coming in through the panes of
broken glass overhead set the vine leaves dancing,
scattering the sunlight among the vividly coloured
leaves. Serafina paused to admire the rich display of
green and gold, red and purple. Her mother would
enjoy painting those leaves. . . The best ones were at

the top near the roof. So were the best grapes! Serafina tucked her hair more firmly into her red woolly cap, hitched her skirt above her knees and, ignoring Michael's warnings, clambered up between the wall and the thick stem of the vine till she could perch on the cross-bar which supported the roof. In fact, the cross-bar was probably holding the whole rickety structure together. The autumn sun was warm and strong, and she found it stifling up there. Taking off her jacket, she draped it over the bar. There were more grapes here than she had thought. . .

'Sally! Come on! We shall be late!'

Serafina hastily cut one more bunch and scrambled down. She squeezed out through the door, which was still locked, even though all of its glass and most of its wooden panels had long since disappeared, and joined Michael, who was waiting impatiently outside.

'We'll soon have to think of something else for Mama, Michael,' she said. 'The grapes are very nearly finished.'

'Never mind that now! You know how disappointed Pa will be if we're not there for our walk. Come, I'll go over the wall first, then I'll take the basket from you.'

'If he wants us to be on time he shouldn't keep us late at morning lessons,' panted Serafina as she hitched up her skirts and scrambled up the tree after her brother.

'It's your fault. You shouldn't have asked him about that last bit of Xenophon.'

Serafina didn't reply—she was saving her breath for the run home. But as she perched on the top of the wall before jumping down she suddenly realised that she had left her jacket in the greenhouse.

'You'll have to go on, Michael. I'll get my jacket and join you as soon as I can. You'll have to try to explain to Pa. . . Here, take the grapes!'

Michael set off at a run, and Serafina returned to the greenhouse. She clambered up the vine once again, collected her jacket, put it on, and prepared to climb down again. But then she froze as she heard the sound of voices. . . Cautiously she peered down, but could see nothing between the broad leaves. The voices came nearer and she heard the sound of a key turning in the rusty lock of the greenhouse. Two people came in. One was Sam Eckford—he never came near the place, what was he doing here? The other's voice was deeper and immensely authoritative.

'This will all have to come down, Eckford. It's dangerous. I'm surprised this vine has survived for so long. Have you been looking after it? You'd have done better to repair some of the boards, or even to remove the whole thing.' The speaker moved forward and Serafina had a tantalising glimpse of him. Tall, athletic figure, black hair—he was the handsomest man she had ever seen, and obviously both rich and fashionable. His travelling-cloak was open, and she had the impression of a snowy cravat and fawn-coloured pantaloons. He had obviously come some distance, and she wondered briefly how he managed to look so immaculately clean!

'No, no, your lordship! I was never told to look after anything but the house. And that was bad enough. It needs a lot doing to it, begging your lordship's pardon.'

'Yes, yes. We'll have to get an army of workers in if

it is to be habitable before Christmas—which is what I want. Get this lot pulled down before I come again, will you?' They were turning away, but the gentleman suddenly stopped. 'What the devil. . .?' Before Serafina realised what was happening a lean hand had stretched up and grasped her ankle. 'What are you doing here? Come down at once!'

Serafina held on to her perch for dear life and kicked hard. It was quite effective, for Michael's old boots were heavy.

'Ouch! Why, you——'

Sam, seeing his master attacked, cried, 'Come down, you little varmint!' and started to pull at the vine.

'No, don't do that, Eckford! You'll have the place down——'

But it was too late. The structure gave a groan and slowly disintegrated. Man and master were buried under the old vine as Serafina slid helplessly along the pole to land gently on the ground outside some feet away. Horrified, she turned to see the damage. What glass remained had fortunately stayed in place so the two men were in no real danger, but they were trapped under the vine and its supports. She hesitated and went back to the ruins of the greenhouse.

'Are. . .are you all right?' she said.

'Good God, it's a girl!' An irate face peered out between the branches—furious grey eyes and cheeks flushed with anger. His hair was dishevelled and his cravat filthy with cobwebs and dust. But he was still very handsome. However, Serafina dared not linger to admire him—the gentleman was starting to push his way out of the tangle of leaves, branches and wooden supports. Ignoring his shout of, 'Wait, you!', she ran to

the tree by the wall, threw herself over and fled for
dear life up the hill. When she reached the shelter of
some trees she paused and looked back. To her relief
they had obviously decided against pursuit. She limped
home, but was not sorry to discover that the walking
party had set off without her. She felt she needed time
to pull herself together!

Later that afternoon when Serafina, having washed
the dirt and dust from her own person, was sitting
demurely with her mother, the children came rushing
in to report on the walk.

'You missed a lot of fun, Sally,' said Rafe. 'We
marched and marched till we could see the sea—just
like the Greeks.'

'Greeks?' Mrs Feverel looked puzzled.

'Xenophon,' explained Angelica. 'And his army of
ten thousand. They marched through Persia to the sea.
We read about it this morning.'

'Hundreds of miles, Mama!' said Rafe, his eyes
shining. 'They were real heroes. And when they saw
the sea they shouted, "*Thalassa, thalassa*!". And so did
we. "*Thalassa*!" Mrs Pennyworth was very surprised. I
don't think she liked it.'

'Oh, goodness, was she there?' asked Serafina.

'She was out for a drive with Hartley. Lizzie
Beaminster was in the carriage with them.'

'Never mind that,' said Michael. 'Mama—guess
what? Lord Aldworth is coming down himself any day
now to see Blanchards. Miss Twitch told us. Perhaps
he's going to let it? What do you think, Mama? Will
he call on us when he's here?'

'I shouldn't imagine so, Michael,' said Mrs Feverel,
to Serafina's profound relief. 'Not this time, anyway.'

She turned to her daughter. 'So, Serafina—your grape-gathering days are over. I'm not altogether sorry, for I had an uneasy conscience about your taking them, even though no one else appeared to want them. But I shall miss my delicious dessert. I wonder if Lord Aldworth will cultivate the vine? Perhaps he would even let you have some?'

'I doubt it, Mama,' murmured Serafina.

There was something in Serafina's voice, something in the blindingly innocent expression on her face that caused Mrs Feverel to look sharply at her daughter. What had Serafina been up to? Mrs Feverel, as so often in the past, decided it was better not to ask.

Nothing more was heard of Lord Aldworth. Apparently he had merely called in at Blanchards on his way from Newhaven. He stayed there only one night, and left for London and his own estate in Berkshire the next morning.

Serafina had been relieved not to run the risk of meeting him again. But she was annoyed to find that his handsome face had a totally irrational tendency to haunt her dreams.

CHAPTER TWO

LORD ALDWORTH reined in his horse and contemplated the view. The morning sun slanted across the countryside, creating a patchwork of light and shade in the broad valley and bathing the hills opposite in its glow. Below, the river glinted in the light as it wound its lazy way to London and the sea, and across the valley in the hollows not yet reached by the sun fingers of September mist curled round the trees and hedges, and covered the fields with an insubstantial veil. Huge beech trees on the hills above shone green and gold in the sunlight. Lord Aldworth took in a deep breath of scented downland air, and let it out in a sigh. To his mind there was no lovelier place than this in the whole of Europe, but he could not wait to leave it. Though he had been back in Berkshire for only three weeks, the situation was already almost intolerable—another week of living at Aldworth with his sister-in-law, his stepmother, not to mention his three stepsisters. . . He grimaced. It was unthinkable.

There was one person who would not be pleased when he told her he was going back to Vienna. He could already imagine what his grandmother would say, and it would not be agreeable. But there was no point in postponing the interview—he would see her tonight. One more gallop then he would return to the house which was now his—damn it!—and work his way through the mountain of chores to be completed before he could leave England with an easy conscience. A comparatively easy conscience. Lord Aldworth was not a man to disguise the truth from himself. He was deserting his proper post, and he knew it.

The sun was still shining as Lord Aldworth approached the Dower House that evening, but its rays were not permitted to enter the drawing-room, where his grandmother, the Dowager Lady Aldworth, waited to receive him. As a thrifty Frenchwoman she took measures to avoid the damage done to curtains and carpets by unshaded sunlight. Complexions, too, were better preserved without it and, even though she was nearly eighty, the Dowager thought of such things. However, a frown marred her carefully preserved features as she listened to what her grandson was saying a few minutes later. They were speaking in French, for Lady Aldworth was the daughter of a French aristocrat. She always used English with the rest of her family, but Charles, she was used to say, was one of the few Englishmen whose French accent she could tolerate, and she usually took pleasure in conversing with him in her native tongue. Not this evening.

'I have never interfered before, Charles; you cannot accuse me of that. You have done exactly as you please ever since you left Oxford. I have to admit that your public career has been exemplary, but your private life is another matter.' She paused, then added scrupulously, 'Though I suppose you have a perfect right to as many mistresses as you choose. You are, after all, a bachelor and in the prime of manhood.'

'I am grateful for your broad-minded attitude, ma'am, but I have to confess that I never have more than one mistress at a time. It can lead to confusion,' he assured her with a grin.

The Dowager was not to be diverted.

'But things have changed now,' she went on repressively. 'You are no longer Charles Dacre, a charming bachelor diplomat. You are the fifteenth Baron Aldworth, with a title and large estates to care for. When your idiot of a brother succumbed to a trifling illness without first having the good sense to get an heir, he left a nice mess for us all. As if your step-mother and three stepsisters were not enough, we now have another widowed Lady Aldworth——'

'Not to mention yourself, ma'am,' interrupted Lord Aldworth with a graceful bow.

'Impudence!'

'And,' he went on, 'dare I point out to you that Gervase had hardly been married six months when he died? It would surely have been precipitate if his wife had borne a child much before their first anniversary—and Gervase was never that in his life, as we both know.'

'He was an incompetent shuffler,' said Lady Aldworth, not mincing matters. 'The point is, Charles, that he didn't take a wife till he was well over thirty! He would have had plenty of time to get all the brats the title needed if he had bestirred himself. Why, your father was only twenty-two when Gervase was born. As for the shrew Gervase married. . .'

'Well, there I have to agree with you. I think I too would feel disinclined to survive if I were obliged to endure her company for long. She has a voice like a screech-owl.'

'Well, what are you proposing to do about it?'

'About my sister-in-law? What can I do but leave her where she is? And avoid listening to her.'

'No, that's not what I meant at all, and you know it! You're already close to thirty yourself. I want to know what you are proposing to do about an heir!'

Lord Aldworth shut the snuff-box he had been admiring with a snap, and turned to face his grandmother. 'I know you do, ma'am. You have, after all, been saying so ever since I returned from Vienna. And I will say again, I have no wish to change my present way of life. What is the reason for all the anxious haste? You can hardly say I am halfway to my dotage, and I feel no diminution of my. . .'

'Of your virility. I do not mince words, me! I must confess you don't look as if you do, either!' She eyed her grandson with grudging admiration. He always dressed fashionably, though not extravagantly, and here in the country his superbly cut dark green riding-coat and close fitting pantaloons did nothing to disguise the set of his powerful shoulders and the athletic grace of his build. For all the care taken with the folds of his immaculately starched cravat, the unconscious elegance of his hand on the mantelpiece, the lazy negligence of his pose, there was nothing effete about Charles Dacre. From his crisp black hair down to his gleaming top-boots he was all confident male.

The Dowager pulled herself together, and said with a return to her former tone, 'You owe it to the family, Charles. Good God, what is wrong with your generation? Your father did his duty—two sons while he was still in his twenties—and now it is up to you to do yours. Accidents can happen to the healthiest among us, and you cannot say that jauntering about the Continent is the safest way to live. From what I've heard there could well be a few husbands who wouldn't mind seeing you off, too.'

'Let them try,' her grandson said indifferently. 'I never took anything that was not freely given, Grand-mère!'

'As if that were anything to the purpose! And now this South American business——'

'What South American business? What do you mean?'

'You needn't pretend, Charles. I am not yet in my dotage either, and I hear a thing or two. Don't worry, I know you have your duty, and, though I could wish you were not involved, I'm not going to tease you into giving it up before it's finished. But you cannot claim it isn't dangerous.'

'I can—it is mere routine. But it worries me that you know anything about it. How many others do?'

'None! My source is discreet, and so am I. We shall forget it, if that is what you wish. But—why not marry first?' When he shook his head in a gesture of repudiation she asked, 'Why do you dislike the idea of marriage so much? Have you never even contemplated it?'

'Frequently,' he said with a short laugh. 'And always with horror! What, abandon the very civilised pleasures I enjoy at present—the challenge of pursuit, the delights of a shared passion and then the final parting, with no regret or recrimination—exchange all that for the kind of life I have observed marriage to bring? You must be mad!'

'You exaggerate, Charles!'

'Forgive me, but I do not! You cannot say that my

father's second marriage was a recommendation! The scenes, the drama—the poor man never had a moment's peace! Four of them—my stepmother and her three dreadful offspring—and they hadn't even a legitimate claim on him! Forever demanding this, complaining about that. And then Gervase and his choice...' Lord Aldworth took his hand from the mantelpiece and moved restlessly about the room. 'Have you any notion of what it is like at present up at Aldworth? I live in a...a hen-coop, surrounded by squawking, cackling females. You may put me in Bedlam if I add another to the collection, to squawk at *me*, to submit *me* to her freaks and her tempers, to accuse *me* of selfishness and worse.'

'You've been spoiled, Charles. In my day a man married first and took his pleasures afterwards. You've been living like a butterfly for far too long.'

'I believe my work with Castlereagh has not been without merit, ma'am,' said Lord Aldworth mildly.

'Oh, lord, I'm not denying you've done marvels in Vienna and elsewhere for your country. But what about your family? When you were a younger son it was all very well to carve out a name for yourself, charging about the Continent, performing heroic deeds. Even afterwards in Vienna, wheedling trade concessions out of what is left of my poor France, and seducing the wives of all the others who are doing the same——'

'The commission has been more than fair with your poor France, ma'am. As for the rest... You overestimate my powers, I assure you.'

'I doubt it,' said the Dowager drily. 'But you must now put that all behind you and settle down to managing Aldworth. Good God, you're not trying to tell me that a few raddled Englishwomen will get the better of you, when Metternich and his lot have tried and failed, are you? You're a diplomat!'

'Diplomacy plays no part in dealing with the numerous Aldworth widows, ma'am—except yourself, of course. A bludgeon is more their weapon.'

'Well, get rid of them, then,' said the Dowager, losing patience. 'If you were to get yourself a wife they would have to move out of Aldworth anyway. Gervase was far too soft with Almeria and her three harpies. They should have been packed off when he married. And the screech-owl should be given somewhere else to live, too—but not this house,' she added firmly. 'You could settle some of them in the Sussex property, perhaps. Old Millicent Dacre's place—what's it called? Blanchards! That's been empty for years.'

'I went to Blanchards on my way back. It's in a bad way and the caretaker has been negligent—the place was overrun with gypsies—but it could be put right. . .'

There was a silence in the room as Lord Aldworth went to the window and stared out at the rolling Berkshire countryside, at the distant Palladian mansion set like a jewel in its park.

'You know I am right, Charles.' His grandmother's voice was sympathetic but firm. 'The family needs an heir—and an absentee landlord does the land no good.'

'Yes, I know you're right. Of course you are right,' he said finally. 'But not yet, Grand-mère.'

'You can't leave it much longer,' she said unrelentingly. There was another silence. Then she sighed and spoke again. 'What if we were to compromise? If I were to find you a nice, biddable girl—not too sophisticated, one that wouldn't expect much by way of attention, a simple girl who knew her duty, and was prepared to perform it without fuss, to give you your heirs and let you go your own way otherwise. . .'

His attention caught, Lord Aldworth came back to her. 'You would never find such a paragon.'

'I think I might. France was full of them in the old days—I don't see why England shouldn't have a few. She has to be well-born, that goes without saying, but she needn't be rich.'

'All the better if she isn't!' said Lord Aldworth cynically. 'She would at least have something to gain from the marriage. But it's a hopeless task. Such a girl would have to be simple to the point of idiocy, Grand-mère!'

'Oh, *mon Dieu*, have I misunderstood? You want her to have brains?'

'Good lord, no! A wife is better off without them. Indeed, a clever wife is the last thing I should want!' Lord Aldworth grinned as he entered into the spirit of the thing. 'Well, Grand-mère, if you can find me a well-bred, biddable, modest, sweet-natured girl. . .'

'Who knows how to behave. . .'

'But isn't going to argue, or think she knows better. . .'

'Who is looking for a rich husband. . .'

'And is exquisitely lovely into the bargain. . .'

'I didn't promise that!'

'Well, why not? If we are going to invent an imposs-ible dream, why not have her lovely too?' Lord Aldworth laughed. 'I'll make a bargain with you, Grand-mère. If you find such an ideal—I say *if*—I'll marry her!'

* * *

Lord Aldworth might not have been serious, but his grandmother was. After he had left her to go back to his 'hen-coop', she sat deep in thought for some time. If this was the only way she could persuade her reluctant grandson to marry then she would find a suitable girl, one way or another. It was a pity, though. She had always hoped that he, the best-loved of her grandchildren, would find a woman he was capable of respecting and with whom he would be willing to share his life properly. He would have had much to give and much to gain from such a partnership. Not for the first time she cursed Charles's father's unfortunate second marriage. And as for Gervase and his harridan—the less said about them the better. The only clever thing poor Gervase ever did was to quit the world and leave the way clear for Charles to succeed. . .

Her thoughts had come in a circle back to her present problem. Where was she to find a wife for Charles? It would be dangerous to wait for next season's crop of débutantes, for Charles was not expecting to stay in England for long. He had come home after Gervase's unexpected death to sort out family affairs, but he would have to return to his post in Vienna to deal with unfinished business there. Once in Vienna he might well succumb to the attractions of a dainty *contessa* or an elegant *marquise*, and postpone fulfilling his family obligations in England. Worse still, he might be called on to act in a business which she knew to be dangerous, for all his protests. He must marry soon!

The Dowager spent much of her time during the next few days writing to a number of friends and acquaintances. She also sent instructions for her apartments in the family mansion in Berkeley Square to be aired and opened. It was tiresome that she would have to spend time out of season in London, but she was determined to spare no effort to see that her grandson acquired a wife. . .

Meanwhile, some eighty miles to the south, the happy anticipation of Serafina's visit to London was disturbed by some disquieting news from Oxford. Gabriel's tutor was uneasy about him, and Mr Feverel hastened up there to spend some days with his son. When he returned he was clearly worried, and, since it was not a matter that he could possibly hide from his wife, both she and Serafina soon knew it all. Gabriel had fallen in with a bad set—idlers and gamblers, all of them. The boy had gone up to Oxford at sixteen, of course, and had probably been too young and too unsophisticated to withstand the wiles of those older than himself. Whatever the cause, he had been incurring debts, the sum total of which was still unknown. It was an anxious time for them all, for Mr Feverel's resources were strictly limited. Though his family was an ancient one, the estate was now small and, since Lucius Feverel had liberal ideas, a major part of its income was taken up in repairs and maintenance.

Serafina hated the thought of leaving her family in this state, but her mother gently pointed out to her that Lady Chilham's ambition to secure an advantageous marriage for her might now be more important than she had realised. So Serafina satisfied her conscience by cancelling two of her new dresses and finally set out for London, determined to succeed. She was kindly received by Lady Chilham and soon settled into the house in Curzon Street.

Here she quickly found that Society's rules were every bit as rigorous as the rules of Latin grammar or the principles of mathematics, and that learning them was every bit as demanding. Lady Chilham was as thorough as Mr Feverel, and much less tolerant. She took Serafina through the tortuous procedures for arrivals, introductions, departures and return visits. She instructed her in what one might say and what it would be social disaster to say, what one might wear and might not wear, what was done and what was not done. As Lady Chilham had feared, Serafina was quick to learn what was required, but it was difficult to convince her that the rigmarole was desirable. She was forced to remind the girl constantly of the goal she and Mrs Feverel, and Serafina herself, all had in view.

Serafina grew to dislike the very mention of 'an advantageous marriage'. No girl could grow up in a family with three younger brothers without knowing that there were physical differences between men and women, but nothing in her upbringing had led her to believe that there should be differences in their mental attitudes. It seemed laughable to her that men, most of whom she regarded as reasonable human beings, should demand such artificial behaviour from the women they hoped to marry; it was absurd that any man would be influenced in his choice of a partner for life by the manner in which she curtsied, or that he would depend on the opinion of his mother, or his aunt, or the patronesses of Almack's, or any of the other arbiters of good behaviour. Then she remembered the young men in Sussex and her failure to attract an offer from all but one of them, the necessity for her to make a good match, and she would sigh and set her mind to satisfying her godmother.

About a month after Serafina's arrival she came in from a stolen visit to the British Museum to hear that Lady Chilham wished to see her immediately. Serafina's heart sank. How had her godmother found out? But when she entered the little salon on the first floor she found nothing to indicate that Lady Chilham was annoyed. On the contrary, though she was sitting calmly enough in her customary place by the fire, there was an air of suppressed excitement about her. She had a letter in her hand.

'Serafina! The most extraordinary opportunity for you has arisen. I only hope we may profit from it. This is from an old friend of mine, Lady Carstairs. Listen to what she writes. "Do tell me if there is any further news of Lady Aldworth's quest to find a bride for her grandson. I am sure it is being treated with all possible discretion, of course, but such an affair must arouse a great deal of interest. I should have thought Charles Dacre was handsome enough to find a girl for himself, but no, it seems the Dowager has been charged with the task. Perhaps he is too busy, in every sense of the word, in Vienna! And the need for an heir is evident. What a prize! The Aldworth fortune is vast, even allowing for the Aldworth widows. If only my own granddaughter were old enough! Don't forget to let me know the instant you hear a thing."'

Lady Chilham folded the letter carefully and put it down. 'She rattles on further, but nothing of any interest to you. You realise what this might mean, Serafina? Have you heard of the Aldworths? They are fabulously wealthy, and Aldworth himself must be one of the most eligible bachelors in England. It would be to aim almost too high. . .'

Serafina cleared her throat nervously. 'I believe they own a property in Sussex, ma'am. Blanchards is quite near where I live.'

'Then you know the family?'

'No, not at all,' said Serafina swiftly, shutting out of her mind a sudden vision of furious grey eyes under a dusty crown of vine leaves. 'Blanchards has not been lived in for as long as I can remember.'

'That is satisfactory. We shall have our work cut out as it is, without the intrusion of your family background.'

Serafina stiffened. 'I beg your pardon, ma'am?'

'Well done! That touch of hauteur was excellently judged. I think you are learning after all, Serafina!'

But Serafina was not to be mollified. 'You referred to my family, I believe, Lady Chilham. Surely it is at least as old and distinguished as anything Lord Aldworth can boast?' She added scornfully, 'It is not rich, of course.'

'I'm sorry if I have offended you, child. There's nothing wrong with your breeding—on either side. But your upbringing. . . That is a different matter. You will naturally deny that there is anything wrong with it, nor do I blame you for your loyalty. But we both know that it is not what Lady Aldworth will look for. That reminds me—I must make a few discreet enquiries. Exactly what is Lady Aldworth's role in this affair? Lord Aldworth is certainly not the man to need any help in engaging a young woman's affections. Rather the reverse, I should say!'

The result of Lady Chilham's researches was to give her a very thoughtful air. She sent once again for Serafina.

'How serious are you about wishing to oblige your family, Serafina?'

Serafina looked surprised, and then her quick intelligence made the connection. 'What is wrong with the Aldworth match, Lady Chilham?'

'Nothing at all, nothing at all. It would be many a young girl's dream. It's just. . .'

'Just. . .?'

'Lady Aldworth has a very clear idea of the sort of young girl she is looking for. Her grandson will marry no other.'

'And?'

'You meet her requirements in only two respects. Perhaps three, if you were to concentrate.'

Serafina should have been very glad to hear that she was not to be put forward as a candidate for Lord Aldworth's hand. She was haunted by a secret fear that, unlikely though it was, he might recognise in her the thief in his greenhouse. But this was too much for her natural pride.

'Which are they?'

'You are beautiful, and well-bred. And with some hard preparation I think you could persuade her that you know how to behave in Society.'

Serafina's eyes were glittering as she asked, 'And in what ways would I not satisfy Lord Aldworth's stringent requirements?'

'The tendency to talk like that is one of them,' said Lady Chilham bluntly. 'Lady Aldworth is looking for someone who will give her grandson an heir, is meek, content to let others do her thinking for her, and is ready to allow Lord Aldworth to continue in his present mode of life——'

'Stop, stop! You have said enough. Lord Aldworth obviously wants a...a Miss Twitch, but with impeccable lineage and outstanding beauty. I can see that he and I should never suit.'

'That is not the question. It would be more to the point to remember that if you could catch him, Serafina, your family would have no more financial worries. But I fear we could never persuade him—or Lady Aldworth—that you were even a suitable candidate.'

'Could we not indeed?' said Serafina, her eyes glittering again. 'I would wager, ma'am, that if I were to set my mind to it I could play the role of the pretty doll Lord Aldworth seems to require as well as anyone. Indeed, I might even enjoy it.'

Lady Chilham looked appraisingly at her goddaughter. Then she said, 'Do you know, I think you just might do it? I had forgotten your performance as that little spinster... You were certainly most convincingly demure... But no, it would not serve, Serafina! It would be to deceive him most shamefully.'

'You say he is rich, ma'am? And extremely eligible? And yet he has such a small interest in the girl he will make his bride that he asks his grandmother to select one for him! I think Lord Aldworth deserves no better. And, as you said, it would, if I succeeded, put an end to my family's worries.'

The two ladies smiled at each other. 'It would certainly be a triumph to snare the Aldworth fortune,' said Lady Chilham thoughtfully.

'And how I would enjoy taking Lord Arrogance down a peg or two!' said Serafina.

'What do you mean? You surely wouldn't cry off at the last minute or anything silly like that, would you?' asked Lady Chilham sharply.

'That is the last thing I should do. What should I gain from that? No, Lord Aldworth would merely gradually discover that he had married more than he bargained for. At the very worst he will abandon me in his country seat, and I shall be free to study as much as I like. And at best he might even come to terms with having a bluestocking for a wife! And until he did one or the other I could make life most uncomfortable for that conceited peer!'

Lady Aldworth, meanwhile, was having small success in her search. The best families in England seemed to be suffering from a dearth of eligible candidates. Miss Trotton de Courcy was malleable and willing, but she had a face like a horse, and laughed like one, too. Lady Amabel Wye was lovely enough, but her manner was imperious, and a disagreeable frown too often marred her fair brow. The Honourable Prudence Carter was too fat, Lord Bacup's daughter too frail. . .and so it went on—each of the girls she had so far seen had some fault or other. In fact, Lady Aldworth was reluctant to give her seal of approval to anyone. Though she herself had suggested such a match, she found it repellent to think of Charles tied to a girl who fulfilled all his selfish requirements. He would need more than such a soulless union to keep him happy for the rest of his life. So it was with no great optimism that Lady Aldworth agreed to pay a call on Lady Chilham. It appeared that there was a god-daughter. . . She asked herself what would be wrong with this one.

Her first impression, however, was good. The chit was angelically lovely—one requisite more than adequately fulfilled. Silver-gilt hair, clear blue eyes under delicately arched brows, a perfectly formed nose and a beautifully moulded mouth—a fraction too wide perhaps, but that was better than being too small. The girl was slender and moved gracefully—her curtsy was a delight to watch. She looked healthy in spite of her ethereal air, and her teeth were good. So was her dress sense. The round gown in pale blue muslin was neither too plain nor too elaborate, and the Paisley shawl over it was handled with skill as she sat down on the chair in front of the Dowager. Good hands and feet, neatly disposed. Altogether very promising!

'Lady Chilham tells me that you live in Sussex, Miss Feverel.'

'Yes, Lady Aldworth.'

'Where, exactly?'

'Hardington Feverel, not far from East Bourne.'

'Really? Do you know Blanchards, our estate down there?'

'Yes, Lady Aldworth.'

'Well, girl? Tell me more. How close is it to your home?'

'It is quite near, Lady Aldworth.'

'Really? Did my grandson call on your papa when he was down at Blanchards recently?'

'No, Lady Aldworth.' The girl seemed to be getting nervous. She seemed almost too simple, thought Lady Aldworth. Even Charles would tire of these monosyllables. Perhaps she was to be disappointed yet again in

her search? But this Feverel girl was so lovely—she
would try once more.

'Let me see... Feverel. Of course! Lucius Feverel,
the scholar.'

'You know him?' Suddenly the girl's face came to
life. The wonderful eyes glowed and her mouth was
curved in a smile. Lady Chilham coughed and Miss
Feverel, with an effort she could not quite hide, calmed
down into her former insipid manner. Lady Aldworth
was intrigued. She decided that this was a promising
line of investigation.

'He is a madman, of course,' she said with deliberate
provocation. What would be the reply to that? The girl
must either agree, thus showing lack of filial respect
for a father she was clearly fond of, or dare to disagree
with her visitor. Lady Chilham shifted nervously in her
chair, but Miss Feverel remained calm. Her answer
when it came was a masterpiece of diplomacy.

'I cannot judge what the world thinks of Papa. I
have lived in the country until very recently. You may
be right, Lady Aldworth——'

The Dowager smiled in grim satisfaction. So the girl
was going to sacrifice her father in her own self-
interest, eh? Or was she too simple to see the implication? But the satisfaction faded at the unexceptionable
words which followed.

'—but I owe him every respect. He has always been
a kind and loving father to me and to my brothers and
sister.' Miss Feverel had been looking down at her
clasped hands but she now raised her eyes and gave
Lady Aldworth a look of hurt reproach. Had the
Dowager but known it, that look was one of Serafina's
most successful weapons. The Dowager barely stopped

herself from begging pardon. She pulled herself together.

'Brothers and sister, eh? You like children?'

'I love my brothers and sister, ma'am.'

The conversation continued in this vein for some time, but though Miss Feverel's manners were subjected to some hard testing she did not falter in her modestly polite responses. Only once was there a hint of something else. Towards the end the Dowager snapped out a question intended to disconcert this paragon.

'Well, miss, you know why I am here and I suppose you have considered whether you would like to be the next Lady Aldworth. Should my grandson decide you'd suit, what would you say?'

The blue eyes widened in surprise at this very indiscreet enquiry. The girl gave a slight smile and said demurely, 'Until he does, Lady Aldworth, it would not be proper for me to say. Anyone must be flattered at Lord Aldworth's condescension, of course.'

This time there was something in the voice—a slight irony? Surely not! All the same it was enough to intrigue the Dowager. The girl had a quality unlike any other she had met. She found herself wondering what Charles would make of the chit, and was inclined to risk introducing them. But first she would have some further conversation with young Mademoiselle Feverel! The Dowager had a suspicion that she might have been engaged in a battle of wits during the past half-hour. And if that were so, then this angelic-looking girl had been one of the most cool, most subtle opponents Lady Aldworth had come across for some time.

CHAPTER THREE

A few days later Serafina received an invitation to visit the Dowager Lady Aldworth at her house in Berkeley Square. It was made clear that Lord Aldworth would not be present.

'She means to have another look at you, Serafina,' said Lady Chilham. 'On the one hand it is very flattering—you have passed the first test, so to speak, and I don't think any of the others got as far. On the other hand. . . I wish I could be with you, but the invitation only mentions your name. . . Still, you managed the last interview perfectly. We shall just go through the courtesies involved in making a call, if you please. And we must look through your wardrobe. . .'

As a result of Lady Chilham's efforts Serafina arrived at Berkeley Square looking composed and very elegant. The weather had turned cold and she was wearing a velvet pelisse in a very pretty shade of dark lilac over her white muslin dress. Her face was framed in a bonnet of lilac *velours simulé*, lined with white sarsnet, and she was carrying a small white fur muff, borrowed from her godmother. Marbury, the elderly butler, afterwards confided to Mrs Phillips, the Berkeley Square housekeeper, that he had never seen anything so lovely come up the front steps before.

Lady Aldworth had a suite of rooms on the first floor. Attempts had been made, somewhat unwisely, by the other Aldworth ladies to oust her from them, but she had foiled them all, and whenever she was in London she occupied what were, in fact, the best rooms in the house. Serafina followed Marbury up the broad staircase and into Lady Aldworth's salon.

'Miss Feverel! How charming you look—come here and sit down.' After the courtesies were complete Serafina found herself sitting on the opposite side of the fireplace from the old lady, facing the long windows. 'It is pleasant to see another face, Miss Feverel. I have been confined to my rooms in this inclement weather.' After Serafina had expressed her sympathy and they had exchanged pleasantries the Dowager said, 'Tell me, Miss Feverel, would you be willing to do an old lady a favour? My eyes are not what they were and there is an article in *The Times* which intrigues me. As you will have guessed I was born in France, and though I have no sympathy for the regime which was recently defeated by the Allies I am enough of a Frenchwoman still to wish to know what is happening to her now. Would you read it to me?'

Serafina could hardly refuse. She took the proffered paper and began to read. At first she managed to stay in character. She hesitated over words of more than one syllable, she stumbled over foreign names, looking apologetically each time at Lady Aldworth. The Dowager merely nodded. But slowly Serafina's interest was caught by what she was reading. She soon became more fluent, referring easily to Metternich, Talleyrand and Aix-la-Chapelle. The soft, sweetly hesitant tone she had adopted in London disappeared, and indignation was in her voice as she read of Prussia's extortionate demands. The article came to an end, and she looked up to find Lady Aldworth smiling at her grimly. She had betrayed herself! Oh, how could she have been so careless? 'I. . . I read a lot with Papa,' was all Serafina could find to say.

But to her surprise the Dowager simply replied, 'Of course, of course. You read well, Miss Feverel—after your initial nervousness. Thank you.'

Serafina thought it was time to take her leave. Though Lady Aldworth had not referred to the change in her personality, she must have noticed it. She would certainly not ask to see her again. So it was with astonishment that Serafina heard her hostess suggest a further meeting. 'Perhaps Lady Chilham would be good enough to take you to Lady Carteret's drum, which is to be held at Marchant House in a week's time. I will see that you receive invitations. I am sure you would enjoy the occasion, and I shall try to arrange for my grandson to be there. He is, of course, his own master, but he normally obliges me when he can. I shall not tell him anything beforehand, but I shall take the opportunity to introduce you both.'

Serafina was still perplexed as she took her leave. She was even more astonished when, as she got to the door, Lady Aldworth said, 'Miss Feverel! The manner is very good—just what Charles thinks he is looking for. Don't overdo it—a touch more vivacity would not come amiss.' She chuckled, then added, 'But you must take more care to sustain it. All the time, Miss Feverel! Goodbye—I shall see you at Marchant House.'

After Serafina had gone Lady Aldworth chuckled again, and then grew serious. The girl was very nearly perfect in her role as an *ingénue*. But it was now obvious that it was a role. The real Miss Feverel was more intelligent and better educated than she admitted.

What a clever minx she was! Well, it might end in disaster, but Lady Aldworth was inclined to think that Serafina Feverel just might be the perfect answer to Charles's objections to a proper marriage. Meanwhile she, Lady Aldworth, would sit back and enjoy the comedy.

The drum at Marchant House, which took place in November each year to celebrate Countess Carteret's birthday, was not generally held to be among London's most brilliant occasions. The capital was not as full as it would be in spring and early summer, nor were the Carterets, though a worthy enough couple, leaders of Society. But it was usually well-attended, and to one as unsophisticated as Serafina it was immensely exciting. She tried hard to look composed and not to stare as she went through a succession of handsomely furnished rooms to the ballroom at the back of the house. She herself caused no small sensation. Since she had not yet been presented her toilette was modest, but Serafina had no need of embellishment. Her simple white silk dress provided the perfect foil for her beauty, and she was the focus of many admiring eyes and whispered enquiries for her name. Lady Chilham was soon besieged by eager aspirants for a dance with Miss Feverel.

Lady Aldworth was there, of course, but there was no sign of her grandson. She greeted Serafina kindly, though she took care not to give the curious any indication that this was her favoured candidate.

About halfway through the evening there was a stir as a small party of elegantly dressed ladies and gentlemen entered the ballroom. They had obviously been dining together and were all in high spirits. Serafina recognised Lord Aldworth immediately. On his arm as they came into the room was a vivacious, dark-haired woman, dressed in a daringly cut gown of geranium-coloured gros de Naples silk. Diamonds glittered at her throat and in her hair, and she was carrying a fan which she was using to great effect. Even as Serafina watched, the lady spread the fan and gazed mockingly at Lord Aldworth over the top of it.

'There's Lord Aldworth, Serafina,' said Lady Chilham. 'The tall man with the woman in red. Gracious me, that's Louisa Paget, unless I'm very much mistaken. I'm surprised; I thought the Pagets were in Vienna still. Just look at that dress—Paris in every line of it! But then she always did spend a lot on her clothes. Heavens, how she hangs on Aldworth's arm. I wonder where Sir Robert is?'

'Sir Robert?'

'The lady's husband. He's not one of the party, that's certain.'

After a while the little band of revellers split up and wandered round the ballroom, talking to friends and acquaintances. Lord Aldworth stopped at his grand-mother's chair for a while but he soon moved on, still accompanied by Lady Paget. Serafina watched him as he shepherded his lady expertly through the crowds, then laughed down at her, put his hand at her waist, and swept her into the waltz which had just begun.

'Just look at those two—they are practically embrac-ing in public! I have never approved of the waltz, however fashionable it may be in Vienna. It gives rise to the sort of scandalous behaviour you see over there,' said Lady Chilham.

'They look so graceful, ma'am—and the gentleman is keeping the same strict distance from the lady as everyone else is,' replied Serafina.

Lady Chilham frowned. 'That might be so—but they don't look as if they are,' she said somewhat obscurely.

Serafina sighed. Lord Aldworth was more handsome than she had remembered, and his black and white evening clothes suited him even better than his travelling garb. How could she possibly attract him? She could never aspire to the sophistication and elegance of the woman at present in his arms. She sighed again, but then saw that the Dowager was beckoning to her, and with a word to Lady Chilham Serafina went over to speak to her.

Lady Aldworth was frowning, and her bony fingers were clutching her cane so tightly that the knuckles were white. The old lady was clearly in a rage, and Serafina was willing to wager that it had been caused by her grandson's appearance with Lady Paget. What was she planning to do? Serafina felt a touch of apprehension, but smiled dutifully and, at Lady Aldworth's invitation, sat down beside her. The Dowager said abruptly, 'Miss Feverel, if you are willing, I will introduce my grandson to you. I am sure he would like to make your acquaintance.'

Serafina allowed her eyes to rest for a moment on the two circling the floor. 'Really, Lady Aldworth?' she said doubtfully.

The Dowager lips tightened. 'Perhaps I should have told him you were to be here tonight. However, I wanted to surprise him. He will come over when he sees I have someone with me, I am sure.'

Serafina was by no means sure of this, but she was

proved wrong. The waltz ended, Lord Aldworth escorted his partner back to her friends, bowed, and could then be seen threading his way towards his grandmother.

Serafina was suddenly in a panic. 'I don't think. . .'

But she subsided when the Dowager snapped, 'Don't be foolish, girl. Stay here!'

Lord Aldworth was suddenly quite near and Serafina clasped her hands together nervously. However, there was no sign of recognition in his face as he looked first at her and then enquiringly at his grandmother.

'My grandson, Lord Aldworth—Miss Feverel.'

The usual courtesies were exchanged, then Lord Aldworth took a small step back and examined Serafina. 'I congratulate you, Grand-mère,' he said. 'Miss Feverel is charming.'

Serafina supposed that she deserved his patronising tone, for it was well-known to all three of them that she was a candidate for marriage, but, try as she might, she could not suppress a feeling of resentment. A faint flush of anger appeared in her cheeks, but Lord Aldworth seemed to regard this as one of maidenly modesty.

'Delightful!' he said.

'Miss Feverel is staying with her godmother, Charles.'

'Really? Now that is good news,' he said. His tone was still one of patronage and Serafina felt a strong desire to box his ears. Since this would hardly further her cause, however, she hid her feelings by looking down shyly at her hands.

'But don't you find it rather boring in London at the moment, Miss Feverel? There are so few entertainments

for such a lovely young lady.' She looked up again
to find that he was smiling down at her—a ruefully
lopsided smile—and for a moment she felt the pull of
his charm.

'I am enjoying it, Lord Aldworth,' she said, stammer-
ing a little.

'That's good! That's very good. Er...where do you
come from? The Home Counties?' Lord Aldworth's
tone was kind but it was obvious that he was making
conversation, and Serafina doubted that he was really
interested in her answer. However, much could be
forgiven of a man who continued to smile at one in
that devastatingly attractive way.

'She comes from Sussex, Charles,' said the Dowager.

'How very interesting!' His eyes strayed a little, and
Serafina saw that he was watching Lady Paget, who
was taking the floor with another member of her
party—a handsome man in his forties. 'Er...would you
dance with me, Miss Feverel?'

They joined a set of country dances. Serafina was
not sure how, but they ended up in the same set as
Lady Paget, and it was obvious that Lord Aldworth's
real purpose was to keep a close watch on what was
happening at the other end of the set. Though she
could do little about it, this annoyed her. But after a
while he pulled himself together and spoke.

'Did my grandmother say you came from Sussex,
Miss Feverel? You are not a smuggler, I hope!' An
avuncular grin was meant to convey that, in case she
thought he was serious, this was a joke.

'Oh, goodness me, no, Lord Aldworth!' she
exclaimed, looking at him in well-simulated horror.
'Ladies in general are not, you know.'

'No, of course not. Stupid of me. Er...so where do you live?' His eye moved to the head of the set.

'Feverel Place at Hardington.'

'I see.' Serafina waited in vain for any comment on this. If he had been listening with any concentration, he must have asked if she knew Blanchards—Hardington was not all that far from the property. But he said nothing, and she began to feel angry again.

'And what do you do with your time in London?' he asked at last, turning to her with another charmingly avuncular smile. Before she could reply Lady Paget's delicious laugh rang out and his head turned swiftly towards the sound.

Serafina took a deep breath and said diffidently, 'I clean the streets and sweep chimneys.'

'Good, good! I expect your godmother has arranged a good few things of that nature.'

Serafina almost spoilt everything by laughing out loud. What a conceited, rude man this was! He had obviously written her off as a mindless nonentity, and was treating her accordingly. She would enjoy the dancing and forget him, and she managed to do so for a while. Then he seemed to pull himself together and make a genuine effort to talk to her, but though she risked no more nonsensical replies it was not difficult to keep up her role of *ingénue*. He said little that would not have been instantly understood by a five-year-old child. The set of country dances finally came to an end and they returned to the Dowager, who was talking to Lady Chilham.

'Thank you, Miss Feverel. I enjoyed that enormously. We must try it again some time. Now, if you'll excuse me... Your servant, Lady Chilham... Grand-mère.' He

was gone. Not five minutes later they saw him escorting
Lady Paget from the room.

When Serafina came downstairs the following day, she
was greeted with the news that the Dowager Lady
Aldworth had just arrived and was waiting to see her
in the salon. Surprised, she went in to find her godmother and the Dowager in earnest conversation. But
Lady Chilham excused herself after a short while, and
Serafina was left alone with her visitor.

'I've come to talk to you about my grandson,' began
Lady Aldworth briskly. 'Lady Chilham has told me
that your father would not object if Aldworth were to
make an offer for you, though naturally they would
have to meet first. I should like to know how you
would view such an offer.'

Serafina would have spoken but Lady Aldworth held
up her hand. 'I know that I have asked you this once
before, Miss Feverel, and was refused an answer. At
the time I was content to let matters take their course.
But the situation was not as urgent then as it is now.
Unless I act swiftly this new affair of his will distract
Aldworth, and once again he will delay fulfilling his
family obligations. You see—I am being frank with
you. I can hardly be otherwise. You can't have failed
to observe his conduct last night with that creature.'

'Do you mean with Lady Paget?'

'So you know her name? It's an old name, a good
name. She has no business to be exposing it to gossip,
and nor has Charles. Why the devil couldn't he confine
his affairs to Vienna or Paris?' She stopped, glared at
Serafina, and then made an effort to speak more
calmly. 'But that's a matter between my grandson and

me. I haven't come here to talk of that. I'm here to ask if you are serious.'

'Serious? I'm not sure what you mean, Lady Aldworth,' said Serafina with a wide-eyed stare.

'For the love of God, don't play-act! There isn't time for it. That innocent gaze doesn't fool me, Miss Feverel—we both know that you are far cleverer than you pretend. I'm not sure I approve of your attempt to deceive me, but that's water under the bridge now. I have come to the conclusion that you are the very girl for my plans.'

Serafina said calmly, 'What plans, ma'am?'

'To get Charles married, of course. I realise now that a genuinely simple girl would never do! Charles would get bored in five minutes and I would lose him before he ever got round to offering for her. I need someone who can appear to be what he wants, yet is clever enough to hold his interest afterwards, and I'm inclined to think that you are the very one. I wish to know if you are serious in your wish to marry Aldworth.'

'I. . . I am serious in my wish to marry well, ma'am. I too have an obligation to my family. But whether it should be to your grandson is another matter.'

'Listen to the chit! Anyone would think eligible bachelors grew on trees, ready for the plucking! You're not in love with any one else, are you? There are no complications of that sort, I hope?' Serafina shook her head, and Lady Aldworth continued, 'Good! Well, now, Aldworth is a man who keeps his promises, and he has promised me that he will marry. I think I can persuade him that you are suitable. He trusts me, I believe.'

Serafina gave a laugh. 'Wait, wait! Unlikely though

it may seem to you, you might have to persuade me that your grandson is suitable for me! Marriage to such an unwilling suitor does not seem very attractive!'

'He is worth a little effort, Miss Feverel. He is well-born, handsome, and rich, as I am sure you already know. But he is not just the charming rogue most people see. He is a skilled and intelligent diplomat, and deeply committed to his country's interests. Given the right partner he could be equally committed to his marriage.'

'Then tell me why he delegates this important decision to you, Lady Aldworth,' Serafina asked bluntly, abandoning her pose completely. 'I have my own reasons—family reasons—for wishing to marry for wealth rather than love, and if Lord Aldworth seeks a . . .a doll, then I am prepared to be one. But why does he wish for such a bride? I hardly think a doll would be the right partner for a man as intelligent as you claim Lord Aldworth to be.'

'Exactly! But Lord Aldworth does not wish to marry at all! I have won his agreement on condition I can find a bride who is silly enough not to interfere with his present way of life.'

'Silly?' asked Serafina in astonishment.

'My word for it, not his. His is "biddable",' explained Lady Aldworth.

Serafina gave an exclamation of disapproval.

Lady Aldworth hesitated, then went on, 'There are good reasons for his attitude, which I will not go into at the moment. But. . . But, Miss Feverel——' she spoke with emphasis '—I think it would in fact spoil his life to marry such a girl. He is already somewhat selfish, and slightly arrogant——'

'Somewhat! Slightly! You are over-partial, Lady Aldworth.'

The Dowager, far from resenting this, smiled. 'If you would agree to get to know him better, I think you would find it possible to tolerate him. His preoccupation with that creature last night was unfortunate, but I shall deal with that. Once Lady Paget is out of the way I think you would find him attentive enough. Will you try it? I have to know.'

Serafina hesitated.

'I shall see that there are handsome settlements, Miss Feverel.' Then, when Serafina still didn't speak, she sighed and said, 'Will you at least agree to see something more of him?'

This Serafina agreed to do.

Lord Aldworth's interview with his grandmother that same day was much less friendly than their earlier discussion. She received him coldly, and began without any idle preliminaries.

'I have found the girl I consider to be ideal for you, Charles. You met her last night—if you were aware of her existence.'

'What do you mean, Grand-mère? I even danced with Miss Feverel!'

'Oh, so you remember her name, do you?' she said sardonically.

'She's a very pretty girl——'

'She is exquisitely lovely, well-born, sweet-natured, and she has all the other qualities you need, Charles. I expect you now to keep your word, and see if the girl will marry you. I only hope you haven't put her off by your obvious preoccupation with someone else.'

'Surely the bargain was that I should be free to go my own way?'

'But even you, Charles——' Lady Aldworth's voice was scathing '—even you would surely not intend to flaunt your amours in front of the girl's very nose?'

Lord Aldworth stiffened and said, somewhat defensively, 'I was not aware that you were about to produce a prospective bride for me so soon. Lady Paget happened to be in London, and is an old friend of mine——'

'And Sir Robert? He is still in Vienna, I hear. Is he a friend of yours?'

'Why, yes.'

'And you think it the act of a friend to expose Sir Robert—a senior diplomat and distinguished servant of your own country—to expose such a man to ridicule, and his wife to gossip and scandal? I am surprised and grieved, Charles. Your affairs in Vienna are, I suppose, your own concern——'

'Indeed they are, ma'am,' said Lord Aldworth angrily.

But Lady Aldworth continued as if he had not spoken, 'I have regarded your career as something of a Don Juan with tolerance, Charles. I have even been amused at the reports of your escapades which kind friends send me from time to time. But this affair with Lady Paget is very different. Your behaviour in this matter is not honourable, and I find it singularly unamusing. In fact I find it distasteful, and I begin to wonder what sort of man you have become.'

Lord Aldworth flushed. 'You are doing me an injustice, Grand-mère. In spite of what you saw, Lady Paget is not my mistress.'

'And you are not attracted to her?' There was a pause. When he remained silent, she went on, 'Leave her to her other friends, Charles, before it is too late. Concentrate instead on your promise to me. Miss Feverel would make you a perfect wife. Spend time with her instead of bringing discredit on the family name with such a dubious liaison.'

There was a long silence. Lady Aldworth was content to have it so. Charles was usually honest with himself. He would admit that her analysis of the situation with Louisa Paget was a fair one.

'Where shall I find Miss Feverel?' he said eventually.

CHAPTER FOUR

AFTER that Lord Aldworth was a frequent visitor at Curzon Street. He remained patronisingly avuncular, and Serafina often had to grit her teeth to stop herself from dropping her pose and saying something outrageous. But as time went on she began to enjoy his company. It was not only that she found it amusing to pit her wits against his. When he put his mind to it he could be a very charming companion, willing to do what he could to entertain her. It was considerably easier to gain admission to various exhibitions and museums under the aegis of a peer of the realm than it would have been on her own, and she soon learned to use her ingenuity to ensure that their various outings were to more interesting places than he thought suitable for her amusement.

She shuddered to think what her father would have said if he had been there to hear the inanities she uttered and the naïve questions she asked. But in the end she could pride herself on the fact that, though Lord Aldworth was frequently amused by what she said, he never for one moment suspected that she was not all that she seemed. In this she was helped by the fact that he did not, basically, see her at all as an individual. He might, as she had heard, have abandoned his pursuit of Lady Paget, but he had certainly not transferred his interest to the girl he was considering as a bride.

Lady Paget herself was less indifferent—or more personally interested—and indeed on one occasion Serafina felt she might have gone too far. They had met Lady Paget and her escort by accident at Somerset House. Lady Chilham, who was also one of Serafina's allies, had asked Lord Aldworth to take them to view a private exhibition there.

'How odd to meet you here, Lord Aldworth,' said Lady Paget. 'I had quite thought you had gone into the country.' Her green eyes rested on Serafina, and Lord Aldworth was forced to introduce them all.

'What a pretty girl! Your niece? Are you here for an educational visit, child?'

'No, Lady Paget. I am staying with my godmother.'

'Ah, yes! Uncles, aunts, godmothers—they are all pressed into service to educate the unwilling young! Poor Aldworth! How we suffer!'

'I should imagine,' said Serafina, with a look of innocently glowing admiration, 'that your fortunate companion must feel proud to be seen with such an elegant guide. I only wish my own aunts were half so lovely—or is he your godson?'

Since it was unfortunately true that Lady Paget's friend was considerably younger than she was, this caused some coldness on the part of the lady, and she withdrew shortly afterwards.

'That was not well done, Serafina,' said Lady Chilham severely.

'Why, ma'am?' Serafina faltered. 'Was I. . .was I too forward? But Lady Paget is lovely! Should I not have said so? She is offended with me?'

Lady Chilham pursed her lips disapprovingly, and walked away to examine one of the pictures. Serafina looked at Lord Aldworth, who was suppressing a grin, but when he saw Serafina's look of hurt reproach he tried to explain.

'Lady Paget is with someone she regards as a friend, Miss Feverel, an equal. Not as someone who needs looking after. I think she was slightly put out at your remark, but do not worry about it. I'm sure she realises that it was innocently meant.'

Serafina was relieved that Lord Aldworth was not there to hear her godmother's subsequent remarks.

With this and other diversions the time passed. November was drawing to its end, and Serafina would soon leave London to spend Christmas at home. Lord Aldworth was a frequent escort, and London was beginning to speculate on their friendship. But he had so far not committed himself.

This somewhat unsatisfactory state of affairs was brought to a close by a message from the Foreign Office. Lord Aldworth's presence was urgently needed in Vienna, and he was to set off immediately. His grandmother was annoyed. Lady Aldworth had hoped that her grandson would visit Serafina in Sussex after Christmas and meet her family—in particular, Mr Feverel. But there was little Lord Aldworth could do about this call to duty. Some highly delicate nego-tiations were in hand, and he was essential to their successful conclusion. He promised his grandmother that he would seek out Miss Feverel as soon as he returned, and pursue the acquaintance with a view to marriage.

'If she is still available it will be more than you deserve, wretched man!'

'I shall return as soon as I can, Grand-mère. Miss

Feverel tells me she will be in Sussex till March. She won't meet anyone there. I should be back by then — or shortly after.' He left with a grudging blessing from her.

The Dowager, anxious to make sure that her plans were not spoiled, assured Serafina before she left that Lord Aldworth had every intention of making an offer when he returned at the end of March. Serafina did not know whether she was pleased or sorry. She was eagerly looking forward to being with her family, and even more to acting naturally again. This eagerness gave her some pause for thought. Did she really wish to spend the rest of her life with a man who was both intelligent and perceptive, but who was neither as far as she was concerned? He was superficially so attentive, yet in reality so indifferent to her that he had never observed her closely enough to see how she was deceiving him. She decided that she must give the matter of their relationship some serious thought in the next few weeks. She was prepared to marry for her family's sake, but not if it meant she would be actually unhappy.

However, all thought of rejecting Lord Aldworth was dismissed when she arrived home. Gabriel's affairs were more desperate than anyone had realised, and Mr Feverel had been forced to dispense vast sums to buy him out of trouble. The family's capital, never large, had been seriously eroded and, though the thought was highly distasteful to Mr Feverel, Serafina's marriage might be their only salvation. . .

January and the first half of February passed too quickly. Serafina wandered the fields with the rest of

the family, skated and sledged, spent a good deal of
time over Christmas rehabilitating Gabriel in his
father's regard, and talking at length with her mother.
She never once expressed any of her doubts about
Lord Aldworth, though she did say that he expected
his wife to be a model of decorum. This gave rise to
some mirth until Serafina showed them just how much
she had learned, and even instructed Angelica in some
of the arts. But most of the time she behaved as she
had before she had gone to London, ignoring the rules
she had painstakingly acquired, and determined to
enjoy to the full these last weeks of freedom.

There came a day of brilliant sunshine, though the
wind was cold. The children were well wrapped up in
woolly caps and scarves for their afternoon walk, and
Serafina kept up a brisk pace. She was in charge, for
her father was once again with Gabriel in Oxford. As
they came back up the drive to Feverel Place Rafe
suddenly said, 'Race you up the oak tree, Sally!' This
was a time-honoured challenge that no Feverel could
resist. Up to now Rafe had always been too young to
race Serafina, and she knew how important it was to
his pride that she should not reject him.

'Right, my boy! Mick, Angy, you be the judges.
Come on!'

Encouraged by the shouts and cheers of the judges,
Rafe and Serafina, one each side, started scrambling
up the old tree which stood at the beginning of the
drive. Serafina was badly out of practice and Rafe
forged ahead, dodging nimbly between the branches.
The light was no longer so bright, and Serafina, in her
excitement, misjudged her distance and found herself
falling. She quickly grabbed a branch, swung on it,

glanced down and had the impression of a figure below
her. She yelled, 'Watch out there, Mick!' and let herself
drop to the ground. There was little danger—all the
children were well used to this technique. So Serafina
was surprised and angry when, instead of leaving the
way clear, Michael stayed where he was. As a result he
lost his balance as she swung herself with some force
against him, and they both tumbled to the ground.
Serafina was furious as she scrambled inelegantly to
her feet.

'What on earth are you thinking of, Mick? Why
didn't you m——?' Her voice died away as she became
aware of the well-dressed but slightly dishevelled figure
on the ground. Michael was some feet away, standing
dumbfounded next to a wide-eyed Angelica. From
above came Rafe's voice.

'Sally! Sally! Are you hurt?'

'Don't worry, Rafe,' Serafina answered automatically. 'I'm quite safe.'

Lord Aldworth got up, dusted himself down, then
looked at them all. Serafina was staring at him in
horror, her mind racing. Whatever was Lord Aldworth
doing here in Sussex, long before he was even due to
be in England? And how was she to explain her
behaviour? This must surely be the end of any
ambition to marry the man. Why didn't he speak? 'Are
you. . .are you all right?' she croaked.

'Of course I am,' he replied in an irritated voice.

'I'm. . .sorry.'

'You're the girl from Blanchards' garden, aren't
you? Tell me, do you make a habit of knocking people
down, or is it a particular vendetta against me?' When
Serafina continued to stare at him, he said, 'Never

mind. What are you children doing here? Is this the entrance to Feverel Place, or have I lost my way? I wish to see Mr Feverel.'

'We are the Feverels, sir,' said Rafe, who had just come down from his perch. 'And I won, Sally!'

'The Feverels!' Lord Aldworth looked more closely at Serafina. 'Take that cap off,' he said suddenly.

'Why?' said Serafina defensively, though she knew very well why he wished to see her hair. Lord Aldworth was not in a mood to stand any nonsense. He stretched out and removed the woolly cap himself. The hair tumbled down in a riot of silver-gilt curls.

'Good God! Am I dreaming? Miss Feverel!' He looked incredulously at the figure before him—its tangle of hair, its jacket covered in green stains, its torn skirt, and Michael's old boots on its feet. 'But no, you can't be, surely! Didn't I hear the boy call you Sally?'

'That's what we call her——' began Angelica.

Serafina came to life and trod on her sister's foot. She had resolved on a desperate course of action. 'Miss Feverel is my sister, sir. My elder sister, Serafina. People who do not know us well often confuse us—we are very alike. Have you come to see her? I'm afraid she has gone to Oxford with my father.' Behind her back she was making discreet signs to the others. Then she went on, 'Can I help you? I am Sally Feverel, and these are my brothers and sister. May I have your name?'

'I'm Aldworth. I own Blanchards. I met your sister in London before Christmas.'

There was a long indrawn breath from the other three children, and they drew closer to Serafina. She took a deep breath and said, 'I am sorry you have had such an unfortunate first acquaintance with the rest of us. Will you. . .do you have to tell Serafina about it? She'll be distressed at my behaviour—but then she so often is. I'm afraid I'm a sore trial to her and to my parents.' There was a stifled laugh from Rafe. Serafina turned on him. 'Go on, laugh!' she said fiercely. 'But it's not at all funny—we'll all be dished if today's events get out. Take him back to the house, Mick, and tell him not to say anything. Don't give him any chance—you know how he talks.' Rafe was efficiently removed out of harm's way by Michael, and Serafina was left with Angelica and Lord Aldworth. 'I hope you don't mind. Rafe gets in the way. . .'

'And you are hoping to cozen me into keeping quiet. Yes, I understand perfectly.' His sudden grin flashed out. 'I'm no tale-bearer, Miss Sally.'

'Thank you! You're a trump!' She grinned back at him. 'I know it's more than I deserve. I'll return the favour some time, I promise.'

'By all means, if it is ever necessary,' said Lord Aldworth, looking amused. 'Now, did you say your father is not at home?'

'He is in Oxford, Lord Aldworth.'

'When will he be back?'

Left to herself Serafina would have said that her father was to be a month in Oxford—she wanted no other meetings between her family and Lord Aldworth in the immediate future. But Angelica, who, as Serafina later told her, was occasionally unbecomingly forward, added her voice. 'He's due back tomorrow!'

'Good! I shall call in two days' time, then.' He turned to go, but, seeing Serafina's worried expression, he attempted to reassure her. 'I shan't tell on you. Your secret is safe with me! Goodnight!' He walked off towards the road.

'I hope your secret is safe *from* him, too!' muttered Angelica when he was out of earshot. 'Sally, whatever possessed you to tell such a whopper?'

'What else could I do? Throw myself on his mercy? Ask for his understanding? You don't know him, Angy. Lord Aldworth would have no sympathy. He's selfish, arrogant and quite ruthless. He would have cast me off without a second thought, and what would we do then for money?'

'He seemed quite nice to me,' said Angelica.

That night three of the Feverels held a council of war—Rafe was considered to be too young, and was left asleep. In order to explain her actions, Serafina had to tell the other two a suitably edited version of Lord Aldworth's plans for marriage to her. Mistresses and the like were, of course, not mentioned. Instead, she drew a picture of a career diplomat, performing great deeds in Vienna, needing an heir, but unwilling to be tied to his wife and family.

'So you see,' she concluded, 'he has to find a...a biddable, meek little wife to stay at home and look after the children. And that is what I must appear to be.'

It was generally agreed that, in the circumstances, Serafina had acted with great presence of mind that afternoon. But, though she had solved the immediate problem, they were now left with a much bigger one— how to sustain the fiction.

'I don't think Lord A will stay long down here,' Serafina said thoughtfully. 'I think this was in the

nature of another call *en passant* on his journey from
Newhaven to London. He probably wished to pay a
brief visit only to make Papa's acquaintance—
nothing—nothing of a more serious nature.'

'You mean he isn't going to offer for you yet?' asked
Angelica. Since the afternoon she had become very
eager to see Serafina married to Lord Aldworth and
had made her approval of him plain.

'I shouldn't think so.' Serafina put on Lady
Chilham's voice. 'Goodness me, Angelica, you are
precipitate! An important personage such as Lord
Aldworth does not make an offer of marriage without
a great deal of thought and preparation. He must
consult his grandmother, his lawyers, his chaplain, his
agents——' Her voice suddenly changed and she said
somewhat bitterly, 'Anyone but the one other person
most concerned—his bride!'

'You're not unhappy about it, are you, Sally?' asked
Michael. 'I'm sure Papa could find another way. . .'

'You must not even think like that, Mick! No, of
course I shall be happy! Lord A has at least as much
address as Hartley Pennyworth.'

The Feverels all collapsed into giggles at this.
Serafina's 'beau' was a family joke.

'No, I'm serious, Sal,' Michael persisted.

'I shall be very happy to marry Lord Aldworth, if he
asks me. He is much the best chance I shall have of
repairing the family fortunes, and also of satisfying my
own ambitions. Is that serious enough? But, unless we
are very clever, I will not have the opportunity. And
that is very serious indeed! What about Mama?'

There was a silence. Mama was most unlikely to
agree to any form of deception. Then Angelica said

slowly, 'Mama might be persuaded at least not to inform on us.'

Serafina was sceptical. 'I can't imagine how!'

'If we could convince her that it would break your heart not to marry Lord A. You could say that you had fallen hopelessly in love with him, and you would die if you had to part from him.'

'You've been reading too much poetry,' said Michael in disgust.

'No, Angy's right!' said Serafina. 'Mama has a very tender heart herself. She would understand that.'

'But you're not so stupid as to have fallen hopelessly in love, Sally!'

'Good lord, no. It has always seemed the greatest folly to me, and I've never had the slightest inclination to do so.'

'But Papa and Mama love each other,' cried Angelica.

'Of course they do, now. But I remember Mama telling me once that their marriage was arranged—she hardly knew Papa before she married him. And I think that might be the best way love is to be found. Marriage to an intelligent man, with whom one can share one or two interests. . .'

'From the sound of it, Lord A isn't going to share many interests with you, Sally,' said Michael bluntly.

'Well, no. But I think he will be abroad a great deal of the time, and I should be free to read and study. The library at Aldworth is famous. I shall visit you here quite often. . . No, don't worry, Michael, I am very happy to be left to my own pursuits.'

'Wouldn't it be splendid if you did fall in love with him?' said Angelica dreamily.

'On the contrary—it would be disastrous! And most unlikely. But I think I could pretend to have done so.'

'Pretend? To Mama?'

Serafina pulled a face. 'I wouldn't enjoy that part of it. But what else can we do?'

'Perhaps Lord A won't meet her?' suggested Michael.

'Papa is bound to introduce them,' Angelica said. 'You know how proud he is of her. No, we must persuade Mama that it would be unkind to spoil Serafina's chances. I'll help!'

Michael was still not happy. 'As long as you leave me out of it,' he said finally.

The conference decided that Papa, if approached in the right manner, would probably not interfere.

The conspirators suffered a set-back when Mrs Feverel categorically refused to have anything to do with the deception.

'But Mama,' cried Angelica dramatically, 'Sally is deep in love with Lord Aldworth. You cannot condemn her to a life of misery!'

'Don't be so silly, Angelica. Serafina is far too sensible a girl to allow her emotions to get the better of her. If Lord Aldworth is so unreasonable then she is better off without him. Now fetch your mathematics primer and go to the schoolroom. I think a little rational study would not come amiss. Where is Serafina?'

'In her room. She really is unhappy, Mama.'

'Bring her here.'

When Serafina entered her mother's room her face

bore a look of determined cheerfulness. Mrs Feverel eyed her sharply. 'What is wrong, Serafina?'

'Nothing, Mama. I. . . I think I must have a cold.'

It was true that Serafina's eyes and nose were pink — she had worked hard to make them so.

'Do you truly wish to marry Lord Aldworth?'

This time Serafina's answer was heartfelt. 'Oh, yes, Mama!'

'Then why did you play such a foolish trick on him? And what are we to do about it?'

'I don't know, Mama! I was in a panic, I suppose, at the thought of losing his regard. And at the moment I should certainly lose it if he were to think me a hoyden. In London I have worked very hard to deserve his admiration, and it seems so sad that it will all be wasted.' She hung her head. 'I wish Rafe had not challenged me, but I couldn't refuse, could I?'

Mrs Feverel said drily, 'No, I don't suppose you could. Nor do I suppose you wanted to!' She looked at her daughter's bent head. 'Perhaps I could speak to Lord Aldworth for you?'

'Oh, no!' cried Serafina. 'I mean, Lord Aldworth has not the least notion that I am in love with him! And at the moment I am sure his instant reaction would be to withdraw. You must not, Mama!' There was a silence. Then Serafina said, 'It is such a pity — he is only at Blanchards for such a very short visit. Oh, *why* did he have to come here yesterday?'

'A short visit?'

'Three or four days, I believe.'

'And if nothing occurred to reveal the truth to him this time, when would you tell him? Soon?'

'If only I had time to give him confidence in me!

Later, I am sure, I would be able to confess everything to him, but we don't yet know one another well enough. Oh, Mama, I could not deceive him forever. I only need a little time!'

'Hmm.' Mrs Feverel frowned. 'I will not join in a deliberate deception, Serafina. I wish to make myself absolutely clear on that point. But if your Papa agrees, and on condition that you tell Lord Aldworth the truth before he commits himself to you, I will help you. I find I shall not be able to receive visitors for a few days. Much as I should like to meet Lord Aldworth, I'm afraid my health is about to deteriorate.'

Serafina's smile was brilliant as she leapt up and embraced her mother. 'Oh, thank you! Thank you, Mama!'

That night it snowed quite heavily. When the Feverel conspirators got up they found nearly a foot of snow on the ground.

'Perhaps Pa will be delayed?' said Michael hopefully.

Serafina shook her head. 'He might, but I don't think we should count on it.'

'Well, perhaps Lord A won't come visiting in the snow?'

'You may be doing your best to console me, Mick, but it isn't good enough! Think! Lord A travels at all seasons all over Europe. He isn't going to be put off by a little snow over a distance of two or three miles! Oh, I know it's further round by the road, but it still isn't far enough to stop him coming. No, we have to prepare for the fact that Lord A and Papa are going to meet tomorrow or the day after.'

'I still think Lord Aldworth has a nice face,' said

Angelica. 'He looked as if he had quite a sense of humour. And look at the way he agreed not to tell Serafina about you.'

'About me?' asked Michael, startled.

'No, stupid! About Sally.'

'Of course. Sorry. I was just confused for a minute. There are really four of us here, though I can only see three—Michael Feverel, Angelica Feverel, Sally Feverel and Serafina Feverel.'

'You're wrong. Serafina Feverel is in Oxford,' said Serafina absent-mindedly. She was working on another idea. 'He did, didn't he?'

'Did what?'

'Agree not to tell. I wonder if I could use that again? If I could get him not to mention Sally when he is talking to Papa?'

'You couldn't!'

'I could try. I don't think Papa would betray me, but it would be better if the occasion didn't arise. He might find it difficult. It would certainly help if Sally wasn't mentioned. . .'

'I'm tired of this,' said Michael suddenly. 'I want to go sledging. We're wasting the snow, and once the sun comes out it won't last long.'

'Of course!' Serafina's eyes lit up. 'We shall go sledging! Fetch Rafe and we'll all go up Pett's Hill. Then you three can sledge down this side and I'll go down the other side to Blanchards. Sally will pay a call on Lord Aldworth this morning.'

'You can't!' said Angelica. 'That's one of the things you told me were never done. A young lady never calls alone on a gentleman.'

'Serafina wouldn't dare, certainly. She's a lady. But

Sally. . . Sally isn't—she's a hoyden. Let's get Rafe and
the sledge. I'll see Mama.'

Conversation was not easy as they trudged through the
snow up the hill which divided the Feverel lands from
those of Blanchards, and it was made more difficult by
the presence of Rafe. So Serafina's co-conspirators
forgot their problems and enjoyed the rare sight of a
Sussex landscape covered in snow. At the top they
parted company, Michael and Rafe setting off first
down the hill, and Angelica following soon after.
Serafina saw them off, then walked over to the other
side, and viewed the path down the south-eastern
slope. She had to screw up her eyes as she did so, for
the sun had come out and its rays dazzled her. This
particular run was unfamiliar, but it looked fairly
straightforward—a shallow incline at first, followed by
a steeper slope leading into the field behind
Blanchards' walled garden. She got on her sledge and
with a whoop she pushed off.

Lord Aldworth sat at breakfast in Blanchards' small
parlour—the only room on the ground floor that was
habitable. He had risen early, for he wanted to see
more of the men who would be working on the house.
He was in Sussex for a number of reasons. The routine
work in Vienna had been dealt with more expeditiously
than he had expected. The other matter had also gone
well, except for some unpleasant suspicions about the
people involved. At the very least there had been some
careless talk, and perhaps there had been worse. How
had his grandmother heard about what she had called
'the South American business'? But for those doubts,

he could reasonably have stayed abroad for another month, enjoying the company of his friends. Indeed, he had been strongly tempted to do so. But his doubts, combined with his promise to his grandmother to marry soon, had brought him back early. He was not a man to shirk his duty, and he had come to the reluctant conclusion that his duty lay for the moment at Aldworth. Serafina Feverel was exactly what he had stipulated—more than he might have hoped for, in fact. Her beauty was undeniable and, though at first he had been bored at the thought of spending time with such a featherhead, she had in fact quite often amused him with her naïve comments. How long this would last once they were married was another matter, but he could surely endure it until he had acquired an heir!

His grandmother's picture of his association with Lady Paget had not been attractive, either. She was right; he had been in some danger there. When he'd heard that Louisa Paget was shortly due back in Vienna it had strengthened his decision to leave early. With time to spare before he was due back in London, he had decided on impulse to break his journey in Sussex for a day or two. If he was planning to marry, then the sooner Blanchards was ready for occupation by one or other—or all—of the ladies at present living in Aldworth House the better. Work on the house in Sussex had been delayed by his preoccupation with affairs in London before Christmas, followed by the trip abroad, and he wanted to set things in motion again. With luck it would now be ready by Easter.

There had been another motive, of course. He had wanted to have an informal look at the home of the girl who was probably going to be his bride. It was a pity she and her father were away, but he had been wrong to call without first sending his manservant with a note. He hoped Mr Feverel would not take it amiss... Then he smiled cynically. Surely no father would take it amiss that a rich suitor was impatient to see his daughter! But how did Serafina, who was the epitome of correct behaviour, come to have such a sister? Sally, she was called. A pity the girl was such a hoyden; there was something appealing about her. He smiled as he recalled her woolly cap, her old jacket and bedraggled skirt, her unladylike yell as she had landed on him, and later the frank appeal for his help. So like Serafina in feature, and so unlike her in everything else!

A drip of water splashed down, just missing the breakfast-table. Devil take it! The unexpected fall of snow had found every hole in the roof of the house, every crack in the masonry. Of course Blanchards lay in a hollow; that was part of the trouble. He wondered whether the field behind could be drained and a conduit put in to lead the water from the hill away from the house. He ought to inspect it—he had never looked beyond the garden. But surely this was hardly the weather for any inspection of the ground. He looked out of the window. The morning had been grey, but now the sun had appeared and the sight of the countryside, dazzling in its mantle of snow, called to him. Putting on his heaviest boots, he went through the garden and out into the field. At least from this slightly higher ground he could see the state of the roof from outside. He turned round and contemplated the house...

A sudden and strangely familiar yell caused him to turn round. It was a shock to see a colourful figure on a sledge hurtling towards him...

CHAPTER FIVE

LORD ALDWORTH leapt easily to one side. But it was unfortunate that the sledge also veered to the same side, and as it overturned and slid to a stop it took his legs from under him. Sally Feverel—for it was she, of course—came to rest in a flurry of snow a few feet away. They looked at one another in silence. Then the girl suddenly burst into a peal of laughter, and after a moment Lord Aldworth joined in.

'I have never in all my life met anyone so prone to mishaps!'

'It's you who are prone, sir. . .' And she went off into another peal.

Lord Aldworth regarded her with fascination. The bright red cap was awry, and wisps of her hair, caught in the rays of the sun, looked like strands of spun gold. Sparkling eyes, the colour of the sky, laughed at him out of a delicately shaped face with cheeks which were rosy with fresh air and exercise. He had never seen anything so. . .so alive! A sudden and strong pull of attraction, not quite like anything he had ever felt before, took him by surprise.

'It's very sad!' she continued. 'I was going to beg a favour of you, too!' Laughter bubbled out of her again, and he was hard put to it not to say that he would grant her anything she asked. Instead, he got up and offered her a hand.

'Let me ask first,' he said. He could feel himself smiling at her like an idiot! 'Are you all right?'

She allowed herself to be pulled up, and they brushed the snow off their clothes. Then she became serious. 'I could have injured you—I'm sorry, truly sorry. I thought I could avoid you by turning the sledge over.'

'You might have injured yourself a lot more. Are you mad?'

'You could say so, I suppose. But you don't grow up with four brothers and sisters without getting used to a few spills and bruises.'

Surprised, he asked, 'I thought there were six Feverels?'

'Oh! Oh, yes,' she said. 'I wasn't counting Gabriel. He has been away for such a long time.'

'What about Miss Feverel? I can't imagine her suffering spills and bruises.'

'No, no. Oh, good lord, no! Serafina was the one who comforted us when we were hurt. You wouldn't believe how good my sister is, Lord Aldworth. It's very hard for me to live up to her.'

'I am sure Miss Feverel is as good as she is lovely. But I shouldn't think you need worry about a comparison. Do you?' The girl before him blushed and looked confused. Delightfully, deliciously confused.

She stammered, 'W-we are so different, Serafina and I. She tries to satisfy every canon of propriety. People would never see her climbing trees, or arguing about philosophy, or any of the other things which are not considered suitable. Whereas I am forever offending. That's why I wanted to ask a favour. . .'

Lord Aldworth became cautious. 'What is it?'

'Well—er—do you think you could avoid mentioning my name to my father when you see him? I love him dearly, but he is so proud of Serafina, and I am such a contrast to her. He will only get angry, and I would rather not have that—especially when you are there. Could you do that?'

'An acquaintance with you, Sally, may not be dull, but it certainly leads to complications! If I do as you ask, conversation with the two people I chiefly wish to see is going to be very difficult. First you ask me not to mention you to your sister Serafina, and now you wish me to avoid your name with your father. . .' He studied the face turned up so pleadingly to his, and found it impossible to disappoint her. 'I suppose I could try. I certainly won't volunteer anything about our. . . encounters. Will that do?'

'But you are nice!' she said, looking astonished.

He was curious, and slightly offended. 'Has your sister told you I am not? I don't think I have been unkind or rude to her, surely?'

'Oh, no! She. . .she thinks you're perfect! Only I thought you sounded. . .sounded. . .'

'Go on.'

'Well, stuffy, and not very interesting.'

'I beg your pardon?'

'You take her to such dull places—to shops and parties, and to see the animals at the Tower, and to Astley's and all the other childish things.'

Lord Aldworth tried, and failed, to suppress a feeling of annoyance out of all proportion to the criticism. He had done his best to amuse Serafina Feverel, at some cost to his own inclinations. Did this chit think he had gone to those places to amuse himself? That his level of intelligence was so low? How dare she? He found himself growing so angry that he decided it would be better to send her home before he said something he would later regret. 'It's getting colder,' he said, turning towards the house. 'I think we should start thinking of getting you home. I cannot imagine you will wish to climb that hill again, so we'll go this way.'

As they went through the garden he said as calmly as he could, 'I am sorry if your sister has found my company boring...'

'Oh, goodness, my stupid tongue—I've made you angry, and that was the *last* thing I wanted! Serafina has not said any such thing! Please do not be offended, Lord Aldworth. My sister would never forgive me if I gave you the wrong impression. She has found great enjoyment in your company, truly. I was speaking for myself. It all seemed such a waste...'

Really, the girl was impossible! There was a bite in his voice as he asked, 'And what would Madam Impertinence do with her valuable time?'

'Don't be angry with me, please! If you only knew how I long to visit London! To hear a debate in the Palace of Westminster—particularly one on Foreign Policy—with someone like you who could explain the people involved——'

'Alas, ladies are not allowed in the debating chamber.'

'How unfair! As if we are not allowed to take a sensible interest in what is happening to our own country!' Her voice trembled with real anger and he attempted to distract her.

'What else would you do in London?'

'There are all sorts of buildings I should like to visit—Westminster Abbey, the Royal Exchange, the

Guildhall... I would go to the theatre to see Shakespeare, not farces, and spend as much time as I could spare in the British Museum——'

'If you are suggesting that I should do all this with Serafina, you are being absurd! Your sister would die of boredom before we had done the half of it.'

She looked at him strangely, and her voice was sad as she said, 'Yes, she would. And gentlemen do not appreciate it when young ladies take an interest in such things. It is better to be Serafina.' She was quiet then until they reached the high road, and he found himself softening towards her again. He wondered if she was tired.

'Would you like me to get out the gig and deliver you to your home?'

She shook her head. 'Thank you, but no. I like walking.'

'Then allow me to escort you.'

'I am obliged for the offer but no, thank you,' she said with great determination.

'I must!'

'On no account! I—er——' She gave him a comic look. 'I am very familiar with the road to Blanchards, you know. I have visited it quite regularly, especially in the autumn. All those grapes... And if anyone from the family saw me with you I should be in trouble again. No, I will not hear of it! Goodbye, Lord Aldworth, and thank you again for promising not to mention me.' She took a step, then paused and said, 'Tell me, do you enjoy your conversations with her? Serafina, I mean.'

Lord Aldworth could not immediately recall ever having had what he would call a conversation with

Serafina, but he put as much conviction as he could into his reply. 'Of course! What a strange question! Why do you ask?'

'Oh, no reason. It's just that I cannot imagine what you talk about. Goodbye again.'

'Goodbye. . . Sally. Shall I see you tomorrow?'

'I don't think so. I shall keep out of the way.' Her grin flashed out. 'I'm regarded as a liability rather than an asset in elegant company, Lord Aldworth.' She set off at a brisk pace up the road.

After she had gone Lord Aldworth felt dissatisfied. He should have gone with her, at least to her gates, but she had been quite decided in her refusal. *Very* unlike her sister. . . What an annoying baggage Sally Feverel was! He should be grateful that his grandmother had found the right member of the Feverel family—Miss Independence and he would soon be at odds with one another. He started back towards the house, but then stopped in thought. That extraordinary feeling of attraction he had felt towards her—he had almost kissed her there in the snow! That was very strange. The girl was nothing like any of his previous amours. . . What was he thinking of? Sally Feverel was the younger sister of the girl he was planning to marry . . .some time. He walked briskly up the steps to the door, determined to put them both out of his mind for the moment. But the animated little face, so like and yet so unlike that of her sister, floated before his eyes. She was an interesting little thing. . . What a strange question she had asked at the end! He stopped yet again. What the devil *did* he and Serafina Feverel talk about?

* * *

Serafina felt dispirited as she walked back to Feverel Place. She had enjoyed sparring with Lord Aldworth and, even more, she had enjoyed expressing her real feelings about their activities in London. But the situation was fraught with danger, and if he once found out before she had had time to lay some sounder foundations for their friendship... Strangely, it seemed more important than ever before that she should marry this man. However, when she reached the house and saw that her father had arrived home, she put all thought of Lord Aldworth out of her mind.

In answer to the family's eager questions Mr Feverel told them that Gabriel was clearly back on the right track again and working hard.

'I shouldn't be surprised if they offered him a chance to do a further degree. His professor is very taken with his work. There's the problem of the estate, though. I really need his help here. Still, it would be an honour.' He turned to Serafina. 'What's this I hear about a visit from your suitor?'

Serafina gave Angelica a look of burning reproach. 'Not me,' mouthed her sister. 'Rafe.'

'I think he's coming to see you tomorrow, Papa. But I don't think he's quite ready to offer for me yet. He is really just paying a social call, as a neighbour, on his way to London. We were...we were quite taken by surprise when he came.'

'I should think so, indeed! In my young days gentlemen didn't pay visits to perfect strangers without checking first that they would be welcome! Still, you were pleased to see him, eh, puss?'

'Oh, yes, Papa,' said poor Serafina. 'Er...may I have a word with you in private, Papa?'

Once in the library she was unable to stop herself from telling her father the whole. To her relief he took it very well. Indeed he laughed so heartily at one point that she grew quite resentful. 'But Papa!' she protested. 'It really isn't funny at all. Lord Aldworth would be extremely angry if he knew.'

'I should imagine he would,' said her father. 'And with some reason. So what will you do about it? Or are you expecting me to sort it out for you?'

'I don't think anyone could,' said Serafina gloomily. 'Not before Lord Aldworth and I know one another sufficiently well for me to tell him myself. Meanwhile. . .'

'Meanwhile you want me to carry on the fiction, is that it?'

'You're too clever, Papa. Yes, that is what I would prefer.'

'Is he such a coxcomb, Sally? I wouldn't like you to marry someone you disliked.'

'I. . . I told Mama that I loved him. That wasn't quite true. But when I was talking to him this morning, when I could speak to him like a sensible human being, I liked him very much.' She paused and thought about it. 'Very much. I think I could be quite happy with him, Papa. If only I can tell him about my deception in my own time.'

'You've asked him not to mention the name Sally to me, you say? That was cunning. Not honest, but cunning. And the poor man isn't to mention Sally to Serafina!' Mr Feverel almost went into another paroxysm of laughter, but sobered when he saw Serafina's face. 'I should say, rather, "poor Sally"! Very well, I shan't go out of my way to betray you. But I won't tell any lies, mind. Do you wish me to have a word with your mother? She will not be so easy to persuade, though I know she wants you to marry the fellow.'

Serafina then informed her father of her arrangement with her mother. He frowned at first, for he disapproved of making capital out of Mrs Feverel's illness. But he was finally won over.

'Our name won't be worth much if this ever gets out, Sally. I hope you realise that. But there, I never cared for what people in general thought of me. A poor lot, people in general. Now, tell me what you've been reading while I've been away. I have some new German books from Oxford for you—there's a particularly fine copy of *Werther*. Now there was a madman—dying for love, the fool! It's well-written, however.'

When Lord Aldworth called the following day the stage was well set. The snow had gone, and Angelica and Michael had taken Rafe for a walk—a long walk. Mrs Feverel was in her room, with a collection of books and periodicals to amuse her, and a bell was to hand for her to call one of the maids if she needed anything. Serafina, dressed in one of her London muslins which had been freshly laundered the day before, was sitting in the library with her father. Her hair was smoothly caught back in a pink ribbon, in marked contrast to the recent riot of curls under the woolly cap. Maggie, her mother's maid, had applied a little Gowland's lotion to Serafina's cheeks to remove the hint of colour brought about by her adventure in the snow. Pink ribbons trimmed her dress and tiny white slippers were on her feet. A piece of her mother's embroidery was in her hands.

'Don't set any stitches I can't afterwards remove, for heaven's sake, Serafina. It's a particularly pretty design, one of my favourites, and you know what you are,' her mother had said as she'd given it to her.

Serafina broke the silence that had fallen on them after they had left her mother. 'Remember not to call me Sally, Papa,' she said nervously. 'Also that I have never willingly opened a book in my life, nor am I at all clever or knowledgeable. Modish young ladies aren't.'

'You have reminded me so often that I should have to be a dolt myself to forget,' said Mr Feverel somewhat testily. 'Though why the devil the man would prefer such a simpleton I cannot understand. But there's not the slightest need for you to look so anxious; I'll accept what you say. Pick up your embroidery, *Serafina*; I see someone coming up the drive. But you in turn must remember this—I will tell no lies, not even for you.'

There was no time for more. Lord Aldworth was being announced.

Serafina took a deep breath and set herself to act as she had never acted before. This man was no fool. It had been comparatively easy yesterday and the day before to persuade him that Serafina and Sally were two different people, for he had never been really interested in Serafina as a person, and in any case he had not seen her since before Christmas. But he had seen Sally twice at close quarters very recently, and the resemblance between the two sisters must seem almost incredible. Only twins could be so alike, and Lord Aldworth knew that Serafina was not a twin. She must convince him of their separate identity by character-acting alone. Sally's carelessness in dress and appearance, her frank, uninhibited manner of speaking, her interest in the world of books and politics were already a contrast to Serafina's exquisite neatness and propriety, her sedate modesty, her lack of interest in anything intellectual—but she must now underline this contrast with her voice and manner. Her nervousness was not assumed as her father went to meet his guest.

'Aldworth, how kind of you to call! At last, after all these years, we meet our neighbour from over the hill!'

'Mr Feverel, your servant, sir. I am sorry that my brother's preoccupations in Berkshire left him little time to visit Sussex. And if I am honest I have to confess that I would have postponed our meeting until I had more time down here—except that I had another reason. . . Miss Feverel, I hope I see you well?'

Lord Aldworth came over and took Serafina's hand to his lips. She blushed, looked down and murmured something suitable. As he looked at her an expression of disbelief crossed the handsome features. 'Amazing!' he said.

This was the moment. She must bear it in mind that Sally would not have talked of meeting Lord Aldworth. As he continued to stare she looked up with an air of slightly embarrassed bewilderment. 'Sir?' said Serafina. 'What do you mean? Is there. . .is there something wrong?'

'You are so like——' He stopped. Serafina continued to look puzzled, while he obviously wrestled with a problem. How could he even mention Sally, when he had promised not to? Even though she was nervous of the outcome, part of her was enjoying his dilemma. But she had to admire his sang-froid as he went on,

'So like a picture I saw recently in Vienna. Botticelli, I think it was.'

'Bottic——?' Serafina's anxiety at an unfamiliar name was patent.

Mr Feverel intervened. He came over to his visitor with a glass of wine and said genially, 'Ah, Vienna. I hear you have recently come from there, Aldworth. You've been working for Stewart and Castlereagh, I believe. How are we doing?'

Lord Aldworth was finding it difficult to take his eyes from Serafina, but he turned to his host at this. 'As well as we could reasonably hope, sir, though it's a slow business. As I understand it, the chief difficulty lies with Prussia. We and the other Great Powers are doing everything we can to persuade her to moderate her claims for reparations from France, but she is very reluctant to forgo anything. It is uphill work.'

'Difficult lot, the Prussians. You only have to read their so-called literature. But I'd have thought Wellington wouldn't stand for any nonsense?'

'He does his best, though he sees everything from a military point of view, of course.'

'It was a good move to withdraw some of the occupation troops from France, wouldn't you say?'

'Indeed. The people are growing resentful of these foreigners living off their country. It's natural enough, I suppose. But a resentful population and a weakened regime in France won't help anyone. Unless we do something about supporting Louis we shall——' He stopped suddenly. 'But where are my manners? I am sure I must be boring Miss Feverel!'

'Oh, no!' Serafina said in her shy, slightly high-pitched voice. 'I like to hear gentlemen talking.' She added with simple pride, 'And I know of the Duke of Wellington.'

Mr Feverel frowned. 'I should hope so, indeed.'

'All the same, I shouldn't like your daughter to think that I came to visit her only to ignore her, or, worse, to bore her!' Lord Aldworth came over and sat down beside Serafina. 'That is a pretty piece of embroidery, Miss Feverel,' he said. 'And executed with skill.' Serafina's blush was wholly natural. If he only knew!

Under the pretence of examining the work Lord Aldworth was having a close look at the face bent over it. 'Remarkable! Quite remarkable,' he said, frowning. 'Tell me, are all your family as handsome, Feverel?'

Under her demure front Serafina was indignant. This was cheating! He might not have mentioned Sally's name, but he was deliberately inviting her father to talk of the rest of the family. She waited apprehensively for the reply.

'I believe they are,' replied Mr Feverel indifferently. 'I have never paid much attention to their looks. Serafina resembles her sister, I believe.'

This was perfectly true—Serafina and Angelica were quite alike—though it was not what Lord Aldworth understood from the remark. 'Astoundingly so!' he said, taking his eyeglass and examining once again the young lady sitting next to him. Serafina was grateful for her father's evasion but thought it was time to change the subject.

'Would you like me to see if Mama requires anything, Papa?' she said nervously.

'If you wish to, my dear. But come back soon. I am sure that Lord Aldworth and I have a great deal to say to one another, but he might object if you were absent for too long. And don't you want to hear what your father says about you?'

'Oh, Papa!' said Serafina, looking reproachful. 'You are a tease. I am sure Lord Aldworth is too kind to listen to your stories! I expect you will talk about politics or books or sport, not about a silly girl like me.'

'Well, off you go!' Serafina made her escape. As she went she heard her father say, 'My wife is an invalid, Aldworth. I should have liked to have you meet her, but that is unfortunately not possible today. Perhaps the next time you call? Are you planning to stay in Sussex long?'

'I'm afraid not. I leave for London very soon. . .' The conversation continued as she went up the stairs.

Her mother was naturally very interested in their visitor. 'Hetty says he is very handsome. Do you think so?'

'Of course. And Papa seems to like him. I wish you could meet him, Mama, but I'm glad you agreed not to see him this time. I heard him say he is going to London within the next day or two.'

'So soon! So your problem will be solved—temporarily?'

'Yes. . .'

'What is wrong, Serafina? You are surely relieved that Lord Aldworth will soon be gone, aren't you? Or will you miss him?' Mrs Feverel's voice was sympathetic, but amused. 'Oh, dear, it is hard enough to be in love! But only you, Serafina, could have made it so complicated too!'

'In lo——? Yes, you're right, Mama. It is hard—very hard. But I am glad he is going. I shall be glad not to have to pretend to him any more.' She paused. Why wasn't she more convinced of this? Her mother raised an eyebrow, seeing her daughter's uncertainty and waiting for her to say more. Serafina went on slowly, 'But you're right, I shall miss him. He is different, somehow, down here in Sussex. I like him better... I mean, even better. And...and what if he is angry with me for the deception and refuses to see me any more?'

'I should imagine that he will indeed be angry. Very angry! But if you truly love each other you can solve that problem.' Serafina looked doubtful. 'You must confess the truth to him, my dear.'

'I will, I promise.'

As Serafina went back downstairs she was hard put to it to know what she felt. Talking to her mother had made her face the problem more clearly herself. What she had said was no less than the truth. On the one hand she wanted Lord Aldworth out of Sussex as soon as possible—the risk of discovery was too great. She had been lucky that Blanchards was comparatively isolated, and that he apparently did not as yet wish to make the effort to meet the other families of the neighbourhood. His arrival at Blanchards had been unplanned and she doubted that it was generally known. But it only needed one question to an innocent neighbour for the whole subterfuge to be exposed. The sooner he was in London the better!

On the other hand... As Sally in Sussex she had a chance to talk to him as she really was, and she was finding the experience more stimulating than she could have imagined. He was a different person when he dispensed with the air of indulgent indifference he adopted towards Serafina, and behaved naturally.

As she came into the room Lord Aldworth was saying, 'The trouble is, sir, that the present powers that be in Europe are all so damned autocratic! They have no moderation—I would say not even much sense! Ferdinand of Spain is the worst—he's going to give us real trouble soon. He's an unpleasant character, and not at all popular with his people. We can't interfere, of course, but we're very keen to keep our trade links with the Spanish American colonies. There's something brewing out there... That's the reason I had to go back to Vienna in such a hurry, to be honest. We wanted to get something signed and sealed before... Ah, Miss Feverel. How is your mother?'

'Feeling a little better. She sends her apologies to you, Lord Aldworth, and hopes to be able to see you before you go back to London.' This was sheer bluff on Serafina's part, for she knew very well that Lord Aldworth would have to make his excuses.

'Alas, that is impossible. I was telling your father that I am going to London quite soon. I've done all I can to set things going at Blanchards for the moment. But I hope... I intend to come back a little later in the year, and perhaps then...? Shall I see you in London before then, Miss Feverel?'

She lowered her gaze. 'I hope so, Lord Aldworth. If Papa permits.' She said in her soft, slightly higher Serafina voice, 'I enjoy life in London. And Lady Chilham says there are even more parties once the season starts.'

'Tell me...tell me what you most like doing. In London.'

So Sally's comments had met their mark! Serafina kept her amusement at this request well-hidden as she replied vaguely, 'Everything. Shopping, I suppose. And I like it when you take me to places you enjoy visiting. The animals at…the Tower, was it?… were nice…' She smiled in sweet reminiscence.

Lord Aldworth sat back, looking satisfied. 'I thought as much,' he said. 'We shall see some more of London when you return to the capital, if Lady Chilham permits. Would you like to visit the British Museum again? Or somewhere else—the Palace of Westminster, perhaps? Or the Royal Exchange?'

The avuncular tone again—he deserved to be deceived! Serafina's response was a masterpiece of reluctant compliance as she said, 'If those are places you would like to visit, Lord Aldworth,' adding despondently, 'I am sure they would all be very interesting. What is the Royal Exchange?'

Mr Feverel, who was clearly not comfortable at this deliberate misrepresentation of his daughter's character, frowned again. He suddenly said, 'Serafina, would you get me the *Cogitationes*? There's something in it which I wish to show Lord Aldworth before he leaves. Something about Spain. It is apposite to our present situation, I believe.'

Remembering to walk with the graceful but slightly mincing gait that she had been taught in London, which was so different from Sally's free stride, Serafina obediently fetched the copy of Bacon from the shelves, and gave it to her father with a charming little curtsy.

'Do you know where all your father's books are, Miss Feverel—even one in Latin?' asked Lord Aldworth, with a look of surprise.

She had not thought to ask where to find the book first! What a fool she was! Serafina looked suspiciously at her father—had he done it deliberately? He knew she had been referring to the work that very morning... Lord Aldworth was waiting...she must think of something quickly—her movement had been too confident to deny that she had known where it was.

'Oh, yes, indeed!' she said proudly. 'I dust them very frequently, Lord Aldworth. Papa doesn't trust the servants to do it. I know all their covers.' She looked at the copy of Francis Bacon's book. 'Especially the pretty ones.'

Mr Feverel leafed through the book and said, 'Ah, yes! Here it is. Read that, Aldworth.'

While Lord Aldworth's attention was on the book Serafina stole a look at her father. He was regarding her with disapproval mixed with admiration—so he *had* tried to trap her! But why?

After Lord Aldworth had left Serafina tackled her father about it with some indignation.

'Sally, I just couldn't sit there watching you make a fool of him. I liked him. He talked like a sensible man about the international situation, and he obviously feels deeply about his work. And you were so...so... cocky. When I agreed to help you I thought you were distressed, but this afternoon you were actually enjoying yourself. So I gave you something to think about.' He smiled at her in triumph. 'And you failed! You walked straight to that book, as I knew you would.'

'You'll admit that I soon recovered my position, Pa!'

'Magnificently! "Pretty covers" indeed!' He chuckled. Then he said more seriously, 'However, I warn you that I won't have much more of this nonsense. When Lord Aldworth pays his next visit I hope he will have been told, by you or someone else. And Sally——'

'Yes, Papa?'

'I approve very much of Lord Aldworth. I like the idea of having him as a son-in-law, and not just because he is rich, either.'

For the rest of the day Serafina was restless. Her encounters with Lord Aldworth had stirred feelings she had not before experienced. In London she had felt a tug of attraction at their first meeting, but that had soon been overlaid with irritation at his lack of interest in her, at the low level of intelligence he expected of her. Here in Sussex she had met him as a different person, and the tug of attraction was even stronger. Her father was right—she had enjoyed the meeting in the library, dangerous though it had been. She had felt alive! Here was a man who was worth challenging—she felt it, and her father also felt it. Her charade had been born of desperation, but now she would not have missed it for the world. For the first time she saw what Lady Aldworth had meant when she had said that Charles was worth an effort. But that was not the Charles Serafina would know—Sally was the girl who had caught a glimpse of the real Charles Dacre.

So it was not really surprising that Sally should decide to risk meeting Lord Aldworth once more before he left Sussex. Who knew what would happen before she saw him next?

CHAPTER SIX

THE snow had completely disappeared, and the mud and slush which it had left on the roads had also gone. The sun was bright in the sky when Serafina walked over to Blanchards the next day. She would have ridden, but she dared not let Lord Aldworth see her in her riding-habit and the very elegant riding-hat that Papa had been good enough to give her the Christmas before. In them she looked too much like Serafina. So she marched over the hill in her woolly cap and the same old jacket and skirt—which were even more the worse for wear since her accident with the sledge. At the gate into Blanchards she paused for thought. She could hardly go boldly up to the front door and ask for Lord Aldworth!

With a shrug she climbed up her usual bit of wall and sat on top of it for a minute or two, grimacing as she saw the bare expanse where the greenhouse and vine had once stood.

'Regretting your past escapades, Sally?'

Startled, Serafina turned her head. Lord Aldworth was standing at the far entrance, her sledge at his feet.

'Have you come for this? I found it in the field and was about to come looking for you to return it.' He came through the garden towards her, staring hard. With a touch of suspicion in his voice he said, 'You are astonishingly like your sister!'

Serafina laughed in apparent delight. '*Merci du*

compliment, monsieur! I know our features are almost identical, but it's the first time that anyone has thought me as elegant as my elegant sister! My mother says that I even lack elegance of mind. But it's so stuffy to be proper. And, though Serafina is so much more presentable, I do think I am just a touch quicker of understanding, don't you? May I come in?' He nodded and made to go to the gate, but with a laughing protest Serafina climbed nimbly down the tree on the garden side of the wall and jumped to the ground. Here she stood facing him, a frank, open smile on her face. 'Can you imagine Serafina doing that? She would sooner die!' With great daring she said, in a travesty of Serafina's somewhat childish voice, 'Oh, Sally, please don't be such a hoyden! What will people think?'

Lord Aldworth, much to Serafina's relief, laughed. 'You're a minx, Sally Feverel! Your sister is right—you should learn to behave.'

'Well, I shall, but not yet. Besides, you already know me as I am—it would be a waste for me to try to behave properly with you! Your visit yesterday went well, I hear.'

'Where were you?' he asked casually.

'I told you—the family usually tries to keep me out of the way when elegant company is expected. Serafina and Pa were considered to be company enough—the rest of the family had to go for a walk! But from what he said afterwards Pa liked you a lot. He thought you intelligent.'

'You sound doubtful. Does my choice of excursions in London still cause you to think me "stuffy"? Lacking in intelligence? You are wrong if you do. Your sister enjoyed those excursions.'

'Did she say so? I expect she was trying to please you.'

'On the contrary. The suggestion that we should visit some of the places you mentioned—the Royal Exchange and so on—appalled her. It was at that point that she tried to please me—she did her best to disguise her feelings, but her reluctance was obvious.'

'In that case, I suppose you were right. But wouldn't it be more intelligent to. . .? Have you never thought of educating her?'

'What on earth for? She is perfect as she is.'

'Oh. I see. Er. . .for what?'

'I don't think that need concern you,' said Lord Aldworth coldly.

'But it does! Serafina is important to me, and I wish to be sure that she will be happy with you.'

'You are being precipitate, Sally——What are you laughing about now, for God's sake?'

'Precipi. . .precipit. . .' Serafina could not get the word out for laughter.

He said haughtily, 'I suppose you will explain, when you have recovered yourself?'

These words, uttered in such a tone, sent her off into another gale of laughter. How could she explain? To say that she had used the word in order to make fun of him to the children? 'Goodness me, Angelica,' she had said, 'you are precipitate! An important personage such as Lord Aldworth. . .' And she had used just such a haughty manner, too. But to tell him this would hardly help to soothe him. She made an effort and said, 'I beg pardon. Only—you sounded so. . .so stuffy!'

'Stuffy!' She had been right. He was angrier than before.

'I am sorry, truly I am, but you should not provoke me. What shall we talk about? Your visit yesterday? Pa said you had discussed the international situation. He must have enjoyed talking to someone who is right in the centre of affairs. Is there really a prospect of further trouble? War, even?'

'No, I don't think so. That would be in no one's interest.'

'I suppose it's important to keep a balance between all those who might wish to pursue their own profit at the expense of the others? Do we? Pursue our own profit, I mean?'

'Of course not! Except perhaps in trade. That's where our interests lie—markets and goods for our merchants. There's a situation brewing in South America——' He broke off.

'Papa told me something of it. The Spanish colonies out there wish for independence. Do you think they should be supported?'

'At the moment,' he said carefully, 'our official position is to support the sovereignty of Spain—though I am not sure how long that will last. Sally, I would much rather not say anything more—we have to tread very warily, and with as much cunning as in any wartime campaign. There are any number of wolves and traps, and I'm doing all I can to see that we avoid them at the moment.'

'You'll have to learn from the lion and the fox, won't you?'

He looked at her in surprise. 'You read Machiavelli?'

'Have I shocked you? A girl, and so well-read?' she mocked. 'Allow me to tell you that I wouldn't let you treat me the way you think Serafina should be treated. I read anything and everything, the more the better. Indeed, "I have studied books rather than men", and I sometimes think I have been right.'

'What a waste of so much beauty!'

'Don't you dare patronise me! Serafina is the beautiful one. Keep your empty compliments for her.'

'You are her equal in beauty, Sally. Or you would be if——'

'If I cared more for such things, Lord Aldworth. But I am not content to be a. . .a plaything. When I marry it will be with the intention of having a true partner for a husband, one who will share his life with me, share his worries and his triumphs, share his interests and work, not. . .not someone who would put me in his home and then forget about me except when he wants heirs!' She came to a sudden halt as she realised that she had allowed her feelings to get the better of her. If Lord Aldworth did marry Serafina, that was exactly what he intended to do with her. This thought was so depressing that she had to turn away from him to hide sudden tears.

'He would be a fortunate man, your husband,' said Lord Aldworth slowly, and turned her gently towards him. 'Look at me, Sally. Why are you crying?'

'I doubt my ability ever to find such a man.' It seemed quite natural that he should take her in his arms to comfort her.

'That is nonsense!' he said softly. 'You could do anything! When the time comes for you to marry——'

'I shall no doubt be forced to compromise.'

Lord Aldworth seemed not to have heard. His arms tightened round her and his eyes were on her lips. He bent his head. His own lips were very close. . . Serafina stared up as if mesmerised. A sudden excitement was racing along her veins. Something momentous was happening. . . Then Lord Aldworth gave a groan, released her, and moved away. 'I must be mad,' he muttered. 'Quite mad!' Without looking at her, he went on, 'Will you take the sledge back with you now? There would be room for it in the gig. I'll get one of the men to take you home.'

Serafina was dazed. Nothing had really happened and yet she had caught a glimpse of something she had never before even dreamed of. It had nothing to do with reason or logic but, whatever it was, it threatened her sane, rational view of life as nothing else ever had. She shivered and said in a subdued tone, 'Yes. Thank you.'

'Sally!'

'Yes, Lord Aldworth?' she said, looking at him.

'I. . . I'm sorry if I frightened you.'

'You didn't frighten me. I. . . I wanted you to kiss me.'

'Oh, God, Sally, I can't! I mustn't!'

'No, of course you must not. I know that.'

She raised her head and looked at him gravely. He went to say something, hesitated, then shook his head. When he finally spoke he sounded angry.

'Come, I'll take you to the stables. There'll be someone there.'

The stables were on the other side of the house. They went through the walled garden and out into the overgrown shrubbery—at this season a tangle of branches and dead leaves, interspersed with laurels. Lord Aldworth kicked a dead branch off the path with unnecessary violence. 'This will all have to be pruned and cleared. There's a mountain of work to be done before——' He cut himself short and they walked on in silence. They came to a place where the path was so overgrown that it had narrowed to a single track. 'I'll go first—there might be some more rubbish in the way,' he said. But a few yards on the path was completely blocked, and he was forced to stop. Serafina, who had been watching where she put her feet on the muddy track, walked straight into him. She slipped and would have fallen, but he caught her.

It was like putting a match to tinder. There was no pause for thought, no hesitation, no holding back. She was seized in his arms and he kissed the breath out of her body. For a moment she had no thought of resistance, indeed no thought at all. She was swept along on a tidal wave of emotion such as she had never before experienced. He was holding her so tightly that she could not move, and yet she wanted to be even closer. He was trembling as he parted her lips with his own. . .

Serafina *was* frightened now—frightened by the sudden force of an experienced man's passion, and even more frightened at the depth of response it had aroused in her. She was torn between an intense desire to let this man do anything he wished with her and an equally strong fear of this total loss of control. She gave a little cry and sought to free herself—and the instant she did he let her go.

'Sally, I. . . Oh, God, what can I say? You're just a child. . . I. . . I don't know what came over me.' He turned away from her, cursing under his breath. Then he turned back and said desperately, 'Such a thing has never happened before, I swear. I behaved like a schoolboy, grabbing what he wants with no thought or care. Have I hurt you?'

The polished, urbane man of the world had vanished. He looked much younger, almost vulnerable, as he stood before her, making an obvious effort to regain his composure, an expression of contrition and concern on his face. Her heart gave a sudden pang and she forgot her own fears in a desire to reassure him. Forcing herself to speak normally, she said, 'Hardly a schoolboy. Not like any schoolboy I've known, at any rate. No, you didn't hurt me. And. . .and I understand what you mean—I felt it, too.' A shiver went down her spine. 'Nothing like that has ever happened to me before, either.'

'But you are still so young! I'm the one who should have known better. And I didn't. Was that your first kiss, Sally?'

Serafina was still so dazed that she answered him with complete honesty. 'The first which. . .made me feel like that. I'm. . . I'm not sure I like it. It wasn't at all sensible. And it doesn't fit in with my ideas of. . . With what I wish to do with my life.'

An unwilling laugh escaped him. 'I'm afraid life doesn't always let us dictate our own terms, little Sally. Surely your reading has told you that? Feelings have a way of coming into conflict with what one knows to be safe, or sensible. And,' he said, with a sudden note of bitterness, 'one's duty. My God, I know about duty only too well. But that's another question. Tell me what I can do to make amends to you.'

Serafina had been reminded by this speech of Lord Aldworth's own determination to live his own life, but she made herself remain calm. 'You don't have to make amends to me, Lord Aldworth. After all, it was——' she swallowed '—only one kiss.' She stared, fascinated, as his eyes dropped to her mouth, and her own treacherous emotions started to respond once again. She took a hurried step back, and said with decision, 'But I think it has given me some right to be plain with you. Plainer than I would otherwise be. I have heard things about you—about your behaviour in Vienna and other places. You needn't think Serafina has been telling tales, either—she thinks you perfect. But I write—and receive—letters, you know. Your association with Serafina in London has naturally roused a certain amount of interest, and there are always some who like to gossip, and others who pass the gossip on. Young ladies are not supposed to know about affairs and...and mistresses, and certainly Serafina would never dream of mentioning them to you, even if she knew about them. But, as you know, I am no lady, and I do ask you about them.'

He had been listening intently, but now his face closed up and he said coldly, 'Forgive me. What happened just now gives you no right whatsoever to ask anything of the kind! It was another thing entirely!'

'Was it? I fail to see the difference.'

'That kiss was the impulse of a moment,' said Lord Aldworth grimly. 'I am sorry it happened, and I shall certainly take care that it does not happen again. But my affairs are exactly that, Sally Feverel. *My* affairs. They have nothing to do with you or anyone else!'

'They surely have something to do with your wife!'

'I do not yet have a wife. In any case, neither that kiss nor my affairs have any relevance to my marriage.' Serafina gave an exclamation of disgust and turned away. There was a difficult silence. Then he sighed and said, 'I suppose I haven't been making allowance for your youthful idealism. I can't blame you for asking the question. Look at me, Sally.'

She turned round with obvious reluctance.

'I can't justify kissing you, and I dislike myself for having done so. But believe me, I meant no disrespect. It was an. . .an overwhelming impulse, and even now I cannot account for it. Can you forgive me, and forget it happened?'

Serafina's delicately balanced composure suddenly snapped. 'I'll forget it! I'll forget it willingly! I don't wish to remember it. But how many other unaccountably "overwhelming impulses" is poor Serafina to put up with if you do marry her? How many affairs is she to hear about from the gossips? Tell me that! No relevance to your marriage, indeed! But don't bother to say anything more. I don't wish to hear it. I must go!'

She tore past him and ran to the stables. When he caught up with her she was standing by the groom. She looked at him stony-faced and waited while he gave orders that Miss Sally Feverel was to be conveyed home. There was a slight delay while the sledge was fetched from the garden where they had left it, but conversation between Lord Aldworth and his visitor was minimal.

Lord Aldworth went back into the house feeling more unlike himself than he had for a long time. For years he had known what he wanted and had used his considerable charm and abilities to get his way. The nature of his work abroad would have made a long-term commitment to one person inadvisable and, in any case, his father's second marriage had given him a horror of that institution. While his brother Gervase had been alive Charles had always sworn that he should not be caught in the same trap as his unhappy sire. Fortunately, he had never met anyone with whom he wished to spend more than a delightful interlude, and all his affairs had been with mature, experienced women of the world—women who knew the rules and kept to them. It had seemed to him that this was an ideal life—work he loved, and pleasure where and when he chose to find it.

But Gervase's death had changed all that. Marriage and an heir for Aldworth were imperative and, though Charles was reluctant to face the prospect, he acknowledged the justice of his grandmother's views. Life was always uncertain, and the sooner the Aldworth succession was ensured the better. Serafina Feverel had seemed to represent a suitable compromise. A lovely, well brought up bride of impeccable lineage, a couple of healthy children born as soon as possible afterwards, and then a life of domestic preoccupation for his wife, and freedom for him to find congenial company elsewhere—even, perhaps, to take up the work he loved again. Not ideal, but the best one could do.

Now Sally Feverel had dared to cast doubt on it all. A slip of a girl, impudent, indecorous, ungraceful—no, not ungraceful. Though they were not what was expected of a young lady, her movements had a wild, free grace of their own. But she was frank to the point of rudeness, she was over-educated, opinionated, lacking in any sense of dress or occasion... She had dared to question what had seemed to him to be a very sensible arrangement, and, what was worse, she had made him begin to question it himself!

When he had first seen Serafina in her father's library he had found the resemblance to Sally almost too much to credit. Could two girls who were not twins possibly be so alike? But he had soon dismissed his doubts. The very different way he felt about each of them had convinced him. Serafina was placid, gentle and undemanding. Her understanding might be a trifle limited, but she would never argue with him. Life with her would be easy, if somewhat boring. Dull. In fact, he had recently found himself wishing that Serafina were not quite such a mouse, that she were a little more like her sister... But no! A wife like Sally Feverel would drive him insane in a week!

On the other hand... Sally would never be dull. She might be infuriating, but he had never yet been bored in her company. She was almost as lovely as her sister, and equally well-born. Dammit, she was fun! And that kiss... His blood quickened at the thought of it. Young and inexperienced though she might be, she would be his equal in passion, he was sure. He smiled as he thought of her laughter, the animation in that delicately moulded face in the snow, her fiercely loyal defence of Serafina's interests. What a girl she was! What...what if he were to change his mind and marry the younger Feverel sister...? He was tempted; he was strongly tempted...

What was he thinking of? It would be the very trap he had so sedulously avoided! Sally Feverel would never meekly acquiesce to his will; she would expect— no, *demand* to be consulted on anything and every-thing. She would not agree to stay at home while he was abroad; she would want to be with him—if only to see the world. And what a disaster for his career she would be, with her unconventional behaviour and lack of Society manners! He shuddered as he visualised the effect of Sally's impetuous ways on the rigid protocol of the diplomatic circles of Europe. He was willing to wager that she would never be content to come second in his affections, but would want him to dance attendance on her all the time. And though at the moment he felt that he might want nothing other than this, what would be left when this present infatuation, this *madness*, had worn off, as it surely would eventually? He would be tied to a wife with a mind of her own, a wife who would demand to know what he was doing and why, and who would fill the house with her accusations and recriminations when he refused to tell her. In short, a wife who would make his life the hell his father's had been.

No, Sally Feverel must be firmly and completely put out of his mind. He was determined to marry someone quiet, peace-loving and biddable, someone who would give him the freedom he had set his mind on. Her sister, Serafina, in fact. He was leaving Sussex the next morning and the memory of what had happened this afternoon would soon fade. By the time he saw Sally Feverel again he would have to regard her with equanimity as his future sister-in-law. He took comfort from the fact that he would probably not have to see very much of her once he was married to her sister. Whenever she came to Aldworth, he would most likely be away. In fact, it might be wiser to make sure that he was.

* * *

Serafina surprised her family when she returned home by going to her room and staying there for several hours. Angelica made an attempt to speak to her, but Serafina merely shook her head and refused to answer. When she finally came downstairs she did her best to appear normal, but this was beyond even *her* powers of dissimulation. In the days that followed she did not improve. When not actively forced into conversation by one of the others she was silent. She excused herself from the traditional afternoon outings, instead going for long walks by herself. And her performance in the Saturday play was totally lacking in the verve they had all come to expect. The Feverels were very worried. Serafina had always been the least temperamental, the most energetic, the sanest of them all. What had happened?

The climax came about two weeks after Lord Aldworth's departure when Rafe, in a misguided effort to cheer his sister up, challenged her to climb the oak tree. Serafina burst into tears and was understood to say through her sobs that she wished she had never heard of the wretched oak tree! At this piece of heresy Mrs Feverel chased the younger ones out, assured her husband that this was something only a mother could do and that she was perfectly well enough to cope with it, and invited Serafina to sit down by her sofa and talk.

'Now, Serafina, I do not intend to animadvert on past history. What is done is done, and neither tears nor temper will undo it. Is your present state of mind due to Lord Aldworth's absence in London, or to regret that you have deceived him? Or is there something else about which I have not heard?'

After some evasion and further questioning Serafina confessed to her mother that Lord Aldworth had kissed her the day before he had left for London.

'So this is what has been distressing you! I understand now. Being kissed against one's will——'

'No, Mama.'

'No?'

'I. . . It was not against my will. I wanted him to.'

Mrs Feverel was shocked but, once she had ascertained that the matter had gone no further than a kiss, she was inclined not to treat it too seriously. 'For I understand that it is Lord Aldworth's fixed intention to offer for you when you return to London and know him a little better. He has already informed your father of this.'

'He has?' Serafina was astonished.

'He mentioned it when he was here, apparently, and has now written more formally to your father to that effect. Quite why he finds further delay necessary I am not perfectly certain, but in view of your little deception it is perhaps as well—it gives you time to tell him the truth before matters become serious between you. He has written a charming letter. Your papa showed it to me when it came this morning. Papa intended to discuss it with you, but you were so unkind to poor Rafe that I felt I had to speak to you first. . . You have not been yourself since Lord Aldworth left, and I wondered if there was something more than mere lovesickness. It seems I was right!'

'What will Papa say to Lord Aldworth?'

'I know he approves of him. But he has always felt that you should make up your own mind about your future husband. Your papa is a rare man, Serafina, as I hope you realise. Neither Lord Aldworth's riches nor his position would influence him, even though the advantages of such a match to the family are obvious. He intends to say that if Lord Aldworth can persuade you to accept him then he will give his approval. He assumes, of course, that you will have revealed your subterfuge before allowing Lord Aldworth to commit himself.'

Serafina nodded. In her present pessimistic mood it seemed most unlikely that Lord Aldworth would want to marry her when he knew how she had deceived him. Her mother continued.

'But since I assume that you will accept him, the kiss, though precipitate, was not a serious matter.'

This reminded Serafina of the true source of her unhappiness. This time there was no humour for her in the word 'precipitate' as she cried, 'But it was, Mama! When Lord Aldworth kissed me he thought I was Sally, not Serafina!'

Mrs Feverel, perplexed, regarded her daughter for a full minute. 'You know, I always regarded you as the most intelligent of my children, but I find it impossible to conceive how anyone could have put themselves into a situation where the placing of a kiss is so confused!'

'You said you weren't going to animadvert, Mama!'

'And I won't, however strong the temptation. You are being punished quite enough by the pickle you are in. What do you propose to do about this. . .misplaced kiss?'

'What can I do? But it is not very pleasant to know that Lord Aldworth had marriage to Serafina in mind before he kissed Sally!'

'Are you quite certain that he was not taking a page out of your own book? Treating you as separate people when he knew you were really one and the same?'

'No, I'm sure he doesn't suspect. He. . .he behaves quite differently to each of us. And he was very angry with himself for succumbing to the temptation. I don't quite know how that kiss happened, Mama, but now I don't know how to go on!'

'I find it quite extraordinarily difficult to advise you. Nor do I think it wise to consult your Papa. I doubt he would know how to help, and in any case I think the kiss is best kept between ourselves, Serafina. Fathers have a different way of looking at such things.' There was a silence, broken after a minute or two by Mrs Feverel.

'You will have a little time in London, I think, before Lord Aldworth makes his offer. If you have decided that you wish to accept it, you will have to use the time beforehand to attach him to you so firmly that he will accept your excuses. You can be very persuasive when you choose, my dear.'

Serafina sighed and nodded.

Mrs Feverel began to say something, stopped, looked doubtful, then took another breath and said, 'I was surprised when Angelica said you were in love. You had always seemed to me to be someone whose sentiments were admirably controlled, and I confess that I doubted what she said. But is it true, Serafina? Do you really love Lord Aldworth?'

'I don't know! I have never felt like this before, Mama.'

Mrs Feverel looked grave. 'You must be sure that you know what you are facing, Serafina. I have not met

Lord Aldworth so I cannot judge him. Your father likes him, and that is a recommendation, but he of course sees him from a man's point of view. When we discussed the question of your marriage initially you seemed content to marry for material advantage, for companionship, perhaps, but not for love. I wonder if that is still the case?'

'It is still necessary. Gabriel's debts——'

'Gabriel's debts are nothing compared with your happiness, Serafina. I would persuade your papa to forbid the match if I thought you were going to be unhappy!'

'Oh, no!'

Serafina's involuntary cry was ignored by Mrs Feverel, who went on, 'What you tell me about that kiss—that it was Sally Lord Aldworth thought he was kissing—would indicate a certain lack of scruple in his approach to women. There are many such men and, as long as they are reasonably discreet and continue to show consideration to their wives, the world does not condemn them. If Lord Aldworth should indeed turn out to be such a man, it would be easier for you if. . .if you were not. . .too attached to him.'

'I understand that, Mama. I will keep it in mind.'

After Serafina had gone Mrs Feverel sighed and took out a letter from her workbox—a letter which she had no intention of mentioning to her daughter. Lady Chilham, unaware of Lord Aldworth's request to Mr Feverel, had written to warn her friend that Serafina should return to London soon.

Lord Aldworth is in town again and is constantly seen with Louisa Paget. We all thought she had

returned to Vienna—she left London last month—
but apparently she merely spent a few days in Paris,
shopping, from the look of it, then suddenly turned
round and came back here! It is my opinion that she
must have learned somehow or other of Aldworth's
decision to return early to England. In her anxiety
to see him again Lady Paget appears to have quite
forgotten that she has a husband waiting for her in
Vienna. The Dowager Lady Aldworth is furious, but
seems powerless to stop the affair. The sooner
Serafina is here the better. I miss her, anyway. It's
time she was back.

Serafina's departure from Sussex was not a joyous
occasion. Her family was sad to see her go—they would
all miss her. Mr Feverel, a born optimist, was sure that
Aldworth would be sympathetic when his daughter
confessed, but Angelica was afraid that he would
refuse to listen, and was already regretting the loss of
such a handsome, eligible suitor for her sister. Mrs
Feverel's views were more complicated. She suspected
that Serafina's feelings were more deeply engaged than
even the girl herself knew, and she was torn between
hope that Lord Aldworth would not make Serafina
unhappy by rejecting her after her confession and fear
that greater unhappiness lay ahead for her daughter if
he were to marry her.

Serafina herself was sure that Lord Aldworth would
not accept any excuses. She had made him ridiculous,
and no man of breeding and pride would tolerate that.
So it was in a mood of melancholy resignation that she
joined her godmother once more in Curzon Street.

'Good heavens, Serafina, I do not know what has

happened to you! There is work to be done, child, and you sit there like one of Lord Elgin's statues! You must go to see them, by the way; all the world is talking of them again. But I must tell you, dear child, that Aldworth is paying Louisa Paget the most marked attention once more. The whole town is talking of it, and it is no secret that his grandmother has sworn she will not attend any function where they will be seen together.'

Serafina suffered a momentary pang, followed by a surge of anger. 'How dare he?'

Lady Chilham looked at her in amazement. 'What do you mean? It is annoying for us, of course, but you have no claim as yet on his loyalty. And you may well never have if that woman is not stopped in her efforts to ensnare him.'

'Lord Aldworth, ma'am, has been good enough to convey to my father his intention to ask me to marry him!'

'His intention to ask. . . I have never heard of such an arrangement before. You mean he has asked your father for permission to pay his addresses to you?'

'Not exactly, ma'am. It seems there must be a short delay before he does so. He wishes to give me time to get to know him better, he says, but I think it is really because he has some unfinished business on hand. Lady Paget, perhaps?'

'It may be so,' said Lady Chilham doubtfully. 'But what an extraordinary way to be going on! I had thought better of Aldworth—if these are continental manners, then I have no wish to know more of them. But,' she continued, brightening up, 'whatever the reason for the delay, you are to be congratulated,

Serafina, on capturing one of the most eligible *partis* in
London. I knew you could do it!' She embraced her
god-daughter warmly. 'Now, what will you wear
tonight to the Granthams'? We must not be compla-
cent—that woman is dangerous... I wonder if we
should give you a touch of colour? You look sadly
pale, child. I thought the country was supposed to be a
healthy place!'

CHAPTER SEVEN

THE pleasure Serafina had formerly taken in her plot
to trap Lord Aldworth had almost completely disappeared, but she was persuaded to make an effort to
look her best that evening—though she strenuously
resisted any effort to add colour to her cheeks. In the
event she looked enchantingly ethereal in a dress of
white Urling's net, worn over a pale blue satin slip and
decorated round the hem with bunches of silk forget-
me-nots. Lord Aldworth, who was standing in a corner
conversing with Lady Paget, drew in his breath at the
sight.

'What is it, Charles?' Lady Paget followed his eyes.
'Oh, the Feverel child—charming, absolutely charming.' She turned back to him. 'You know, it is really
quite depressing once one is past a certain age! I spend
a fortune on a Paris creation, I enjoy the services of a
first-class lady's maid, who spends hours dressing me,
and what happens? A child like that, in a dress which
was probably made by the village dressmaker, quite
outshines me!'

'Quite!' said Lord Aldworth.

'Charles!'

He looked at her with an apologetic smile. 'I'm
sorry, my dear. I'm afraid I didn't hear what you said.
Was it about Miss Feverel?'

Lady Paget was offended, but dared not show it.
Though Charles had frequently sought her company in

the past few weeks, she did not deceive herself that his heart was in their flirtation. As she had discovered in those early days in Vienna, and later in London, when he chose he could make any woman feel entirely desirable, the centre of his world, a goddess among women. His devotion, while it lasted, was comprehensive. But this feeling was noticeably absent from their present affair. He occasionally smiled at her in the old way, and then, in spite of herself, her heart would quicken. But suddenly, without warning, his attention would fade and she would feel she had lost him again. Lady Paget was a clear-sighted, intelligent woman, but Lord Aldworth's present behaviour was puzzling her. It was characteristic of a man who was interested in another quarry, and on Lord Aldworth's past record that would not be at all surprising. Though it was vexing. And highly inconvenient.

But who could the new object of his affections be? She had dismissed Serafina Feverel as a possible rival without a second thought. The chit was very lovely, but she had nothing to offer a sophisticated man of the world such as Charles. No, he was reluctantly obeying the orders of his harridan of a grandmother in his cultivation of Miss Feverel. Even though Lady Paget had found it galling, she had understood why she had been so suddenly dropped before Christmas. The poor man had to set up a marriage of sorts after his brother's death, and she had been sure that her time would come again when Charles eventually grew tired of the girl's simpers.

But matters had now become more serious, and more urgent. This was not the time for Charles to lose whatever interest he had once had in her. . . . She stole

a glance at her companion. His eyes were still on
Serafina Feverel. He could not be in love with her!
Men were often fools, but she would give her best
Parisian bonnet to the Little Sisters of the Poor if
Charles Dacre had been caught by a pretty face with
nothing behind it! He wasn't even looking at her in
that way—more. . .regretfully, as if he were looking at
a ghost, or a shadow. How odd!

Her musings were cut short.

'Louisa, I ought to say a word to Miss Feverel. I had
no idea she was coming to London quite so soon. Will
you excuse me? I am sure you understand why I am
not proposing that you should accompany me?' He
looked at her with his familiar glinting smile.

She forced herself to say calmly, 'Of course, Charles.
It is kind of you to spare me Lady Chilham's icy
courtesies—I swear I shall catch cold from them one of
these days! In any case, I see Denham over there,
trying to catch my eye. He can amuse me while you
are gone.'

'My dear, you are, as always, the perfect companion—
tolerant and almost too understanding! I shall not be
long.'

He walked away, a tall, confident figure. Lady Paget
frowned. There had been something in his tone then—
a touch of contempt? Surely not. She watched him as
he crossed the room and wondered what her best plan
of action would be.

Serafina had seen Lord Aldworth and his companion,
of course, and she had been surprised by another
sudden surge of anger. How dared he, indeed? She
thought waspishly that there was no necessity to ask

what sort of 'overwhelming impulses' bound him to Lady Paget. They were perfectly natural ones of the baser sort! But she looked suitably demure as he came over and spoke to Lady Chilham.

'I see you have your god-daughter back with you, Lady Chilham. You must be happy to see her again. Indeed, we are all the happier for seeing Miss Feverel in London again—and in such beauty.'

Looking somewhat sceptical, Lady Chilham assured him that she was delighted to have Serafina with her, and thanked him for his complimentary remarks. 'Though they are perhaps too extravagant. Surely in the whole of London there must be one or two who ...do not share your pleasure, Lord Aldworth?' She allowed her eyes to rest fractionally on Lady Paget.

He had the grace to look somewhat disconcerted by this direct attack, but recovered and turned to Serafina. 'Miss Feverel, what can I say? This is an unexpected pleasure!'

Serafina was faced with an almost irresistible urge to ask him if she had been precipitate in her return, but restrained herself. It was not the moment.

'Are your family well, Miss Feverel?' he continued. 'Your parents, and brothers and sisters?'

Serafina suddenly realised that she was sitting on a keg of gunpowder! Lady Chilham was unaware of the separate existence of Sally and Serafina, and might well betray her before she was ready. She must turn the conversation away from her family without delay! For once, her air of nervous hesitation was not assumed as she replied, 'Thank you, Lord Aldworth, they are all well. I hope Lady Aldworth is not ill—I have not seen her here tonight.'

This was an unfortunate remark, as she realised the moment the words were out of her mouth. She knew perfectly well why Lady Aldworth was not present, as did most of London. She blushed as Lord Aldworth said thinly, 'My grandmother is indisposed at the moment. I am sure, however, that she would enjoy a visit from you now that you are back. May I call on you tomorrow, Lady Chilham? I hope to see you then, Miss Feverel. Your servant, Lady Chilham, Miss Feverel.' With a graceful bow and a smile that did not reach his eyes he was gone.

'Really, Serafina, I sometimes think you have more hair than wit! Whatever persuaded you to refer to his grandmother? You know why she isn't here; I told you myself only today!'

'It was a natural enough question,' Serafina said defensively.

'But not one to please Aldworth!'

'That was not my aim——'

'Well, it should be! He hasn't come up to scratch yet, my girl. You could still lose him.'

'That is the very thing I wanted to talk to you about, ma'am. But it must wait until we are more private...'

'Serafina! What were you thinking of? Aldworth will never forgive you for making such a fool of him,' wailed Lady Chilham when Serafina told her of her double identity. 'Oh, it is really too bad of you—to have captured the interest of the most eligible bachelor in London and then to throw it away with such wilful idiocy... I hope you realise that if a word of this gets around you will have ruined your chances with anyone else, as well? Oh, how could you? After all my work...'

Serafina's heart sank at this confirmation of her own worst fears, but she rallied and said tentatively, 'I thought if I waited a little before telling him he might become sufficiently attached to overlook it, ma'am.'

'You cannot be serious! A man would have to be besotted to do so, and Aldworth of all people would never allow his feelings to run away with him to such an extent.'

'In that case, ma'am, I am lost indeed, but I have nothing to lose by trying. Will you...could you now forget what I have told you, and only remember to be silent about Sally?'

Lady Chilham looked outraged and shook her head, but Serafina's powers of persuasion were considerable, and she was finally prevailed upon to do as her god-daughter requested.

The season was now showing signs of stirring, and it promised to be a glittering one. The storm and stress of the Napoleonic wars were over, and no effort was spared in the pursuit of pleasure. The ladies of Society were busy planning balls, routs, assemblies and receptions, each one striving to outdo the next. Fountains of flowers, pyramids of fruit, tents of feathers—nothing was too extravagant for the ambitious hostess who wished to create a stir. The Prince Regent's latest extravagances—his increasing interest in Brighton and the pavilion there, the scandalous behaviour of Lady X or Lord Y—were the main topics of conversation. Serafina sometimes grew impatient with this frivolous world, but rigorously excluded any hint of such feelings from her demeanour. She exerted herself in public to be as beautiful and as biddable as Lord Aldworth could possibly wish, but in the privacy of the Curzon Street house she continued to read the newspapers and learn of the world outside England.

Not everywhere was as peaceful. Napoleon was vanquished, but the spirit of the French Revolution was far from dead. The ideals of liberty, fraternity and equality, the desire for independence, were still giving the autocratic rulers of Europe some trouble. The American colonies had been free from British domination for some time, of course, but now the South Americans were fighting fiercely for their independence from Spain. And the British Government, aware of its status as a parliamentary democracy and, more cynically, interested in the possibilities for trade, was finding itself increasingly, if unofficially, in sympathy with the rebels.

But none of this was discussed at the functions which she attended, and if it had been she would not have permitted herself to join in. She was waiting, with a mixture of hope and fear, for Lord Aldworth to make his offer. She often caught him looking at her with an expression she found difficult to define, but he made no attempt to declare himself. He too seemed to be waiting. And meanwhile he was seen in Lady Paget's company often enough for the gossip to continue. The Dowager Lady Aldworth decided that she had had enough of London, and removed to her house in Berkshire.

Before she did so she sent for Serafina. 'Well, Miss Feverel, what have you to say? Why are you standing at the side waiting for Charles to fall into the arms of that harpy?'

'Why are *you*, ma'am?'

'Because I cannot stop it, that's why! Charles seems to have lost all sense. He absolutely refuses to listen to anything I have to say. I have never known him so... so deaf to any advice.'

'I cannot stop it either—and it would be out of the question for me to give him advice, or even to approach him on the subject of his relationship with Lady Paget.'

'You're no fool, however. I have the impression that you could think of something if you chose. Surely the fact that my grandson is about to make you an offer gives you some influence over him?'

'Lady Aldworth, you know better than most what sort of relationship Lord Aldworth wishes to enjoy with his chosen bride. Do you really think she could have any influence whatsoever on him—especially before she is married? And he has not yet even asked me.'

'He will, he will. He has said so. He had made up his mind before Christmas—before he went to Vienna. But since his return...he has been so different.' She frowned. 'I don't understand him. And I don't understand why he insists on waiting before approaching you. It's that Jezebel!'

'Lord Aldworth does not appear to me to be happy in Lady Paget's company...'

'Nor should he be!' The Dowager shot Serafina a look. 'So you've been watching him, eh?'

'Discreetly. He goes through the form of paying her attention, but I am almost sure that his interest in her is not as straightforward as it seems. He sometimes appears to be as indifferent to her charms as he is to mine.'

'Does he indeed? I have avoided seeing them together for some time, so I cannot judge. Indifferent to Lady Paget, eh? That's more encouraging. But in that case, why...?' She stopped and seemed to be debating something. Finally she said slowly, 'What do you know of Charles's work, Serafina?'

Serafina had a fleeting vision of Sally's discussion with Charles in Sussex. Sally knew a little, but not Serafina. She sighed and said, 'His diplomatic work, ma'am? Almost nothing. He never discusses it with me.'

'No, he wouldn't, of course. But if it isn't his interest in Lady Paget which prevents him from making a formal offer, then it must be his work.'

Serafina was surprised. 'What do you mean, Lady Aldworth?'

The Dowager was silent for a moment. Then she said, 'I'm about to betray a confidence. I don't like doing it, but I think you should know, and I am as certain as I can be of your discretion.'

'What is it?'

'Charles sometimes does highly...secret work for the government. Not often now—he did a lot more some years ago in France.'

'When Napoleon was in power?'

'Yes. He speaks French like a native, of course.'

'And?'

'He is probably postponing his marriage plans until a particular assignment is over—and I have an idea that, whatever it is, it is not part of his normal diplomatic activities.'

'But why should that delay anything?'

'He says it isn't dangerous, but perhaps he thinks it might be.'

'I see. And I am. . .unworthy of his confidence. Perhaps he shares that with Lady Paget—she is, after all, part of the diplomatic world.'

Serafina must have revealed how depressed she was, for Lady Aldworth suddenly sounded old as she leant forward and begged, 'Don't give up, Serafina! I am relying on your skills to rescue Charles from a disastrous mistake. The more I see of you, the greater is my conviction that you are the very one to make my grandson happy. Get him to offer for you, Serafina. Once he is officially betrothed he will give up any thought of Lady Paget, I am sure. The rest will follow.'

Serafina was too conscious of her own difficulties in the matter to respond positively to Lady Aldworth's plea. 'You place a heavy burden on me, ma'am,' she said sadly. 'I will do my best, but it may not be enough.'

Nevertheless Serafina thought hard about Lady Aldworth's recommendation, and eventually decided on a course of action which might help.

Lord Aldworth was not, of course, Serafina's only admirer. She seldom lacked partners at any function she attended, and her room in Curzon Street was rarely without a floral tribute of some kind. The most recent was a lavish arrangement of exotic blooms, and Serafina had cringed at the crass sentimentality of the verse which had accompanied it. Her first impulse had been to throw the card in the fire and take the first opportunity which presented itself to make it clear to the sender that such effusions were not welcome. But with Lady Aldworth's words in mind she had restrained herself, and instead placed the flowers and their message in a prominent position in Lady Chilham's salon. Here she waited for Lord Aldworth. He had taken to calling quite regularly—almost, Serafina thought resentfully, as if she were an elderly relative in need of the comfort of a daily visit.

As she sat in the salon, surrounded by the heavy scent of the flowers, Serafina reviewed the past few weeks. She could hardly claim to have made much progress in her efforts to attach Lord Aldworth. Except for his calls, which seldom lasted very long, she saw him less frequently now than she had before Christmas. And even when he was with her he would quite often sit in silence for several minutes, frowning at Lady Chilham's Aubusson carpet as if something about the design displeased him. He occasionally invited her for a drive or a visit to some exhibition, but he seemed strangely reluctant to be seen in public with her. For a man who was contemplating an offer of marriage his behaviour was certainly odd.

Was it that he had become aware of her duplicity? She examined the evidence for this and rejected it. The trouble, whatever it was, did not concern her directly, she was sure. True, she sometimes caught him looking at her with a fleeting expression of regret in his eyes— perhaps he was finding it more difficult than he had thought to forget Sally? Her heartbeat quickened at the thought, but she quickly grew calm again. Even if it was so, that was not the chief reason for the change in him.

Serafina got up and walked about the room

impatiently. The scent from those flowers was giving
her the headache; she was finding it difficult to think!
She stopped by the long windows and rested her
forehead against the cool glass. There was nothing
she could do directly; so much was certain. At the
moment he regarded her as a stupid, doll-like creature,
unworthy of any sort of confidence. Should she confess
now—this afternoon? It took less than a moment's
reflection to discard that idea. He would pack her off
to Sussex and she would never see him again! Very
well, she would have to keep up her deception and do
what she could by indirect methods. It would entail
some risk, but when had she ever refused a challenge?

At this point in her musings her visitor was
announced.

Lord Aldworth entered the room, elegant as ever in
a blue superfine coat, a spotless cravat tied in its usual
intricate folds, and pale pantaloons over gleaming top-
boots. He bent over her hand in a graceful gesture,
murmuring a greeting, but as he straightened again an
expression of distaste marred his handsome features.
He surveyed the room through his glass. 'Ah,' he said,
staring at the flower arrangement.

Serafina took up her role, and looked distressed.
'You do not like the flowers! I thought they were very
pretty, but perhaps I am mistaken?'

'Not at all, Miss Feverel. I am merely surprised at
Lady Chilham's choice. Their—er—perfume is somewhat overpowering.'

'Lady Chilham did not choose them; they are mine,
Lord Aldworth. Mr Allen sent them. With such a very
lovely poem.'

'The devil he did!' Serafina was pleased to see that Lord Aldworth was looking slightly affronted.

'Yes, shall I show it to you? Or. . .perhaps I should not. Mr Allen may prefer me to keep it private.'

'I am not having other gentlemen writing private love letters to you, Serafina!'

'It is a poem! I liked it as much as anything I have ever seen in Papa's books. Mr Allen is so clever——' She stopped as Lord Aldworth calmly removed the card from her hand, as she had intended he should. 'Lord Aldworth! You should not!'

'Allen wrote this. . .poem to you?'

'Yes! Is it not lovely? Of course, I am not really an angel, but don't you think it was clever to use my name like that? "Seraphic Serafina, angelically fair"?' She sighed happily. 'Papa called us all after angels, you know. Even Rafe is really Raphael.'

'What about Sally?'

Serafina held on to her happy expression with difficulty as she cursed her carelessness. 'Sally? What do you mean? Her real name is Cherubina,' she said, improvising rapidly, and blessing the day that she and Angelica had debated what her parents could possibly call another girl. 'Oh, you are asking why we call her Sally? When she grew older she hated Cherubina— though I think it is a pretty name. But Sally can be very determined when she wishes. Sarah is her second name—it is Mama's name too, of course.' She appeared to lose interest in her sister as her eyes returned to the card in his hand. 'I know I'm not nearly as beautiful as Mr Allen says, but the sentiments are expressed in such a lovely way. Pray give the poem back to me, Lord Aldworth! I am going to keep it forever!'

'I think not. I could not permit it,' he said sternly.

'But I like it!' Serafina put her hands together and looked up at her visitor with hurt reproach. The look worked its usual magic.

'I am sorry, my dear,' said Lord Aldworth more gently. 'Allen must be told that you are not free to accept such...missives. I am surprised that Lady Chilham allowed it!'

'I didn't know! Am I not?'

'Not what, Serafina?' he said, looking down indulgently.

'Not free?'

'Well, of course you are not! Did your father not tell you?'

'He said that you were intending to...intending to...'

'To ask you to marry me? I am.'

'But...' Serafina raised large, puzzled blue eyes to Lord Aldworth. '...you haven't yet,' she said timidly.

Lord Aldworth looked down into the blue eyes gazing into his and cleared his throat. 'Er...there are reasons why any announcement cannot at present be made public,' he said. He sounded pompous but Serafina could see that he was experiencing some difficulty in resisting the lure of blue eyes and red lips so close to his own.

'As you wish, Lord Aldworth,' Serafina said submissively, but with patent disappointment. She made to move away but Lord Aldworth's arm stole round her waist and he pulled her back.

'Do you wish to marry me, Serafina?' he murmured.

She was almost overwhelmed by a passionate and totally unexpected urge to wind her own arms round his neck and pull his face down to hers, to repeat the kiss they had exchanged in the garden at Blanchards. Oh, God, she thought, alarmed, he's going to kiss me and I don't know if I will be able to act my part! With a supreme effort she controlled her panic. A little agitation was surely permissible. 'I. . . I. . . Yes, I think so.'

'May I kiss you?'

Her eyes flew once again to his. There was a look of complacency about him which was her salvation. She offered her cheek.

He laughed. 'Oh, no,' he said. 'Your lips, my dear, those lovely lips. . .' Pulling her to him, he kissed her full on the mouth. Serafina remained passive, her eyes and lips firmly shut, her feelings firmly under control. 'You may open your eyes, Serafina.' Slowly she opened her eyes and looked at him. Lord Aldworth was examining her face as if searching for a resemblance. . . He sighed, then smiled encouragingly and said, 'What a child you are! But you'll learn.'

'Are we betrothed, Lord Aldworth?'

'I think you may call me Charles, don't you?'

'Oh, I couldn't——' She smiled shyly. 'Very well, Charles.'

'Serafina, I have an odd request. I am delighted— and proud too, of course—that you have agreed to be my wife. But may I ask that you keep our engagement secret for the next month or so?'

She looked puzzled but said, 'Of course, but why?'

'I cannot explain.'

Nothing venture, nothing gain. Greatly daring,

Serafina said sadly, 'It's Lady Paget. She is so much more beautiful than I.'

'No, you are wrong. That is to say, Lady Paget is part of the problem, but only a part. You need not fear that my feelings are engaged elsewhere. . .certainly not with Lady Paget, whatever the appearances. My work is complicated and sometimes not for discussion. I wish to finish a particular part of it before our marriage plans become general knowledge. Will you trust me?'

Serafina looked at him uncertainly. Could she learn any more by further questions? She rather thought not, and she dared not risk arousing any suspicion that she was less compliant than she seemed. 'Very well, Lord Ald—Charles. Do you wish my godmother to be kept in ignorance too? I shall try, but. . .'

'I think I know enough of her to trust her discretion. But you had better leave things to me. I don't think I need say more to your parents—they are already aware of my intention to marry you.'

No suggestion that she might refuse him—only the assumption that things would go as he desired! It was a pity, thought Serafina, that this strange urge to be kissed by Lord Aldworth, this even stranger desire to share his troubles and comfort him did not blind her to his conceit and arrogance!

'Yes, Lor—Charles. Of course I will,' she murmured. 'Whatever you wish.'

Lady Chilham came in at that point, and Serafina sat quietly by while Charles gave her godmother the news and extracted a promise of secrecy from her. He left soon after.

As soon as he had gone Serafina was embraced

warmly. 'So you did it! How did he take your confession?'

'I . . . I didn't tell him,' said Serafina defiantly. 'No, dear godmother, please do not scold. My reasons were sound. Firstly, he has conveniently insisted on keeping our betrothal private for the next month, so I still have time to tell him the truth before it is made public. If he then wishes to disown me he will be able to do so without a scandal. Second, being engaged to him gives me some privileges—a very few, it appears—and I wish to use these to help him. He is troubled in mind, and it has something to do with our friend Lady Paget. Not, as you are no doubt thinking, because he has formed any lasting passion for her. In fact, from the manner in which he spoke of her I should say rather the reverse. This intrigues me, and I want to find out a little more about it. I have a better chance of this the closer I am to him.'

'Why are you doing this, Serafina? It goes far beyond the bounds of a simple wish to make an advantageous marriage.'

Serafina grew scarlet as she stammered, 'I . . . I h— have always had a nose for intrigue, ma'am. I cannot resist it.'

Lady Chilham looked penetratingly at her god-daughter. 'Hmm,' she said. 'As long as you don't find Charles Dacre too intriguing. You wouldn't be the first to break her heart over him, not by any means.'

'What do you mean, ma'am? I? Fall in love with Lord Arrogance? You are sadly mistaken!'

Lady Chilham was not convinced, but allowed the matter to drop. Instead she said, 'What on earth is that smell? Good God, Serafina, what on earth are you thinking of, putting Mr Allen's flowers in the salon? What if Aldworth had noticed them?'

Serafina's eyes danced. 'Oh, but he did, ma'am! And I rather think they helped matters along enormously.'

'Oh, did they, indeed? Well, you may now have them removed. I shall tell Bates to put them in your bedchamber.'

'On no account, please! Could they perhaps be put in the hall where there is a movement of air? It might disperse their somewhat overpowering fragrance. If not, they can be thrown away. They have served their purpose.'

The relationship between Lord Aldworth and Serafina changed surprisingly little following his proposal. His visits continued to be frequent, though short, and though he kissed her both when he arrived and when he left his attitude remained friendly rather than lover-like. Much as she resented this calm lack of any real feeling, Serafina was on the whole glad of it. The slightest hint of passion might have caused a breach in her defences against him. As it was she often spent the minutes after his departure wishing for she knew not what and cursing the day she had learned what it was to be kissed properly, as a woman, by the real Charles Dacre. Then she would excuse herself to Lady Chilham and go for an unfashionably energetic walk in Green Park, surrounded by nursemaids and their charges, or she would take up her *Guide to London* and visit one of the places of interest in the capital, concentrating hard on what she saw. Lady Chilham watched her with anxious eyes but said nothing, not even to discourage her from these solitary expeditions.

It was on one such walk that Serafina caught sight of Lady Paget. Since she had no wish to indulge in one of the barbed conversations in which the lady specialised, Serafina took measures to avoid being seen. But what was such a fashion-conscious woman doing in Green Park at this hour?

She was soon to learn. A gentleman, dressed neatly but soberly in brown, came hurrying up to Lady Paget and greeted her with a decidedly foreign-looking bow. Serafina recognised him, though she did not know his name. He had been at the Granthams' in the company of the Spanish ambassador, and Serafina's curiosity had been roused because he had looked so out of place. Later she had decided that his Excellency had thought so too, for the man had soon disappeared. Now here he was again, in decidedly odd circumstances. Serafina could not imagine what sort of business could bring Lady Paget and this unpleasant-looking little man together at such a very unfashionable hour and in such a very unfashionable place. It was clear that they had no wish to be discovered for they wasted no time. A few minutes' concentrated conversation, then the Spaniard set off towards Piccadilly and Lady Paget hurried in the direction of St James' Park. Serafina walked slowly back to Curzon Street, pondering on what she had seen, but unable to find an explanation. It had not been a lovers' tryst, she was sure.

CHAPTER EIGHT

WHEN Lord Aldworth called the next afternoon she was still debating how she could get him to tell her more about the man she had seen in Green Park. Finally he asked her what was wrong.

'What do you mean, Charles?'

'You seem abstracted. And I have something particular that I wish to say to you.' Serafina pulled herself together and sat attentively while he went on to tell her that he might have to go away for a short while.

This must be what Lady Aldworth had talked about. 'Where. . .where are you going?'

He frowned, as if her question was too direct. 'Now, my dear, you must not become too curious. My work often takes me to strange places, and I cannot be answerable to you all the time. I shall be back within the fortnight, and then we shall set about telling the world that we plan to marry. Will you like that?'

Since it seemed to be expected of her, she looked delighted and breathed, 'Oh, yes, Charles! I would like it above anything. But I wish I knew when you were going, exactly. . .?'

He frowned again. 'I am not quite sure. Quite soon. So if I do not call on you for a little while you must not worry.' When she remained silent he said somewhat coldly, 'You look dissatisfied, Serafina. Is it not enough that I have promised to return in a very short time?'

Serafina wanted to cry, No, it isn't! If you are going into danger I want to know about it, I want to help you! I want at least to share your worries! How dare you shut me out like this? But she restrained herself.

'I'm sorry, Charles,' she said. 'I really didn't mean to offend you. I only wanted to know if you were going before the rout at Carlton House. Gentlemen often have things they must do which they do not wish their wives to worry about. I must remember that in future. But you did promise to escort us.'

She held her breath while he looked at her closely but then he decided that she was sincere.

'When is it? The day after tomorrow? I cannot make any promises, my dear. Shall I ask Denham or one of the others to take you if I am not here?'

'That is kind of you. Godmother and I would not like to miss it. Everyone says it will be a splendid occasion.'

They talked of other things for a while, then Serafina took a breath and said, 'Charles, I saw someone at the Granthams' a little while ago, but I have forgotten his name. It would be so awkward if I met him again. Do you think you could help me?'

'I will if I can, of course. What does he look like?'

Serafina described the man she had seen in Green Park.

Charles's face was expressionless and his tone neutral as he said, 'You were introduced to him? By whom?'

Serafina said, 'I. . . I cannot remember. Oh, please tell me who he is, Charles! I have been in a quake in case I met him again! Indeed, I nearly did, the other day. He was in Green Park, but fortunately he didn't see me.'

'Miguel Barros? In Green Park?'

'That's the name! Thank you, Charles. I knew you would help me! Now I shall know what to call him—Sen. . . Señor Barras.'

'Barros. But if you wish to please me, Serafina, you will forget him. He is not a man I wish you to know.'

'I don't know him, really. Only I saw Lady Paget with him in Green Park. It seemed a strange place for them to be. . .'

'*What*?'

Serafina was quite genuinely startled by Charles's sharp exclamation. He said more calmly, 'You must be mistaken. Lady Paget would sooner be seen dead than in Green Park with the nursemaids. I am surprised you go there.'

'It's pretty! The cows and milkmaids, and all the children. It's very nice there. But I did see Lady Paget with Señor Barr. . . Barros, Charles. I am sure I was not mistaken.'

'Well, you might have done, I suppose. But I trust you will not mention this supposed meeting to anyone else. I wouldn't like to have you thought a scandalmonger, and I still think you might have been mistaken.' When she would have spoken he added firmly, 'Take my word for it, Serafina. Forget the matter. Shall I call on you tomorrow? At five o'clock? We could go for a drive in the park if it is not too cold.'

Serafina decided on submission. 'I shall be here.'

At the door he seemed to sense that all was not well. He stopped, took her in his arms, and smiled at her in such a way that her heart turned over. 'I shall be glad when I have finished my business, Serafina. We shall put the notice of our engagement in the *Gazette*, and then it won't be long before we are married and our life at Aldworth can begin.'

The thought of the confession which must precede that happy situation caused Serafina to shiver. He misunderstood.

'You needn't be afraid. I shall be a most considerate husband, my dear.' He kissed her gently, and she in her anxiety allowed herself to respond, just a little. His arms tightened and he kissed her again. Though she trembled in his grasp she dared not show more feeling. He stepped back and surveyed her. Serafina refused to look at him but instead kept her eyes on the floor. He laughed. 'Lady Modesty! But I think you're learning, Serafina!'

Serafina returned from an outing with Lady Chilham the next day resolved to look her best for the drive with Lord Aldworth. It was gloriously sunny, and she had a new promenade outfit which she wished to put on. The muslin dress was simple enough, but the dark blue spencer and white bonnet edged with blue and white plaid silk which went with it were extremely flattering. Wherever Lord Aldworth was going she was determined that he should remember her!

It was disappointing, therefore, to find a note waiting for her, written in his firm, clear hand. Lord Aldworth presented his regrets, but he was unable, after all, to take her for the promised ride. He hoped she would understand. He had arranged for his friend, Lord Denham, to take Serafina and Lady Chilham to Carlton House on the following evening. He hoped she would enjoy the evening, but not so much that she would forget her most devoted admirer et cetera, et cetera.

It was more than disappointing. When Serafina thought over her conversation with Lady Aldworth she suffered some disquiet. Was the mission, whatever it was, dangerous? Surely not. Europe was now at peace, Britain's power and prestige well-established. Surely no one would dare to harm an envoy of His Britannic Majesty? She tried to dismiss her anxiety, but the niggle of doubt remained.

The following evening Lord Denham arrived in good time to take them to Carlton House. His lordship's open admiration of Serafina was sufficient explanation of his readiness to perform this service for his friend.

'Thank you, Denham,' said Lady Chilham graciously as the ladies came into the hall. 'It gets so crowded in Pall Mall, and I hate arriving late.'

'Do you know Carlton House, Lord Denham?' asked Serafina. 'I have never been there, and I am so looking forward to it.'

Lord Denham smiled down at her and confessed that he knew it well. 'Though each time one goes there one wonders what one will see, or where one will be! The Blue Velvet Room might have been changed overnight to the Yellow Salon, or the Gothic dining-room to the Roman library! The Prince Regent is notoriously. . .fickle in his tastes, I'm afraid. But the refreshments will be first-rate. The Prince never stints on entertainment. Pray, let me help you with your cloak, Miss Feverel.' Serafina's cloak was taken from the footman and placed reverently round her shoulders, much as a connoisseur of porcelain would handle a Ming vase. Serafina hid a smile, and thanked him prettily.

Serafina had heard of the marvels inside Carlton House, and in spite of Lord Denham's warning she was eager to see them. But as she and her companions filed through one room after another she was conscious of a sense of disappointment. The furnishings were magnificent, of that there was no doubt. But for her taste it was too overpowering. It lacked restraint, refinement— and the atmosphere was suffocating. The Prince Regent received them affably, teasing Denham on his good fortune in escorting the prettiest girl in London and holding Miss Feverel's hand with every sign of appreciation. Serafina was glad to escape—such princely attention was a trifle overwhelming.

The evening wore on, the crowds grew, the entertainment was indeed lavish and Serafina was hardly ever without a partner, but she became more and more dispirited. Where was Charles now? Was he in danger? What was she doing here at this stupid party, in these overheated rooms, among this babbling, peacock throng? Though she made every effort to disguise it she became more and more agitated. Lady Chilham noticed how pale she had become and asked her if she was feeling unwell.

'I... I think, if you do not mind, ma'am, I should like to sit somewhere cool. I have a slight headache.'

She was taken at once downstairs to the conservatory, which was a decidedly exotic affair, built in the Gothic mode, but with classical statues and urns. Overhead the elaborate fan vault was filled in with little bits of coloured glass, and at the far end there was a Gothic screen decorated in gilt, vermilion, blue and yellow. It made her eyes ache to look at it. But the conservatory was practically deserted and blessedly cool, scented with banks of flowers and plants. Long windows towards one end opened on to the garden. Here her godmother found her a seat in a secluded alcove, saw that she was comfortable and left her, promising to return soon with a drink of water.

Serafina sank gratefully back against the cushions and closed her eyes. Images of Charles haunted her — in London, in Sussex, talking to Serafina, talking to Sally. Where was he? And how was she ever to get out of the fix she had put herself in? She was hard put to it to stop herself from crying. This was ridiculous! What was wrong with her?

She was disturbed by the sound of voices. By some trick in the structure of this extraordinary room she could hear them quite clearly, though they must be some feet away. They were foreigners, apparently — Spaniards. She closed her eyes again and hoped that they would not disturb her... Then the mention of a name caused her to sit up and listen with all her attention.

'Lord Aldworth left London this afternoon.'

'Where is he going?' A soft, silky voice with a quite characteristic lisp — where had she heard it before?

'Sussex, *señor*.'

'And then to France?'

'Not immediately. The arms ship will not arrive at Newhaven for a day or two. Did Lady Paget not say that Lord Aldworth would be travelling to France with it? And that he would meet Garcia somewhere near

Dieppe? But I do not know where he intends to stay until he sails, Señor Barros. I shall find it out.'

'I know it already. Lord Denham told me. Aldworth has a house down there, just a few miles from Newhaven. This begins to fit together.'

Serafina had placed the voice. It was Barros, the man who had been speaking to Lady Paget in Green Park. But... She grew cold as she took in what he was saying—Lady Paget? Lord Denham? What did that mean? They were Charles's friends! Or...were they? The other man spoke.

'The ship will be well-guarded, *señor*.'

'That is obvious. So we must attack Aldworth before he goes on board. At this Blanchards. We need more detailed information from him about the meeting place with Garcia. And there is a letter of authorisation, apparently...'

'Lord Aldworth won't give in easily.'

'It may take a little while, Felipe. But everyone gives in, eventually. Or they die.'

'You would kill him? An English lord?'

'I hope it won't be necessary. But we have our own boat, and the Channel is both wide and deep... Someone is coming. It will be the ambassador. Let me talk.'

There was a sound of footsteps coming in from the garden. They stopped by the two men.

'Good evening, Your Excellency.'

'Who is this?'

'He is not important, Excellency. He has been helping me to gather information.'

'And?'

'Lord Aldworth has left London and is now on his way to France. But I think we can intercept him.'

'Good. There must be no violence, mind! All I wish is that Aldworth and Garcia do not meet. That arms shipment must be stopped. You can pursue Garcia later.'

'It will be, Excellency. Leave it to me.'

'Then I shall go back. His Highness will be wondering where I am. Come with me to the door, Barros. Send your fellow away.'

Serafina's heart jumped as she heard footsteps approaching. There was no escape—they were going to see her! She put her head in her hands and waited.

'Miss Feverel! Are you ill?'

She gave a start, looked up, then rose and gave a deep curtsy. 'Your Excellency! Oh, please forgive me! I didn't see you. I have such a headache...' She allowed her voice to trail away.

'Sit down, sit down! I hope we didn't disturb you?'

'When?' asked Serafina blankly.

'Just now. You didn't hear us talking?'

'I heard voices... I think. But my head was aching so...' Her voice trailed away again as she sank on to her seat.

'Of course. But why are you alone like this?'

'Lady Chilham has gone to find someone to bring me a drink of water. I am so ashamed of myself, Your Excellency. The Prince Regent has been so kind... I hope he will forgive me.'

'Who would not forgive such a very lovely young lady? I hope you will soon feel better. I'm afraid I must go back to your prince. Shall I tell him about you?'

'Oh, no! Thank you. My godmother will be here very soon. Pray do not disturb yourself on my account.'

He bowed and walked away. As they moved away

Barros said rapidly in Spanish, 'Do you think she heard us, Excellency?'

'What was there to hear? In any case, we were some distance away and speaking in Spanish. I know Miss Feverel quite well. An exquisite creature, but as stupid as she is lovely. We need not worry that she understood anything. Incidentally, do you know that she came here with Denham? An intriguing situation, wouldn't you say?'

The two men laughed, then parted. Barros gave Serafina a quick glance as he passed her and went out of the doors at the end into the garden.

As soon as the two men had gone Serafina jumped up and ran to search for her godmother. She was lucky. Lady Chilham was just appearing at the door. Behind her was a footman with a glass of water in a very fine crystal goblet, but Serafina ignored him.

'I must go home at once, ma'am,' she cried. 'I. . . I feel faint!'

'But, Serafina, I have no idea where Lord Denham may be. He arranged with me that we should meet in half an hour! It would be impossible to find him in this crush.'

'I must go!' The desperation in Serafina's voice convinced her godmother.

'Very well.' She turned to the footman. 'Kindly find some transport to Curzon Street for Miss Feverel and myself. Then you will find Lord Denham and inform him that my god-daughter has been taken ill and I have taken her home. Quickly, man!'

In a very short time Serafina and her godmother were back in Curzon Street.

'Now, tell me what is wrong, Serafina!'

'Ma'am, I beg you to understand. It is very important to me that I go down to Sussex immediately!'

'But why?'

'Lord Aldworth is in danger.'

'Whatever are you talking about, Serafina?'

'The Spanish ambassador—I heard them talking. And the other men! They intend to kill him!'

Lady Chilham looked at her in horror. 'You must really be very ill, my dear. It has turned your brain! Let me feel your forehead.'

'Please, Godmother, please let me go. I must go!'

'Bed is where you must go, my girl! I shall send for Dr Hobson tomorrow——'

'No! I am not raving! The Spanish ambassador was talking with Miguel Barros in the conservatory—he doesn't want Charles killed, but they are going to!'

'What farrago is this? As if His Excellency would contemplate anything of the sort. He is a most gentlemanly creature. And who is this Barros?'

'It's because of the South American rebels!'

'What South American rebels?'

'Have you not read about them? *The Times* has had several articles on them.'

Lady Chilham looked sadly at her god-daughter. 'You poor thing. I'm sorry you miss Aldworth so much, my dear, but you must not go chasing after him, you know. I always feared you were more attached to him than you admitted. But he is perfectly safe—he will be back shortly, and then you will be married quite soon. Now, try to forget all this rubbish about South America and rebels and killing. It isn't at all suitable for a young girl. I always said no good would come of all that reading. It has gone to your head.'

'Charles is in danger, I tell you!'

'Of course, of course,' said Lady Chilham soothingly. 'I'll get Denham to look into it.'

'No, you mustn't! They mentioned him too. It sounded as if he might be one of them! And Lady Paget.'

'Now that is too much! Really, Serafina, I will not tolerate any more of this nonsense. You will please me by going to bed immediately. I shall send one of the maids with a sleeping-powder, and Dr Hobson will see you tomorrow. Goodnight, child.'

'But Godmother——'

'Goodnight, Serafina!'

Serafina saw that it was hopeless, and abandoned her attempts to convince Lady Chilham. But she had not given up. As she meekly allowed herself to be undressed and put to bed her mind was racing. It was already half-past four. Her resources would not stretch to a private chaise—besides, where would she find one? But she knew that one of the new fast coaches left Gracechurch Street at six forty five a.m. and arrived in Brighton in the early afternoon. Both Gabriel and her father had used it. She could be at Blanchards not long after. Escaping from Curzon Street presented no problems to Sally—there was a tree just outside her bedroom window—but getting to Gracechurch Street would be more difficult... A hackney coach from Berkeley Square? It was risky at that hour of the morning, but it would have to be done. Somewhere in the closet was an old cloak she had discarded... When the maid brought the sleeping-powder Serafina was apparently already asleep. Betty

placed the glass on the table next to the bed and
tiptoed out.

Serafina waited a little while till the household was
quiet again. It would not be long before the lower
servants were getting up to start their day, but no one
would think of disturbing the mistress and her guest
till noon or later. She must write a note—perhaps she
should simply tell her godmother that she had gone
home to Feverel Place? Lady Chilham might understand that better. That done, she swiftly packed a small
bundle together, put on her simplest dress, gathered
up the cloak, and went to the window. . .

The streets were deserted, but there was one solitary
hackney coach in Berkeley Square—it had probably
delivered a customer home from some function or
other. She pulled up the hood of her cloak and ran
towards it. The driver took a little persuasion, but he
eventually agreed to take her to Gracechurch Street.

Waiting for the coach to leave was tedious, but
Serafina attached herself to an obvious countrywoman,
who had spent the night at the inn and was now having
a generous breakfast. When Mrs Bunniman heard that
Serafina was travelling to see a sick relative she
immediately took her under her capable wing. As a
result, some of the problems faced by a young girl
travelling alone were avoided, and the journey passed
in reasonable comfort, except for the length and detail
of Mrs Bunniman's stories.

In spite of the stories Serafina had time for consideration on the journey. Feverel Place lay on the direct
route between Brighton and Blanchards. She would
stop briefly at her home, both to get some assistance
and to change into Sally's clothes. The time would be

well-spent, for if Charles was alone at Blanchards he would be astonished and possibly angry at Serafina's sudden appearance, and if he was not alone—if, God help him, the Spaniard had already got there—then she would definitely need someone else with her. Michael would come, she was sure.

But after she had dismissed the chaise at Feverel Place her plans received a set-back. Her family was not there. Susan, the gardener's little daughter, came running round from the back to tell her that they were in Brighton! Mr Feverel had decided very recently that a stay in the resort would benefit Mrs Feverel, and had taken a house on the Steyne. The family had removed there the day before, together with most of the servants. Susan's father had been left in charge, but he had gone to East Bourne to look for some plants. There was no one there except herself to help Miss Feverel.

Refusing to let herself be daunted, Serafina hurried into the house, changed into her old skirt and jacket, snatched up some food from the larder and stuffed it into her pockets, then made for the stables. She was soon galloping over the hill to Blanchards. As she drew near she became more cautious. She left her horse in the field behind the house and walked discreetly round to the front.

A great deal of work had been done on the building since Serafina had last seen it. The roof had obviously been mended and the paintwork refurbished. But the shutters in the front of the house were all closed and the place looked deserted. Had Charles already left for France? Or was he not at Blanchards at all but somewhere else? She drew swiftly back into the shadows of a large beech tree as a figure came round the side of the house. But it was not Charles. Nor was it Sam Eckford. It was a stranger—a swarthy, stocky, unpleasant-looking stranger. He shouted something in Spanish and disappeared into the house. Serafina's heart was beating unevenly. This was what she had most feared. She was too late—Barros and his men were already at Blanchards! But where was Charles?

She slipped between the bushes and shrubs, making her way to the back of the house again. She had spent so much time in her youth exploring Blanchards and its grounds that she knew every path, every gate, every wall. It was not difficult for her to remain unobserved, even had anyone been looking. In the courtyard at the back stood a travelling coach—an old-fashioned, cumbersome affair—which looked exactly like the one her grandfather had used when he had come visiting. Many a time she had played in just such a coach, for it was full of little nooks and crannies, fascinating to children. There were horses in the stables, too—five or six. As she watched, a roughly dressed character, looking more like a gypsy than a nobleman's servant, came out of the stables leading one of the horses. It was saddled, and after a minute the first man she had seen came out of the house and mounted.

'I shall not be long, Aitken,' he shouted. He was speaking in English, but it was clearly not his native tongue. 'I have some business at the inn but it won't take long. See if Barros wants help inside.'

'I'm paid to look after the horses, not people,' was Aitken's surly reply.

'You won't be paid at all if you don't do as you're told. Get inside! They're upstairs.' The Spaniard rode off, and Aitken looked up at one of the windows which was slightly open, cursed at it, and went in.

There was no question in Serafina's mind that she should now go back to summon help, but the temptation to find out exactly what was happening first was too strong, her anxiety for Charles too great. Tucking her skirts up, she ran lightly across to the creeper which covered the wall at this point. It was an old friend—she and Michael had never been able to get into Blanchards, but that particular window had a most conveniently placed twist of branches immediately below it. She started to climb.

When she got to the point where she could see into the room she was hard put to it not to betray herself with a gasp of dismay. Charles was facing the window, his arms and legs tightly bound and a bandage over his eyes. He was speaking to someone out of sight— Miguel Barros, presumably. Serafina ducked and listened intently.

'Curse you, I've told you till I am tired! I don't know what you're talking about. How dare you keep me here like this? I demand that you release me!'

'You may go with our goodwill when you have given us the letter and the information you carry in your head. If you continue to deny their existence, Lord Aldworth, you will continue to be kept prisoner.' The voice was the same soft, lisping voice that she had heard in the conservatory at Carlton House. Charles started to protest, but Barros cut him short.

'Forgive me, but I am really quite tired of this! If you will not tell us, then you must allow me to tell you. We know that England plans to aid the enemies of Spain by providing arms for the rebels in South

America. No doubt your government would deny this as strenuously as you have been denying it. But we have known of the existence of such a plan for some time.'

There was a silence. Then Charles said calmly, 'You must be mad! Castlereagh would have to be unbelievably stupid to defy the wishes of the rest of the Allies in such a way. I cannot imagine he would countenance such a thing. But in any case, what has this to do with me? What the hell do you think you are doing here, treating me like this? Even if such a ridiculous plan did in fact exist, why should you think that I have anything to do with it?'

'Lady Paget has been most helpful——'

'Ah, now I see.' Charles's voice was full of amused scorn. 'You are a fool, sir. I am surprised that you have allowed yourself to be so duped.'

'Duped?'

'Perhaps you do not know the lady very well? Then I must tell you that she is an attractive woman with an overgrown sense of drama. She likes to be at the centre of attention, and I have recently been neglecting her. No doubt she thinks to revenge herself by this outrageous farce.'

'Farce? This is no farce, milord.'

'What else would you call the machinations of an unbalanced woman? I hope you haven't paid her, or promised her anything?'

'She will receive a share of the emeralds.'

'It gets better! What emeralds?'

'Stop pretending!' Barros's voice rose, but he took a breath and continued quietly, 'The plan was drawn up by you and Sir Robert Paget. You met a man called

Pedro de Garcia last January in Vienna—the inn was called the Zum Goldenen Topf. You made the arrangements then, and since that time you have been waiting for him to return with payment, in the form of emeralds from New Granada, for the arms your perfidious government has agreed to release. You, Lord Aldworth, are now on your way to France in order to meet him. The shipment of arms is due off Newhaven within the next forty-eight hours. Do you need more?'

Charles was still calm, but a note of tension had crept into his voice. 'How very detailed! Where did you hear this. . .farrago?'

'Initially from Lady Paget.'

'Not Sir Robert?'

'Aha! So you have been suspecting your old friend? Is that why you have so assiduously courted his wife?'

'I courted Sir Robert's wife because, before she grew tiresome, she was a damned attractive woman—and—er—very willing. Barros, think carefully about what you are doing. For no reason at all, as far as I can see, you have chosen to believe the unsupported word of a jealous woman. You are in grave danger of making a fool of yourself, to say nothing of causing a very unpleasant diplomatic incident. His Excellency, who is a man of honour, will not thank you for this. Now release me before the affair gets out of hand.'

'You are a brave man, milord, but a foolish one. You will not persuade me that it is nonsense—we have had the story checked and rechecked. Lady Paget may be a discontented woman tied to an elderly husband, and she is certainly a greedy one, but she is no fool. And I believe her to be very fond of you still. She was most concerned that you should come to no harm.

Now, before we are forced to disappoint her and try
...less agreeable methods of persuasion on you, will
you admit to the truth of the story? Then, if you will
tell us where you have hidden the letter of authorisation and give us the rest of the necessary information,
we shall let you go free—subject to certain conditions.'

'I would certainly not agree to any conditions whatsoever with vermin such as you.' The bored contempt
in his prisoner's voice roused Barros to anger. There
was the sound of a sharp slap. 'You do see what I
mean?' The contempt and boredom were still there.
'My hands and feet are tied, and I am blindfolded. A
worthy target for vermin, wouldn't you agree?' said
Charles.

Barros said unpleasantly, 'You are right, of course.
My employers may be gentlemen, but I am not. I work
for Spain, but I am also as greedy as Lady Paget. I too
have been promised a share of the emeralds, and to
succeed I would do almost anything. Do not deceive
yourself, milord. If you continue to refuse to tell me
then I shall kill you. Or wait! Perhaps I have a better
idea! Would you like me to have Miss Feverel brought
from London to join you here? I could have her
delivered by tomorrow evening—in plenty of time to
take her to France with us. It could be an enjoyable
experience—she is very lovely.'

'You would not dare!'

'But I would. It would not even be difficult. Miss
Feverel would be an easy target—she is beautiful, but
not very clever, I think. Shall I ask the men to bring
her?'

The silence was longer this time. Then Charles
finally spoke. 'There is no letter, whatever Lady Paget

might have told you. And there is no password. I alone
am the key. Garcia will reveal himself only to me, and
only I can make him known to the captain of the ship.
In return Garcia will hand over the emeralds. To me.
No one else will do. So if you kill me you will have
nothing. Why don't you give up? You cannot succeed.
I might be able to arrange for you to have your share
of the jewels if you do as I suggest.'

'You forget, milord. I may covet the jewels, but I am
also a patriot. Let me think.' There was yet another
silence, after which Barros said, 'I am inclined to
believe that there isn't a letter. We have searched you,
your baggage and the coach extremely thoroughly. For
the rest—you might be telling the truth, though I doubt
it. But it appears that we have to take you with us if
we wish to see either the jewels or the arms.'

'You will never succeed in taking over the ship!'

'I do not intend to. We shall take you to France
ourselves. The arms are less important to us than
Bolivar's agent. And the emeralds. So—you will come
to France, Lord Aldworth. But if, as I suspect, you are
thinking of playing any tricks, you will be the first to
die, I assure you.'

There was a knock. Footsteps could be heard moving
away towards the door and Serafina risked a look
through the window. She saw that Barros had gone out
to talk to someone on the other side, leaving the door
almost closed. Charles was trying vainly to loosen his
bonds. She ducked down again quickly as the door
started to open and Barros came back.

'Felipe has returned. Our vessel is ready and waiting, and by the time we reach the port the tide will be
high. We shall go immediately. What is this? Surely

you haven't been trying to release yourself, Lord Aldworth? A foolish and useless endeavour! But just as a precaution... Aitken! Aitken! Fetch my bag from the next room, if you please.' A moment or two passed, then Aitken returned. There was the sound of a struggle and a chair turned over. 'Hold him down!' Barros said curtly. Serafina was filled with horror. What were they doing to Charles? A faint, sweetish smell came drifting out, and when she stole a quick glance into the room she saw that Charles was lying quite still on the floor.

'That should keep him quiet for a while. Long enough to get him to Newhaven. But we'll leave him tied up, just in case...'

CHAPTER NINE

SERAFINA decided that she could do no good where she was. She must race home and send to Newhaven to alert the coastguards. She was sure that a man on a good horse could overtake that heavy coach. Cautiously she climbed down and looked around. It was still quite light, and she had no idea where Aitken was—she would have to risk it. She had not got very far when Aitken appeared at the back door, but fortunately she was hidden from him by the carriage. She froze. Then to her horror a horse and rider came into the courtyard, and started to make for the stables. Serafina was in a panic. If she was discovered now there would be no possibility of help for Charles or anyone else—herself included! But just when discovery seemed inevitable there was a call from the house and the rider dismounted and went over to the door, where he stood discussing something with Aitken. Now was her opportunity to hide—but where? She looked round and noticed that the door of the travelling coach was slightly, but invitingly open. Without a second thought she slipped inside and crouched down on the floor. She was just in time. The men walked past within inches of where she had been standing seconds before, and went into the stable.

Serafina forced herself to think calmly. There was no chance of escape from the coach while Aitken and the other man were anywhere in the yard. She was effectively trapped inside. Even now one of them was passing again on his way into the house. But what would happen if she could not escape before they all drove to Newhaven? Her blood ran cold at the thought of discovery—she must find some sort of hiding place, she must! Her grandfather's coach which, as far as she could see, had been exactly like this one, had been intended for long journeys during which the traveller might wish to sleep in his own coach. The seats had been like these—broad and deep. And underneath there had been... Ah! Yes—there it was! A leather flap under the seat which pulled down and held more valuable luggage in behind it. It had been perfect for hide-and-seek in the past, but would she fit in there now? She wriggled and squirmed and discovered that she could—just. She pulled the flap down in front of her and lay there trying to regain her breath. It would not do if they heard her, and someone was approaching! Two men, carrying a heavy burden, got into the coach. There was a thump as they dumped something on to the seat opposite, then they sat down themselves over her head. The coach set off...

Afterwards Serafina remembered the hour that followed as one of the worst, most excruciatingly uncomfortable experiences of her life. If the road to Newhaven had been any longer she would have betrayed herself by being sick! She dared not relax, for a pothole or even a steep slope might have sent her rolling forward into view. She clung to the strut at one side and held her foot against the other as the coach swayed and jolted along, and wondered why Charles had chosen to travel in such an antique when he had a perfectly comfortable chaise. Unless... If the coach really was the twin of her grandfather's then it had a small cache in which to hide jewellery and money from the greed of highwaymen. Was there, in fact, a letter, though Charles had denied it? Was he playing some deep game of his own? And had he hidden it where no one who did not know the secret could possibly discover it? Perhaps. There was no way of finding out at the moment.

At last the nightmare came to an end. The coach came to a halt and Serafina could smell the sea and hear the sound of the waves crashing on to the shore. They must be at Newhaven. She tensed as the men got out, but they were apparently engrossed in extracting their unconscious prisoner and carrying him away. She must be patient. It would be some time before the ship could set sail, and the coach could not be under observation all the time. She would wait inside a little longer—they would come back for the luggage. Daylight was fading but there was still a little light inside the coach. While she was waiting this might be the time to test her theory. She lifted the flap cautiously and peered under the forward seat. On one side was a small piece of wood—a flaw in the panelling, one would have said. So far, so good. Gently she eased it out with her fingernail. Under it was a tiny knob, which she pressed, quickly putting her hand over the piece of panelling before it made a noise as it fell out. She had been right! Behind it was a small recess in which lay a letter and a bag full of money.

The bag was heavy, and when she peered inside she could see a large number of gold and silver French coins. Charles must have had it ready for his journey. Thanking heaven that she was wearing her old jacket,

Serafina put the bag and the letter into one of her pockets and then, hearing the sound of returning footsteps, she slipped back into her hiding place.

'Take the luggage on board as quickly as you can, Aitken. We're sailing in a quarter of an hour! Hurry! The longer we stay here, the more dangerous it gets, and the tide is perfect. You take the coach back to the house. Make sure you put it in the coach-house, and see to the horses. We don't want any questions. You have your story ready?'

'Course I do!' muttered Aitken. 'Where's my money?'

'You'll get it when the luggage is on board, not before. Get on with it! I'll just make sure that his lordship is…comfortable in his quarters. He should wake up soon.'

Grumbling and cursing, Aitken untied the boxes and started carting them towards the ship. Now was her moment! Serafina slid cautiously forward, then lifted herself up to see out. Aitken was bent double under a large box, making his way slowly to a fishing boat moored alongside. By screwing up her eyes she could make out its name—*Maria Cristina*. Barros was just going on board. At some point or other Serafina must have made up her mind, for now, without any hesitation, she got out of the coach on the landward side, almost falling as the money bag pulled her over to one side and her stiffened limbs refused to take the weight. She paused for an agonising moment or two, then sidled round and, taking a deep breath, darted to the shelter of a pile of boxes near the edge of the quay. Here she crouched until she saw her opportunity. Aitken was back at the coach, Barros had gone below, and the crew was occupied forward. She slipped like a shadow onto the ship, and made for the stern, where she had seen huge piles of fishing nets. Hoping to heaven that the captain and crew were too concerned with their human cargo to do any fishing, she burrowed her way between the nets, made herself comfortable as best she could, and lay down. Whatever happened now she could do no more. Soon the orders to the sailors increased, there was much scurrying to and fro, and the *Maria Cristina* started to move. The strain of the past twenty-four hours took its toll, and Serafina. . .fell asleep.

Shouts and cries, the mewing of seagulls, the noise of wheels on cobblestones—Serafina gradually became aware of all of these. She had been cold in the night, but now she was warm—almost too warm. A vast expanse of blue sky met her eyes as she slowly opened them. She lay there for a moment as memory returned—memory and the scent of danger. There was also a strong smell of fish all round her. Cautiously she lifted her head, thankful that she was still wearing her beloved woolly cap. She had found it in her pocket when she had woken briefly in the middle of the night, and had put it on. The *Maria Cristina* was just edging alongside a stone wall. Serafina ducked down again as a sailor came past, whistling. He leapt up on to the wall and busied himself pulling the boat by means of thick ropes which he wound round capstans on the quay. He was watching the animated scene on the quayside as he did so—much to Serafina's relief, for he would certainly have seen her otherwise. He finished

what he was doing and stepped away out of her sight.
There was the sound of a woman's voice and laughter.

'Manuel! Come down here and finish your work!'
shouted a voice of authority in Spanish. Manuel
reappeared, swaggering along the quay towards the
other end. Serafina breathed again. But she must get
off the boat as soon as possible. Over there were a
couple of rungs up the side of the wall, but how could
she get up them without being seen? Perhaps Manuel
would be as interested in the ladies at the other end?
She peered over the nets. Yes, his back was towards
her and he was flanked by two buxom fisherwomen.
He had an arm round each, and was clearly flirting
with them. Several other members of the crew came to
join him, laughing raucously, and there was soon a
crowd on the quay at the far end of the boat. A man
who was clearly in charge came hurrying down towards
them all, waving his arms and shouting. Now, if ever,
was her chance. She ran to the side, scrambled up the
rungs, and was on dry land in a trice. Quickly she
merged with the moving throng on the quayside.

Wherever she was, she was in France, and it was
quite clearly market day. Stalls of fish, fruit and veg-
etables, cheeses of all kinds, household goods and a
few clothes lined the streets. Women in voluminous
skirts, sabots, and heavily starched white bonnets
walked along them, sampling this, feeling that, bargain-
ing with the shopkeepers. Booths selling wine and cider
were ranged along the front by the boats, their cus-
tomers sitting on barrels and bollards, quaffing from
huge tankards. It was a noisy, lively, colourful scene.

Serafina eyed the stalls and felt faint with hunger.
She had woken in the night and consumed the pathetic

remnants of the food she had stuffed into her pockets at home. It had been something, but not nearly enough, and now the smell of freshly baked bread was reminding her of how little she had eaten for two days. Her fingers curled round the bag of money that she had found in the coach and, without taking it out of her pocket, she extracted several coins. They were silver francs. Even one was too much for bread—she must buy something else first. A change of clothing wouldn't be a bad idea, for her clothes reeked of fish. As she watched the girls walking so gracefully in their swinging skirts and aprons, pretty caps or stiff white bonnets on their heads, baskets on their arms, the glimmering of an idea came to her.

She wandered away from the main shopping area and sought out a quieter street in which were a number of shops with various items of clothing for sale. She spent a little time examining the wares laid out in front, becoming conscious of the stares and significant sniffs as she walked along. She smiled ruefully at a pleasant-looking woman who was standing at the door of one of the smaller places.

'I've had an accident, *madame*,' she said, affecting a strong Spanish accent—the women would know that a Spanish vessel was in port. 'On my brother's boat. I think my clothes are ruined—all of them, including the ones in my bags. He's given me some money to dress myself, but I don't know if it will be enough.' She held out a few of the francs.

'My poor little cabbage! I'll find something for you. Come in. I think you will need a wash, too, *hein*?' The shopkeeper went along the shelves and selected some garments. Then she beckoned to Serafina and showed her into a tiny room at the back. She fetched a bowl of water and a cloth, and left the new clothes on the chair by the door. 'Call me if you want anything else,' she said. 'And there's a privy outside where you can throw the water when you've finished.'

It wasn't long before Serafina was once again sweet-smelling, and dressed in a full skirt, a white blouse and a large apron. She hid the precious letter in her bodice and, after taking out a few more coins and putting them in her pocket, she tied the bag of money on a piece of cord round her waist and hid it under her skirt.

'Ooh, la—la!' said the woman when she reappeared. 'Why can't I look as pretty as that in the clothes I make? But you'll need stockings and sabots. And perhaps a cap? Would your brother pay for a cap, chérie? I've a very pretty one here, quite cheap.' When Serafina finally left the shop a prettier serving maid would have been difficult to find. With regret she abandoned her own outer clothes in the dustbin by the privy. They were quite ruined. Smiling her thanks, she paid the woman, and set off to look for food. A roll and some cheese washed down with a cup of fresh milk made her feel better straight away. Then she went in search of other necessities, the first of which was a large basket, rolls and cheese to fill it, and a starched napkin to cover it.

Then she went back to the quayside. Here she bargained for a wicked-looking knife which was used for cutting fish, and put it under the rolls. She was almost ready. Out of the corner of her eye she saw that Miguel Barros and the other Spaniard—Felipe?—were striding purposefully to the hostelry at the end of the quay. It was a post-house—it looked as if they were going to hire some horses. After a few minutes they rode out of the yard and down the main street with the air of people who were going some distance.

Serafina took a deep breath and walked swiftly up to the inn.

'And what might a pretty little ladybird like you want?'

The innkeeper was smiling, but definitely curious.

'I... I was looking for Señor Barros. He asked me to meet him here,' she said.

'The Spanish gentleman? He's gone off to Bourg-Dun. He won't be back for a few hours. Was there something...special you wanted?' The look in his eye suggested that he might be willing to provide it.

'No, no,' she said hastily. 'I'll wait for him on the boat. But I'll take something to drink for the others.'

She bought a bottle of wine, which she put in her basket, and a jug of cider, and started off down the quay.

She had to run the gauntlet of cries and cheers from the fishermen drinking at the booths, but managed quite well until one, slightly drunker than the rest, actually tried to stop her by putting his arm round her. Serafina, hampered as she was by her basket and the jug, was helpless, but the burly owner of the booth pushed the man aside. 'Let her be, Jules! Can't you see she's on her way to someone else? Now, sit down and stop making a fool of yourself.'

The fisherman subsided and Serafina thanked the stallholder and went on to the *Maria Cristina*.

'*Bonjour*!' she called. She wasn't sure what dialect was used in this part of France, but she was equally certain that the Spaniard wouldn't know either. Nor would he notice any accent.

'*Señorita*!' He nodded and smiled, but stepped forward and barred her way as she came down the plank.

'I have food for the prisoner—a Monsieur Barros ordered it from the inn over there, before he set off to Bourg-Dun.' She turned and pointed to the posting inn. The burly stallholder was still staring at them. 'Don't worry about him,' she said. 'That's just my father. He likes to keep an eye on me. Well? Are you going to let me pass?'

'Señor Barros said we weren't to let anyone on board...'

'That's strange. His instructions to me were very clear, and he paid for all of this! The wine and food for the prisoner, and the cider for you... Oh, well, I'll take it away again. I hope he won't want his money back, though.'

'Wait! He must have meant strangers, not serving girls—at least, not pretty ones like you.'

Serafina dimpled. 'I hope there aren't too many of you left on board—it's not a very generous amount of cider... Pedro?'

'The others have gone off into the town. And my name's Juan. But I prefer wine, anyway,' he said, eyeing the bottle.

'The cider is better than the wine, I assure you, Juan. Monsieur Barros said that the wine was for the criminal, and that's about all it's fit for! Is he...is he very dangerous?'

'He's well-watched. There are two of us here and we both have weapons. He won't get loose.'

Serafina gave a realistic shudder. 'Just two? You are

both so brave! I shall leave the cider with you, yes?'
And take the prisoner's breakfast in.' She smiled
entrancingly again and offered him the jug. He put his
weapon down and took it, standing aside as he did so.
'Leave some for your friend!' she said with a roguish
look as she went round to the cabin.

In the gangway outside the cabin was another sailor.
He was armed with a large pistol, and an even larger
knife was in his waistband.

'*Oh, mon Dieu!*' cried Serafina. 'What a terrible
sight! A pistol and a knife! But I suppose with only
two of you to guard the whole boat you need such
dreadful weapons. *Ooh, la-la!*' She eyed the cabin
door. . .

Inside the cabin, Lord Aldworth was experiencing
difficulty in not giving in to something close to despair.
For the hundredth time since being surprised at
Blanchards by Barros he cursed the careless tongues at
the Foreign Office. Louisa Paget he had known to be
an informer, and had used her, carefully feeding her
false information about the time and place of his
rendezvous in France. That had been useful this morning when he had sent Barros and the other man off on
a wild-goose chase to Bourg-Dun. But someone must
have gossiped about Blanchards. He hadn't told her of
that, and he hadn't thought it necessary to be on his
guard there, either.

What was going to happen when Barros returned?
His chances of survival, never very great from the
moment Barros had overwhelmed him, were now
extremely slim—non-existent, in fact. He had lied to
Barros about the letter and the arrangements for the

exchange in order to gain time, but once the Spaniard realised that he was not going to give them any information of value his end was inevitable, and probably painful. Barros had been too cunning and too cautious. They had trussed him up so carefully that it was impossible to escape, as he had hoped. His limbs were aching, tied as they were with hands together and legs bound by the ankles to the bed. And this wretched blindfold prevented him from judging distance or anything else! They had released him for a short while last night and this morning—but two of them had waited in the cabin with their pistols ready. He had been able to do nothing. Then he straightened his shoulders. He must not give in! While there was life there was always hope—a little. He could hear voices now, and someone was coming towards the cabin. . .

'*Oh, mon Dieu*! What a terrible sight! A pistol and a knife! But I suppose with only two of you to guard the whole boat you need such dreadful weapons. *Ooh, la-la!*'

He must be mad or dreaming! That voice! He dismissed the thought for the fantasy it was. Sally Feverel could not possibly be anywhere near. It was an illusion—a similarity of timbre and quality, though it was speaking French. He strained his ears all the same as the door opened.

'Do not leave me alone with this villain, I beg you! Oh, how I wish Monsieur Barros had gone somewhere else to buy his food!'

The French, though nearly perfect, had a slight accent.

'You'll be perfectly safe, *señorita*. I shall stand by

the door with my pistol ready. Just make sure you do not get between it and the prisoner.'

'You mean I am to feed him! To approach him? Never!'

'He can feed himself.'

'How? He cannot see, and he has no hands.'

'I suppose you'd better take the blindfold off his eyes,' said the guard reluctantly.

'What about the rope round his wrists? I'm not going near him when his hands are free!'

'Don't be afraid, *señorita*. Just remember what I said about not shielding him.'

A pair of hands held Charles and gave him a warning squeeze. The knots were undone and the kerchief removed. He turned his head and met Sally's eyes. He tried to speak, but Sally forestalled him. 'He doesn't look such a desperado, does he? In fact I feel a bit sorry for him. I shall give him some wine first.' She poured some wine into the glass on the table and held it out to him. He raised his bound hands mutely.

Sally knelt down in front of him, and the guard said immediately, 'Move, *señorita*! I would not wish to shoot you.'

Sally gave a scream and jumped up. She said angrily, 'Then you must free his hands yourself. I cannot undo knots from the side, me. It is impossible!'

Charles could see that the guard was perplexed. To get too near the prisoner would be dangerous, especially if his hands were released. At last he said slowly, 'Take my knife and cut them. I will stay here.'

'He will not hurt me?'

'I give you my word, *mademoiselle*,' said Charles in perfect French.

'*Oh, mon Dieu*, the villain speaks French!' she exclaimed. She looked uncertainly at him and then turned to the guard, who nodded and levelled his pistol purposefully. Serafina took the knife, moved gingerly to Charles's side and cut the rope round his hands. She jumped quickly away and put the knife on the table. Then she picked up her basket and, having rearranged the food a little, she put it on the bed beside him.

'Bread and cheese, *monsieur*.'

Charles looked down. The handle of a knife could be seen under the napkin. Sally moved away and went over to the guard.

'There! That's a relief. I was afraid he would grab me. But then you were here, were you not? You would have saved me. . . Pedro?' She looked up at the unfortunate man with melting blue eyes.

He gazed down bemused, and murmured, 'My name is Luis.'

Sally dropped her voice a little and said, 'Your friend on deck—Juan—said you would be free this evening perhaps. If you are not already engaged would you have time for a little French girl and her sister? We sometimes like a change from the French boys. . .'

'Your sister? Is she as pretty as you?'

'Much prettier. With black hair and. . .and. . .' Sally's hands were much more expressive than anything she could have said. 'Would you like to see her? She's on the quay. Come—you can see her from this porthole.'

The guard cast an uneasy glance in Charles's direction, but saw that he was munching stolidly.

'Come! He won't trouble you. What do you expect him to do, tied to the bedpost as he is? Leap on you from behind? I hope you're not going to disappoint

Arlette and me. She likes her men brave and strong—as well as handsome.'

The guard allowed himself to be led over to the porthole. 'Now, that's my father—you see that burly fellow up there? But he is going out himself tonight. And next to him is Arlette. . . Oh, she isn't there! Wait, I think she's just behind him. Can you see her? Black hair and a white blouse cut low in the front. Maman says she has no shame, that one! You'll have to crane your neck. . .'

The guard was clearly enjoying the sensation of holding Sally while they both attempted to peer out at the same time. He was a pathetically easy target. Charles jerked him back then hit him hard. He went down without a murmur.

'Quick, the rope and the kerchief!' But Sally already had them ready. Luis was soon on the bed, trussed up and gagged.

'This isn't the moment to ask how or why you're here—there isn't time. But thank God you are,' he said.

'Now for number two,' she said, grinning up at him. 'Don't forget Luis's pistol. I have his knife.' She picked up the basket again and tripped out. 'Thank you, thank you, *monsieur*!' she trilled. 'I'll see what your friend Juan says.'

When Serafina went on deck she found that Juan had been finding the cider quite to his taste. The jug was empty, and Juan had a slightly foolish grin on his face.

'Ah, *señorita*. . .'

'Oh, Juan,' cried Serafina reproachfully. 'You've finished it all! Never mind, you shall have some more tonight. Luis says you will both be free. He'd like to spend the evening with me and my sister. Will you come too?'

'Wha' time?'

'*Zut*! I forgot to ask! I'll wait here while you go and ask him.'

'Gorra stay here. On duty.'

'Oh, but you can just pop down for a second, can't you? I dare not. Papa is still looking this way—he'll start to wonder if I go below again. He's very strict——' she lowered her voice '—but he'll be out tonight.'

Juan cast an eye at the burly stallholder. 'All ri'.'

He stumbled round the corner. There was a thump, and the sound of something falling. Serafina went back and helped to gag Juan and tie him up before he was taken to join his friend. Charles shrugged on his coat, which was looking decidedly the worse for wear, then he locked the door and they walked unhurriedly off the boat, dropping the cabin key over the side as they went. Once in the crowd, however, they left the quayside as quickly as possible.

'We'll carry on talking French, if you don't mind. You're good enough to fool most people, and I don't want to draw attention to us.'

'In that case you'd better get some other clothes! You're a touch conspicuous in those!'

Charles laughed as he looked down. 'I must remind you of the occasion in the greenhouse at Blanchards! Decidedly dirty.'

'But still handsome,' said Serafina involuntarily. 'I remember thinking how handsome you were.'

He stopped and looked down at her. 'Really?' he murmured with a glint in his eye.

'Yes, but don't let it go to your head. It needs to be clear at the moment. And I've. . . I'm——' She stopped and swallowed. Reaction was setting in and she was feeling distinctly strange.

'Sally! Don't give way now! You've been such a heroine. Wait! We'll sit here in the shade for a moment.'

They sat in silence for a little while, then Serafina said, 'I feel better now. I'm sorry, Charles. What a poor thing I am! I don't even know what happened. When we got off the boat I was feeling very cheerful, and then suddenly I wanted to sit down and howl my eyes out.'

Charles looked at her, his eyes warm and sympathetic. 'I've had the same sort of thing happen to me in the past, Sally. It's nothing to be ashamed of. You were quite superb on that boat. If I hadn't known who you were I'd have sworn you were a minx who had never left her father's tavern in Dieppe. And. . . I owe you my life.'

'Rubbish! You'd have got out somehow.'

'We'll never know. But we're not out of the wood yet. We need money and transport. I have some English money, but it won't be nearly enough. The rest was left in England, and at the moment I don't know where or how to get any more.'

'Will this do?' Serafina turned away from him, lifted up her skirt and removed the bag of money.

'Where the devil did you get that?' He examined it. 'It's mine!' Charles gave her a penetrating look. 'Just what have you been up to, Sally? Are you a witch?'

'I'll explain, but it will take quite a time. Shouldn't we be moving on?'

'You're right. Well, this solves the problem of our finances—there's enough here and more. We can buy all we need. As you say, I really need some other clothing. A smock? And a beret? And then when I have those I could perhaps purchase a horse and cart.'

'We need something faster than that! A chaise or a curricle, surely?'

'I can afford to buy a horse and cart. I'd have to hire a chaise. If you were Barros what would you do when you found I had escaped?'

'I'd go after you—oh, I see. I'd enquire at all the post-inns, of course!'

'And when you found someone who answered to my description, you and some of your band would ride after him. Quite. I don't want to face Barros until I am better equipped to.'

'But how far is it to——? Where are you going, Charles?'

'Paris.'

'Paris! But that must be a hundred miles! Why?'

'It's the place Garcia and I arranged to meet if either of us didn't turn up at the rendezvous. He'll be there waiting for me. But the most urgent problem at the moment is getting away from Barros. Sally, we have a lot to discuss, including what I'm going to do with you. And I'd like to know by what miracle you came to be here, too. But there isn't time. We have to get out of Dieppe before Barros returns.'

'It's better if I go and buy clothes. I can say they're for my father. Stay here!'

CHAPTER TEN

HALF an hour later Charles and Serafina were driving at a slow but steady pace along the road to Paris. Their cart was shabby but in good repair and, besides a small load of hay, it carried some provisions and a few extra clothes. Charles, smoking a long pipe and wearing a dun-coloured smock and a shapeless hat, no longer looked quite so distinguished. In fact, thought Serafina with a certain degree of satisfaction, he was the picture of a respectable, though not very rich farmer, returning home from market. She herself now sported a stiffly starched white cap and a flat straw hat with a wide brim which shaded her face. A bright blue fichu covered her shoulders. She looked the epitome of a respectable farmer's wife.

After all the activity of the morning Serafina was content to sit in something of a daze for the first part of the journey, watching the Norman countryside roll by and letting its peaceful beauty restore her. Charles was quiet too, apparently sensing her need for peace, and perhaps himself needing time to recover from his experiences. His night must have been, if anything, even more uncomfortable than hers. As time went on, however, she began to think again—Barros would surely soon return to Dieppe from Bourg-Dun. What would he do? How long would it be before he decided to search the road to Paris? She became uneasy. It was a relief to hear Charles say comfortingly, 'You can stop looking behind us, Sally. It will be an hour or so yet before Barros could catch up with us, and I'm leaving the high road before that. In fact. . .here's the turning.'

'Why are we leaving the Paris road?'

'We aren't. Trust me—I know the country between Dieppe and Paris like the back of my hand. I ought to. This is a very pleasant alternative road along the other side of the forest, and it's cooler here, too. We can relax a little.' They travelled on in silence for a short while until the high road was well behind them. Then, 'I think explanation time has come, don't you?' said Charles.

'Tell me first what this is all about. I thought you were a diplomat.'

'I am. But sometimes I. . .do other things. Not often now—I did more during the war. As you know, my grandmother is French, and I speak the language fluently. So do you, I notice. Tell me where you learned it.'

'My father invited the widow of a French emigré to live with us until she was able to go back to France in 1816. She spent a year with us, and we all spoke to her in her own language. I still correspond with her.'

'Could you go to her now? It might be a solution to one of our problems,' asked Charles sharply.

'I'm afraid not. She lives in the Auvergne.'

'I see.' He thought for a moment. 'Well, it seems as if I shall have to take you to Paris with me. I can't leave you on your own in the wilds of Normandy, and you'll be safer with me than with anyone else. Safer from Barros, anyway.' He smiled at her with a glint in his eye.

She said hastily, 'You were going to tell me about your work.'

He nodded. 'I think you deserve to be told. But it's not for general consumption, Sally.'

'Oh! You disappoint me. I was about to stop the next peasant we see to discuss it with him!'

He smiled at her remark but then grew sober again. 'I meant even after we get back to England. At present what I am doing for the government is highly unofficial, and, if questioned, my superiors would deny all knowledge of my activities. They concern a man called Bolivar. Do you know who he is?'

'The Venezuelan who is leading a rebellion against Spain in South America? Yes, of course.'

He looked at her with a smile in his eyes. 'Of course,' he murmured. 'Most of the people in England have never heard the name, but Sally Feverel knows him.'

'With a father like mine it would be difficult not to. Carry on.'

'Bolivar has access to some of the most valuable emerald mines in the world in New Granada. He has the wherewithal to purchase arms to carry on his struggle—more than enough. But except for a few hundred rifles from the United States he can't find anywhere else to buy them. The major countries of Europe wouldn't dream of supplying him, because he's rebelling against one of their allies.'

'And we are? Supplying them, I mean?'

'That's where I come in. We aren't—officially. But when Richard Rush, the American ambassador, approached us a little while ago we. . .listened, shall I say? A colleague of mine—Robert Paget—'

'Ah, yes,' murmured Serafina. 'Lady Paget's husband.'

'Yes,' he said curtly. 'Yes, well, Robert arranged a meeting in Vienna between Bolivar's agent and ourselves. The terms were agreed and now the arms are ready and my job is to carry out the exchange—emeralds for arms. Barros's task is to stop it.'

'What will happen now? The ship carrying the arms was due in Newhaven soon, wasn't it? Where will it go now?'

'Are there no secrets left? Where did you learn that?'

'I'll tell you later. What happens to it when you aren't there to board it?'

'It will go back to Portsmouth and wait for further orders.'

'I see. So Sir Robert Paget was...is a colleague in all this? Er... Where does Lady Paget come in? I thought... We thought you were...'

Charles looked down at Serafina broodingly. 'For a short while I was—if you are asking whether I was in love with her. She was never my mistress. But then I discovered that she was dishonest—a cheat and a liar. It killed any feeling I had for her. Since Christmas I have been using her to deceive Barros.'

'Your feelings about deception seem to be somewhat illogical, Charles. Surely you have indulged in a little double-dealing yourself in the past? In Vienna, for example?'

'I take it you're referring to my affairs again. I told you once before, Sally—they are not important. Fidelity in marriage doesn't seem to count for very much in Vienna. I respected very few of the people I knew there. I liked them—they were witty, informed, polished—but there were very few whose integrity I trusted. Sir Robert was one, which is why I...never quite lost my head over Louisa Paget. I don't deceive people I respect, Sally. I would not, for example, lie to you.'

A cold finger touched Serafina's heart. She said slowly, 'And integrity is important to you... Would you be as unsympathetic as you sound if I lied to you, Charles? Or if Serafina lied to you?'

'I can't imagine either of you doing so, especially not Serafina. But yes, I would. How could you respect or trust anyone who lied to you? Why? Are you about to lie to me?'

'No, I am not about to lie to you. Sally Feverel is always herself with you, Charles.'

'Well, then, tell me how you came to turn up on Barros's fishing boat in time to rescue me.'

Serafina's mind was made up. She had considered making her confession here on the road to Paris, for Charles was grateful to her, and the time had seemed more propitious than any other. But what he had just said made it impossible. How could they continue in each other's company all the weary way to Paris after a revelation such as hers? It would be impossible. No, she would keep her confession for a better occasion. There would be one. She said slowly, 'I heard you were at Blanchards. I... I wanted to apologise to you because I hadn't been very polite the last time we had seen each other. But then I saw the strangers, and I became suspicious...'

From there on it was easy. She told Charles everything that had happened between her arrival at

Blanchards and their meeting on the boat, finishing by saying, 'I've given you the money. This was in the cache as well.' She handed him the letter.

Charles looked at it and grasped her in his arms. 'You wonderful girl! You can't imagine how much trouble this is going to save me when we get to Paris. I. . . I'm overwhelmed, Sally.' He kissed her. Then he kissed her again. And again, and that kiss continued until a whinny from the horse as he felt the reins drop caused them to draw back from one another.

Serafina's nerves were again stretched to their limit. Not only had she just come through a harrowing forty-eight hours, she was now being subjected to the greatest temptation in her life. This man, she knew in her soul, was probably the only man she would ever love, and as soon as he knew the truth about her there was a strong possibility that he would never wish to see her again. The temptation to seduce him during their journey to Paris, to bind him to her with chains he could not in all decency break, was almost over-whelming. But some inner sense of honour held her back. She was committed to the original deception, but she would not make it impossible for him to cry off from their engagement.

She was trembling, but she pushed him firmly away as she said, 'Charles, you must not. I know you mean nothing by it, but it isn't fair—either to me or to Serafina. And we have a long road to Paris.'

He took the reins again, but didn't move the cart on. Looking at her with a puzzled frown, he said slowly, 'Each time I kiss you, Sally. . .it means a little more.'

'It mustn't!'

'No, I know. I'm sorry. Oh, devil take it, Sally, I'm

always saying that to you. I don't know what it is about you. . . Look, I swear I mean you no harm, and I intend to keep my word to Serafina. I know I mustn't make love to you, or even kiss you. But somehow, when you're there. . . I kissed you just now without even considering whether I should or not—I was so delighted to see that letter. Then one kiss didn't seem enough. . . Oh, God damn it, I know I mustn't seduce you! That would mean breaking my promise to Serafina and marrying you instead. . .' He looked at her for a moment. 'No, it would be an impossible situation. And a marriage between us wouldn't work either!'

'I think you're right, Charles. It would be an impossible situation. But. . .why do you say that a marriage between us wouldn't work?'

He said carefully, 'If you married me, we should have two choices. Either you would take Serafina's place in my life and stay most of the time alone at Aldworth with our children while I travelled abroad. I cannot imagine that you would tolerate that, nor would I wish to subject you to it.'

'Or?'

'You would travel with me. And you would soon find that my life as a diplomat would suit you no better. It's never normally as adventurous as this. It usually consists of what you would hate most—what you would call stuffy people at stuffy dinners, exchanging gossip. London, Paris, Vienna, Berlin—they're all the same. Protocol, precedence, formality and gossip—you wouldn't be happy. I should imagine you would find it very difficult, if not impossible, to conform. And. . .my work is important to me, Sally.'

'No,' she agreed quietly. 'I shouldn't be happy.' She heaved a sigh, then grinned at him bravely. 'Well, now that we have cleared the air, let's be friends on this adventure. I shall regard you as I do Gabriel, and you shall overcome this strange desire you have to kiss me. Done?'

Charles looked a little grim, but he said with resolute cheerfulness, 'Done!'

And so it was for the rest of that day, and for the two days that followed. They ambled steadily through the French countryside, stopping at remote inns, buying provisions as they needed them, and never once catching a glimpse of Barros and his men. Charles's manner, which was at first somewhat restrained, slowly relaxed, and the time passed pleasantly in animated conversation or companionable silence. Their minds were in perfect harmony and, if anything, the secret, silken threads which bound them grew stronger by the hour. But Charles treated 'Sally' as she had asked—as Gabriel or Michael would have treated her.

On the third day they had to make a considerable detour to ford one of the numerous small streams which flowed into the river Epte. They had intended to stay at Gisors but found themselves late in the evening with a good few miles still to go. The horse was visibly flagging, and though they went on for a little way, hoping to find somewhere to stay, it was in vain. Finally they decided to spend the night outdoors in a wayside clearing. It would not be much more uncomfortable than one of the inns—they had hay in the cart, and the night was warm. Charles saw to the horse, and made a bed in the cart for Serafina. Then he gathered up his thick woollen cloak and spread it on the ground near by. In answer to Serafina's look of enquiry he said, 'There are limits to my resolve, Sally. I don't intend to find out where they are. I'll be more comfortable down here.'

Serafina nodded mutely. They had managed not to share a room at the two inns where they had stayed— to share the narrow confines of a cart would be even more dangerous. She went to the nearby stream and rinsed the dust and sweat of the day from her face, then returned to the cart. Here she lay down. The hay felt rough to her face, so she took off her fichu and spread it under her head. Charles made his own preparations for bed, then they lay down and talked for a while until daylight faded, the moon came out, and the world was asleep around them. Then their talk became more desultory and finally stopped. Serafina lay gazing at the stars in silence until she, too, slept.

Charles woke with a start to find the rays of the sun on his face and a blackbird singing in his ear. He had slept more soundly than he would have imagined. He sat up and surveyed the clearing. The horse was munching some grass near the tree to which it was tethered— perhaps that was what had woken him. The cart was close by, and he could just see Sally's foot hanging over the edge. He got up and made his way softly to the stream.

Sally was still asleep when he came back. He stood by the cart, unable to take his eyes off her. She was lying on her back; her wonderful hair, released from its confining cap, was spread out over the blue fichu— pale, molten gold on a ground of azure. He had always thought her a pretty girl, but now that her face was in repose he could see how classically pure her features were. She was quite extraordinarily lovely—a perfect model for *Beauty Discover'd Sleeping*, an unconscious but none the less almost irresistible invitation to a kiss. One hand cradled her cheek, the other was flung out over the hay. Her right leg was bent, but the other lay straight, so that her foot overhung the end of the cart, and he noticed with a smile that her boot had fallen off. For a moment, Charles Dacre, the connoisseur of beautiful women, took over. How often in the past had he contemplated a sleeping woman, traced the line of her nose, her throat, her bosom...? He caught his breath as he saw that Sally, unused to the restriction of a laced bodice, had loosened its strings for greater comfort, and her blouse—a peasant woman's blouse, large and generously cut—had fallen away to reveal more than a hint of the exquisite curves of her breast... He was seized with a desire greater than any he had ever before experienced, and he had taken a step forward before he knew it. Then he stopped short with a groan. This was Sally, and he must not! He groaned again at the irony—never before had he felt so strongly moved, and never before had he suffered the slightest scruple about taking what he desired. But this was Sally. He must not ruin her life, as he knew he could. He stood for a moment while this strange emotion, this new and curiously tender wish to protect her, battled with the most powerful feelings of desire he had ever felt.

'Charles!' Sally had opened her eyes. 'Oh, Charles!' She was looking at him sleepily, but with such joyous delight that he forgot all resolution, all restraint. As she sat up he grasped her in his arms and lifted her bodily out of the cart, holding her against him and covering her face with kisses. She gave a little cry and leant back, gasping in ecstasy as his mouth roamed over her face, her throat, her bosom. Then, feverishly returning his kisses, she slowly put her arms round his neck, and together they sank down to the ground. . .

'Them's nice goings-on, I must say!'

Charles was suddenly still. He turned and looked up. Over his shoulder Serafina saw a vast figure with a red, bucolic face looking at them in patent disapproval. Next to him was a boy who, in contrast to his father, was gazing at them in open delight. He moved a little in an attempt to get a better view of Serafina, staring at them all the while.

'Stop staring, Martin, do!' The older man gave Martin a shove, and Martin staggered and yelled in fright as his foot went down a rabbit hole.

'What do you do that for, Pa?' he shouted. 'I only wanted a look. She's pretty.'

'That's as may be, but how many times do I tell you not to stare? There was that bearded woman at the Martinmas fair—she wasn't all that pretty, but you couldn't take your eyes off her either. . .' The two argued for a minute, and this gave Charles the opportunity to get up, stretch over for Serafina's fichu, and pass it to her. Refusing to show any shame, she turned to face the cart and then calmly put herself in order, ending by twisting her hair up and putting her cap on. The straw hat followed. She turned back to the men and looked at them. Martin was now subdued and his father back in control again.

'What's your business here, friend?' he asked.

'It's private,' said Charles curtly, keeping himself in front of Serafina.

'Well, it may look as if it did ought to be, but it ain't—not on the public highway, it ain't. I've a good mind to let the magistrate know 'bout you two. Vagrants, that's what you be—vagrants!'

'We are not vagrants. We are on our way to... Magny.'

Father looked sceptical, but made no attempt to challenge this, perhaps because Charles had sounded decidedly aggressive.

'I think you'd better be gettin' on, then. Before I do let 'im know, like. Good mornin' to you, friend. I don't suppose I'll see you on my way back. Come on, Martin.'

Father set off purposefully, and after a moment Martin followed. As he went he could be heard saying, 'I think she's prettier than the bearded lady, Pa...'

Charles let out a breath. 'That was close,' he said. 'If they had tried to take us to the magistrate, we'd have been sunk. God, Sally, I'm sorry! I must be mad. To fall on you like that...'

'You didn't,' she replied, not looking at him. 'I invited it. It seems I'm as bad as you at remembering.'

'But I'm older. I should know better.'

'Oh, for heaven's sake, Charles, don't let's argue about who is more to blame!' exclaimed Serafina. 'We must just make sure it doesn't happen again. Unfortunately we have to stay together until we reach Paris, otherwise I would suggest we part company. But that is impossible.' She stared at him angrily. Then her lips started to twitch. 'Martin had never seen such a spectacle in his life... His face...' She started to laugh.

Charles joined in. 'At least he has taste. He thought you were prettier than the bearded lady.' They went into paroxysms of laughter, and the tension between them eased. 'I think you're prettier than a bearded lady, too, Sally,' gasped Charles. 'Though I haven't seen her, of course, so I can't really judge...'

After a moment or two they grew serious again. 'All the same, Sally, all the same... If those two hadn't turned up...'

'Well, they did, and I'm glad they did. Don't let us repine over what might have happened but didn't.'

'I take it as a useful warning. No more nights under the stars, my girl. In any case, after Gisors I think we shall have to stick to the high road. The others are not so good, and I'm running out of time. Come on—we'll pack up the cart and go. Luckily I have a friend in the town who will give us a good breakfast.'

Halfway through the morning they drove into Gisors, past the huge château-fort which dominated the town, and wound their way through the narrow streets until they reached a quiet inn on the other side. Here Charles got down and, saying briefly, 'I shan't be long,' went in through the low door. He was as good as his word. Hardly a minute had passed before he emerged with another man—thick-set and swarthy.

'This is Jean-Marie Loubet, Sally. He'll provide us with a good breakfast, and news of the town.'

Serafina smiled at Jean-Marie, but said, 'News?'

'I think Barros might have been here. It would be natural. He would guess that we are making for Paris, and Gisors is an obvious place to stop. But come in.

We can talk over breakfast—or nuncheon, if you prefer.'

They were able to repair some of the damages of the journey in that small but surprisingly comfortable inn. Jean-Marie disappeared soon after they arrived, but his wife looked after them well.

'I've asked Jean-Marie to find some faster transport for us. The horse and cart have served us well, but time is passing and I must be in Paris now as soon as possible. He's finding out if Barros has been here, too.'

A little while later Jean-Marie returned. He brought with him news, and a curious assortment of clothes.

'The word is in the market-place that good money will be paid for news of an Englishman who speaks French like a native, who may or may not have a blonde woman with him.' He glanced at Serafina. 'Forgive me, *mademoiselle*. I merely quote what is being asked. And Pierre Douleaux was boasting that he'd be rich before nightfall.'

'Pierre Douleaux?'

'It seems,' said Jean-Marie carefully, 'that he came across a suspicious-looking couple on the road to St Eloi.'

Serafina blushed scarlet and, not looking at her, Jean-Marie went on, 'The—er—lady had blonde hair.'

Charles muttered something which, on the whole, Serafina was glad she could not hear. 'So Barros and his agents are looking for us. And if this Douleaux person tells them that he saw us near Gisors they'll be on the watch at the gates on the Paris road.'

'Yes, but. . .' Jean-Marie paused for effect '. . .they may not recognise you.' Charles started to speak, but Jean-Marie interrupted him. 'Look!'

He held up a set of clothing—the black breeches and dark upper clothes of a notary, complete with flat hat.

'They'll still look for the "blonde woman", Jean-Marie!'

'Of course. But she will not exist. Look!'

Once again Jean-Marie held up some clothes—a boy's suit, again with a flat hat, from which hung a fringe of coarse, dark hair.

'You're a genius!' exclaimed Serafina.

'You don't mind?'

'Of course not, Charles. Unless you think modesty is more important than our lives?'

'Since you put it like that... And it might be better at that...' His significant look was not lost on Serafina, and she grew scarlet once more.

Charles grinned and took a quick glance at Jean-Marie, who was preoccupied with sorting out the clothes. 'The temptation will be considerably less, Sally,' he said in a soft voice.

'And I have a gig for you, with a good horse, and other horses booked on the way. I'll give you the names of the inns to call at. Barros won't find you,' said Jean-Marie.

After a day and a half they reached Argenteuil, just outside Paris. Charles drew up before they entered the small town and said, 'This is where we stop, Sally. I'm going to leave you here with some friends of mine.'

'You can't! I'm coming to the embassy with you.'

'Oh, no! Think for a moment—you've been travelling more or less in my company for more than five days. What would that do to your reputation if it were known? I've been considering how to get round the problem ever since we left Dieppe, and this is what I've decided. I have some good friends here, and I think they would agree to take you in. If anyone ever asked, they would claim that you had been with them since you left England. Please, Sally.'

Serafina saw the justice of what he said. Charles was notorious for his affairs. Her name would be irreparably damaged if it got out that she had spent so long unchaperoned in his company. No one would believe the truth. Trying not to sound as depressed as she felt, she said, 'Very well. I'll do as you say.'

'Good girl! Er. . .the only thing is. . .' Charles looked highly uneasy and Serafina wondered what on earth could cause this self-possessed man such embarrassment. He cleared his throat. 'My friends, I am sure, will help us all they can, but it would make their position much easier if. . .'

'Yes?'

'If they believed you were my fiancée—if they thought you were Serafina!' He went on rapidly before she could say anything, 'I know that deception is abhorrent to you, but our position—even to good friends like the Brecys—is somewhat equivocal. Madame la Comtesse especially would be uncomfortable. She is a very conventional creature at heart. Naturally your parents and Serafina will have to know the truth later, but until we get back to England I really think it would be advisable. I promise not to abuse my position,' he added wryly.

Serafina stared at him. She could hardly believe it! The irony of the situation was almost too much to bear. She started laughing, but the trouble was that once she had started she couldn't stop. The tears started to roll down her cheeks and, without her quite knowing how, she was suddenly crying as if her heart would break.

'Sally! Oh, God, Sally, I'm sorry. I'm a clumsy fool. If you hate the idea so much we'll forget it.'

'It. . .it's not that,' she sobbed through her tears. 'I think you're right—it would be better. I think I must be overwrought.'

He smiled at her. 'There's an inn over there. I'll take you there and bespeak a private parlour, where you can recover a little. Perhaps the landlord has something to restore your spirits. Come.'

Serafina allowed herself to be led into the inn. The innkeeper was sympathetic when told that young Etienne was feeling unwell, and bustled about fetching a more comfortable chair and opening the window for more air. He saw the 'boy' seated in a cool private parlour with a tisane and a glass of weak brandy and water in front of him. He waited for further orders, but when Charles nodded he went out, closing the door quietly behind him. After a while Serafina was quite calm again, and better equipped to deal with the topsy-turvy situation in which she found herself.

Charles said softly, 'I really ought not to delay things much longer. If I didn't meet Garcia at Dieppe as planned, the arrangement was that he would make his own way to Paris, taking a roundabout route. He should be there tomorrow. I'd like to see you safely installed with Armand and Giselle de Brecy, but I must see them first. Will you wait here while I call on them?' Serafina nodded. He sighed and lifted her chin. 'You'll like them.'

When she still didn't speak he went on, 'The business

about the engagement. . .it has a great deal to com-
mend it, you know. It isn't as if many people would be
involved—just the Brecys, in fact. My only thought is
to protect you, Sally. The thing is, I'm not quite sure
how they would regard you if you weren't. . .engaged
to me. It might be embarrassing for them and for you.'
He paused. When she refused to look at him he said,
'But if you really cannot bear the thought of it, I'll
abandon the idea.'

'I'll agree to anything you say, Charles.'

'Good. I'm sure it's best. You will have to put your
skirts on, of course, before Giselle sees you, but we
have our other clothes in the baggage, and there's a
wood just before the château where you can change. It
would be too strange to do it here. The landlord is
puzzled enough.' She looked at him enquiringly. 'Your
hat! I'll have to think of some reason why you can't
remove it. The blonde hair might come as a bit of a
shock on top of that black fringe.' He fetched the
landlord and explained that he was about to see the
Comte de Brecy, and would prefer to ask the Comte's
permission before taking his son to the château. He
asked if he might leave the boy in the parlour.

'Of course. Mind you, the Comte is a kind man, and
I am sure there would be no difficulty. . . But there, it
is perhaps better not to take things for granted. And
your son does look very pale—he has been crying, is
that not so. . .? Has he been upset?'

Charles looked stern and said repressively that his
son was not always as obedient as he would wish. The
landlord looked at him doubtfully, then said, 'Well, he
will soon recover from his headache here, *monsieur*.
Argenteuil is a quiet town and he will not be disturbed.

Now that the abbey has gone there isn't much to bring the crowds... Should he perhaps remove that heavy hat?'

Charles said solemnly, 'That was the very cause of Etienne's distress. It is absolutely forbidden for him to remove his hat in the daytime for the whole of this month, my good fellow, a fact which Etienne sometimes ignores. Our sect is strict in these matters, and he must learn. With suffering comes patience and ultimate joy—remember that, Etienne!' Then, promising to be back within the hour, he left. Serafina had some difficulty in keeping her face sober. Charles was outrageous!

She was quietly sipping her tisane when she heard the sound of two horses drawing up. Their riders dismounted and came into the inn. She heard the innkeeper exclaiming and apologising. A hatefully familiar voice said, 'Never mind, never mind! We arranged to meet some friends on our way to Paris and we appear to have missed them. I don't suppose an English gentleman has stopped here, has he? Perhaps in the company of a fair-haired lady?'

CHAPTER ELEVEN

SERAFINA's heart leapt into her mouth. It was Barros! Oh, God! What if he came in? She jumped up, but flight was impossible. Then she calmed down again. The last person he would expect to see in France was Serafina Feverel—even if she were recognisable, which she wasn't. She seated herself again, further way from the light, and pulled her hat down over her features.

The innkeeper seemed to think that it was his fault that no such person had called at the inn. He was even more apologetic when Barros asked to be served with some wine in his parlour.

'I'm sorry, *monsieur*. So very sorry. It is already occupied. A sick boy—travel sickness. He's very pale, and I think he's been crying... His father left him here for a while. *Monsieur*!'

Barros had flung open the door and was staring in. He ignored Serafina, sitting in a dark corner with her head in her hands. His eyes raked the room, then he went out again.

'I just wanted to make sure,' he said curtly.

The innkeeper was affronted. He said coldly, 'Perhaps *monsieur* would prefer to drink some wine elsewhere? There is a very adequate hostelry on the other side of the town. *Monsieur*?'

'Another inn, you say? Where?'

Within seconds Barros was on his way. Serafina wiped the sweat off her face and breathed again. But

then a thought occurred to her and she jumped up and
ran to the innkeeper. 'Can you tell me where the
Château des Colombes is, sir? In which direction? It
isn't on the other side of the town, is it?'

'No, no, boy. It is a step or two back the way you
have come. It isn't far. Is your father seeking work
with Monsieur le Comte?'

'I. . . I don't know,' faltered Serafina. 'My father
doesn't tell me much. . .'

'Such a strictness,' marvelled the innkeeper. 'Come,
you must go back into the parlour. Your father might
return at any minute and he will be angry again. Have
you still some tisane left? Look, you haven't finished
the brandy, either.' Serafina smiled timidly and sat
down again. She sipped the brandy. The innkeeper
went on, 'Mind you, my boy, it's better to have some
discipline than none at all—look at that fellow who
came in here just now. There's manners for you! A
foreigner, he was—Spanish by the looks of him. He
didn't frighten you, did he?' He tutted, then smiled. 'I
hope he likes the Trois Corbeaux. It's a hole!'

Charles came back soon after and Serafina flew out
to meet him.

'Barros!' she whispered urgently. 'He was here.'

'There, there, Etienne,' said Charles, with one eye
on the innkeeper, who was staring. 'You needn't worry
about a thing. Monsieur le Comte would be pleased to
receive you tonight. He is a kind man and sympathetic
to our cause, I think.'

He paid the innkeeper and they got in the cart and
drove off.

'Charles, I'm worried. Barros was asking for you. He
is determined to track you down.'

'I'll be at the embassy before he finds me. Besides, he won't catch me out again. I'll be on my guard this time—and I am armed.' He took out the pistol. 'Meanwhile you'll be safe with Armand. There's really nothing to be afraid of.'

'That's why you want me to stay here, isn't it? Because of Barros. Whatever you say, you know there's danger.'

'I want you to keep out of sight of any English people who might talk about you! Even as my fiancée you would still be exposed to some gossip. There is a slight—a very slight—risk that Barros will try again. But the odds are small. Please, Sally, don't make things more difficult than they are. I hate leaving you, you know that.'

A little way down the road they turned off into a wood where Serafina changed into a girl again. She discarded her hat with relief, laughing again at Charles's ingenious tale. Then they drove through some iron gates and up a long drive, stopping eventually with a bit of a flourish in front of a small château.

'Well done!' cried an exquisitely dressed gentleman at the top of the steps. 'The horse is not exactly the purest Arab strain, and the phaeton is a touch rustic, but the style... Ah, that was perfect!' His voice changed as he came round to assist Serafina. 'And *mademoiselle* is enchanting! Charles, you have the luck of the devil. I congratulate you. Your servant, Miss Feverel.'

'My dear, this is Armand de Brecy. In spite of his foppish appearance he is a good friend of mine.'

'I shall call him out—you will see it, *mademoiselle*.

One day he will go too far, and then... Come—my wife will be ready now to meet you. She is inside.'

Giselle de Brecy had a charming smile, but Serafina could see why Charles had wanted to make their story as respectable as possible. The Comtesse might be kind-hearted and ready to help her husband's friend, but she would not tolerate anything really irregular. Her loyalty and sympathy were stretched to the full as it was. The Comte had been a colleague of Charles in the old days, and he was eager to discuss them, but Charles was impatient to be gone. It was important to meet Garcia, especially as he now knew that Barros was also descending on Paris.

'You'll be careful, Charles?' asked Serafina, unable to hide her anxiety. They were alone on the drive for a few minutes before Charles set off for Paris. Armand de Brecy had found some clothes for his friend and, though the fit was not perfect, Charles looked his familiar handsome self again. The Comtesse de Brecy had found similarly suitable clothes for Serafina.

'Of course! There's no real danger now.'

'How can you say so, when you know——?' Serafina bit her lip. This would never do. Charles had to go to the embassy, she knew that. It was not sensible to make a fuss. 'Good luck, then.'

He looked to where the Comtesse was framed in the doorway, then bent forward and kissed Serafina's brow. 'Don't go far, my dear—it would be advisable not to leave the grounds of the château. I ought to be back within the week.'

'Goodbye, Charles.' In spite of her best efforts Serafina's voice wavered.

'Oh, to hell with propriety!' Charles ground out. He

seized her in his arms and kissed her hard. Then he
left without another look.

As she went in again, Serafina was conscious that
her hostess was looking at her with a slight air of
disapproval. But when the Comtesse saw how unhappy
she was she softened, embraced her warmly, and suggested a walk in the pleasure garden. Listening to the
soft voice talking about the flowers in the beds all
around, Serafina slowly recovered.

Charles sent a note every day, and after two days he
told them in guarded terms that he had found 'the man
he sought' and that their business had been conducted
satisfactorily. He would soon be with them again.
Serafina rejoiced and the Brecys made plans for a
celebration—a *fête-champêtre* for the four of them in
the forest of Laye, near St Germain. The servants were
set to making all sorts of savouries and sweetmeats,
and the wine was put to cool in the icehouse in the
grounds of the château. The Comtesse arranged for
her dressmaker to make up some pretty muslins, which
were simple but perfect for the warm, sunny weather.

So it was that Charles returned to an excited household determined to celebrate the success of his mission.
The Brecys persuaded him that no harm could come
of the expedition—St Germain-en-Laye was seldom
visited by Paris society in May, for the Bois de Boulogne
was so much more convenient.

The day was brilliant, the procession truly impressive. An open barouche carried the Comte de Brecy,
his wife, and their two guests. The ladies looked
enchanting in their thin muslins—the Comtesse in pink,
Serafina in blue. They wore villager straw hats with

ribbons to match their dresses, and were carrying
dainty parasols—all to protect their complexion. The
gentlemen were in the first stare of fashion, Charles
having equipped himself in Paris. Behind the barouche
was another, larger coach containing the servants and
all the refreshments, and everything else that was
necessary for their comfort. The drive took over an
hour, for they had to cross the Seine, but it seemed to
pass in a flash.

Serafina was determined to enjoy herself. Since the
Brecys had no notion of how Charles's fiancée had
behaved in London, and Charles thought of her as
Sally, she decided to be her natural self. But, in fact,
the weeks in London had taught her a lot, and the
Serafina on the way to St Germain was no longer the
Sally of the old days. She had always been graceful,
but now, though she was not conscious of it, her
movements had more natural elegance. Sally's exuberance had been toned down and, though she had lost
none of her spontaneity, she had acquired polish and
refinement. Her discussions with Charles on the journey from Dieppe to Argenteuil had not only taught
her a great deal about the world he lived in, she had
learned a lot about the art of conversation, too. She no
longer interrupted impulsively, nor was she quite so
eager to make her point at the expense of others. The
conversation in the barouche flowed easily and naturally, with a great deal of amusement and polished
wit. She was secretly entertained at the look on
Charles's face when he realised that hoyden Sally was
more than holding her own with his fashionable
friends!

The picnic was a great success, the food excellent

and the wines exquisite. After it was over, the Comte announced that he and his wife were proposing to enjoy the fresh air and sunshine without moving from the spot. He added with a knowing look that he expected Charles and his fiancée would like to wander through the trees... The Comtesse looked doubtful, then approved of a walk—as long as it did not take too long, and they did not wander too far.

'They seem to be even more strict in France than they are in England,' said Serafina as she and Charles strolled through the glades and clearings.

'It's even worse in Spain,' said Charles. 'Until they are actually married young men and women never see each other without a duenna present.'

'Charles, tell me about Barros.'

'He seems to have dropped out of sight. I saw Garcia at the embassy and, once the letter and the emeralds had been exchanged, we thought it wise for someone different to escort him to Portsmouth. The arms ship will be waiting for him there now, and I shall see him when we get back. If Barros is still in Paris he will be watching *my* movements, not those of anyone else.'

'So you are still in danger?'

'He won't make a move unless he sees Garcia with me. And now that can't happen. Garcia has left Paris.'

'What a relief! So our troubles are over.'

'They won't be completely over until I see you safely back in England with your parents. I sent a message, by the way, both to Sussex and to Serafina in London. It didn't say much—even the diplomatic couriers are not completely discreet—but I said you were staying with friends near Paris and I asked Serafina to arrange to visit Feverel Place straight away. That will keep her out of London for the moment. Then I can deliver you to your home on my way to Portsmouth.'

Serafina pushed away the thought of the confusion which would be created both in Curzon Street and in Sussex. And her family would probably still be in Brighton!

'You are taking a great deal of trouble on my behalf, Charles.'

'You took more than a great deal on mine, Sally. I can never repay you for what you did.'

Serafina looked up at him and smiled wistfully. He murmured something and took her roughly into his arms. When her ridiculous hat got in the way he pushed it back, so that it hung by its ribbons while he kissed her. Then he groaned in despair and buried his face in her hair.

'What am I to do, Sally? I can hardly bear the thought of losing you. In spite of the danger, in spite of the discomfort, the week with you was the happiest in my life, and the moments in that clearing—I sometimes think I shall go mad if they are never to be repeated. You were seldom out of my mind all the time I was in Paris, and I couldn't wait to come back to you.' He kissed her desperately again, then put her from him and turned away. 'But it won't do!' he said with angry emphasis. 'I can't subject you to the sort of life I must lead. I dare not! You would die under all the petty restraints and artificialities, the criticism you would face for being yourself. The girl I love would disappear. All that enthusiasm for living, that lovely spontaneity would vanish, buried under the demands of a diplomatic career. Louisa Paget, for all her faults, had the same zest for life before she married Sir

Robert. Look at her now—a bitterly disappointed woman, seeking satisfaction in her intrigue and the quest for wealth.'

'I hope you do not compare me with Lady Paget, Charles?'

'Of course not. Your honesty, your integrity place you beyond comparison with her.'

Serafina was silenced. Then she said carefully, 'And Serafina? Are you going to marry her, feeling as you do?'

Charles hesitated, then said, 'I don't know. I am committed to her, you know that. It would be difficult to betray that commitment. And. . . Serafina is different. She would be content with so much less than you—her children, her home. I could make Serafina happy, I think.'

'I see. . .' Serafina gave an unladylike sniff, and a tear rolled down her cheek.

'Oh, Sally, Sally!' Charles pulled out a handkerchief and wiped her eyes. Then once again he held her to him, tightly, painfully. . .

'Well, Charles! So this is why you were so anxious to get away this weekend! An idyll in St Germain, eh?'

Charles released Serafina and whirled round, sheltering her from the speaker. This was an elegantly dressed woman, not in the first flush of youth, but still lovely. She was standing at the edge of the clearing next to a distinguished-looking gentleman of about forty, and there were several other well-dressed ladies and gentlemen behind them. They were all regarding Charles and Serafina with some amusement.

'I don't blame you in the slightest, my dear. Such a very pretty little companion! Why have we never seen

her in Paris—or Vienna? Or is she a new...
acquisition?'

'Don't tease him, Lady Harcombe. Can't you see
he's embarrassed? It must be for the first time,' said
the gentleman, openly smiling. 'I'm sorry to have interrupted you, Charles. Come everyone!'

'No, wait! Ambassador!' The gentleman turned back
in surprise at Charles's peremptory tone. 'You misunderstand the situation completely, Ambassador.'
Charles drew Serafina foward. 'Miss Feverel is my
fiancée. May I present her to you, sir?'

'Indeed?' Sir Charles Stewart, British ambassador to
France, spoke in a neutral tone, but his companions
were openly sceptical.

Charles grew pale with anger, but restrained himself
and said with careful courtesy, 'Miss Feverel is at
present a guest of the Comte and Comtesse de Brecy
at Argenteuil, sir. They invited us to a picnic in the
forest here to celebrate the completion of my mission,
and Miss Feverel and I were taking a walk while our
host and hostess rested. I believe you know Armand
de Brecy?'

The ambassador looked highly embarrassed himself.
'Charles! My dear fellow! What can I say? If you can
bear to introduce me I shall give Miss Feverel our
deepest apologies for our unworthy thoughts about
her—and for any distress we've caused her.'

Serafina, conscious of what Sir Charles had
observed, was having no difficulty in looking suitably
distressed. Charles was still cool as he made the
introductions.

The ambassador said, 'Lucius Feverel's daughter? I
met him at Oxford many years ago. A brilliant man,

though some of his articles on international affairs have been a thorn in our flesh! Miss Feverel, once again I cannot tell you how vexed I am that our careless tongues have upset you. Please forgive us. Though since we had no inkling that you were in France. . .'

'Miss Feverel is here on a private visit, sir.'

'Let Miss Feverel speak to me herself, Charles—if she will.'

Serafina said, 'I'm afraid it was my fault that you were not informed of my visit, Ambassador. Charles would have been pleased to announce it, but I have too much pride! I did not wish the world to know what a silly creature I am. I'm sorry to have to admit it, but I persuaded the Comte de Brecy and his wife to invite me to stay with them. I was so anxious for his safety that I practically followed Charles to France! Perhaps I do deserve some censure.'

Sir Charles looked amused at this graceful way of relieving him of some blame. 'Not at all! But you are not at all silly, Miss Feverel. And now I know why Charles was so determined in his refusal of our invitation to the ball tomorrow night in honour of Prince Yurievski and the rest! You must change your mind and bring Miss Feverel with you, Charles. I will not allow you to say no. And if the Comte de Brecy and his wife will agree to come also, Miss Feverel will not need any other chaperon.'

'Sir, we couldn't possibly impose on the Brecys in this way. Tomorrow night is surely too short a notice?'

'In a moment, Charles, you will have me believing that you are ashamed of Miss Feverel! You seem very reluctant to let her be seen. . .?'

'Not at all! I am very proud of her. But. . .'

'We shall go to find the Brecys. I cannot imagine that Armand will refuse.' He offered Serafina his arm and she curtsied and took it. Together they went back to the Comte and Comtesse, followed by Charles and the others. Compliments were exchanged, the ambassador used his considerable skill to present his invitation tactfully, and when it was accepted he added, 'Perhaps you would all join us at dinner beforehand? If Miss Feverel is about to be a diplomat's wife—for which, I may say, she seems eminently suited—she ought to experience the full rigours of a diplomatic occasion!'

To Serafina's surprise the Brecys were pleased about the invitation. 'My dear, it will be a splendid affair,' said the Comtesse. 'What a baptism of fire!'

'That is exactly what it will be,' said Charles grimly. 'A baptism of fire. The poor girl will be exposed to some of the most critical eyes in Europe.'

The Comtesse looked surprised. 'But your fiancée will manage beautifully, Charles! She is absolutely *comme il faut*. You can have no doubts that she will cope!'

Serafina could see that Charles had grave doubts of Sally's ability to cope with some of the greatest sticklers for etiquette in Europe but, in the circumstances, he was unable to express them. However, a more urgent problem was exercising her own mind.

'What shall I wear?' she asked. '*Madame* has been kind enough to give me these muslins, but a ball... They will hardly do. I cannot go, Charles.'

'Of course you must!' The Comtesse hesitated briefly, then said, 'I have a ball-dress that I have worn only once, and that was last year when Armand and I were in Madrid. No one here has seen it, for we live rather quietly at the moment. It is just right for the occasion and I think, with a very slight alteration, that it would fit you. Come, *mademoiselle*, I will show it to you.'

Serafina was persuaded to try the dress on. It was the most beautiful dress she had ever seen—Parisian to the last bow. There was a slip of white satin, finished at the bottom with three narrow pipings of blue silk, looped and twisted. Inside each loop was a fleur-de-lis made of tiny pearls and crystals. Over the slip was a layer of white lace, caught up to one side and looped with bows of the same blue silk. The bodice was plainly cut, made of white satin under a delicate net richly embroidered with shimmering crystals and gleaming pearls. It was held under the bust with a rouleau of blue. Serafina looked like someone quite different in it—as ethereal as the London Serafina, but. . .more sophisticated, more self-assured. Her three admirers were unanimous that she should wear it.

'And when Hortense has dealt with your hair you will be a sensation, even in Paris,' said the Comtesse ecstatically.

'But surely you will wear this yourself, *madame*?'

'You flatter me! Since the birth of little Thierry I am far too. . .generously built! But do not worry. I have a perfectly adequate dress to wear, *mademoiselle*.'

The alterations were soon effected. The Comtesse sent for her jewel cases and selected a necklace in the form of a *collier* of crystals and pearls, and a delicate crescent of the same crystals and pearls which would hold Serafina's pale gold curls in place on top of her head.

The following evening Serafina, in her borrowed plumes, looked as if she had spent her life in the courts of Europe. Charles handed her a bouquet of small white roses and deep blue ribbons, and assisted her into the de Brecy carriage. The Comtesse de Brecy, looking extremely handsome in a poppy-red dress and diamonds, was already inside. The Comte joined them and they rolled away.

'Are you nervous, Serafina?' said Charles with a smile.

'No, not really. I'm looking forward to it, I think. Are you?'

'I have seldom been more nervous in my life. And it is all on your behalf.'

'My behalf?'

'I. . .' He looked at her smiling face. 'I want you to enjoy it.'

Serafina was certain that Charles had changed what he had been going to say. And she had a fair idea what his original thought had been, for it had already been expressed earlier in the day by the Comtesse. She had asked *madame* to tell her something of the people she was likely to meet that evening and the things she might need to know.

'I should not like to disgrace Charles,' she had said. 'And things are different here in France.'

The Comtesse had been very pleased to help, and they had spent a profitable hour. But before they had gone down to join the gentlemen again the Comtesse had said, 'I shall be there to help you, but you need have no fear, *mademoiselle*. I cannot imagine why Charles is so nervous—for he is, you know. I find it rather touching, don't you? It seems to me that you have everything in your favour—youth, beauty, and a great deal of spirit.'

She had thought for a moment, then said, 'You lack experience, I suppose, and Charles knows, as I do, that diplomatic circles can be very cruel, with little sympathy for anyone who is guilty of a solecism. There will be some who will regard you with envy, and their eyes will be all the more critical because of it. I confess, I do not like it, this world—that is why we use the excuse of little Thierry to spend most of our time here at Argenteuil on our estate. But I do not fear for you, and you must have no fears for yourself, or for Charles's reputation. He will be the envy of all the gentlemen, that is certain! You must enjoy it!'

'Then I will! Indeed, I would be a poor creature if I didn't after all your kindness—this lovely dress, the jewels and all the other things, your maid's attentions ...and the help and encouragement you have given me. Thank you, *madame*.'

And now Charles was having doubts again. Serafina put up her chin and resolved that she would not fail— or at least if she did she would go down with all flags flying. No one was going to dare to be ashamed of her!

The journey took about an hour and on the way she quizzed all of them again on the protocol for the evening, and the personalities of the guests who would be there. It was treated in a light-hearted manner, with a great many scandalous anecdotes, especially from the Comte de Brecy, but Serafina learned a lot. And since she had a very good memory she had mastered most of it by the time they reached the embassy.

* * *

The ambassador's dinner party was a large affair, with over thirty guests. Serafina's first ordeal was waiting in line on the stairs to be announced. Word had got round that Aldworth—who was well-known for his jaundiced view of marriage!—had now shackled himself to a dream of a girl, a real diamond. Naturally everyone was anxious to see the beauty, and Serafina had to put up with a large number of well-bred stares and whispers. Charles grew a little restive, but Serafina smiled at him calmly and ignored the rest. The Brecys were a great help. They talked on unexceptionable topics during what seemed to be an interminable wait. At last they reached the top, where the ambassador was waiting.

The major-domo announced them. 'Lord Aldworth, the Comte and Comtesse de Brecy, Miss Feverel.' Sir Charles, who had been elegantly but informally dressed at St Germain, was imposing in full regalia—black silk knee-breeches, decorations and all. His manner was still as charming, though with a line of guests extending down the stairs, foreign nobility among them, he had little time to spend on a comparatively unknown English girl, however beautiful she was. Serafina went along the line of dignitaries, curtsying correctly wherever necessary, and eventually entered a beautiful room lined with mirrors and with a splendid chandelier in the centre. A vast table was laden with crystal, silver-gilt cutlery and candelabra, white napery, and flowers. When the Comtesse de Brecy took her to the list of guests to find her place, Serafina, who naturally came low on the scale of precedence, found herself placed some distance from Charles, who was to sit on

the opposite side of the table nearer the ambassador
and his guest of honour.

'Hmm, you've been put next to young Ashleigh,'
said Charles. 'A rising star, it's said.'

'And the Vicomte de Vaubois is on her other side,'
said the Comtesse. 'Oh, Charles, you will have to take
care! You might lose Mademoiselle Feverel if you are
not careful. The Vicomte is a charmer, too!'

At that moment a young man who was almost as tall
as Charles, but slighter, with a thin, clever face, came
up and asked if Charles would introduce him. This was
Mr Ashleigh. They all chatted for a moment, then the
Comtesse's partner, the Comte de Guions, came up
and bore her off. Mr Ashleigh and Charles grinned at
one another.

'You have to give the ambassador his due,' said Mr
Ashleigh.

'Indeed,' Charles replied. 'Giselle de Brecy is one of
the few women in Paris who is placid enough to keep
our friend under control.' He saw that Serafina was
puzzled. 'Surely Armand told you about Philippe de
Guions?'

'I don't think so.'

'The Guions are an old Gascon family, Miss Feverel.
They are notorious for being hot-tempered, and
Philippe is worse than most. His father was the same.'

'Surely you've heard of the battles he and Philippe
had when they lived in London during the wars, my
dear?' said Charles. 'They were famous.'

'I think I must have been too young.'

Mr Ashleigh laughed. 'I would have liked to have
been there when Papa de Guions yelled that all sons

were ungrateful, unmannerly wretches and the Prince Regent took it personally.'

'Old Guions was never made welcome at Carlton House after that, it's true. It was a pity, though. He was always accusing Philippe of unfilial behaviour, but they were really very fond of one another. It was just that *monsieur* didn't allow his son any independence, and Philippe resented it!'

A stir at the door indicated that the guests of honour—Prince Yurievski and his wife—had arrived. Everyone bowed and curtsied as the ambassador led Prince and Princess Yurievski to the table. The rest of the guests followed suit. Mr Ashleigh took Serafina off to her place with an air of a man who knew he had the prize. Charles looked at them with a mixture of apprehension and amusement, then collected his own dinner partner, the wife of an Austrian diplomat, from the group who had just come in.

Charles's manners were usually effortless. But, though she could not possibly have guessed it from his behaviour, he had to work hard that evening to pay his partner the attention he owed her. Several times he found his eyes straying to where Sally was sitting. Whenever he looked the conversation was always flourishing, sometimes with young Ashleigh, sometimes with Vaubois—never exclusively with either, and never with anyone else. At least she had remembered something of company manners! But did she have to look so...so happy? As if she was enjoying every minute of what ought to be an ordeal! As for the two young men ...they were quite clearly fascinated. Ashleigh knew his manners well enough to give the lady on his other side a fair share of his attention. But Vaubois! An arrogant young cub, if ever he saw one! And Sally was looking positively fascinated by him. Both Ashleigh and Vaubois were nearer Sally in age than he was, of course. Charles turned to Madame von Logau.

CHAPTER TWELVE

ON THE international scene it was admitted that cracks were appearing in the Grand Alliance—cracks which the British Government's attitude to South America was not helping to cure. Word of Charles's latest mission to help Bolivar had seeped out in the way those things did and the Austrians, to say nothing of the Russians, were not altogether pleased. But all difficulties were put aside on the evening of the ball held in the British embassy for the Tsar's delegation. It was afterwards generally agreed that it was one of the season's successes. There were several stars at the ball—not least Prince Yurievski——but the unknown Miss Feverel was certainly another. She danced through the night with hardly a break, and her partners spoke afterwards of her charm, her wit and her poise. Not even the sourest dowagers could find a genuine cause for criticism—unless it was that she seemed to have an unfair share of all the most interesting gentlemen!

Serafina enjoyed it all—what girl would not be flattered by the attentions of half of Paris society? But the man she really wished to impress was Charles himself, and nothing in his manner suggested that she had succeeded. He could hardly have failed to notice how popular she was, but she wanted him to acknowledge that he had been wrong to dismiss her as unsuitable for sharing his life, to see that she was more than

capable of coping with whatever demands were made
on her. He had danced with her once, but had seemed
somewhat distant. Charming, but distant. As the evening wore on she waited impatiently for him to ask her
again. When the invitation came she was surrounded
by admirers and he had to make his way through to
her.

'I hardly dare take you away,' he said a little coolly.

'Quite right, Aldworth! Leave her here!' cried
Vaubois.

'Oh, no, Vicomte! I am betrothed to Lord Aldworth.
I must do as he wishes,' said Serafina, with a bewitching
smile at the Vicomte. She put her hand on Charles's
arm, and allowed herself to be led into the ballroom.

'No one could deny that you are a success, Sally.
Are you enjoying it?'

'Of course!'

'What were you were talking about so eagerly at the
dinner-table! Ashleigh could hardly take his eyes off
you, and Vaubois didn't even try.'

She looked at him with a hint of mischief in her eye.
'Do you really wish to know?'

'Only if you wish to tell me.'

'Well, the Vicomte and I talked about the Vicomte.
Then we talked a little—a very little—about me, then
we talked about the Vicomte again. Mr Ashleigh and I
talked about the new translation of Shakespeare into
German. Then we talked about you.'

'About me?' Charles was startled.

'He admires you enormously—much more than he
does me. I was quite cast down,' Serafina said mourn-
fully, gazing at him over her fan.

'You are a minx, Sally. Ashleigh is smitten along with all the rest.'

'Yes, but only for tonight. And I encouraged him to talk about you. I must say, Charles, I found it fascinating.'

'What did he say?' asked Charles, somewhat uneasily.

'Oh, nothing to compromise you. Mr Ashleigh is an extremely discreet young man. He didn't tell me about Lady Harcombe. . . You mustn't stand still in the middle of a waltz, Charles.'

Charles, thus admonished, started dancing again. 'Who did?' he asked grimly, after a pause.

'I can't remember—one of the tabbies.'

'It all happened long ago, Sally.'

'It really doesn't concern me, Charles. Nor do any of the others. After all, you had to do something before you met——' Serafina stopped short. She had been going to say, Before you met the girl you fell in love with. For a moment, under the influence of this evening, intoxicated by this waltz with Charles, the signs of jealousy she saw in him, Serafina had deceived herself into believing their own myth: Charles did love her, whatever name he called her. He had asked her to marry him because he could not imagine life without her. They were going to live happily ever after in Aldworth, London or even in Europe—it didn't matter to either of them, as long as they were together. But suddenly the bubble was burst, and cruel reality showed through. She rather thought that she was never going to marry Charles—not as Sally, not as Serafina, let alone all the rest. So she said instead, 'Before your brother died and you needed an heir.'

'Sally——'

'Heavens, Charles, don't sound so serious! I shall begin to think you don't know how to behave!'

He smiled in spite of himself, but then grew serious and said softly, 'We cannot talk here, Sally. But I promise you that we shall have a proper discussion before long. It's a pity that this affair came along. It meant that we had to postpone leaving for England.'

'But I wouldn't have missed it for the world! I love it!'

The dance came eventually to an end, but Charles kept hold of Serafina and led her over to a group in the next room which included the ambassador.

The talk there seemed to be more serious than the occasion warranted. The discussion had apparently turned to the question of South America, and in spite of His Excellency's efforts it was getting heated. The Vicomte de Vaubois was hotly defending the colonials' right to self-determination, and this was being disputed by the Gascon, the Comte de Guions, and the Austrian, Graf von Logau. Disaster loomed, and Serafina saw the ambassador give a discreet nod to Mr Ashleigh to fetch the Comtesse de Brecy. It looked as if her peacemaking efforts were going to be needed.

'*Monsieur*,' said Graf von Logau, civilly enough, 'consider these Spanish colonists for a moment—they have no idea how to run a country. Spain has looked after their interests for so long.'

'Ah, Charles, there you are,' said His Excellency gratefully. 'And Miss Feverel, too. What do you think of the orchestra?'

Serafina assured the ambassador that the whole

evening was perfect. Charles asked if Prince Yurievski was staying long in Paris.

'I believe he returns on Friday to St Petersburg,' said the ambassador. 'A beautiful city—but cold in winter. Have you been there, Graf von Logau?'

Graf von Logau was not to be distracted. 'Not yet, Excellency. But the Tsar will not be any more pleased than Metternich at this encouragement your government is giving to Bolivar and his ilk. I tell you, the Spanish colonials are not yet fit to govern themselves.'

'The colonials have every right to do so——' began Vaubois.

'Be silent, young man! I have listened long enough to your radical maunderings!' said the Comte de Guions, growing redder. 'Colonies are like children. They have to be kept under control until they are fit to look after themselves! I was very disappointed to hear that Lord Aldworth had taken part in some escapade to deliver arms to the rebels. Very disappointed.'

'Children have a habit of growing up, sir,' said Charles mildly. 'The British Government was forced to let our colonies in North America go their own way some time back. But I believe we are now on the way to building up a good relationship with them once more—this time based on trade and equality. Should Spain not do the same for her "children"?'

'Bah!' The Comte de Guions suddenly turned on Serafina. 'What do you think of it all, Miss Feverel? Do you approve of what Lord Aldworth is doing?' He put it into a woman's terms for her. 'Do you agree with setting up children to defy their own parents?'

The attack on an inexperienced young lady was

unfair—everyone except Guions felt it. Charles and the ambassador spoke together.

'Really, Comte——'

'Miss Feverel can hardly be expected to have formed a view...'

But Serafina was not disturbed. 'Well, *monsieur*, I would not dream of disagreeing with anything Charles did—not in public, anyway.' She gave him one of her enchanting smiles. 'But, forgive me—as I listened to you I was wondering what you would have said twenty years ago? When your father was alive?'

Since the Guions' family battles were well-known to most of the people there, the group dissolved into laughter. Even Guions himself smiled. Some good-natured teasing followed and the atmosphere changed. With a sigh of relief the ambassador called for more wine for the gentlemen and led Charles and Serafina away.

'Brilliant, my dear. Quite brilliant. Charles, this young lady will be wasted as your wife—we ought to have her on the strength.'

'I can't spare her, sir.'

The ambassador smiled as he saw the look Charles gave Serafina. 'I understand,' he said. 'I understand perfectly. Take good care of her, Charles.'

Soon the evening was over. When the four drove back to Argenteuil dawn was breaking over the roofs of Paris. Serafina was exhausted. So much was happening—and so much more was still to come, most of it not pleasant. She resolved there and then never to regret the past week, but to remember it when she was an old, old lady—a maiden great-aunt, telling tales to the Feverel grandchildren.

* * *

Soon it was time for Serafina and Charles to leave the Château des Colombes. Giselle and Armand pressed them to come again soon, after they were married. Serafina was hard put to it not to show how unlikely she thought that would be. The hired post-chaise was brought round, and their slender amount of luggage strapped on. An elderly lady, a certain Madame Houblon, had been engaged to chaperon Serafina for the journey. She would join her daughter and son-in-law in London when her duty was done. Charles produced a fourth member of their party—a tough-looking individual, John Derby, who was a member of the embassy household, and who would apparently serve as Charles's valet.

At the last minute Giselle de Brecy handed Serafina a dressmaker's box. 'It is for you,' she said. 'I could not possibly wear it again, even if it fitted me. I shall always remember how lovely you looked in it at the embassy ball.' Serafina embraced her impulsively, and placid, correct Giselle held her tightly. 'Come back, Serafina,' she whispered. 'Please come back.'

With much waving and some tears on Giselle's part, the coach moved off on the way to Calais and England.

They drove along comfortably enough—the roads were quite good and the weather favourable. In contrast to their journey from Dieppe the pace was brisk, as Charles wanted to reach Portsmouth as soon as poss-ible. Garcia would wait as long as he could, but the arms were already overdue. So they pressed on, intend-ing to be in Calais in time to get the packet boat to Dover in three days' time.

Madame Houblon was a pleasant enough woman,

but her presence hindered any real conversation. Serafina was not altogether sorry—time enough for revelations when Charles returned to Feverel Place after seeing Garcia. But they soon discovered that the chaperon was not a good traveller, and some time had to be spent in occasional stops for her to have 'a breath of fresh air'. Charles chafed at the delay, but there was nothing he could do about it, except pay a little more at the post-houses for first-class horses which would make up the time. In spite of their delays, they kept up to schedule, and found themselves on the road through the Forest of Crecy to Montreuil, their last stop before Calais, with a little time to spare. It was late afternoon on a very sunny day, and the carriage had become very hot. The forest looked invitingly cool, and when Madame Houblon requested them to stop Charles gave the order willingly enough.

'You don't want to stop here, sir,' said the post 'boy', a wizened, elderly man, who rode on the leader. 'It's a bit isolated here.'

'Oh, please!' exclaimed Madam Houblon. 'I am so very hot!'

'Just for a short while, perhaps, Charles?' said Serafina. 'Madam Houblon is very flushed—and I too find the carriage stifling.'

'Three minutes,' said Charles. 'But don't go far.'

The ladies descended and went a little way into the forest. Charles turned to the post boy. 'What is wrong?'

'Well, I could be mistaken, but I disliked the looks of a certain cove what was asking about an Englishman and his party this morning. Before you stopped at our place. Foreign, he was.'

Charles nodded, then took out his pistols and went

to speak to John Derby, who had been travelling on
the box. When he turned round again Sally and
Madame Houblon were vanishing into the trees. 'Sally!
Come back! I said not to go too far.' There was a
wavering cry and then a yell. Sally's yell. Charles leapt
through the undergrowth in the direction of the sound.
As he ran he heard an exclamation and some loud
swearing, followed by a sharp smack. He burst into a
clearing and stopped short. Barros was standing there,
holding Sally in front of him like a shield. His face was
bleeding. At his side were two others, one clutching a
half-fainting Madame Houblon, the other pointing a
cocked pistol in Charles's direction. Sally was struggling valiantly, but Barros had a very firm grip of her,
and even as Charles watched he twisted her arm up
behind her. She gave a little cry and was still.

'Half a loaf is better than nothing, milord Aldworth.
Garcia, I hear, left Calais some days ago. The arms are
probably already on their way to South America. But
there are still the emeralds. Where are they?'

'Release Miss Feverel and Madame Houblon and I
will tell you.'

'Oh, no! I've been tricked once before by that sort
of arrangement. The emeralds! Or first the old lady
then the fiancée will die.'

'Who is going to kill them? Your henchmen? They
don't look as if they relish the idea of killing defenceless women in cold blood.'

'Your fiancée is not a defenceless woman, milord.
You see my cheek? I think I could kill her myself with
pleasure. But the men will do as I order them. And if
they will not I shall kill them too. Fetch the emeralds.'

'If you harm either of the ladies any further I swear you will die, Barros,' said Charles.

'Much as I would like to teach Miss Feverel a lesson, I would prefer to live, and enjoy the advantages the emeralds will bring. It will be a complete and painless exchange—the emeralds for the ladies, I assure you. Why are you hesitating? I am not a gentleman, so my word is not valid, eh? But I am a realist, milord. I am not as anxious to shed blood as Miss Feverel, and I am more likely to escape if it is merely a matter of theft.'

'The emeralds are in the carriage. I will fetch them if I can take Madam Houblon and one of your men back with me.'

Barros thought for a moment. 'Very well. Luis—you go.'

The man holding Madame Houblon put one arm round her and supported her as she tottered back to the carriage, followed by Charles. Here she subsided on to the seat. Charles said to the driver of the carriage and the post boy, 'Wait here. We shall be back to go to Calais as planned in a short while.' Then he said to the valet, 'Follow me at a distance. If anything goes wrong, shoot to kill—first Luis here, then Barros.'

Having thus ensured that at least one of Barros's men would be eager to see that things went well, Charles opened a small case on the seat, took out a leather bag, and walked back to the clearing. He held it up. 'The emeralds.'

Barros said, 'Take the girl, Juan!' Then he turned to Charles. 'Bring them to me.'

Glancing at Luis, Charles said to the valet, 'Remember what I said!' Then he walked up to Barros and handed him the bag. Barros up-ended it and tipped a

couple of the stones out on to his hand. He smiled.
'Good! Come, Juan! Come, Luis!' Juan threw Sally to
the ground and while Charles knelt down to rescue her
the three Spaniards ran to their horses and galloped
off.

'You must go after them!' Sally struggled to get up,
but Charles put a restraining hand on her.

'Let them go! We must make all speed to Calais.'

'But, Charles——'

'Do as I say, my love.' Ignoring her protests, he lifted
her up in his arms and carried her to the carriage. Here
he put her carefully down, signalled to the coachman
to drive off, and pulled the door shut behind him. The
driver needed no urging to hurry to the next stage—he
was as anxious as they to reach it. He wanted no
further truck with all these foreigners.

'You're hurt!' Charles took Sally's chin in his hand
and looked with concern at the abrasion on her cheek.

'He hit me...back,' she murmured. 'But my arm is
more important. May I borrow your handkerchief?'

'What happened?' asked Charles, looking in concern
at the long, deep scratch which was still welling blood.

'Juan's knife. He must have got a new one. It was
stuck in his belt, and as he threw me down it caught on
my arm. It's not serious, but it makes a mess. Ow!'

Charles had taken off his cravat and was binding it
tightly round the wound. 'That ought to do till we get
to Montreuil. But let me know if it hurts any worse.'

'Worse than what?' she asked, pulling a face. But as
time went on she settled down and even slept for a
little.

They spent the night at Montreuil and set off the
next day for the last stage. Madame Houblon was very

nervous, but Charles assured her that all would be well,
that the devils had got what they had come for. A
certain tone in his voice caused Serafina to look at him
sharply. Her suspicions were further raised when
Charles insisted on an extra guard and the inn's fastest
horses, even though they were well up to time.

'To set Madam Houblon's mind at rest,' he said,
when he saw Serafina looking at him. She nodded, but
was not totally convinced.

They reached Calais early in the evening, and were
able to go on board almost immediately. John Derby
accompanied them and stationed himself outside the
cabin Serafina was sharing with Madame Houblon. The
only incident to disturb them was a scuffle on the
quayside about half an hour before the packet sailed,
when a trio of foreigners were turned away, somewhat
roughly, from the gangplank.

The crossing to England was not very comfortable.
A most unseasonable storm blew up, and in the end
the eight leagues from Calais to Dover seemed more
like twenty—and took longer. Madame Houblon, of
course, felt sick almost as soon as they left the harbour,
so Serafina left her to the good offices of the steward
and went on deck. Huge storm-clouds were banked
above, but there was still a glimmer of light in the sky
to the west, and she could see Charles up at the bows.
She made her way through the various bits of rope and
cargo and joined him.

'You shouldn't be here. It's going to be rough, I'm
afraid. Where's Madame Houblon?'

'Already succumbing. In the cabin. Charles, I must
ask you. Why did you let Barros have those emeralds
so easily?'

'Easily? He was threatening your life!'

'You gave in too quickly.'

He looked at her with a little smile on his face. 'I'm glad Barros didn't think so.'

'He doesn't know you as well as I do.'

'He might know me better now.'

Serafina looked at him sharply. 'The emeralds weren't real ones? But Barros looked at them! He examined them!'

'Only a couple, which you might say—rolled out to order. Fairly small ones, too.'

'What a risk! What if one of the others had come out?'

'The others were carefully restrained by a fine but very loosely tied net.'

'What were they? Glass?'

'Very good glass. The best.'

Serafina was silent for a moment, then she grew indignant. 'All the same, what would have happened to me if Barros had found out? The ambassador told you to take very good care of me! Did he know?'

'No one knew except myself, John Derby and Armand. And you were well looked after, Sally—at least, you were all the time you stayed near the coach. But you strayed away—I only took my eyes off you for a few seconds. . .'

'It was that wretched woman. She insisted on being private. . . Where are the real ones?'

'I'll tell you later. When it's all over. How's your arm? I see you have a nice black eye.'

'Black eye? Oh, never say so!' she wailed.

'Well, it's nearly a black eye, but it'll fade quite soon.

Pull your hat down over it,' he said reassuringly. 'The arm is more worrying.'

'It itches, but the salve you put on it when we got to Montreuil seems to be working.'

'You'll have a scar for a bit. But it's not permanent.'

'A scar, a black eye, an abduction, my life threatened. . .and you were the one who dared to tell me that an acquaintance with *me* led to complications! But I dare say you've forgotten that.'

He grew very still. 'I think I remember everything you've ever told me.' His fist came down on the rail. 'I wish to heaven I could see my way out of the coil I'm in,' he said violently. 'I've been such a fool. I never realised, you see. . .'

'What, Charles?'

'That I would fall in love. Really fall in love, with someone who would share. . .everything.'

Serafina almost told him then. But a desire to wait, to postpone what was bound to be a difficult scene until they were in the privacy of her home, held her back. She put her hand over his. 'It might turn out all right,' she said.

'How? How can I make Serafina so unhappy? It would be better to give both of you up.' He swore under his breath, then as a gust of wind sent the boat heeling over to one side he said, 'You'd better go in, Sally. It's dangerous. And in any case you mustn't stay out here with me any longer.'

She went to go. He drew her back and held her against him for a long moment. 'Oh, Sally, Sally!' he groaned. Then he turned her round, kissed her very gently, and then released her.

* * *

They got into Dover very late. It had always been unlikely that they could get to Hardington in one day, but the delay made it impossible. Charles was taciturn, wrapped in his own thoughts, and Madame Houblon still felt queasy. The time spent in driving along poor roads through Hythe and Winchelsea to Hastings seemed endless. They spent the night there and went on the next day to Hardington, arriving at Feverel Place in the early afternoon. Serafina was relieved to see the house full of activity—her family was back from Brighton.

'Sally! Sally! Where have you been? What's wrong with your face?' The children came running out to greet her, full of questions which the travellers ignored for the moment. They got out stiffly and Serafina helped Madame Houblon up the steps. Mr Feverel was in the hall. In contrast to the children, he appeared to be neither surprised nor delighted to see them.

Charles was businesslike. He checked that Mr Feverel had received his message, and said that he was in a desperate hurry to get to Portsmouth. Serafina introduced Madame Houblon, and said that she was on her way to London. The children's eyes were growing rounder by the minute, until their father sent them away. 'Lord Aldworth——'

'Sir, I am deeply conscious that I owe you all sorts of explanations. And I intend to satisfy you. But I have a very urgent commission in Portsmouth which cannot be delayed. Sally will explain. It will take three days only. On the third day I shall be here again, when I shall be pleased to answer all your questions. May I ask your kindness for Madame Houblon? She is very tired after our long journey and needs rest, otherwise I would have taken her with me to Brighton now. May I——dare I ask your help in getting her there tomorrow for the London Mail? She has done some service to your daughter.'

'I shall be pleased to help *madame*,' said Mr Feverel with a brief smile for the lady. Then he added somewhat grimly, 'And I shall expect you in three days' time.'

Charles said goodbye to Serafina at the door of the chaise. Their parting was necessarily brief and unemotional.

'I have left some salve for your arm with your other luggage. Keep using it. And the bruise on your face is fading. I'm sorry, Sally—for everything. At the moment I have no idea what to do and, to tell you the truth, I am glad not to have seen your sister, though it is surprising. She was not expecting us, of course.'

'I. . . She is possibly out somewhere. Our arrival was, as you say, unexpected. I am sure she will be here waiting for you when you return.'

His face shadowed over. 'Yes. Goodbye, Sally. I shan't forget these past days—ever.'

'You must go. Goodbye, Charles.'

When the chaise disappeared from sight, Serafina felt desolate. The family crowded round her again, demanding to know of her adventures, but all she could think was that Charles had gone. The idyll—for it had been an idyll—was over. Never again would she and Charles share their laughter, exchange their thoughts with such perfect freedom. She would never again experience the passion which had been aroused in her by his kisses, never know its fulfilment. When

Charles returned in three days' time she could no longer postpone telling him the truth.

'Serafina!' It was her father. 'Your mother wishes to speak to you. But first I should like a word, if you please. In the small study.' Serafina did not remember when he had last used such a tone to her. Though Mr Feverel had been civil enough during the arrival and departure of Lord Aldworth, his manner had been cold. He was clearly holding fire until he could have a full explanation from his daughter's fiancé on his return from Portsmouth. But now it became evident that he was, in fact, very angry, and it was an ominous sign that the interview was to take place in the study, and not in the library. Mr Feverel's library was a place for reading, repose and discussion—never for anything unpleasant.

'We shall be brief, Serafina. Your mother is waiting to see you, and I do not wish to keep her in suspense for much longer. But first I should like an explanation of these.' He handed her three pieces of paper. Two were on official embassy notepaper, the other was from Lady Chilham. Serafina read them. The two official ones were as Charles had said. He explained that Sally was with him and safe, and in the one to London he asked Serafina to go down to Feverel Place immediately. Lady Chilham had sent it, unopened, together with a letter of her own. Presumably Charles's letter to Serafina had been opened and read by her father.

'Your mother has not seen these. Fortunately, since we have ourselves only just come back from Brighton, we did not receive them immediately—they were waiting for us here. I cannot imagine how your mother would have felt if she had known earlier that you were not safe with Lady Chilham as we thought, but had disappeared into the blue. Lady Chilham herself, as you will see from her letter, was very distressed. You had told her you were coming home here, and she had assumed that was the case. She had written to us, and was waiting to hear, when this letter arrived from the embassy in Paris. I have already written to Lady Chilham to set her mind at rest.' There was a pause. Then he said, 'What does it all mean, Serafina? And why is Lord Aldworth still of the belief that there are two of you?'

Serafina was forced yet again to confess that she had still not disabused Lord Aldworth.

'But the matter is getting out of all bounds! Now you have involved the embassy and heaven knows who else in your ridiculous masquerade! I shall have things to say to Lord Aldworth myself when I see him again, but before I do you will meet him here and tell him, without prevarication, what you have been doing. How you have managed to sustain the deception I cannot imagine. Lord Aldworth seemed to me to be a sensible man when I met him here. He is apparently not only dishonourable, but a fool as well.'

'He is far from dishonourable, Papa! The whole thing was my fault!' And Serafina gave her father a necessarily brief outline of the reasons both for her actions and those of Lord Aldworth.

Her father listened intently, then said slowly, 'I don't understand all of this—you must tell me again. But now you must see your mother. Remember that she knows nothing of these letters.'

'But what shall I say?'

'That is for you to decide, Serafina,' said her father,

becoming angry again. 'You are the clever one in inventing half-truths. See if you can satisfy your mother with them. And don't upset her! And don't tell her any lies, either!'

'But Papa——'

'Save your breath for your mother! And put something on your face to hide that bruise!' He went out.

Serafina was relieved that her father's instruction gave her an excuse to go to her room. She would have a moment or two to recover some of her spirits—in her present state, her mother would have the whole story out of her in two minutes. The loss of her father's regard was a bitter blow. When the full explanation was made to him he would see reason about her escapade in France, particularly as it had been for a noble cause. He would think better of Charles, too, when he learned how much Charles had done to protect her good name. But when that was all finished her father would still condemn her for her unforgiveable omission to tell Charles the truth.

When Serafina finally plucked up her courage and sought her mother out she was pleased, even in her distress, to see that the sojourn in Brighton appeared to have done her a great deal of good. She was sitting by the window, entertaining Madame Houblon. The two were talking animatedly as Serafina entered.

'My dear!' Mrs Feverel embraced Serafina warmly, and made her sit down on the stool in front of her. 'Madame Houblon has been telling me such a tale! I gather you were the toast of Paris! But how is this, Serafina? Paris? And what about the villains who threatened your lives?'

Serafina saw that her father's warnings had been

unnecessary. Before she had had a chance to prevaricate to her mother, Madame Houblon had revealed enough to make it impossible. But, instead of frightening Mrs Feverel, the news seemed to have excited and interested her. With a look at Madame Houblon, Serafina said, 'Mama, I will tell you everything—and I have the loveliest dress you have ever seen to show you. But Madame Houblon must be tired, and I think we should see her comfortably installed in her room, don't you?'

Madame Houblon was shepherded away and Serafina was left alone with her mother.

'I think you are suffering from the journey too, my love. I think it would be as well if we left all these explanations till tomorrow, after our guest has gone. I shall tell the others that you are to rest for now. But tell me, Serafina—is all well with you?'

CHAPTER THIRTEEN

WHEN Serafina remained silent Mrs Feverel said anxiously, 'It is not, I can see. What is wrong, Serafina?'

Serafina hesitated, then said, 'I expect I am tired, Mama.'

'Ah, my child, don't! Don't shut me out!'

'But I promised Papa! And he is angry enough with me!'

Mrs Feverel smiled lovingly and said, 'We both know that your papa cossets me far too much. I am really feeling very well at the moment. And if you were to hide the truth from me, purely out of consideration for my health, that would upset me more than almost anything you could tell me. We shall leave the account of your adventures till tomorrow. Tell me for now why you are so unhappy.'

The tears came then. 'Oh, Mama!' sobbed Serafina. 'I have been deceitful and sly, I know. But the punishment is so very hard! First Charles, and now Papa.'

Slowly Mrs Feverel pieced together Serafina's somewhat incoherent confession. 'So you still haven't told Lord Aldworth about Sally-Serafina and, though you believe him to be as much in love with you as you are with him, you're sure he will repudiate you when he hears the truth. Is that it? And you are upset because Papa is angry with you too?' When Serafina nodded mutely she went on, 'He has some reason, my love.

You have put him in an impossible position with Lord Aldworth.'

Serafina stared at her mother with tear-drenched eyes. 'I hadn't thought of that! Oh, Mama, what shall I do?'

'I think I can mend the rift between you and Papa. But Lord Aldworth...the case is not absolutely hopeless, but I fear it will need time. You are right—he will probably be hurt and very angry with you at first. But don't despair—gentlemen need time to forget damage to their pride, but if he truly loves you he will come round eventually. Now, I think you should go to your room, and I shall tell Hetty to bring you something on a tray for tonight. Tomorrow is another day, my dear.'

Mrs Feverel had obviously done some sterling work on her husband. After Madame Houblon had said her farewells and departed in the Feverel coach for Brighton the children were dispatched on a walk, much to Angelica's disgust, and Serafina and her parents sat together in Mrs Feverel's room. In the clear morning light her mother could see the remains of the bruise on her cheek, and demanded to know how it had been caused. Serafina gave both of them a full account of her adventures, trying as she did so to explain how impossible she had always found it to tell Lord Aldworth the truth.

Her father listened intently, then said, 'Well, Sally, I confess I was angry with you—and I am still not pleased with your continued deception. But I will say that I am proud of your courage. And invention.'

'I am full of admiration and gratitude, too,' said Mrs

Feverel, 'for the care Lord Aldworth seems to have taken for Serafina's reputation.'

'Sally's reputation,' said Mr Feverel somewhat grimly.

'It was unfortunate that the ambassador found you both at St Germain, but what a triumph it led to!' said Mrs Feverel. Then her lips twitched and she started to laugh. 'But...but tell me, my dear Machiavellian daughter, how did you feel when Lord Aldworth asked you to pretend to be Serafina?'

Mr Feverel started chuckling too, and at the end he embraced Serafina and said, 'I have to forgive you, Sally. The situation must have been worthy of the best Greek farces. But...' he grew serious again '...I don't envy your having to confess to Aldworth after that episode. He will feel that you made a complete fool of him.'

Behind Serafina's back Mrs Feverel was shaking her head at her tactless husband. Then she said swiftly, 'We must decide how much to tell the children. They would enjoy a somewhat expurgated version—the villains for Rafe and Michael, and the ball for Angelica. Where is the famous dress?'

Serafina jumped up and ran to fetch it, but came back a few minutes later with a downcast face. 'The box isn't with the things I brought from France! Yet I know it was in the chaise... Charles must have taken it with him! I'm sorry, Mama—you will have to wait till he...till he comes back.'

The next day Serafina was in a fever of apprehension. Charles would be here before the day was out. Her feelings were not helped by her father, who invited her to his library to discuss what she was going to say.

'I shall see Aldworth first, Sally. And I have decided to tell him that, as far as I am concerned, he is to act as he sees fit.'

'You're going to tell him about me?'

'No, I think you must do that, though, if you wish, I shall stay with you while you do. But I cannot in all honour hold him to his word to marry you. If he still wishes to do so I shall be delighted, of course.' Her father's tone did not show any great optimism.

'I shall see him alone, Papa,' Serafina said unhappily.

Lord Aldworth was prompt. He came back to Feverel Place in the late afternoon and, though he must have been travelling for a major part of the three days since they had seen him last, he looked as immaculate as ever. Serafina watched him through the window of the small parlour which adjoined the library. He was carrying her dress-box. After a moment she heard his voice in the hall, refusing refreshment, explaining that he had called in at Blanchards before coming. Then the library door shut. Serafina waited in dread for it to open again.

It seemed an age before Charles was shown into the parlour, by which time Serafina's delicate lace handkerchief was torn to shreds. When he came in she was standing with her back to the window, in the shadow of the heavy velvet curtains.

'Serafina,' he said gravely, and came over to kiss her hand.

Serafina's throat was so dry that her reply was lost. She curtsied in silence. Charles took a step back and said, 'Serafina, I have concluded from what your father has just said to me that he does not hold me to my promise to you—that your sister has already told you of...of what happened between us in France. I can't express to you how ashamed that made me feel.'

He stopped and Serafina said, 'Charles, I——' But he interrupted her.

'I would have given anything in the world not to have hurt you, but I believe it would hurt you much more to be married to a man who is fond of you, but ...who is in love with someone else. Your own sister, in fact. It would be a damnable situation, and you are worthy of better than that. The same applies to Sally. Though I... Though my feelings towards her won't change, I don't intend to ask her to marry me either. She is young—she will no doubt forget me in time— and I... I will not allow myself to be a cause for distress and disharmony in such a close-knit family as yours.' A sob escaped Serafina. He said desperately, 'Oh, my dear, don't! I am not worth it! You will find someone else, I swear—someone who will love you as you deserve.'

'Charles, listen to me——' She put her hand on his arm and the Paisley shawl she was wearing fell back, revealing the long scar made by Juan's knife. He stared at it.

'What the devil...?' He took her chin in his hand and examined her face. 'Sally!' There was a dreadful silence. Then he said in a voice trembling with anger, 'What the hell do you think you are doing? This is not a matter for tricks and play-acting. Not for me! How dare you, Sally? How could you?'

She must tell him now—she must. Serafina opened

her mouth but the words simply would not come. She shuddered and hid her face in her hands. Another sob escaped her.

'Oh, my darling, don't!' He held her to him and hugged her close. 'Can't you see the situation is impossible? I've thought about this till I was almost out of my mind, but I can't marry you after rejecting Serafina. You would have to live estranged from your family for the rest of your life. You could never be really happy again, even if we were together. But Sally——' He gently removed his hands from her face and lifted her chin. 'Sally, I can't imagine not loving you. Whatever happens you've become part of me, and it will be the hardest thing I've ever done in my life to leave you.' His eyes were on her mouth again. Her heart lurched and the world went spinning round as he kissed her. She gave a little cry and threw her arms round his neck, pressing close to him, seeking comfort, raining little kisses on his face, trying to reassure herself that if they loved each other as much as this he would—he must— forgive her. And all the time tears rolled down her cheeks.

'Sally, oh, Sally!' Charles practically lifted her off her feet as he kissed her again with desperate passion. 'If you knew how I've longed to do this! If you knew how much I adore you, how damnable it will be to part from you!' He held her tightly, then gradually his passion faded and his grasp was more gentle. Slowly he released her. 'This is doing neither of us any good. Let me think for a moment. If Serafina were to find someone else, I suppose then... But it might be years. Would you wait? I have no right to ask you that. And

I must see your sister before I say more. My darling, lovely girl, I must see your sister. Will you fetch her?'

This was the moment. No evasion, no escape. She swallowed and said quietly, 'My sister is here, Charles. I am Serafina.' There was a silence while he looked at her blankly, almost as if he suspected her of another trick. 'And I am Sally too. We are one person—we always were.'

The silence this time was longer and even more dreadful. Then he said, 'Oh, my God!' and walked away from her to the other side of the little room. He stood with his back towards her for a moment or two, then he turned and said, 'All the time... Oh, God! What a fool I've been! All that heart-searching, all the sleepless nights...the agonies. That ridiculous speech I've just made... You heartless, lying little jade; you were laughing at me all that time!'

'I wasn't!'

'Of course you were!' His anger grew. 'Enjoying the power you had over me, hugging your secret knowledge to yourself, watching every sign of self-reproach, self-recrimination... Oh, my God, I even had to persuade you to pretend you were Serafina in France! Hell's teeth, how you must have laughed to yourself then. You... Jezebel!'

'Please, Charles——'

'Don't talk to me! Don't say one word!' His voice trembled with the intensity of his feelings. 'You could not persuade me to think differently, whatever you said. Why, Louisa Paget is an innocent in comparison to you!'

'Charles!'

'Why did you do it? For some unimaginably cruel prank?'

'No! It started because you came back early from Vienna and caught me in that tree. I had to pretend I wasn't Serafina.'

'Ah, yes! Of course. The rich Lord Aldworth was too great a prize to risk losing?'

'Yes,' said Serafina, and could not think of another word to say. This was no time to talk of love. He was angry, so his words were harsh, but the substance of what he said was no less than the truth. She deserved his anger. He came back to her and she winced as he took her chin in a cruel grip and his eyes blazed into hers.

'Oh, that look of melting reproach! You had me fooled with that one—you were very convincing. And Sally's nobility in defence of Serafina—how did it go?' His voice mimicked hers in cruel mockery. '"Charles, you must not... It isn't fair—either to me or to Serafina. And we have a long road to Paris." Damn you, exercising self-control on the long road to Paris almost killed me! Did you not know that? Did it please you?' He thrust her away from him. 'Of course not— you were disappointed. Now I understand the affecting scene in the clearing, the artless disarray, the carefully dishevelled clothing. You must have been furious with those peasants! If you had succeeded in getting yourself compromised I would have no choice now but to marry you! But, thank God, though you had me so enchanted that I didn't know what day of the week it was, I was lucky.' He stood for a moment, his jaw working. 'Your father knew, didn't he? I see now why he released me from my promise. He at least has some vestiges of honour.'

'Vestige? How dare you? My father has always insisted that I should tell you. Mine was the fault, not his! Take that back, Lord Aldworth.'

'Or what? You'll break off our engagement? You are too late—it's broken, irretrievably broken, Serafina. Or do you prefer to be called Sally? Whichever it is, it doesn't really matter—I shall not be using either again. Indeed, I hope never to see you again.' He strode towards the door.

'Charles!' He stopped, his back towards her, and she took a step towards him. 'I did love you, Charles.'

His voice was icy as he said, 'You don't know the meaning of the word. If you had loved me, you would have told me the truth long ago. Goodbye, Miss Feverel!'

He turned on his heel and walked out of the room. Serafina was fixed to the spot. She could neither call after him nor follow him. She stood there, listening to the sounds of his departure—the curt excuses, her father uttering conventional words of farewell, the sound of his horse on the drive—then silence. Her heart was filled with that silence. It spread chillingly throughout her body till she was shivering. She was still standing there, still shivering, when her father came back into the parlour.

In the weeks that followed Serafina showed true courage—not the impulsive, headlong courage which had launched her into her foreign adventures, but steady, dogged, determined courage. She devoted her time and energy to her family—accompanying the children on their walks, helping her mother wherever she could, and working with her father in his library. She sat late into the night, studying mathematics and logic and puzzling over problems of philosophy, though she never opened any of the books of literature and poetry of which she had been so fond. Her family grew to dread Serafina's determinedly cheerful conversation at mealtimes, to wince at the heartbreaking artificiality of her laughter, and to avoid comment on the pitifully small amount she ate. Mr and Mrs Feverel had many private discussions about her, but Mr Feverel deferred to his wife's judgement in the matter and was patient. Something would turn up. It had to, before his beloved daughter faded away completely.

What turned up eventually was a visitor, in the form of Lady Chilham. Mrs Feverel had succeeded in making her invitation so persuasive that Serafina's godmother had agreed to overlook the manner in which she had been treated, and had come down to give her god-daughter the chance to apologise. Which Serafina did, soberly and sincerely.

'I see what you meant, Sarah,' said Lady Chilham when Serafina left them. 'The child will soon vanish altogether. And those eyes! We must do something.'

'Is Lord Aldworth in London?'

'At the moment he is in Berkshire, but Lady Aldworth says he is coming to London soon.'

'You still see Lady Aldworth?'

'Oh, yes! She is as anxious as ever to see Aldworth married. To Serafina, too. But—I have to say it, if I die for it—I cannot see that happening.'

'Would you. . .could you invite Serafina to stay with

you for a little? I know it is almost impertinent of me to ask, knowing how angry you were with her, but. . .'

'Now that you have told me more of the story I see that what she did was pardonable in the circumstances, I suppose. In any case, I would have to be an inhuman monster not to wish to help her now. But would she come?'

'I think I could persuade her. Could she return with you?'

'Of course. I'll leave it to you to ask her, then. I'll do anything you recommend.'

'What do you intend to do with the rest of your life, my dear?'

Serafina and her mother were sitting on the terrace outside Mrs Feverel's room. Lady Chilham had gone for the day to Brighton, taking Angelica with her, to see the Prince Regent's seaside pavilion.

'I. . . I don't know, Mama. I thought I would stay here with you.'

'That's a dull life for a beautiful young girl. Have you totally abandoned the thought of saving the family fortunes?'

'I cannot marry—ever!'

'For a sensible, rational girl, such as you have always claimed you are, that seems to me to be a most irrational statement. Forgive me if I give you pain, but since you have obviously given up the idea of any reconciliation with Lord Aldworth——'

'What makes you say so?' said Serafina, startled.

'You are not making the slightest push to meet him again.'

'He will refuse to meet me.'

'How can he change his mind about you while you remain in Sussex and he is eighty miles away in Berkshire? I doubt he will come to Blanchards again—not for some time anyway.'

'I couldn't face him, Mama!' said Serafina desperately.

'In that case, why not see if there is in London another gentleman who is more like the ideal you described once—a rational, sensible man of reasonable means? Perhaps you might eventually find it possible to marry him? Believe me, it is not comfortable being a spinster without an establishment of one's own. Love is not necessary; look for respect, interests in common—all the things you mentioned once before. And if Lord Aldworth should see you. . .who knows?'

'I could not go to London, even supposing that Lady Chilham would entertain the idea, if I thought that Charles was to be there.'

Mrs Feverel bent her head over her embroidery. 'Your godmother tells me he is in Berkshire. And. . . she would like you to stay with her again, Serafina.'

So it was that Serafina came to stay once again in the house in Curzon Street.

The London season was now in full swing. Parties, balls, routs, drums, *fêtes-champêtres*—nothing was lacking. The débutantes which Lady Aldworth had once decided she could not wait for were there in force, hoping to make a suitable match—even an advantageous one. But in spite of her unhappiness Serafina still outclassed them all. Her pallor, her fragility aroused a strong desire in the hearts of the gentlemen who met her to cherish her, to protect her against the slightest breeze. And, though she no longer adopted any false poses and was her natural self, she was sufficiently subdued not to arouse comment on changes in her manner. Miss Feverel might not be the sensation of the season she had promised fair to be earlier in the year, but she was soon an accredited beauty.

She had seen nothing of Charles, nor anything of Lady Paget. When she enquired about the latter she was told that Lady Paget had rejoined her husband, and was not expected to be back in England before the following year, when Sir Robert was due to retire from public life. The former she did not mention. Slowly a little of her heartache disappeared. She found herself taking more of an interest in the world around her, even paying visits, now quite openly, to the sights she had wanted to see. She began to believe herself cured—or curable, at least.

She met several men—young and old—who seemed interested in forming a closer relationship with the lovely Miss Feverel, and she did not reject them out of hand, as she secretly wished to do. She accepted invitations to exhibitions, balls, and all the rest, but not one of her partners could claim that he was favoured more than his rivals. Lady Chilham began to despair.

'You must not let Lord Aldworth ruin your life, child!'

'You mistake that matter, Godmother. I have very nearly forgotten him!'

'Then why don't you accept Blake? He's rich, eligible— and very attentive. What more do you want?'

'He hasn't asked me!'

'You could have him do so with a snap of your fingers! Don't think you can put me off, Serafina.'

'But I don't want to be tied down yet—I enjoy the fuss everyone makes of me. I promise to think about it—later.'

Then one evening, when Serafina was changing, Lady Chilham came into her bedroom looking distinctly anxious. 'I. . . I have to tell you, my love, that Aldworth is in London. He's been working at the Foreign Office for the past week, though no one has seen him socially. Now Laura Clifton tells me he will very likely be at Home House tonight. Do you wish to cry off?'

Serafina had grown pale but she looked calmly enough at her godmother. 'I don't think so. I have to see him again some time, I suppose. Don't worry, Godmother. I shan't create a scene.'

'I never thought that for one moment! You may have had shortcomings in the past, but lack of breeding was never one of them. Put your prettiest dress on.'

Serafina smiled wryly. Her prettiest dress would never be worn again. It was here in London because her mother had insisted on her bringing it. But it would stay in its Parisian box. With a sigh she called the maid and continued with her preparations. She did, however, put on an extremely becoming white dress with flounces of net trimmed with Chinese roses. Looking her best would give her courage. And she broke her rule and allowed Martha to put the merest whisper of colour in her cheeks. . .

Lady Chilham seemed almost more nervous than she was. 'Remember, there is no need for you to be more than conventionally polite to him, should you meet. To ignore him altogether would rouse comment. . .'

Serafina hardly heard her. Her heart was racing, and her mother's words were ringing in her ears—'How can he change his mind about you while you remain in Sussex and he is eighty miles away in Berkshire?' Well, Charles was now less than a mile away. Perhaps her mother was right. Perhaps this evening might be the beginning of a reconciliation.

Events at Home House were always well-attended—the Countess was a generous and popular hostess—and tonight was no exception. As usual, Serafina was soon surrounded, but all the same she caught a glimpse of a familiar face in the crowd making his way purposefully towards her. What was Mr Ashleigh doing in London? When he reached her he made a charming bow, and in the teeth of all her admirers asked her to dance with him. To their chagrin, she awarded his audacity with a delightful smile and went with him. As they made their way to the ballroom he said, 'This is a real pleasure seeing you here, Miss Feverel. But where is Charles?'

Behind her a voice said, 'Here, David. So you're in London again!' Serafina jumped and dropped her fan. Both men bent to retrieve it, but Lord Aldworth stepped back immediately and left it to Mr Ashleigh to return it. Then, looking at her with all the warmth of an Arctic sea, he said, 'Good evening, Miss Feverel.'

She was unforgiven. David Ashleigh was looking puzzled and embarrassed. 'Er—I don't quite. . .'

'Understand?' said Serafina with a bright smile. 'Haven't you heard, Mr Ashleigh? Lord Aldworth and I have decided that we should not suit after all. Pray don't let us miss the beginning of the set! Lord Aldworth.' She nodded and walked gracefully away. With another puzzled look at Charles Mr Ashleigh followed her.

*　*　*

Charles followed them—with his eyes. That damned woman still had the power to stir his heart in a manner no other could. But he would master the feeling, if it killed him. She was a lying cheat, and he was better off without her. Look at her now—flirting with young Ashleigh, who was looking as besotted as he himself had been. Well, Ashleigh would cope—he was not likely to be as great an idiot as Charles Dacre. No man was likely to be as great an idiot! He turned away in disgust, and left Home House shortly after.

Serafina danced gaily to the end of the set, and accepted with gratitude her partner's offer to fetch her a cool drink. He escorted her to a table in one of the ante-rooms, and disappeared. Serafina sank back with a shuddering sigh and closed her eyes. On the way to being cured? What a foolish, foolish illusion. The pain was as great as ever.

'Good evening, Miss Feverel.' That soft voice with its silky overtones. . . Her eyes flew open—Barros was standing before her.

'Señor Barros,' she said coldly. 'It should be unnecessary for me to tell you that I do not wish to speak to you. Please leave me.'

'I will—but I thought I should tell you first. . .' He switched to rapid Spanish. 'I have been making enquiries about Miss Serafina Feverel—and her sister, Miss Sally.'

'How dare you?'

'Oh, I have little to lose, *señorita*. My career is already finished. About these enquiries—do you wish to know what I discovered? I will tell you anyway. I now have a very clear picture of what happened at Carlton House and on the quay at Dieppe—though what happened between the two is still somewhat obscure——'

'The quay at Dieppe? Whatever do you mean?'

'You were there.'

'You are talking nonsense, *señor*, and I refuse to hear any more. If you will not leave me, then I must leave you.' She rose to go.

'How is your sister, Miss Feverel. Not the non-existent Sally, but the equally non-existent Arlette? I hate to remind you of the unfortunate occurrences in the Forest of Crecy, but Juan saw you there and was certain that he had seen you before. So was Luis. It seemed impossible, of course, but once we started making enquiries in Dieppe we found it was not so impossible to establish the facts.'

Serafina saw Mr Ashleigh making his way towards them through the crowds. She said disdainfully, 'I suppose you are thinking to blackmail me with these lies.'

Barros looked at her sombrely. 'I am a Spaniard, *señorita*. You have ruined me with your tricks. Now you will pay—but not in money.' He walked swiftly away, slipping with ease through the throng.

'Are you all right?' Mr Ashleigh was regarding her with concern.

'I...yes, thank you. Of course. The heat...'

'I'm sorry I was so long. There's a frightful crowd here.'

'There always is.'

He handed her a glass of lemonade. 'I thought you would prefer this to champagne. But if you would like something stronger...'

'No, no, this is delicious.' Serafina made an effort to

pull herself together. 'How long are you expecting to be in London, Mr Ashleigh?'

'I'll be working at the Foreign Office for a month or so. I'm fortunate—I've come bang in the middle of the season.' He hesitated and said, 'I should like to call on you tomorrow, if I may? But for now I think I should find Lady Chilham and take you home. Forgive me for saying so, but you do not look at all the thing, Miss Feverel.'

'Nonsense,' she cried. 'It's only the heat. Pray do not make a fuss, Mr Ashleigh—my godmother will take me home soon, I promise you.' With that he had to be content, and it was soon evident that Serafina intended to enjoy the rest of the evening to the full. But Mr Ashleigh was no fool. As he watched her dancing, laughing and, it had to be admitted, delicately flirting, he contrasted what he saw with the girl at the ball in Paris. That girl had been totally, delightfully relaxed and natural. The London Miss Feverel was as brittle as fine glass—one breath and she would shatter.

Mr Ashleigh called the next day with a handsome bouquet, and the determination to have some private words with Miss Feverel. He persuaded her to come for a drive with him, and in no time they were bowling through the streets towards Hyde Park. In Paris they had discovered a mutual interest in books and they chatted on this topic for some minutes. Then he said carefully, 'I've been working with Charles this past week.'

'Really?' said Serafina. 'Do look at those children, Mr Ashleigh—are they not delightful?'

'He is rapidly acquiring the reputation of being the hardest taskmaster in London. And the least civil.'

'Charles?' Serafina was startled out of her pose of indifference. 'I find that hard to believe. He was always the epitome of courtesy.' Except when roused to anger with her, she thought.

'There are some who say he has been disappointed in love.'

'Mr Ashleigh,' said Serafina rapidly, 'please go no further. Lord Aldworth's feelings are no longer my concern.' Then she spoilt everything by saying wistfully, 'Is he really unhappy, would you say?'

'Very. Oh, I am aware that it is none of my business, but I have always had such admiration for Charles's work. He was very kind to me, too, when I first started. He. . .he is the best of fellows, Miss Feverel. . .'

'I know,' said Serafina, and looked at him with such misery in her eyes that he drew his breath in. 'But you cannot possibly understand—or mend—the situation between us.'

'Forgive me,' he said. 'It was an unwarrantable intrusion.'

After that he took pains to make light conversation until they returned to Lady Chilham's.

Lady Chilham's maids did not know of Serafina's determination to leave the dress she had worn in Paris undisturbed in its box, and one day one of them took it out to be pressed, so that it would be ready for use when needed. Serafina was shortly afterwards confronted in her bedroom by a weeping maidservant, who was holding the dress over her arm and something in her hand.

'I'm ever so sorry, miss. I handled it ever so gentle—

but this here bead come off. And now I can't see where to put it back on! Nowhere looks right to me.' She held the bead out.

'It's all right, Martha. That didn't come off this dress at all. It's green. Give it to me and take the dress back. I'll see if I can think where it comes from.' Martha curtsied and went away, much relieved. Serafina, puzzled, examined the bead. After a moment she lifted her head and sat thinking. Then she went in search of Lady Chilham.

'Godmother, I should like you to examine this. To see if it is what I think.'

Lady Chilham got out her glass and looked carefully at the object Serafina had handed to her. 'Where on earth did you get this?' she asked. 'It's a very fine emerald!'

'I thought as much. They must have hidden the emeralds in my dress-box. That's why the box was missing when he went to Portsmouth. I must send this back to him.'

'Who, Serafina?' asked Lady Chilham patiently. 'What? I don't understand a word you are saying.'

'The emerald doesn't belong to me, ma'am. I must send it back to Lord Aldworth.'

Serafina hurried back to her room, her heart beating excitedly. From what Mr Ashleigh had said Charles was as unhappy as she. Perhaps there was hope for them after all? And returning the emerald was a heaven-sent opportunity to communicate with him. She wrapped the jewel, and penned a short note—one which was formal, rather than friendly, but which left room for him to reply kindly if he chose. The two were dispatched with a messenger to Berkeley Square.

CHAPTER FOURTEEN

THE next day Serafina waited with eagerness for Lord Aldworth's reply. When it came she ran to her room and tore open the letter. A small package fell out. Stunned, she read:

> Lord Aldworth presents his compliments to Miss Feverel. He thanks her for the emerald, but is returning it herewith. He is sure that the British Government would not wish her efforts towards the success of his recent mission to go unrewarded.

The note was simply signed 'Aldworth'.

Fuming with rage, Serafina dashed off another note, equally brief:

> Miss Feverel thanks Lord Aldworth for his charming letter. However, service to one's country is its own reward. She regrets that she could not possibly keep anything which reminds her of an episode in her life she would far rather forget. The emerald is returned.

After that she found it easier to move about in Society, undeterred by the fear of meeting Lord Aldworth. She had torn him out of her heart, and his place was occupied by a rage which sustained her through all their meetings. She scorned to avoid him or ignore him. She was as coldly polite as he was himself. She heard no more from Barros, and had indeed totally forgotten about him, consumed as she was by her fury at Lord Aldworth.

But Barros had not forgotten her. He had already set in motion the wheels of his revenge.

The first whispers about Miss Feverel floated through Society and were ignored. Then someone in the French embassy confirmed that Miss Feverel had indeed been in France with Lord Aldworth, apparently engaged to him. The scandalmongers did not have long to enjoy that snippet before they were disappointed to hear that Miss Feverel had, quite properly, been a guest of the Comte de Brecy and his wife, and that, though she had travelled back to England in Lord Aldworth's company, a connection of the Brecys had chaperoned her on the journey.

Quite where the next bit came from no one ever learned. But soon all London seemed to know that the Brecy story was only half true—a fabrication, invented in an attempt to protect Miss Feverel's good name. In fact—and everyone had this on good authority—she had been jaunting through France with Aldworth, unattended. A whole week, said the gossips with scandalised delight, completely alone with one of Europe's most dangerous charmers! That she had clearly failed to hold him to any promises he might have made to her was obvious—you only had to look to see that he hardly exchanged the time of day with her now. Poor, poor Miss Feverel! She was completely ruined, of course, unless Aldworth made an honest woman of her, and that, in view of his past history, seemed unlikely.

Although most of Society's disapproval was directed towards Miss Feverel, Lord Aldworth did not entirely escape blame. Until now the objects of his gallantries had all been mature women of the world, and always already married. Society had not altogether condemned him for enjoying the favours of ladies who were so obviously able to take care of themselves. But in this case it was generally felt that he had taken advantage of someone who was young, inexperienced and, not to put too fine a point on it, not very clever.

The victims of scurrilous rumours were often the last to become aware of them, and Serafina was no exception to this rule. The first she heard was when Lady Aldworth called at Curzon Street and asked to have a private talk with her. She was happy to meet the Dowager again, for she had enjoyed their exchanges in the past, but she was also surprised. Surely Lady Aldworth could not still be cherishing the hope that her grandson would marry her? It was now obvious to all London that any attentions Lord Aldworth might have paid to Miss Feverel in the past were over, and that the pair were completely indifferent to each other! Still, she received Lady Aldworth cordially, and was puzzled to find that her visitor's manner was distinctly chilly.

'How may I serve you, Lady Aldworth?' she asked when they were seated.

'You can tell me if there is any truth in what they are saying about you and my grandson,' said Lady Aldworth bluntly.

Serafina said cautiously, 'I am not sure I understand what you mean, ma'am.'

'Of course you do—don't prevaricate with me, miss! Is it true that the pair of you attended a ball at the

British embassy in Paris claiming to be officially engaged?'

'Er...yes,' said Serafina.

'Why was I not informed of this "official" engagement?'

'The circumstances...'

'Is it true that you stayed for nearly two weeks with Armand de Brecy and his wife?'

Serafina said carefully, 'I stayed with Monsieur and Madame de Brecy before the ball, yes.'

'For nearly two weeks, Miss Feverel?'

There was a pause. Then Serafina said, 'Before I answer any more questions I should like to know why you are asking them, ma'am. They seem a little pointless in view of the fact that Lord Aldworth and I no longer think of marrying.'

'You left London soon after Charles—the day after the reception at Carlton House, in fact. You were next seen at the embassy in Paris, about twelve days later. It is being said in London's clubs and drawing-rooms that you spent a major part of the time in between with Charles—alone. The world thinks you were indulging in a little romantic idyll with him, Miss Feverel,' said Lady Aldworth.

Serafina could not disguise her shock. The colour left her cheeks and she drew in a deep breath.

Lady Aldworth regarded her for a moment, then said, 'You don't deny it?'

'I... I will tell you nothing.'

'So it's true! I would never have believed it...' She got up and said with undisguised contempt, 'You're a fool, girl. That's not the way to win my grandson—he can enjoy that sort of liaison any time he wishes, and has frequently done so in the past.' As she walked to the door she added, 'I thought you cleverer than that. It seems I was mistaken in your brains as well as in your character. Good morning!'

Serafina felt both frightened and angry. 'I suppose you would agree that I have a right to defend myself?'

'What can you possibly say? The world has no time for excuses. If the rumour is well-founded, you are ruined, Miss Feverel, whatever the excuse. You would only be redeemed if Charles were to marry you as soon as possible. Even if, as I suspect, you had become embroiled in Charles's mission, and the time spent in France was not your fault—even then, the world would still not forgive you. As I have already told you, I think you have been a fool.' She paused. 'I will do my best with Charles, however. He ought to do something for you.' Then she went out without waiting for any more.

Lady Chilham, who had been out when the Dowager arrived, now came hurrying in. 'Serafina! Oh, my poor girl! You must send for Aldworth immediately! Indeed, I am surprised he has not already called.'

'Why, Godmother?'

'Somehow or other what happened in France has become public knowledge—Lady Clifton was saying——'

'I already know what they are saying. Lady Aldworth was here just now, and was. . .kind enough to tell me everything. She did not trouble to hide her disapproval.'

'How dared she? If she knew what you had done for her beloved grandson. . .'

'It would make little difference. She told me I had been a fool. I think she condemns me more for that than for any possible misdemeanour in France,' Serafina said wearily.

'Serafina, this is not the time for self-pity. I shall write to your father immediately, of course. Aldworth will be here very soon, I am sure, to offer you the protection of his name—he is, after all a man of honour—but it is as well to be prepared.'

'You believe Lord Aldworth will ask me to marry him? When he thinks so little of me?'

'That has nothing to do with it. He must!'

'And if I do not wish to?'

Lady Chilham was scandalised. 'Don't be so ridiculous! It does not come into question. You must!'

'It seems that Lord Aldworth and I are about to be driven into a marriage whether we wish it or not,' said Serafina, half humorously, half in despair, as she left the room.

She went upstairs and sat at the window of her bedroom, staring at the tree outside. But she didn't see the sparrows busy among the leaves, nor the garden below, nor the sky above. She was thinking of what marriage to Lord Aldworth would be like, and contrasting it with what it could have been. Most of the time her face was sad, but a fugitive thought occasionally made her eyes glow, and a tremulous smile appear on her lips. What if. . .? What if this wretched business caused Charles to change his mind about her? If they could rediscover their lost love? Then seconds later she would frown in self-disgust. She was a mindless doll, after all! This was not the time to discover that she still loved him, would marry him with joy if he truly wished her to be his wife. Lord Aldworth had made it only too clear that such miracles did not happen.

When Lady Chilham came bustling into her room in excitement, to tell her that Aldworth was below and wished to see her, she was suddenly in a panic. This was too soon—she had not yet decided what she should do! She said agitatedly, 'I cannot receive him. Tell him to come another time!'

'Serafina! Must I remind you of your predicament? You cannot afford such luxuries. Now, make yourself pretty and come downstairs. I shall talk to him until you are back.'

But when Serafina entered the salon a quarter of an hour later the two people already there did not appear to be finding a great deal to say to each other. Lady Chilham sat by the fireplace looking grave, and Lord Aldworth was staring out of the window. He turned as Serafina came into the room and gave her a small bow. There was no warmth in his expression.

'Well,' said Lady Chilham a touch nervously, 'I am sure you will wish to discuss this matter between yourselves. I shall be in the next room, Serafina.'

She went out, and there was silence. Then Serafina said, 'May I offer you a seat, Lord Aldworth?'

'Thank you, I prefer to stand.'

'As you wish—you will forgive me if I sit down.'

He began abruptly, 'Miss Feverel, I am here to ask you to marry me.'

'Oh? Why?'

'I think you know very well. As we are both now aware, you are far from stupid.'

'But—forgive me if I appear to criticise—you do not sound like a man who wishes to marry me.'

'I do not. But circumstances have made it imperative. It would be unthinkable to allow you to suffer

further censure without my taking measures to end it.
I am not unmindful of the fact that I owe you my life.'
Serafina had forgotten this completely, and it now
seemed slightly irrelevant.

'Pray do not allow that trifle to influence you, Lord
Aldworth.'

'It must.' He paused, then said, 'Quite why these
rumours are spreading through London with such cir-
cumstantial detail I have no idea—perhaps you can
enlighten me? But whatever their source I must silence
them.'

'Perhaps you think I started them,' said Serafina,
twin flags of anger appearing in her cheeks.

'It would be a dangerously risky stratagem. But
then—you have never lacked courage.'

'I suppose it does not occur to you that I might not
wish to marry you?'

'Oh, come!' he said, a sardonic smile on his lips. 'It
was your aim from the beginning. Why else did you try
all those tricks? And now there is every reason for you
to marry as soon as you can. I recognise my obligation.'

Serafina felt as if her heart was being squeezed. The
pain was intense. She said desperately, 'Charles——'

'Oh, no! No tender protestations, I beg you. I am
offering marriage, not. . .not love.'

'You did love me—you said so.'

He paused, then went to the window again. Looking
out, he said, 'I loved a figment of my imagination. A
girl—awonderful, laughing girl—called Sally. She
doesn't exist.' He turned back. 'But Serafina Feverel
exists, and is in need of my name. She can have it—on
the same terms my grandmother offered at the beginning. You see, we have no need of subterfuge now. I

know what you want. You know what I am offering. We shall have a plain, open bargain, with no hidden devices.'

'What is this bargain?'

'I am offering marriage and a very handsome settlement. You will provide me with an heir or two.'

'And while you may not have quite the biddable wife you were seeking, you intend to claim the freedom to live your own life otherwise. Am I right?'

'Exactly. We shouldn't need to see a great deal of each other at all, especially after the children are born. Now, have I your leave to send a notice to the *Gazette*? It should be done without delay.'

'I will not marry you!'

'What did you say?'

'I said I will not marry you. Not on those terms. Not now, and not ever!' He looked astounded, then a flush appeared on his cheeks and he started to stride towards the door. Serafina leapt up and stood in front of him. 'You will do me the courtesy of hearing me out!' She waited until he went to the window again and sat down there, leaning back and crossing his legs with an air of detached patience.

'A short while ago you adopted such a high moral tone with me, Lord Aldworth—accused me of lies and deceit, called me a jade and a. . . Jezebel. And then you removed yourself from my life in the cruellest possible fashion.'

'Forgive me for being plain with you—you deserved it!'

Serafina ignored this interruption and went on, 'At the time I had nothing with which to defend myself— even the love I had for you then could not excuse me.

I *had* deceived you, I *had* lied—if not directly, then certainly by implication. In fact, though I wanted to explain why I had acted as I did, my love for you silenced me, because I felt your pain as much as my own—perhaps more. But that is over!' She stopped and swallowed. 'It is over,' she said.

He stood up and bowed. 'Bravo! This performance is worthy of a bigger audience, Miss Feverel——'

'The only audience I want is one man, Lord Aldworth. If you have any sense of justice left, you will hear me out.'

He shrugged and sat down again.

'Just now,' said Serafina, 'you as good as accused me of deliberately plotting my own downfall in order to entrap you. You have not taken the trouble to disguise the contempt you still feel for me. And yet you ask me to marry you!' She paused, then, her voice trembling with scorn, she said, 'And what a travesty of marriage you are offering!'

She now had his full attention. He looked outraged at her words. 'Travesty or not, how does it differ from the one you were so eager to enter into in the spring?'

'When I first heard of you I thought you arrogant and selfish. I told your grandmother so. But I was prepared to put up with that, to be something like the wife you required, and did my best to learn how. If. . . Sally had never materialised, I would have kept my part of the bargain, though it wouldn't have been easy.'

'Then why is the thought of it so intolerable now?'

'Because last spring I had never known what it was to be in love.'

'Oh, come——'

'And as far as I can judge nor had you. Not the kind

of love which Sally and Charles once had for each other.' Serafina's voice faltered and she turned away. But she soon turned back to him and said clearly, 'This is why I reject your marriage and, indeed, despise you for offering it to me. And why I would rather leave London and retire to Sussex. Now that I know what love can be I will refuse anything less, and if I cannot have the glory, then I will not make do with the dross. The love I had for you may be over, but unless I feel that same unity of spirit with someone else I will die a spinster. Anything less would be a betrayal.'

Lord Aldworth's eyes had not left Serafina's face during this last speech. He got up, started to say something, then stopped. Then he said harshly, 'Beautifully expressed. I still think you deserve a bigger audience. But if you are sincere—I say if—I will tell you that you are fortunate to have that choice, together with the luxury of despising me. I have other obligations. If you persist in refusing to marry me, then sooner or later I will seek and find someone else. I must.'

'I will not change my mind.'

'Your family?'

'They will understand my reasons. You need not fear my father,' she added, curling her lip.

He stiffened. 'I respect your father, whatever I feel for his daughter. If you should find that Sussex is not so ready to accept you, my offer of marriage is still open. But in spite of your attempts to influence me otherwise the bargain remains the same. I too remember the glory. But Serafina has none for me.'

'You mistake me. I have no desire to revive any

feelings between us. As I said before, it is over, Lord
Aldworth. And I will. . .not. . .marry. . .you!'

'In that case there is no more to be said. I will see
myself out, Miss Feverel. Good day.'

Lord Aldworth strode impatiently along Curzon Street
towards Berkeley Square. He could hardly escape fast
enough from yet another occasion when he had been
made to look a fool. How dared Serafina Feverel reject
him? His acquaintance with that wretched girl had
been disastrous from first to last, and the sooner he
was rid of all thought of her the better. He dismissed a
sudden, idiotic fear that her image would never stop
haunting him, destroying his sleep and making the rest
of the world seem grey and valueless—as it did at the
moment, dammit!

David Ashleigh was waiting for him when he got in.
'I've been doing as you asked, Charles. I've had some
of our people looking into the source of those rumours
about yourself and. . .and Miss Feverel.'

'You needn't be so delicate about mentioning the
lady's name,' said Charles brusquely. Then, because
Ashleigh had been doing him a favour, he made an
effort to sound more amiable. 'Have you found anything? You must have, or you wouldn't be here.'

'There's a Spaniard—Barros. He's been poking
about in France—in particular the roads from Dieppe
to Paris. He has some sort of network over there. You
did well to escape from them yourself.'

A sudden vision of Sally in that ridiculous straw hat,
sitting on the cart beside him, her face alive with
laughter, made him wince and turn away from his
visitor. 'I couldn't have done it alone.'

'No. Quite.' Mr Ashleigh cleared his throat. 'He is fairly specific. About a place near Gisors. And my enquiries also suggest that Lady Paget has had a hand in spreading the rumour, too. Some of the whispers have come through her friends. She has access to diplomatic sources, of course.'

Charles was silent. He had not seriously suspected Serafina of spreading those rumours herself, whatever he might have implied to her, but it was a blow to discover that the damage had been done deliberately, by his own enemies and former friends. He was more responsible than he had thought for bringing disaster on Sally. It was a poor way to reward her for her courage and audacity. Then he stiffened as he reminded himself that Sally—the Sally he had known— did not exist.

'What are you intending to do about it?'

Charles looked up with a start. 'What's that? I'm not quite sure. There's little enough I can do about Barros. And Louisa Paget is finished anyway.'

'What about the girl—Miss Feverel?'

Charles looked at him coldly. 'I'd like to know what makes you think it is any business of yours what I do about Miss Feverel.'

Mr Ashleigh's cheeks were suffused with colour but he stood his ground. 'I. . . I am impressed with the lady. If she is ostracised by Society then it will be totally unjust, and you know it. . .sir.'

'What do you suggest I do?'

'Why, ask her to marry you! And if you do not, then I will. . .sir!'

'I did, and she refused me, my dear boy. You may have better luck with the lady. Why don't you try?'

Mr Ashleigh looked at Charles in amazement. 'I could have sworn. . . Thank you. I think I will.'

Charles felt a sudden surge of irritation, but he restrained himself, and said as warmly as he could, 'Good luck—and my thanks for your work, David.' With relief he saw his visitor out and went back to his den.

Throughout the following week Charles had an opportunity to observe just how courageous Serafina Feverel could be. Society wasted no time in making their view of her quite plain. She was frequently ignored and sometimes even snubbed. Her crowd of admirers had vanished, but Mr Ashleigh was a constant friend and they attended several public events together. There was a sudden dearth of invitations to private ones. Miss Feverel was pale but perfectly composed. She responded with pleasure to those of her friends who continued to acknowledge her, and seemed not to see the rest. Charles, watching her for any sign of distress on the one hand, or any indication that she might be finding consolation with Mr Ashleigh on the other, saw nothing of either. He had heard from Lady Chilham that Serafina had written to her family and preparations were under way for her to travel to Sussex very soon. Charles could not wait for her to be gone from London. She dominated his life while she was in the same city. Once he could no longer see her, no longer feel himself obliged to keep an eye on her he might start to forget Serafina Feverel and to enjoy his own old life again.

The day before she was due to leave London he caught sight of her in Green Park. She was standing, somewhat forlornly, looking at the children playing, and he was hard put to it not to go over to her. But he remained where he was and stared away towards the Mall. When he next looked she had a companion—a man. He was bent towards her, his head close to hers... Serafina made a gesture of repudiation and started to walk away. The man caught her wrist and held her. Charles did not hesitate this time. He strode up to them both as swiftly as he could. 'Barros!'

Barros turned, and when he saw Charles he smiled. 'Good morning, Lord Aldworth.'

'Release Miss Feverel at once!'

Barros lifted Serafina's wrist then dropped it. 'Certainly,' he said. 'I have said all I wish to say.'

Charles glanced at Serafina. She looked composed, but he noticed that the knuckles of the fingers holding her reticule were white. 'What has he been saying to you, Serafina?'

The words tumbled out of her as if she was trying to rid herself of something loathsome. 'He said that we were both leaving London tomorrow, he and I, both in disgrace. That I had caused his downfall, and that he had taken his revenge. He asked me if I enjoyed being an outcast, and wondered why my father had not called you out for not...not offering to marry me.'

Charles swore, and then turned in fury on Barros and knocked him clean off his feet. When Barros tried to get up, Charles knocked him down again, and then stood over him, his fists at the ready. After a moment he said, 'I was right—you are vermin, Barros, best got rid of as soon as we can. No! Don't try to get up. Just lie there and listen to what I have to say. I have laid no official complaint against you for what you did in

France. Any disgrace is of your own making. But, by God, I will pursue you to the ends of the earth if I hear that you have approached Miss Feverel or have mentioned Miss Feverel's name again. And unless you leave England today I shall arrange the sort of diplomatic incident your ambassador will find not at all to his liking. Understand? Now go!'

Barros scrambled to his feet, cursing in Spanish, and hurried away. Charles said, 'I'm sorry you were subjected to that scene.'

He regarded her anxiously, but she replied calmly, 'You were very expert. Michael would have admired your technique, I am sure. Thank you for rescuing me. He is an unpleasant man.'

'Has he approached you before?'

'Yes, at the Home House, but I had forgotten. Other things were on my mind. Thank you again, Lord Aldworth.' She held out her hand.

'I'll see you back to Lady Chilham's.'

She said with decision, 'That isn't necessary. It isn't far.'

Charles said firmly, 'You put me off escorting you home once before. I am not being put off this time.'

He watched as she remembered the previous occasion. A look of great sadness filled her eyes, and she said, 'It would have been better if you had taken me home then. You would have found out... Very well, Lord Aldworth.' They moved towards Piccadilly.

At Lady Chilham's house she turned and offered him her hand again. 'I do not expect to see you again. I leave London early tomorrow.'

'How will you. . .? What will you do in Sussex?'

'What I always intended to do before my godmother

put ideas into my mother's head. I shall stay at Feverel Place and study. Pray do not concern yourself about me. I shall be quite happy. My family are so. . .so eager to have me back, and all so loving. I am looking forward to it. Goodbye, Lord Aldworth.' He had taken her hand but could not seem to let it go.

'You are not going to marry Ashleigh?'

She had been smiling, but now her expression grew cold. 'That is not your concern. But I did tell you, I believe, in what circumstances I should consider marriage. They are most unlikely to occur. Now I must go.' She drew her hand firmly out of his and vanished into the house.

Charles walked back to Berkeley Square with a curious pain in his chest for which he could not account. At last he would be free of her presence—this woman who had plagued him for so long—and now all he wanted to do was to hurry back and beg her not to go. Ridiculous! Some exercise was called for. He went to the stables and demanded his horse. But, though the gallop through the fields to the west of Hyde Park was invigorating, it did nothing to alleviate the pain.

CHAPTER FIFTEEN

LORD ALDWORTH was not finding it as easy as he had hoped to enjoy his life now that Serafina Feverel had left London. He started to consider quite seriously whether to ask for another mission which would take him out of England—but not to France. Meanwhile he found little solace in the amusements usually associated with gentlemen seeking distraction.

Some time after Serafina's departure he arrived home surprisingly early after a very dull evening gambling at White's to find that his grandmother was still up. When she invited him to partake of a glass of wine with her he accepted with alacrity. Her French common sense was what was needed to dispel his gloom. That, and several glasses of her excellent wine, perhaps.

'So,' she said, 'having turned you down, the little Feverel girl has gone to Sussex. She's a fool, but she's gallant, that one.'

'She's not the fool she made herself out to be, Grand-mère. Far from it,' said Charles with feeling.

'I think she has been foolish beyond measure recently. If you mean that when you first met her Miss Feverel deliberately hid her undoubted intelligence behind a façade of stupidity, you are right, of course. But then, I was never deceived by her. Not for long, at any rate.'

Charles was in the act of sitting down, but this

startled him so much that he stood up again. 'You knew?'

'I observed, Charles. Which is more than you ever did. And I was interested in the chit. Which is more than you ever were.'

'Do you mean to say,' said Charles, his temper rising, 'that you and Miss Feverel plotted against me together?'

'Don't take that tone with me! You deserved it. It wouldn't have been hard for you to see what Serafina Feverel was really like if you had taken the trouble. She was clever about it, but not clever enough to deceive someone who really paid her any attention. Sit down. I don't like staring up at you. Help yourself to some wine first.'

Charles slumped back and gazed into the ruby tones of the wine in his glass as he thought about what his grandmother had just said. It was true. Before Christmas he had been so fascinated by Louisa Paget that he had not taken much notice of meek little Miss Feverel. Sally had said as much, too. The thought of Sally caused him the sharp, familiar pang. But, he reminded himself, Sally was Serafina. Serafina had in fact warned him herself. He gave an exasperated sigh. Even now he found it difficult not to think of Sally and Serafina as two separate people.

'What is it, Charles?'

'Why did you help her? Miss Feverel?'

'She was absolutely right for you—or so I thought at the time. The marriage you had planned—I know I suggested it originally, but that was out of desperation. I wanted you married. But it would have been completely unworthy of you, Charles. Just as Miss Feverel's planned match was unworthy of her. You each wanted something which, if it had gone as you intended, would have ruined you both.'

'She said she thought me arrogant and selfish.'

'I know. She said as much to me soon after I met her. And you were. Conceited, too.'

'Ha! If I ever was, Miss Feverel has cured me.'

Lady Aldworth bent forward. 'Then why did you ruin her? Because you wanted to teach her a lesson in return? If so, that was really unworthy—despicable, even.'

'That was the last thing I wanted, Grand-mère! I did my best to protect her... I didn't know where those rumours came from. I even suspected Serafina Feverel of starting them herself.'

'Why in heaven's name would she do that?'

'To force me into marrying her.'

'You can hardly still believe that to be so. She has refused you—indeed, left London.'

'I know. And I now know who was responsible, as well. But you may believe me when I say I never intended Sally... Serafina any harm. Those damned names!'

'Names? What are you talking about? Has Miss Feverel two names?'

Charles gave his grandmother a twisted smile. 'You don't know the half of it, Grand-mère.'

'Then tell me the whole story. We have time.'

'I suppose it really began when I came back unexpectedly from Vienna after Christmas...'

Time passed, and the candles burned low and were renewed, but the Dowager still sat listening as Charles unfolded the tale of Sally and Serafina. She quite often laughed out loud at the girl's audacity as he went on, and Charles suddenly found himself laughing with her. He began to enjoy it, even to feel admiration at the skill with which Serafina had played one part against the other, how she had manipulated her characters. And, what was more, he began to realise how many clues there had been to what she was doing, if only he had thought enough of Serafina to notice them. But thoughts of Sally had so dominated him that Serafina had remained a dim shadow, a pale imitation of her sister.

When he came to the story of his capture, and Sally's impulsive and desperate journey to France, his grandmother grew quiet. She chuckled once or twice as he described how Sally had bewitched Juan and Luis, but then grew serious again, interrupting him to exclaim, 'But she was magnificent! What courage! What enterprise! She did all this for you?'

He nodded. Somehow in all the drama that had followed he had lost sight of the real heroism Sally— no, Serafina!—had displayed on that boat in Dieppe. In his feeling of humiliation later he had even resented the fact that he owed her so much. Charles began to feel ashamed—he had been much less than just to this girl.

'Go on, go on,' said his grandmother impatiently. He realised that he had fallen silent, and resumed his narrative.

The impossibility of sending Serafina back, the decision to take her to Paris and the subsequent wanderings through the leafy lanes of the Vexin—these were touched on, but how could he convey the magic of that journey, even had he wished? Sally's spirit, her gift of listening, her laughter—all Serafina's of course. When he came to the point at which he had asked Serafina to pretend to be Serafina, he thought his grandmother would choke, she laughed so much. His own lips twitched, and he remembered how Serafina had laughed—if only they could have shared the joke then! But she had afterwards cried as if her heart would break.

Serafina's triumph at the embassy ball was already known to Lady Aldworth. She sat there with a satisfied smile on her face and said, 'I knew it! She's the very one for you!'

There was a sudden silence. 'She won't have me, Grand-mère.'

'You must have been remarkably maladroit when you asked her, Charles. What? This girl goes through all these perils for you, shows you her devotion in a thousand different ways, and then you believe her when she says she won't marry you? Of course she will!'

'I have hurt her too badly. You don't know. . .'

'Tell me.'

Charles reluctantly described the scene in the small parlour at Feverel Place. His grandmother's face grew more and more disapproving and she was finally so shocked that she said, 'What made you behave like that to a girl who had done so much for you, and who loved you?'

'She said she loved me. But how could I believe her? If she loved me so much why didn't she tell me about herself sooner?'

'When?'

'Why not at the beginning?'

'You would have dismissed her as a possible bride

immediately. I never knew anything about Sally, of course, but I myself didn't tell you that Miss Feverel was clever for exactly the same reason. No, Charles, she wanted to make a good match and that would have destroyed it. Her reasons at that time were no more or less honourable than your own, and equally hard-headed. She didn't love you then.'

'Then why didn't she tell me later—in France?'

'It would have been better if she had, certainly. But how could she be sure that you would not reject her out of hand—as you rejected her when she did finally tell you—and leave her to fend for herself? Or worse, force her to travel with you all those miles in mutual antipathy?' She paused to let this sink in. 'Then later, once you reached Paris, you yourself suggested the double deceit of Sally pretending to be Serafina. I suppose by then she had decided to wait till you got home before provoking what was always bound to be a very awkward situation.'

Charles stared at her. This was a point of view he had never considered.

His grandmother looked at him shrewdly, then went on, 'But why are we conducting this inquest? Do you honestly believe she lied when she said she loved you?'

'I don't know... I didn't know what to think. And then when I saw her in London...'

He went on to describe his subsequent behaviour in London and Lady Aldworth exclaimed, 'I am no longer surprised that she refused you! I would have myself! But you are not normally so cruel, Charles. Why did you treat Miss Feverel like this?'

Charles got up and offered his grandmother some wine, then poured a glass for himself. He drank deep, then said, 'I thought at the time I was justified. But I now think I really wanted to hurt her. I thought she had been laughing at me all the time we had known each other, and I wanted to make her hurt as much as I was hurting. Not very noble, was it? And certainly not the action of a gentleman.' He drank again. Lady Aldworth watched him, a troubled frown on her face. This was a Charles she had never before seen. The Charles she knew was handsome, debonair, light-hearted except in his work, confident in his attraction for women, and, it had to be admitted, somewhat ruthless. His commitment to his career was a redeeming feature, but though she had felt that somewhere there was a different Charles, one capable of devotion, almost the only evidence she had ever seen of it was the love he bore her, his grandmother. Now she *was* seeing that Charles, but he was deeply unhappy.

'What are you going to do, my dear?' she said gently.

'What can I do? Tell me!' He suddenly raised his head and she was shocked at the look in his eyes. She hastened to comfort him.

'You must go to see her.'

'I can't!'

'You must! Go down to Blanchards. From what you tell me the house is comfortable, but much still needs to be done outside. See to that, and wait for the moment. Then, when you think you are ready, call on her.' She leaned foward and put a wrinkled hand on his knee. 'You have offered her settlements and an establishment. If that is all you still have to offer, she may refuse you again, Charles. You will have to think of something else she might want.'

* * *

Charles delayed only long enough to put one or two urgent affairs in order before going down to Sussex. His grandmother saw him the night before he went and embraced him warmly.

'You will be successful, Charles. I can feel it in my bones. And then you and Serafina will live at Aldworth, and I shall see my great-grandsons there at last. Good luck, my darling.' When he reached the door she said, 'And when you are down at Blanchards make sure it will be absolutely ready for your step-mother and the rest! It's time we were rid of the screech-owl, too. We shall want some peace and privacy at Aldworth!'

Blanchards looked much the same. One or two of the trees were turning, but it was still high summer. He had seen the agent in London, and work was in hand on the gardens and fields round the house. The travelling coach was still in the coach-house. He roamed about the house restlessly. It was too soon to go to see Serafina, but there was nothing else he wished to do. He made up his mind to go for a ride.

Up on the downs there was a fresh breeze. He rode to the top and gazed down on the English Channel— Beachy Head to the left, Newhaven down below him on the right. How had Sally found the courage to board that boat, going off into the unknown?

'Hello!'

He turned round. Rafe and Michael were behind him, each on a sturdy pony. Michael was looking embarrassed.

'Hello, Rafe! Michael.'

Michael flushed and said brusquely, 'Good afternoon, Lord Aldworth. Come, Rafe!'

'No wait! Don't go—I'd like to talk,' Charles said. 'I'm sorry—we have to get back——'

'That's a whopper! We've got all afternoon,' said Rafe. 'And I want to ask Lord Aldworth about those villains. The ones that gave Sally a black eye. Have they been punished for their dastardly deeds? She's not been the same since, you know.'

'Oh, come on, Rafe! You talk too much. Lord Aldworth can't possibly be interested in gossip about us.'

'I assure you I am. What is this about your sister? She isn't ill, is she?'

'She's perfectly well, thank you,' said Michael, scrupulously polite. 'It's just that she's a bit quieter than she used to be.'

'It's Mr Ashleigh. She's always quieter when he's been here.'

'Hold your jaw, Rafe!' said Michael fiercely.

'Does Mr Ashleigh often visit her?'

Michael's lips were firmly shut. He was obviously not going to say any more. Fortunately Rafe was less discreet.

'He's been twice. And Sally cried a lot after he had gone. I don't think he ought to come any more.'

At this Michael grew even redder and said gruffly, 'I don't think you ought to listen to what a little boy tells you about his family, Lord Aldworth. It's cheating, a bit. Anyway, I. . .we thought you didn't care about her any more. And now it really is time we went.' He gave a little nod and caught Rafe's bridle.

'Will you tell your sister that you have met me here?'

'No,' said Michael briefly. 'And nor will Rafe unless he wants a thrashing.' Then, amid angry protests from his brother, he firmly led the ponies away.

Their departure left Charles in a thoughtful mood. So David Ashleigh had taken him at his word! He supposed it was to be expected—Serafina and David had much in common, though he would have said that David was a little staid for Sally's more exuberant moments. But perhaps she no longer had those? The boys had said that she was quieter. Perhaps she and Ashleigh were even better suited than he had thought? And the boy had said that Serafina was always upset when Ashleigh left. Charles set his horse off at a gallop—it appeared that he had come down to Sussex not a moment too soon. . .

At Feverel Place Serafina was sitting in her favourite place on a stool by her mother. Her father was away at a conference and the three Feverel ladies were having a comfortable, non-intellectual chat, such as Mr Feverel deplored.

'I hear that Hartley Pennyworth is married.'

'Yes—to Lizzie Beaminster, of all people,' said Mrs Feverel. 'It seems to be working. Lizzie is hardly a match for Mrs Pennyworth senior, but she makes no attempt to compete.'

'You should see Hartley, Serafina!' cried Angelica. 'He's getting fatter by the minute, and his air of complacency. . .!'

'Good luck to him. I knew Lizzie Beaminster was the one for him.'

'And what about you, Serafina? Mr Ashleigh seems

very eager. He is a pleasant young man, and very knowledgeable.'

'I like him,' said Angelica eagerly. 'He's quite good-looking, though not as handsome as——' she stopped.

'Lord Aldworth.' Serafina finished the sentence for her. 'No, he isn't.'

Mrs Feverel and Angelica spoke together. 'Did you know that Miss Twitch——?'

'Papa says that the rainfall this year——'

Serafina smiled and said, 'You are both darlings. But you should stop trying to cosset me. And I wish you would abandon these attempts to marry me off, and realise that I intend to be the best maiden aunt the Feverel family has ever seen. All I shall need is lots of nieces and nephews! So, Angy, as a first step, let's start training you for your introduction to Society. That's something I can do to perfection—I can even deal with an ambassador's ball. Why, perhaps I could give classes in the neighbourhood, with a recommendation—"as seen in Paris"!'

'One of the family working for a living is enough, Serafina. Though Gabriel seems to be enjoying his stint as librarian at Arundel. I think he will be quite sad when he goes back to Oxford in October. But what a relief that his debts are being paid off—slowly, but still. . .' Mrs Feverel paused. 'But can you imagine what the neighbourhood would say if Sally Feverel were to set up as an arbiter of good behaviour? Mrs Pennyworth senior would have apoplexy.' The three Feverel ladies burst into laughter.

When Michael and Rafe came in from their ride it was clear that Rafe was big with news—news which Michael was determined to suppress.

'What is it, Rafe?' asked Serafina with a smile.

'Oh, it's nothing,' said Michael. 'Don't encourage him, Sally.'

'It is, it is!' cried Rafe excitedly. 'But Michael says I'm not to tell you.'

'That's not very fair, Mick—you know how imposs-ible it is to keep Rafe from telling everything he knows. Aren't you being a trifle unkind?'

Michael gave a sigh, and with a stern look at Rafe he said, 'It's only that Blanchards is occupied again.'

Serafina lost a little of her colour. 'Is it being let, then?'

'No, it's him!' shouted Rafe, skipping out of Michael's reach. 'Lord Aldworth! And I wanted to ask him about the emeralds and those men. But Michael wouldn't let me. What's the matter, Sally?' His voice faltered, and he turned to his mother. 'Why is Sally looking like that?'

Michael advanced on Rafe with a menacing air, took his brother by the ear, and dragged him out of the room. Mrs Feverel put a hand on her daughter's shoulder.

'It's all right, truly!' said Serafina. 'Angy, do go out and stop Mick doing whatever he's threatening to do to Rafe. He's only a little boy—he doesn't know how to keep secrets. Tell Mick I sent you.' Angelica went out and Serafina let out her breath in a shuddering sigh.

'Serafina——'

'Pray don't worry, Mama. I...was stupid. It was a shock. I'm perfectly all right now. Really.'

There were sounds of argument outside the door. Rafe burst in and ran to Serafina, hiding his head in her skirt. 'I didn't mean to upset you,' he sobbed. 'I didn't know you'd look like that. I'm sorry, Sally.'

'What nonsense you're talking, Rafe. Look like what? See, I'm quite my usual self, and to prove it I'm going to tickle you any minute now!'

As far as the family was concerned, Serafina remained her normal composed self for the rest of that day. She was quiet, but then she very often was nowadays. But in fact the tension within her increased by the hour. Charles was once again quite near—near enough to call at any moment if he chose. Why had he come to Sussex—was it merely to see that the work on Blanchards was finished? Surely he could have done that through his agent? Her heart raced as she thought that he might have come down to see her... But the day passed without a sign of Lord Aldworth. She spent the night that followed lying awake, wondering, hoping, despairing. The pain in her heart might have dulled during the weeks since their parting, but it had never gone away. Poor David Ashleigh's visits to Sussex were merely a reminder of Charles and what she had lost, and each time he left the pain was worse for a while until it dulled again. She fell asleep towards dawn, and when she woke there were tears on her cheeks.

Her case was not helped by the anxious looks directed at her over the breakfast-table. The family had been a wonderful support to her since her return from London, but sometimes their concern oppressed her. She announced that she would spend the day in the library, preparing some notes for her father, and, reassured by her air of calm, they left her to do as she wished.

She spent the first part of the morning on her notes

without, in fact, achieving very much. But then, when the sun got higher, she decided she would work outside. She gathered up her book and notepad, and a couple of apples from the kitchen, put them into a bag together with a small cushion, and went out into the garden. But the sunshine and fresh air enticed her further, and she wandered down the drive as far as the old oak. Here she stopped. It was here that the Sally-Serafina saga had started all those months ago... Her mind skittered away from the memory like a frightened animal, and it was suddenly difficult to breathe. She would think of something else. The tree had always been a favourite place for her. She had hidden here so many times to escape the attentions of Hartley Pennyworth. She smiled—he wouldn't be calling again. Poor Lizzie Beaminster!

As she looked up through the leaves she could see glimpses of the branch which had been her refuge then. It was tempting... No one would know, no one would find her. And she could see if...if anyone came up the drive. In two minutes Serafina was safely ensconced with her apples and her work, her back comfortably cushioned against the trunk, her legs stretched out along the branch. She worked for a while, but the sun was warm, even among the leaves, and Serafina's sleepless night caught up with her. Her eyes gradually shut, and she dozed.

Charles had woken that same morning with a feeling of excitement and dread. Today he would visit Feverel Place. Serafina was at home, he knew that. Perhaps she would agree at least to see him, to give him an opportunity to tell her how he regretted what he had done in the past. Then, later, when he had visited her once or twice more, he might be able to overcome her prejudice against him, convince her that he had changed. . . But what about Ashleigh? Perhaps Serafina was already experiencing with him that—what had she called it?—that 'unity of spirit', without which she would not marry. His blood ran cold at the thought. He must see her.

He rode along the lanes, so engrossed in considering what he was going to say that he had reached the beginning of the drive which led to Feverel Place before he realised. Here he reined in. This was the oak tree out of which Sally had fallen all those months ago. She had knocked him flat then and, he thought whimsically, he had never truly been his own master since. One thing was certain. If by some miracle Serafina Feverel did agree to be his wife, he would never be wholly his own master ever again. Nor did he wish to be. Marriage to Serafina would be like nothing he had ever envisaged—more exciting, more unpredictable, more all-consuming. Certainly nothing like the contract he had twice offered her. His brows drew together. Would she forgive him?

An apple dropped out of the tree and rolled towards him. An apple? In an oak tree? He peered up through the foliage and had a tantalising glimpse of a figure perched on a branch some way up. Its legs were stretched out along the branch and it was leaning comfortably against the trunk of the tree. He dismounted and moved nearer.

'Sally!'

The figure gave a start and leaned over to look

down. Another apple dropped down, followed by a book. 'Oh! It's you! Who told you I was here?'

'I found you for myself, Sally-Serafina.'

'Why are you here?'

Charles looked up at the face framed in the leaves—perhaps a little thinner than it had been, perhaps a touch paler, but infinitely dear, incomparably lovely, the embodiment of everything he now desired. The carefully prepared speeches were forgotten. 'I love you,' he said simply. 'I couldn't keep away.'

A delicate flush appeared on Serafina's face. 'Oh!' she said softly. There was a short pause, then her eyes began to sparkle. 'Is that all?'

'I want you to marry me.'

'To bear your heirs while you live your own life?'

'Certainly!' It was his turn to smile as Serafina looked a little disconcerted. Then he added, 'But my life will be your life too, my heart. One life—together.'

'Oh, Charles!' Serafina stared down at him, smiling mistily, an expression of wonder and delight on her face.

They gazed at one another wordlessly, then Charles said, 'Er. . .this is very difficult. Shall I come up to you, or will you come down to me? It's very awkward proposing when I can hardly see you.'

'I'll come down. Oh, Charles!' Serafina started to climb down, but as soon as she was within reach Charles caught her and lifted her down the rest of the way. He didn't release her, but held her close.

'Sally?'

Serafina flung her arms round his neck and pulled his head down to hers. 'Serafina wanted to do this so often, Charles, but she never dared.' She kissed him, and in that kiss was all the deep commitment of Serafina, all the exuberance of Sally.

He laughed unsteadily. 'I never thought you'd forgive me. . .'

'Shh! It's forgotten. We both made mistakes. But that's all over. Now it's just Charles and. . .and who? Sally or Serafina—which do you want?'

'My darling, I love them both! I can't live without either! But neither of you has yet said that you'll marry me.'

'Then you may have us both, Charles,' said Serafina, with a generous wave of the hand. 'Sally for weekdays and Serafina for best. We'll both marry you.' They kissed again, but when Charles would have released her Serafina said, 'No, wait! That one was for Serafina. Now you have to kiss Sally.'

'How about Cherubina?' murmured Charles after a minute or two.

'Cherubina?'

'Wasn't there a Cherubina? Or was that just Sally's real name? I've forgotten, but it doesn't matter—I'll kiss her too.'

Laughing and murmuring to one another, they passed an ecstatic few minutes before Serafina said, 'My goodness, what would Mrs Pennyworth say? Such behaviour! And I was just thinking of setting up to be an arbiter of propriety, too! Allow me to tell you, Lord Aldworth, that you have a shockingly deleterious effect on my behaviour.'

They started walking up the drive. They had not gone far when they were greeted by shouts from Rafe, who came hurtling down from the house and nearly knocked them over. 'Sally! Sally! You're with him! I knew it would be all right.' He did a kind of war-dance round them both, then said, 'Race you up the tree, Sally!' and raced off to the oak tree, where he hopped about impatiently.

Serafina looked enquiringly at Charles, who grinned and nodded. With a whoop of sheer delight, Sally picked up her skirts and chased off after Rafe.